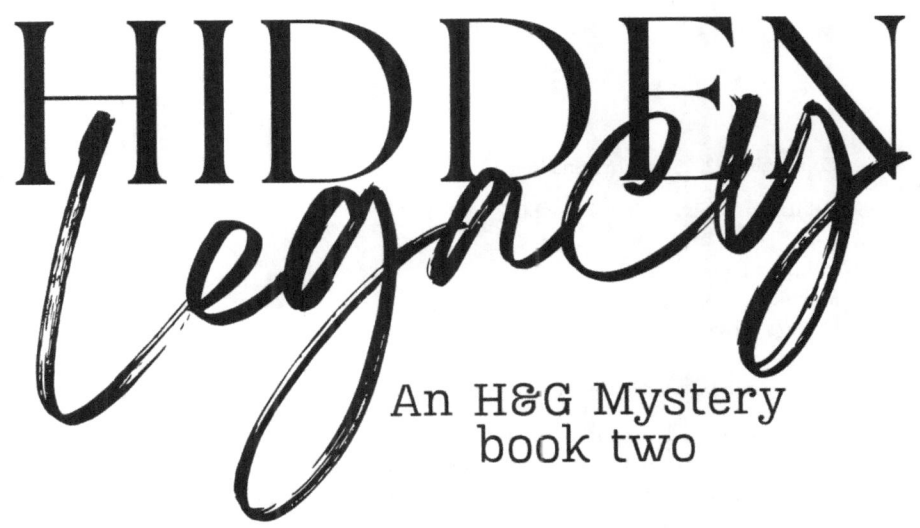

HIDDEN
legacy

An H&G Mystery
book two

CHRISTINA ROST

Scrivenings
PRESS
Quench your thirst for story.
www.ScriveningsPress.com

To the Christians who steadfastly live out their faith in regions where they face persecution for their beliefs. May God protect and preserve you as you fulfill the Great Commission.

"The greatest legacy one can pass on to one's children and grandchildren is not money or other material things accumulated in one's life, but rather a legacy of character and faith."
~Billy Graham

PROLOGUE

Korea
1939

A spark of lightning tore through the bedroom window, then fled. Prickles of gooseflesh feathered across Young-ja's neck. She gripped Edward's hand tighter as they knelt beside the bed and prayed. *Show me what to say, Lord. I want to help carry his burden.*

"Lord, please guide us." Her husband's voice deepened to match the growl of the distant thunder. "In these uncertain times, give us the courage to live for You."

Her rib cage constricted. Ever since the seminary in Pyongyang closed its doors, they'd measured time by single, uneasy breaths. Now, with war on the horizon, uncertainty enveloped them like a cocoon.

"Watch over us, and—"

Banging on the door followed by a string of shouting severed Edward's prayer.

Young-Ja's eyes shot open.

"Stay in the room and bolt the door." Edward jumped to his feet.

"What? Why?" She stood, pulse racing.

The racket intensified.

He grabbed her shoulders. "Do as I say. There are soldiers at the door."

Forcing a nod, she waited until Edward left to turn the latch. *God, protect my husband.*

"Where is your wife?" Raging voices closed in as boots thundered across the floor.

Young-Ja pinched her eyes shut.

"She's not here." Edward's voice hardened. "She's with family. In the country."

"You're English? One of the seminary students."

A deafening thump collided with the wall and Edward grunted.

"Your God will not help you tonight."

Her eyes shot open as she bit down on her lip to stave off a whimper.

"Deliver me, O Lord, from my enemies." Edward's plea melted with the rumble in the heavens.

Another crash slammed against the wall. Edward moaned.

Pressing her cheek against the door, Young-ja strained to hear past the pulse thundering in her ears.

The soldiers' persecution rose in a crescendo, then quieted.

"Young-Ja." Edward's strained voice carved through the closed door. "Open the door."

She yanked at the latch and peered out. Edward sat on the floor, slumped against the wall. Falling to his side, she cradled his battered face in her hands. "What happened? What did they want?"

He motioned to the crumbled parchment sitting next to him as he struggled to get to his feet.

She stared at the Japanese writing. "An order? For me to appear at the shrine?"

"They're trying to get to me through you." Edward's blood-smeared jaw set like smooth marble. "They want the missionaries gone, and they'll do whatever it takes."

"I won't go. I won't bow." She'd heard of others who'd made the trek to pay homage to the idols, then professed they'd not bowed in their heart.

"You're not going anywhere." He pulled a cloth from his pocket and took a swipe at the blood on his mouth.

"What are we going to do? What about our family? Our friends? How many of them received the order?"

"We're leaving." Edward rose, threw the soiled cloth onto the floor, and stormed into their bedroom.

Knees shaking, she trailed after him.

"I'll get word to the others." He opened their armoire and pulled out books and a few pieces of clothes. "I need you to pack a bag."

"We're leaving tonight?"

"I need to protect you, Young-Ja. I'll die before I let them hurt you."

After all these years he remained her steadfast protector. Her love. "We have a few weeks before they require us to go, shouldn't we wait and—"

He turned to face her, fear blanketing his features. "No. We're going now."

Tears stung the back of her eyes. *God, is this what You want?*

She nodded, then crouched next to her trunk. With shaky hands, she opened the lid and poked around until she found her most treasured possession—their family Bible. She opened the cover and traced their names with her fingers. Next to their names were their children's names and five other families who'd worshiped and prayed together for years.

"Leave it."

She jerked her chin up. "No, Edward, I—"

"Someone might search us on the way."

"I can't …" Her heart squeezed. "What will happen to our legacy? Will all of this be forgotten?"

"If God allows,"—Edward laid a hand on her arm—"we'll return."

3

Her shoulders fell as she swiped at her tears. After shoving a wad of clothes into her bag, she dug to the bottom of the trunk until she found what she was looking for—a remnant of oilcloth and a leather belt. She wrapped the Bible in the cloth, then, after securing it with the belt, she coiled the extra leather around twice before threading it through the buckle.

"I'll be back."

"Wait." Edward reached for her arm.

Slipping out of his grip, she picked up the garden blade by the door and scurried outside. When she reached a small patch of dirt, lightning raced across the sky.

Young-Ja fell to her knees. With the Bible tucked under her arm, she clawed at the earth with the blade until she made a hole the depth of her forearm.

God, don't let this chain be broken. Protect our legacy. As another bolt of lightning split the sky, she placed the Bible in the shallow grave and replaced the soil, disguising the area with vegetable plants and rocks.

Showers broke from the heavens as she rushed back into the house. Whatever happened to them, or to their legacy, God alone had the final word.

Edward slung both of their bags over his shoulder. "Are you ready?"

She glanced once more around their home, searing the memory into her heart. "I'm ready."

Like the Israelites fleeing Egypt, they escaped into the darkness, leaving Pyongyang and their old life behind, before the dawn of the rising sun.

1

E mersyn Renée Zucker wasn't sure what she needed more, a hike in the woods, to snuggle a puppy, or an oversized cup of creamy coffee.

She grabbed her messenger bag, then stepped out of her car. Breathing in the warm, mid-May air, she sighed. It was only Tuesday. This was going to be a long week.

Emersyn trudged from the parking lot to the front door of her go-to coffee shop in Newport News. As she stepped across the threshold, she smiled. The upcycled décor, framed covers of whodunnit novels, and the comforting scents of espresso and aged wood wrapped her in a warm hug.

For now, she needed coffee.

She eyed her favorite booth in the corner. Three teen girls stared at their phones. Great. Why weren't they in school?

Sliding into the long line, her mind did loops like a rollercoaster. Her last week of college. She had three essays due, a curriculum outline on the life of bees, and a final week of student teaching art appreciation at Maplewood Preparatory School. After all that, she could take the summer off to relax.

"Your usual?" The barista with a jet-black pixie cut smiled wide.

Emersyn eyed the seasonal menu. "I'll try the blackberry

mocha this time. Large. With an extra shot. And make it to-go, please."

She surveyed the room again. She only had a few minutes to work, but finding a seat might be difficult.

Her gaze drifted back to her favorite booth. The teens took a quick selfie and shimmied out of the booth. Perfect.

The reclaimed bench seats beckoned her to the back corner. Cozy and quiet, the booth had a great view out the window. Now she could get some work done before her martial arts class. She'd agreed to teach the younger belts for the next two weeks while her instructor visited family in Seoul.

"Whole milk. Right?"

She turned back to the barista. "Yes. Thanks."

While she paid for her coffee, she continued to eye her favorite seat.

"Your name?" The barista waggled a marker in the air.

"Em—I mean Renée."

"Hiding from someone?"

"Something like that ..."

Pivoting on her heel, she took off for the blue velvet bench seat with gold buttons.

Emersyn pulled her laptop from her messenger bag and set it on the table. She wasn't hiding, just recovering from her last attempt at a happily-ever-after. Her new rule for dating: no more wealthy heirs in need of a high-society wife. She huffed out a sigh. Why was love so complicated?

While she waited for her caffeine, she opened her laptop and clicked on the local news app. Her ex's photo loomed on her screen. If Guy Atwater won this cycle, he'd be the youngest mayor on record. She stared into those chocolate brown eyes. Guy was handsome, intelligent, and driven. But he was a shark.

She read all the letters after his name and internally deciphered them. He'd be a great politician. Maybe even a great husband and father. As she thought about their last phone call, Emersyn clicked off the article. Nope. She wanted to date someone down to earth, not someone who wanted to merge estates.

Her gaze lifted and zeroed in on the for-sale sign taped to the lower corner of the front window. She'd missed that when she walked in. Why did things have to change?

She pawed the edge of the table until she found what she was looking for. *Em's bench.* As a teen, she'd carved the words with the antique pocket knife her papa had given her.

"A pocketknife can sharpen a pencil or slice through a rope. It all depends on what kind of trouble you plan on getting into."

Papa believed the pen was mightier than a sword. But it didn't hurt to have a sword with you either.

Her gaze swept over to the counter. Two iced drinks and a frappe. All of Newport News had decided to give in to their caffeine addiction today.

She eyed the for-sale sign again. Instead of dwelling on Guy, she should buy the coffee shop. Isn't that what one did after a breakup? Shopped? Or ate gallons of ice cream?

A smile spread across her lips. She'd buy the place and add an ice cream bar. Name a dessert after Guy. Maybe call it the *Shark Sundae.* Then she'd hang a plaque above her booth that read, "This booth is for teachers, starving artists, and daydreaming writers."

"Renée." A barista hollered her name along with two others.

She scooted out of the booth and trailed between the crowded tables to the front counter. Giving a quick nod to the high schooler behind the counter, she glanced down at the row of drinks. She reached for the first paper cup and read the name. *Reid.*

"I think that one's mine. Americano, two sugars." As a deep, honeyed voice floated behind her, gooseflesh covered her arms.

She turned and held out the drink like a peace offering. The tantalizing smell of leather and bergamot mingled with fresh ground coffee. "Here you go."

"Thanks."

"Sure. Anytime." She eked out her response with a shrug.

Behind a pair of dark, masculine frames, gray-blue eyes glinted with a hint of amusement.

"That one must be yours." Mr. Americano reached around her and retrieved her cup.

He smelled like an uptown bookshop. "Yeah. Blackberry mocha."

"Here you go." He handed her the cup, his fingers brushing against hers. "Blackberry mocha? Sounds sweet. Is that your regular?"

"Uh, no. I buy seasonal. In the fall, I'm all about the pumpkin. And cinnamon. And the spice."

His grin deepened along with his dimples.

Emersyn's skin heated. Spice? Really? She needed caffeine. And quite possibly a nap. Or maybe a time jump to another century. "Um, thanks again. For, uh … grabbing my drink."

Forcing herself out of Mr. Americano's orbit, she sidestepped to the right, made a beeline for her booth, and flopped into the seat. "Maybe I should click my heels and land back on planet Earth."

As she took a sip of her mocha, Emersyn stole another glance at Mr. Americano. She'd never seen him before. With his chiseled jawline and wavy hair, she would have remembered someone who looked like they'd stepped right out of a superhero movie.

He wore a charcoal suit, cut to fit, and stood almost a head taller than her. He'd opted for no tie with a blue pinstriped shirt and two buttons open at the collar. While she sipped her mocha, she daydreamed about what he did for a living. Banker. Lawyer. Or maybe a professor. *I wonder if there's a cape under that suit.*

She set her cup down and wiggled her fingers. His brief touch still lingered over her skin. Ridiculous. It must be the stress of finals.

Mr. Americano said something to pixie haircut behind the counter, and she blushed. After a quick back and forth, the girl fished a muffin out of the display, dropped it into a paper bag, and handed it to him.

Emersyn opened her laptop but kept her gaze lingering. Mr. Americano scanned the room, then frowned. Not even a superhero could find a seat today.

Biting back a smile, she glanced at her screen. Time to stop daydreaming and get to work.

"It's a bit of a packed house in here."

Emersyn jerked her head up. Mr. Americano? Her pulse jumped to treadmill levels. "Oh, yeah. It's busy today."

"Would you mind if I shared your booth?" He gripped his laptop bag and shot her a mournful look. "I hoped to get a few things done before I get back on the road."

Yes! Wait. Take a breath. Act natural. She clicked her heels under the table. "Are you a starving artist or a writer?"

His brow shot up. "What?"

"Molder of young minds?"

"None of the above." He flashed her a charming smile. "Just a guy looking for some Wi-Fi."

A shudder tumbled from the back of her neck to her toes. He's adorable. "I guess if you put it that way, I can share." She scooted her bag off the table and motioned to her laptop. "I need to read over a few notes before my next class. I shouldn't be long."

"Please, don't rush." He slid into the seat opposite her and set down his coffee cup and muffin bag. "I'm invading your space. Besides,"—he nodded between their cups of brew—"it will be nice to share breakfast with someone."

Warmth tickled her skin. When was the last time she shared breakfast with anyone other than her study group? Or Donna, her housekeeper?

"Are you a teacher?"

"I ... I'm ..." Emersyn worried her bottom lip between her teeth. "Student teacher. I graduate this month."

"Congrats. Where will you be teaching in the fall?"

"A local private school." She hesitated. Careful. You don't know him. "What brings you into *this* coffee shop today?"

"Work. Well, pleasure." Mr. Americano pulled out his laptop and opened it. "Honestly, a little bit of both."

The glare from his screen reflected in his specs while he tapped on his keys and took intermittent bites of his muffin. When he looked up, he threw her a playful grin.

"I guess I should introduce myself since I'm invading a portion of your world today." He laid down his muffin and extended his hand across the table. "I'm—"

"Reid. Americano, two sugars." She shook his hand. "Sorry, that sounded weird. I envisioned that wittier than it came across."

Reid laughed and withdrew his hand. "It was very witty." He took a sip of his coffee, and a curl of his ebony hair fell over his forehead. Reid swiped at the curl then pushed his glasses up on the rim of his nose. "Not on a level of Dickens' wit. But close."

He's into the classics. Perfect.

"What's *your* name?" Reid popped the last piece of his muffin into his mouth.

"My name?" Her chest tightened as a city bus filled the window in front of the coffee shop. In large, sweeping script, an advertisement for the *Zucker School of Art* spread across the side.

Reid shifted in his seat, following her gaze. When he turned back, concern covered his face. "Everything okay?"

"Oh, yeah." She waved him off. "I thought I saw someone I recognized." She stuck out her hand, then realized they'd already shaken hands. Heat prickled her cheeks. "My name's Renée."

He wrapped his fingers around hers, holding his grip there for a second longer than before. "It's nice to meet you, Renée." After he released her, he glanced down at his screen and punched in a few keys. "That's a beautiful name. French origins, right?"

"It is." *If he speaks French, I'm done.*

"*Parlez-vous français?*" His smooth accent rolled off his tongue like a song.

Her toes curled in her boots. "*Oui.* A little."

Reid looked up and shot her a bemused look.

"I struggle with learning languages." Shrugging, she took a drink of her mocha. "Music and art are more my thing."

"I love music, but I can't play an instrument to save my life. Do you play something?"

"Piano."

For a fleeting second, his expression fell. "So did my mom."

She took note of the past tense. Was his mom no longer around? She could relate to that wound.

"Is it always this busy?" Clearing his throat, Reid did another perusal of the coffee shop.

"No. But then again, I'm usually here in the evenings." She waved her hand around the booth. "I never have a problem getting my favorite seat after six." She shrugged. "Finals week. Maybe that's why it's busy."

"I remember those days."

"You make it sound like you're older than *Father Time.* How long have you been out of school?"

He chuckled as he wiped his mouth with a napkin. "A year. I'm twenty-five. I deviated from the direct path in school for a while."

"Decided to live in Paris?"

He arched a brow. "How did you know?"

Tipping her chin down, she lifted a brow back and waited.

A grin towed at his lips. "Oh, I get it. The French."

"Simple deduction. I studied in England for a year."

"Really?"

"I have close friends who live in London. I think they wanted to keep an eye on me." Emersyn recalled how Kelly and James hovered like nervous hens after Papa passed away. She loved them, but sometimes she wished they were a little less ... well, a little less like hens.

Reid continued to type on his keys. "I didn't go to school in France."

"What did you do while you were there?"

"It's top secret. If I tell you, then …" He flashed her an ornery look and lifted his cup to take a drink.

She leaned across the table and whispered, "Please don't say you're FBI or something." Living so close to the DC area, she'd run into plenty of clandestine government workers. "Is Reid even your real name?"

Reid stopped mid-drink and coughed. "What?" After he placed his cup back on the table, he tugged at his collar. "Of course, Reid's my name."

"Go ahead, fess up. FBI? CIA? NSA? Another three-letter acronym? Silver spoon heir whose ambition is the White House?" She squinted her eyes, trying to goad him further. "Or is this the point where you tell me you can't divulge that information?"

Reid curled his fingers around his napkin, then released it. A flicker of pleasure flashed in his eyes. "You have quite the imagination, Renée."

The way his voice deepened when he feathered her name with a French accent shot fire through her veins. *Please tell me you're just a normal guy.*

"I'm sorry to disappoint you." He leaned forward and held her stare. "I'm just a regular Joe. I work in IT."

"Is that so?" She leaned back in her seat and folded her arms. "Well Reid, you're just the man I'm looking for."

Lucas Reid Bennett's heart pumped in his ears. "I am?"

"You are." Renée's face brightened before she redirected her gaze back to her laptop.

Here it comes. Lucas readied himself to see a society picture of him with his family, no glasses—he only wore those when he worked on his laptop—dressed to the nines, at a charity event, or shaking hands with the Senator.

"Can you help me with this?" She pivoted her screen to face him.

He adjusted his glasses. A half-organized website filled her screen and tension fled his body. She's right. He was the guy she was looking for. Warmth tingled across his neck. *Don't get ahead of yourself.*

Lucas pulled her laptop closer and scrolled through the pages. They were a mess. The padding was off, and she had too many plugins. He tried some of the navigation buttons. They worked, but several went to pages that didn't exist. He read the menu—bio, curriculum, and products for sale. What was she selling? Tutoring? Not website design.

Glancing up, he caught the frustration in her eyes, her full lips bent in a pretty pout.

"What is this?" He swallowed to wet his throat. "I mean, I know what it is. What's it for?"

"It's my website. Well, it's supposed to be." She folded her arms on the table, then laid her head down, dampening her next words. "I hate technology."

He chuckled. He loved technology. Reaching out, he nudged her arm. "It's not so bad. Believe me, I've seen worse."

When she lifted her head, her bouncy, auburn ringlets fell like springs across her shoulders. "You have?"

He nodded. "Is this part of your final?"

"Yes. But it's a double-edged sword. I'm required to have a website for school next year. All my curriculum needs to be available online."

"When do you need it finished?"

"Next week."

"Have you thought of hiring someone?"

She leaned back and fiddled with the strap on her bag. "I wanted to do it on my own. That's probably a bit ambitious at this point."

"I'd offer to take it home and work on it but—"

She pulled her laptop back in front of her. "I … well, like I said, I want to do it myself. When I need to upload my curriculum every semester, I don't want to call an IT guy."

"What do you have going on this evening?" He checked his watch, tearing his gaze from her doe eyes.

"Nothing. But you don't have to come back. Maybe you could just give me some pointers."

He looked up. She'd need more than a few pointers. "I only live an hour away, up in Richmond. It's not a problem."

"What about work tomorrow? You'll get home late."

He pointed to his laptop. "I'm mobile."

"Oh, that makes sense."

Digging through his laptop bag, he found a business card. *Reid Clark.* His stomach clenched. After one of his college buddies said he looked like a character in a comic book when he wore his specs, the name stuck. Everyone he knew used pseudonyms online. Gamers especially. Like authors using pen names, it wasn't that unusual. So why did he feel bad about lying to Renée?

He fingered the card. It was easier this way. He needed to keep his family out of his business—or hobby, as Dad called it—and he needed his clients to take him seriously. Not schmooze with him because he was a Bennett.

Lucas slid the card across the table. Guilt gnawed at his gut. For a second, he thought about scratching out the name and giving her his real one. No. Give it time. He couldn't be completely honest with her. Not just yet.

Renée picked up the card. "Reid Clark." When she looked up, her eyes sparkled. "Has anyone ever told you that you look like—"

"Many times." Reflexively, he pushed his specs higher onto the bridge of his nose.

"I'll meet you back here around seven." Cheeks pink, she

averted her eyes and fiddled with her coffee cup. "Make sure you don't stand me up."

"I wouldn't dream of it."

When she lifted her gaze, his heart lodged in his throat. "Good, because I don't share this booth with just anybody. Only the most noble of software designers."

He swallowed hard. Noble? Maybe he should come clean. Let her know he was an heir to one of the most exclusive estate houses on the east coast—*Bennetts Estates and Antiques*. Their showrooms brought in millions, but it was the private shows in hidden warehouses across the country that put their name in the spotlight.

If she found out he'd lied about his name, she might not think him so noble. Rich maybe. But not noble.

Pushing away those thoughts, he closed his laptop and shoved it in his bag. "I'll be here."

Her lips curved into an adorable smile. "Good."

Chuckling, he slid out of the booth and gathered his trash. With a final look back, Lucas shot her a wave, then ducked out the door.

2

L ucas's stomach rumbled as he pulled into the garage of his Richmond townhome and turned off the engine. Was it already lunchtime?

After crashing at his friend's condo last night, he'd only had a cup of single-shot coffee and a protein bar.

Warmth surged through his veins. He didn't need any more coffee. Last night, he'd sipped on more caffeine than his body needed while walking Renée through the steps to fix her website. He showed her how to load her curriculum, and after he organized her menu and added a contact plugin for her students, she'd looked at him like he'd hung the moon. Or slain her dragon. Whatever the look in her eyes, he hoped to see it again.

He grabbed his overnight bag and laptop out of the trunk, closed the garage door, then took the steps two at a time to the first floor. When he opened the door, silence greeted him.

"Lights on." He said the voice command half-heartedly and light flooded the room.

Home sweet home.

As he dropped his bag on the floor, a thud echoed down the hall. He'd need to pick up some throw rugs this week. After a year the place still felt sterile and new. What color throw rugs?

The blue-green hue of Renée's eyes flashed across his mind. They reminded him of the Atlantic Ocean. When he fell asleep last night, the color mingled with his dreams, and he didn't want to wake up.

"Why didn't I ask to see her again?" He placed his laptop bag on the coffee table and flopped into his favorite club chair. "Because you're an idiot, that's why."

While he'd worked on her website, their conversation bounced from her love of hiking to his obsession with baseball. She was a blackbelt in martial arts, and they both agreed history should be cherished, not ignored.

He pinched the bridge of his nose. "But did she seem interested?"

After they closed down the coffee shop, he walked her to her car, where she thanked him, and promised she'd call if she had any issues with her website.

Not good. He'd slipped right past the friend zone to tech support.

"Open blinds."

At his command, the blinds lifted, bringing more light into the room.

"Tell Renée to call."

The home assistant complained it couldn't complete his request.

He huffed a sigh as he fished his laptop out of his bag and opened it. Maybe if he did some work, thoughts of Renée would vanish from his mind. *Please, God, crash her site.* He laughed. *I'm kidding, God. But maybe You could have her call her IT guy?*

He pushed the power button, and his screen jumped to life. With two more investors, office space, and a date to go online, his dreams of launching his new retail app, *Legacy*, were shaping up to be a reality.

Can I do this? He shrugged off his concern. It didn't matter. When *Legacy* went live, nothing could hinder him from going forward. Nothing.

A vibration shook the bottom of his bag. He set his laptop aside and pulled his phone out. He didn't recognize the number. "Hello."

"Mr. Bennett. You've been ignoring my emails."

Ice crawled through his veins. "Professor Carlson?" He'd been out of school a year, but he'd recognize that voice anywhere. "I'm not ignoring them. I have nothing to say to you."

"On the contrary. We have a lot to discuss."

"No. We don't."

"When does *Legacy* go online?"

"That's between me and my investors."

"Investors? Interesting." Carlson snorted a laugh. "The rich boy from Richmond needed more than his silver spoon to fund his hobby."

Lucas clenched his teeth.

"Unless, of course, you've left the spoon at Daddy's table." Another pause. "That's it. Isn't it? Daddy Bennett doesn't know about your side hustle."

He pinched his eyes shut. The last thing he needed was to give Carlson any ammunition to hold over his head. The man had no basis for his claims that he helped generate *Legacy*. Other than greed.

"The Bennett bank account isn't funding you and now you're floundering out in the real world like the rest of us." Carlson snickered. "How's it feel?"

Lucas's eyes shot open. "Did you have a point to this call? If not, I'm hanging up."

"I've hired a lawyer, Mr. Bennett."

Heat wrapped around his collar. Carlson had crossed a line. If he wanted to play hardball, then so be it. "Good. I have ten. See you in court."

Lucas ended the call and pitched his phone onto the table. *Legacy* was his brainchild. He'd written every square inch of the program.

Springing from his seat, he stomped into the kitchen and

pulled a prepared meal out of the freezer. "A lawyer. Really?" He slammed the tin pan onto the counter. "Unbelievable."

He'd spent months preparing for *Legacy's* launch. Months begging investors to take a chance on him. Months editing code, and months hiding his progress from his family. A sour feeling crawled around in his belly. *What if Carlson tells Dad?*

Lucas yanked the lid off the single-serve pan and turned on the oven. He didn't want to hide *Legacy*, but his dad, Sinclair Walker Bennett, the patriarch of the Bennett empire, would have nothing to do with his new idea. The app was, in Dad's words, "a college kid's school project. A silly pastime."

His neck muscles twisted like spaghetti code. Dad hadn't cared that he'd won all those awards in STEM. Or if he did, he didn't show it. Dad was too concerned with the status quo. Keeping old clients happy and keeping a century-old family corporation buried in the dark ages.

What about new clients? Lucas slumped onto a metal stool. He didn't want to skirt his dad, but he wanted to step out on his own—not brand himself with an old family legacy. *I want to put my stamp on the world.*

Renée's face flashed across his mind. He wanted to be someone she'd look up to. Her knight in shining armor. Short-circuiting her technology villains with a single click of his mouse. He bit back a laugh. "It's official. I'm a nerd."

The oven beeped. He jumped out of his seat, slid the pan into the oven, and set the timer. In twenty minutes, he'd have a hot meal. In twenty minutes, he'd be eating alone. Again. Hopefully, that would change one day.

His thoughts trailed to memories of Mom as he grabbed a glass and filled it with water. "Play relaxing piano."

After a few seconds, piano music floated from the built-in speakers in the ceiling.

When she was alive, his father was happy. Carefree. Then his father remarried, and everything changed.

Lucas's throat burned, and he took a drink. There's no point in living in the past. He needed to look to the future. To *Legacy*.

He retrieved his laptop out of the living room, set it down on the counter, and punched in a few keys to get past the firewall leading to his software. An anomaly caught his eye. He typed again and searched out the problem. It was only an update. Nothing problematic. If everything kept moving forward, he'd be online by the fall.

His phone buzzed again making his heart jump. "If that's Carlson ..." Lucas grabbed the phone and took a swipe at the screen. Dad. Wonderful.

> There's a meeting tomorrow at three. Plan
> to be there.

His gut coiled into a knot. He'd been out of school for a year, traveled the world, and now he'd need to face his fate—taking his position at *Bennetts*.

> Can't make it.

Could he avoid taking up the mantle at *Bennetts* for a few more months?

> There's nothing more important than this.

Pounding from his chest rushed to his ears. Nothing he ever did would be more important than the family business. Ever.

> I'll see if I can change my schedule.

Tapping his fingers on the counter, he waited. There was no response.

That's how it always ended. Dad's demands weren't up for debate. There was no wiggle room if you were the sole heir to the Bennett family fortune.

But he wasn't. Was he? The sole heir. What about Preston? His stepbrother.

Lucas slid his fingers over his phone and typed out a second message.

> There's a three o'clock meeting at
> Bennetts tomorrow. Dad wants us there.

His pulse ticked up a notch. He was tired of being the one on Dad's radar all the time. Maybe it was time to give Preston some family responsibility.

He took a second to send a follow up text.

> No excuses.

Not bothering to catch Preston's response, he pulled a set of silverware out of the drawer and placed it next to his water. When the timer went off, the scent of baked spaghetti floated through the air.

I wonder if Renée likes spaghetti. The thought filled him with warmth. How could it be that after only a chance meeting, his heart cried out for her company?

Sitting down with his meal, he said grace, then slipped a fork full of spaghetti into his mouth.

She'd mentioned she had graduation and family coming into town, but maybe he'd need to drive to Newport News for a cup of coffee.

And commandeer her favorite booth.

A smile tugged at his lips.

This time, if they ran into each other, he'd move beyond tech support and ask her out on a date.

3

Emersyn breezed into the clapboard building of the *Yorktown Courant*. It had been her great-grandfather's idea to revive the archaic newspaper, and after his passing, she'd remained committed to keeping the little press afloat to honor his legacy.

"Morning, Sam." She stopped in front of the desk beside the door.

"Happy Thursday. The paper rolled out on time this morning." Samantha Mitchell, her best friend and part owner of the press, looked up from her laptop. "You look surprisingly energetic. How's your week going?"

Reid's dimpled smile flitted across her thoughts. "It's been a great week."

She stepped around Sam's desk and glided into the small office off the main room. The creaky floorboards beneath her groaned.

After she dropped her messenger bag on her desk, she stepped back into the front room and made a beeline for the coffee pot. She poured the brew into her favorite *Jane Austen* quotes mug and added about a half cup of cream.

Turning on her heels, she faced Sam. "I have a few assignments to finish, but they won't be hard." She took a sip of her coffee and frowned. It needed something. "I can't wait to walk across that stage."

"How's the website?"

As she slipped into the wingback flanking Sam's desk, Reid's voice filled her ears. *Americano. Two sugars.*

"Good." Her voice squeaked. "It's all fixed."

Sam's brow shot up. "You fixed it? How?"

"I … uh, well, it was the oddest thing …" Emersyn took a long drink of her coffee before diving into the story of how she'd met Reid.

"You're telling me a random hot software designer stumbled into the coffee shop, strolled up to your table, and offered to fix your website."

"Yeah. Something like that."

"It sounds like one of those sappy chick flicks. Did he ask for your number?"

"No. He was just being nice."

"Mm-hmm." Sam fished a piece of gum from her drawer and popped it into her mouth.

"What do you mean? Mm-hmm?

"Your cheeks are about as pink as my bubble gum."

Reflexively Emersyn's hands went to her cheeks. "So? I got in a run this morning. It's sunny out."

Sam catapulted from her seat, her purple boho skirt fluttering around her like a ripple in a lake. "You like him. Admit it." She scooted to the front of her desk and propped herself at the corner. "It's like a fairy tale. Cinderella. Or something like that. Did you leave a shoe behind?"

"Fairy tales are for fiction. Besides, after my last relationship—"

"Of whose name we shall not mention." Sam waved a hand in the air as if brandishing a magic wand.

"Exactly." Emersyn folded her arms. "I'm a little handsome guy shy."

"Eww. You said his name." Sam swiped her gold dragon

mug off the desk and walked over to the coffee maker for a refill. "When does your family fly in from London?"

"Next week. Right before Graduation." She couldn't wait to see Kelly and James. And little Noah. They were staying for three weeks. She'd already made plans to take them to her favorite hiking spots. "It'll be nice to have family filling up the house again."

"I bet. That little Noah's adorable." Sam slipped into her desk chair and set her mug down on a home décor magazine. "Make sure you bring them by. Your Uncle James always makes me laugh." She pinched her brow together in a mocking scowl and added a theatrical British accent. "With his stern words of advice and his tales of pirates."

She laughed as she sipped her coffee. Kelly and James weren't her real aunt and uncle, but they were as close to family as she had. "I'll bring them by. I might even convince Kelly to write an article for us while she's here."

"That would be great. We need all the good publicity we can get." Sam leaned forward and picked up the glitter pen off her desk. "I know how much the *Courant* means to you and Abram's memory, but this year's sales have been abysmal."

Emersyn nibbled on her bottom lip as she set down her mug. When she'd shared her idea to resurrect a newspaper from America's fledgling days, Sam didn't hesitate to jump on board. Now they were young entrepreneurs navigating the world of news and small business while fighting against the trends.

She released a sigh. "Maybe we should hire a marketing manager."

"We could, but they can get pricey." Sam twirled the pen between her fingers. "Another option—we could put the *Courant* online."

A knot formed in her gut. What about the ink? The paper? The smudges on her fingers?

"Here me out." Sam dropped the pen, clicked a few keys on her laptop, then pointed to her screen. "I've done some research. If we go online and a monthly paper, turn it into more like a newsletter, we could save money and keep the paper alive."

"So, what you're saying is the *Courant* is on life support."

"I'm afraid so."

"There's got to be another way." She rubbed her temples with her fingers. "Doesn't anyone care about nostalgia anymore? We'll do this, and it will move from paper to blog in an instant."

"Blogs are trendy."

"Blogs are … ugh. They're so overrated. Nobody reads them anymore."

Sam shot her a doe-eyed look. "I do."

"Fine. I'll think about it." She picked up her mug and took it back to the coffee bar for a refill. "This coffee's terrible. I'm buying an espresso maker."

"Subpar coffee's the least of our worries. I'm afraid I have some more bad news."

Stopping mid-pour, she turned to face Sam. "More?" She'd just fixed a leak in an antiquated roof and updated the wiring. She had plenty of funds at her disposal, but she wondered if hoisting a publication from the catacombs might prove more challenging than she'd expected.

"Lady M quit."

"What?" Placing the carafe back on the heat plate, she trudged back to Sam's desk. "Tell me you're kidding."

"Nope. She called in this morning. Something about a second chance at love." Sam's expression fell. "Our Lady M called from her honeymoon in Vegas."

"Second chance at love. Really?" Emersyn groaned. "Did she at least write this month's column?"

Sam's lips formed a tight line.

"Sam. Tell me she wrote the column."

"She didn't send anything to me."

"This can't be happening."

"I'll see what I can find to replace it."

Groaning, she did an about-face and headed toward her office to sulk.

After slumping into her desk chair, Emersyn set her coffee on a stack of unread mail and hung her head in her hands. "What am I going to do? Lady M's our most popular monthly read." She developed the column after reading about the famous Golden Age lady detectives. Lady M, a fictional character, solved mysteries around Virginia. For two years the column had been printed as a monthly whodunit, and for two years readers clamored to read it.

Now with Lady M on the lam, who was she going to hire to fill the gap?

"You could do it."

Emersyn jerked her head up. Sam stood in the doorway.

"What? Me?"

"Think about it. You love sleuthing. You avoid social media. Your grandfather was an enigma. You're practically *Batman*. You'd be perfect."

"No. I couldn't. I've got a full-time teaching job starting in August." She glanced around her tiny office. "I've got enough on my plate keeping this investment afloat."

Sam flopped into the club chair sitting at the front of her desk. "There won't be a paper if you lose Lady M. There won't even be a blog."

She was right, but ... "Wait. Why don't *you* do it? You've got a flare for the dramatic. You pretend to be someone different on stage every weekend."

Sam hailed from a family of poets and thespians. That's how they'd grown up together. Her papa supported the arts, and Sam's mother and father owned a local playhouse.

Sam shook her head. "Uh-uh. Nope. I don't like writing or deadlines. I was made for the stage, not to hide in the shadows like some sleuthhound."

Emersyn folded her arms in front of her and laid her head down. "What are we going to do?"

"Em."

"What?" The question came out muffled.

"Look at me."

She lifted her head.

"Your friends call you Em and now you need a writer for the Lady M column. Don't you see? It was tailor-made for you."

Scowling, she grabbed her coffee and took a long drink. It was lukewarm. Gross.

"I'm telling you, it's perfect." Sam's grin widened.

"Perfect." Emersyn huffed. "Just perfect."

Sam stood. As she walked back to her desk her laughter trailed behind her. "Yes, ladies and gentlemen, we have our Lady M."

Emersyn swiveled her chair and stared at the historic black and white photo of the newspaper building. The *Yorktown Courant* launched in the winter of 1931, with the efforts to turn the rural Tidewater town into an inviting place to settle and raise a family. She wondered if the first owners ever questioned the sanity of their decision.

She spun back, grabbed her laptop out of her bag, and powered it on. At least the original owners weren't being threatened with turning their paper into a blog.

As she scrolled through her emails, she hoped she'd find a final email from Betsy Ann Stanley, otherwise known as Lady M.

Betsy had been a private investigator for twenty years before she retired. Proficient in sleuthing and with no family, she had been the perfect candidate.

Emersyn's gaze landed on the email she hoped to find. Clicking it open she scanned its contents.

Dearest Miss Zucker,

I'm stepping down from my role as Lady M.

I've met someone.

You'll understand when the right one appears. It's like ...
magic.

Her thoughts turned to Reid with his dark-framed glasses and aristocratic cheekbones. When their fingers touched, it was like ... magic. Warmth curled in her stomach like a cat prepping for a nap. Would she ever see him again?

She slipped her hand into her bag and pulled out his card from the side pocket. *Reid Clark.*

He'd told her to reach out if she had an IT issue, but he hadn't asked for her phone number. Why?

As she traced her fingers over the card, she replayed their evening in the coffee shop.

He'd asked about what she taught in school, and she quizzed him about his knowledge of state parks. As the night wore on, they conversed like old friends. She hadn't wanted the night to end. But what about him?

If you ever need an IT guy ...

She shoved his business card back into her bag and returned to the email from Betsy.

A good PI never leaves a case unfinished. I've included several stories to finish out the summer and a list of leads.

Congratulations on your graduation.

Betsy

"Lady M didn't leave us in a lurch." She rolled her chair to the side and looked out at Sam. "She sent me the stories to cover the summer and a couple of leads for a few additional articles."

"Well, look at that." Sam pulled out a hot pink nail file and made two passes across her thumbnail "Now all we need is a new Lady M."

Ignoring the hint in Sam's voice, she ducked back into her office. *Could I be Lady M?*

She might not have a choice.

Clicking the document attached to the email, she scanned Betsy's list on additional leads.

The last one caught her eye.

Fraiser's Missing Deerhound.

Fraiser's Deerhound Pub was known for its large deerhound statue at the entrance. According to Betsy's notes, it had gone missing. With finals and her last month of student teaching, she hadn't even noticed. This was perfect. *Fraiser's* was just down the street. After graduation, she could track down the hound and have a reason to eat some Scottish fare.

Emersyn printed off the notes about the deerhound, then shoved them into her messenger bag.

Papa had sent her on scavenger hunts as a child, so this wouldn't be any different.

She packed up her laptop and slung her bag over her shoulder. Taking her now cold coffee to the sink in the bathroom, she dumped it out.

"I'll do it." She waltzed up to Sam's desk and placed her hands on her hips. "At least until we can find someone new."

Sam grinned. "I've got a whole closet full of wigs. Let me know what you need."

She imagined donning a trench coat and dark sunglasses while skulking under streetlamps. "I'll do that. But it won't be until after graduation."

"Maybe Kelly can help."

"Maybe." She pointed a thumb at the coffee pot over her shoulder. "That coffee's got to go. I'm heading out to grab a latte. Do you want anything?"

"I'm good." Sam waggled her eyebrows. "Maybe Mr. Website will be there."

"I doubt it." Mr. Website, Reid, Americano-two-sugars, was probably staring at his laptop not giving her a second thought.

As she walked to her car, her heart wedged against her ribcage. *I can do this. Right? Play another role.*

Miss Renée at school.

Emersyn Zucker, the heir at philanthropic events.

Lady M at the newspaper.

She'd taken on more aliases than a jewel thief.

A smile tugged on her lips as she pulled out of the parking spot and went in search of a happier cup of coffee.

Sleuthing might be fun. There was no telling what she might uncover.

4

Lucas pulled into his assigned parking spot at *Bennetts* downtown Richmond office and turned off the car.

"Today should be interesting."

Dad had not been pleased that Lucas had invited Preston to their meeting yesterday. Or that he'd tried to pitch his new ideas to the board without clearing it with him first.

But if Dad wanted him to take the helm at *Bennetts Estates and Antiques*, he'd needed to hear him out. Not only about launching the business into the twenty-first century, but also about launching *Legacy*. It was a two-for-one deal. If the man wanted Lucas to show initiative, then he'd show it.

After that, he'd work on making plans to head to Newport News for that cup of coffee.

Tapping out a beat on the steering wheel, he thought about Renée. What was he going to do when he got there? Hang out, nursing an Americano, until she stopped in?

He leaned his head back against the headrest and blew out a breath. How was he supposed to battle Dad this morning with his mind somewhere else?

"Focus ..." He stepped out of his two-seater and armed the alarm.

When he walked through the double doors, Dad's assistant pointed down the hall. "He's waiting for you."

"Great. Is he in a good mood?"

She flashed him a scolding look.

He strode to his dad's door, rapped once, then stepped inside.

Dad huffed but didn't look up. "It's about time."

"I came in as soon as I could."

"I didn't appreciate that stunt you pulled bringing Preston to the investor's meeting."

Lucas pulled back his shoulders, gripped his hands behind his back, and waited for the firing squad.

"I need you to be more present. Here. In this building." Dad stared up at him from his plush, leather chair like a hawk sizing up its prey. "If you're going to step in as head of this business you need to prove yourself."

"We went over this. I won't be taking over the business. At least not right now. I thought you agreed that—"

"Take a seat." Dad motioned to the chair flanking the desk.

Muscles pinched tight, Lucas lowered himself into the chair.

"It's the family business." A calculating smile slid across Dad's face. "Of course, you're taking the helm."

"I'm working on something. An idea I—"

"Are you talking about that app again?"

Holding Dad's stare, Lucas's pulse quickened. *God, help me to stay calm.* "It's called *Legacy*."

"That was a hobby." Dad waved a hand in the air as if brushing aside a fly. "Kept you out of trouble while you were in college."

"It's not a hobby."

"You're twenty-five years old. It's time to grow up. You'll take the reins and run this company the way it's been done for generations."

Lucas pressed his hands onto the armrest.

Dad's eyes narrowed. "Do you really think I'm going to hand this business over to Preston?"

"Why not? He's family. Isn't he?"

"You're my son. He's not."

"What if I sell back my shares?"

Dad slammed a fist on the desk "I've worked all my life building this for you, and you're going to toss it away?"

"No, you worked all your life building this for *you*."

"That silver spoon you eat off of is because I've given it to you."

His stomach lurched. How had it come to this? His father and him bickering like enemies. Why couldn't Dad let him be his own man?

Dad sat back and folded his arms. "Does this have to do with me remarrying? It's been years since Letitia and I tied the knot."

Lucas pried his fingers off the armrest and steepled them in his lap. He didn't want to talk about his stepmother. Not now. Not ever.

Dad's expression darkened. "Well?"

"No."

"You're not a very good liar."

Heat surged around his neck. If Dad only knew he'd been lying about *Legacy* for months. *God, forgive me.*

Dad unhooked his arms, stood, and prowled over to the window. He picked up a crystal paperweight off the windowsill and held it up to the sun. The colors bounced off the walls like a kaleidoscope.

"Here's what's going to happen. You're going to step into the role you were destined for and work with me for five years." He set down the paperweight and pivoted to face Lucas. "By then, you'll be thirty. If you decide you want to turn your back on your family, I give you permission to sell your shares and leave." A shadow slipped across his expression. "You can sell the whole company if you want to. If my legacy dies with me, then so be it." Dad picked off an imaginary lint from his dark lapel. "I'll be retired and living on a yacht somewhere in the Caribbean."

"With Letitia?"

"Of course, with Letitia. Who else would I be with?"

"Speaking of liars."

Dad's hand shot up. "Don't. Don't bring up the past. Letitia had her reasons. I've forgiven her. So should you."

Lucas's spine stiffened. After Mom died, Letitia Eleanor Rossi stepped into their family out of nowhere, toyed with his dad's grieving heart, then waited to say 'I do' before confessing she had a child to add to the mix. Four years younger and spoiled to the core, Preston Antonio Rossi had become his stepbrother overnight.

"I get it, son." Dad turned and eased onto the corner of the desk to face him. "You have dreams you want to pursue. We all do. But sometimes you need to pursue your dream after you've done your duty."

Lucas shifted his gaze and stared out at the summer sky. How would Dad feel knowing he was already pursuing his dream? Once *Legacy* went online, he'd be Dad's competitor. A fist wrapped around his heart and squeezed. *Maybe I should come clean right now?*

"Loyalty, son."

He jerked his head back to face his father. "What?"

"Loyalty and family. Blood family. These are the most important things to me."

Sand coated his throat. Did he really want *Bennetts* to fall into the hands of shareholders? Ever since he was a little boy, he'd imagined working side-by-side with his father. What had changed?

Lucas pulled himself out of the chair and ambled over to the window. "Have you considered my ideas about a more modern approach to business?"

"Are you talking about going online?"

He spun to face his father. "Yes."

"We've been in business for over a century. I don't see why we need to change anything."

He sent a silent plea heavenward, hoping Dad would listen to his pitch this time. "Every company has a presence online."

"Not *Bennetts*. This is a family business. We do work face to face. If we change, we become like one of those warehouse stores."

"Those warehouse stores are making millions."

Dad scowled. "We make plenty."

Bennetts did make plenty, but they'd probably missed out on thousands of customers while the world waxed mobile. People wanted to pull out their phones, make a purchase, and have it waiting for them when they got home.

Lucas cleared his throat, weighing his next move. "The past few years our revenue has been down."

Dad pulled himself from his perch and rounded his desk. "There's been a lot going on the past few years." As he slid back into his chair, Dad smoothed his hand down the front of his suit jacket. "The economy fluctuates. Just like business. If you'd spend more time here, you'd know that."

"I understand, but during those times of flux, if we were online, we'd have broadened our client list not decreased it."

"What about our focus on provenance? Nobody's going to care where a piece came from if they swipe through a thousand images on a screen."

"I disagree." He approached the desk but remained standing. "I have ideas that would allow us to not only study the provenance of a piece but also place our customers in an interactive experience with the product." Lucas's pulse jumped. "Not every purchase would be online, but using the internet to reach worldwide is the business of the future. With this approach, we'd bring together buyers and sellers, connecting countries and cultures, enabling families to learn about each other through their legacies."

Dad leaned forward and steepled his fingers on the desk. "I'd be more inclined to hear those ideas if you agree to my terms. Five years."

Lucas inhaled then exhaled slowly. Keeping *Legacy* a secret for five years would be impossible. "One year."

Dad settled back in his seat. "You expect me to hand over the reins by next summer? It would be like throwing a guppie in with the sharks."

Lucas flinched and looked away.

"I'll reconsider in four. You need to prove yourself."

Time to play hardball. He risked a look into the steel grey of his father's eyes. "Two years. Then I get to implement what I want at *Bennetts*. If you can't agree to that, I'll walk away."

Dad's brow shot up. "You'll walk away? Are you prepared for what that means?"

Sweat pooled under his arms. Was he? "Yes sir."

For several seconds silence pressed in around them.

Dad was good at this. Waiting. Calling people's bluff. Making you sweat. A cackle escaped Dad's lips. "Sit down, son. Before you pass out."

"I'll stand." Lucas squared his shoulders.

Dad continued to hold his gaze. "Okay. Two years."

"Okay?"

"Start working with me now. Today." Dad paused. "I need to see that you care about *Bennetts* and the future of this business, then in two years, it's yours. I'll step down."

Lucas wrestled with the grin tugging at his lips. Twenty-four months. He'd be working all hours of the day, but he could do this. Who needed sleep anyhow?

Before he slipped back into the chair, he stuck out his hand. "Deal."

Dad shook his hand, his look approving. "I admire your tenacity. Or is it your arrogance? It took guts to hold the line." Dad released his hand and nodded to the seat. "Sit. We'll start now. I have two tasks for you."

He struggled to harness the hamster running through his thoughts as he took a seat. "What do you need me to do?"

"A prominent businessman passed away. I need you to meet with his daughter and help them decide to liquidate their estate. Think of this as your initiation."

"Who is it? Anyone I know?"

"Edward Renaldi, the owner of Renaldi's Equestrian Center. He was a dear friend of mine. His daughter, Genevieve, is his only living heir. She's afraid of horses, or some such nonsense, and she wants to sell the equestrian center and the mansion that goes with it."

"Isn't she expecting *you*?"

"Letitia and I are leaving for Denver in the morning. I planned for you to go in my place."

He opened his mouth to protest, then pursed his lips. Before they'd even spoken this morning Dad had already woven him into the business. "What do I need to know? About the estate?"

"Genevieve Renaldi isn't married."

"What?"

"Here me out. She's twenty-seven. Only two years older than you. Smart. Educated. She's a pediatrician and has a practice in Fairfax."

"Are you setting me up at an estate purchase?" Lucas's blood boiled.

"No. I'm not setting you up. I just wanted to pass on that she was single. Her family is ... well, she comes from a great Italian family, and like I said, Edward was a good friend of mine. I thought since you're taking the family business seriously, you should think about settling down."

"Do you have her pedigree papers? I'd like to look over them before I call her."

"Lucas Reid. Why are you being so difficult?"

"I told you, I want to meet someone on my terms. Not someone in the market for a pure-bred husband." A flash of

Renée sitting across from him with her blackberry mocha crossed his mind.

"I didn't say she was in the market for a husband." Dad rubbed his hand across his jaw. "I know Mom would've liked to see you married. I want to make sure you find the right person. Someone who compliments you."

Lucas folded his arms and bit down on the inside of his cheek. First business, now his love life. Dad was a master manipulator. "You might think this is ridiculous, but I want to meet someone like you met Mom. A chance meeting. Nothing planned." He blew out his breath and counted to five. "I want to fall in love with someone, not combine assets into a tidy portfolio."

Dad's expression fell. "That kind of love, with me and your mom, only happens in those sappy romance movies." His eyes turned glossy. "You need to find someone who'll support you and stick it out through the storms of life. Find someone who cares about *Bennetts* as much as you do."

Lucas frowned. What about love? His father met Mom while he was home on leave from the Navy. According to Dad, when he first saw her, his whole world fell off its axis.

Like when I met Renée.

"Give Genevieve a chance." Dad's demanding tone settled like a weight. "Take her out to dinner. Get to know her. Look over the estate items and set up a time to return to give her an offer. When I get back, we'll see if *Bennetts* can make a deal." Dad relaxed back in his seat. "Now for the second task."

Uncurling his arms, Lucas ran his palms across his thighs. "I thought the second task was to strut the Bennett name in front of Genevieve like an eager peacock."

Dad shot him a glare. "I was just giving you her status. What you do with it is up to you."

Good, because all he could think about was going back to the coffee shop and finding Renée.

"We've had a few incidents at our warehouses."

Dad's words yanked him back. "What kind of incidents?"

"There was a break-in at the Albuquerque warehouse, and in Denver, we had a fire. That's why I'm going to Denver then to Albuquerque, to see if we need to beef up security."

"Was anything stolen in Albuquerque?"

"I'm running the inventory now. I'll keep you updated." Dad opened a drawer and pulled out a file. "We had another fire outside of our Oklahoma City location two nights ago."

"Two fires?"

Dad nodded, his expression turning grim. "I'm sending you to Oklahoma City to check on things."

Lucas opened the file and skimmed the report.

"I want you to talk with the fire investigator. I need someone I trust to comb through the inventory." Dad hesitated. "I don't think these were accidents."

Lucas lifted his gaze. "Someone's targeting us?"

"I received this in the mail last week." Dad fished an envelope from his desk drawer, pulled a slip of paper out, and handed it to him.

Lucas scanned the words.

I'm owed my cut. I'll get it one way or another.

When he looked up, Dad pinned him with a stare. "It was addressed to you. Any thoughts on who might have sent it?"

He swallowed hard, gut clenching. "No."

"I didn't think so. I suspect it might be someone from Cavanaugh's."

"Why?"

"I outbid them on the Salina's estate. Salina's art is worth millions." Dad took the letter from him and placed it back in the drawer. "It's possible word got out that you're meeting with Genevieve. Cavanaugh's been chomping at the bit to get a hold of Renaldi's estate."

"But why now? The feud between you and Buster Cavanaugh has been going on for years."

His father shrugged. "I don't know. Who else could it be? This letter, along with the fire in OKC, makes me wonder if they're trying to send *you* a warning."

"Maybe." His breakfast turned in his stomach. "Or, it was a coincidence."

"I want you to go to Oklahoma City and find out." Dad's expression brightened. "While you're there, you can reach out to some of our local clients. See if you can set up any personal showings. You shouldn't be there longer than a week."

Lucas frowned. Galivanting all over the country wasn't what he had in mind when he agreed to step up his role at the office. A week away playing sleuth took him away from working on *Legacy*.

"When should I leave?"

"Your flight leaves Monday. In the morning."

He pulled out his phone and scrolled through his calendar. Juggling two businesses would be tricky. "Don't plan anything for me after this."

"Ah. That's right. Your yearly summer trip with your old roommates."

"Yeah." Lucas bit back the half-truth. He *was* meeting up with his friends for a few weeks, but after that, he'd focus on gathering the final batch of investors for *Legacy*. "I leave the first week of June."

"Where are you going this year?"

"Tokyo, then on to Seoul."

"Great cities. See what contacts you can make while you're there."

His jaw clenched. "I'll see what I can do."

"I have a meeting in thirty. My assistant will send you your flight info." Dad remained seated. "I'm glad we came to an agreement today. Let me know what you uncover in OKC and good luck on the Renaldi estate."

Lucas rose and while he strode out of Dad's office, he couldn't help but wonder who bested who today.

When he reached his car, the words from the note circled through his thoughts.

Was it Cavanaugh's trying to get under his skin? Or was Carlson trying to expand his threats to *Bennetts*?

He sank into the driver's seat and huffed out a breath. Either way, his plans for coffee in Newport News had been shoved to the back burner.

It's probably for the best.

With double the workload, he didn't have time to fall in love.

5

E njoying her quiet Sunday evening, Emersyn sipped on a mug of hot tea while she sat in her living room, cocooned in a blanket, and enthralled in a Victorian mystery novel. She hoped to take a break from thinking about her finals and glean inspiration from one of her favorite fictional lady sleuths.

In this story, there were rules female detectives lived by as they hid in the shadows and rarely received the praise they deserved for their success.

Rule number one—dress inconspicuously. She smiled, remembering Sam's offer to loan her a wig. She might have to take her up on that.

Rule number two—carry a walking stick for personal defense. She waggled her martial-arts-trained fingers. Weapon. Check.

Rule number three—never trust a man in a cheap suit.

She giggled as she set down her mug and read a few more pages. The author transported her to the fog-laden Thames River where the body of a murdered journalist lay bloated and bug-eyed on the craggy banks. Creepy.

The doorbell chimed, and Emersyn jumped. She waited as her housekeeper, Donna, answered the door.

"Em, you have a guest." Donna glided into the sitting room.

"Who?"

Expression beaming, Donna nodded toward the entryway. "Come see."

She set down her book and followed her into the foyer.

"Surprise!" Kelly Landon stood in the entry with her arms open wide. "I smell Earl Grey. Please tell me you haven't gone to the dark side with James."

"Only on days when I'm engrossed in a good book." Leaning into Kelly's embrace, the scents of English lavender circled her.

"Okay. I'll allow it." When she stepped back, Kelly's eyes twinkled. "Don't tell James, but I agree, book reading days are perfect tea days. Not book writing days. I need the dark, creamy brew to write."

Kelly glanced around the entryway and released a sigh. "I'll always remember the first time I walked over this threshold." She looked down at the black and white tiles, then skipped across a few squares like a child playing hopscotch. "I was convinced I'd fallen down a rabbit hole the day I met Abram."

Emersyn's insides warmed. Papa had a unique way of drawing people into another world. A world filled with mystery and adventure.

"Come on, leave your luggage, we'll get it later." She motioned for Kelly to follow her into the sitting room. "What are you doing here? Graduation isn't until next weekend."

Donna trailed behind them, peppering Kelly with a bevy of questions. "When's your next novel coming out? How are James and Noah? Was anyone famous on your flight?"

Kelly slipped into the oversized club chair facing the couch. "Everything's great back home and the flight was long but disappointingly without celebrities. The novel's working, but I've got a lot of research to do."

Donna faced Kelly, arms akimbo. "Whatever you write, I'm sure will be a best seller. But for now, you need coffee and lots of cream."

"Yes, please." Kelly nodded like an enthusiastic puppy. "Airplane coffee makes me want to cry."

All three of them laughed as Donna slipped out of the room with a promise to bring back a plate of shortbread cookies to snack on.

Emersyn resumed her place on the couch, this time tugging the blanket up to her chest and tucking it over her lap. "I can't believe you're here."

"I thought it might be fun to have some *girl* time before the boys get here. We haven't done that in a while." Kelly tipped her chin down. "You sounded a little distracted on the phone. I wanted to make sure all was well."

"I'm fine." An itch tickled her throat, and she reached for her Earl Grey. "Just a little preoccupied with graduation and … a few other things."

Donna swept back into the room carrying a tray with a cup of coffee, a fresh pot of tea, and a plate of shortbread cookies. "I come bearing snacks."

Kelly's eyes turned glossy. "Thank you, Donna."

"Of course. It's good to have you here, even if it is only for a few weeks." Donna brushed away a tear. "Is there anything else I can get you girls?"

Emersyn tugged the blanket closer. The memories they shared with Abram wrapped the room in a cozy embrace. "Let's make up the blue room for Kelly and James. After James and Noah arrive, little Noah can stay next door in the adjoining room."

"Perfect. I'm so glad you're back." Donna squeezed Kelly's arm before she swept out of the room.

"I love the blue room." Kelly took a leisurely drink of her coffee as she nestled back in her seat.

"I know you do. Papa loved it too." Her eyes misted and she cleared her throat. "I moved the large desk from the library into there, so you'd have somewhere to write."

"Thank you." Kelly placed her coffee back on the tray.

"Speaking of the library, we need to go exploring again. I'm convinced more treasures are hiding in there."

Emersyn picked up the teapot and refilled her mug. "Papa liked to hide things."

"It all started when he was a little boy." Kelly smiled. "He told me he hid his treasures under the floorboards in his parents' apartment."

"I remember that. Last month we moved the grandfather clock in the hall while spring cleaning, and a string was hanging out of the back."

Kelly's eyes brightened. "What was attached to the cord?"

"A small velvet bag with a black-and-white photo of a young man and a string of pearls."

"Was there a name on the photo?"

"Yes. Henrich Krause. I think he may have been a childhood friend of Papa's."

"Sounds like another mystery your papa left behind for you to unravel." Kelly took a cookie off the plate and dunked it in her coffee before taking a bite.

"We should work on tracking down Henrich's family together. Maybe the pearls are a family heirloom."

"Returning an heirloom …" Kelly finished off her cookie, and a contemplative look covered her expression. "I might be up for that."

"How are James and Noah? Do you still enjoy city life in London?"

"I do. James is filling in for the physical education teacher at Noah's school this fall, so the boys will be together all day." Kelly kicked off her sneakers and pulled her legs up under her. "That will leave me some quiet time to write."

"What are you working on?"

"A romantic suspense set in medieval England." Kelly reached for her mug, releasing a contented sigh after she took a drink. "When you're there every day, walking through the ruins of the past, it's easy to get lost in the history."

"I can see that."

"How's the *Yorktown Courant* doing?" Kelly put her mug down, then pulled the crocheted blanket from the back of the chair into her lap.

"I lost my Lady M last week."

"Oh, no."

"Yeah. She met the love of her life and ran off to Vegas."

"Wow. People do crazy things for love."

"They do." She paused a moment as she imagined herself calling Lucas. Could she be so bold as to make the first move?

"I hope your runaway Lady M is happy." Kelly schooled her features. "But I'm sorry she left you in a lurch."

"It's okay. I'm going to work the column for a few months while I look for someone new." Emersyn took a sip of her tea, then said, "I don't like to advertise for the position. I want to make the transition from one Lady M to another seamless."

"That makes sense."

"Thankfully Lady M left me a handful of stories to finish out the summer."

Kelly played with the tassels on the blanket. "I hope you can find a new Lady M. She's grown quite the fandom online."

Emersyn cringed. Everything flourished online. Maybe she should reconsider Sam's suggestion.

"You'll be a great temporary Lady M." Kelly interrupted her thoughts. "You've always loved puzzles. It runs in your blood."

She bit back a laugh. "I guess it does."

"I know you want to teach, but this might give you a chance to explore the research side of journalism." Kelly glanced out the window and a faraway look blanketed her features. "Sometimes it only takes one push before you fall into your calling."

"What are you thinking about? You look deep in thought."

She turned back, shrugging. "Oh, it's nothing. I was just recalling how Abram loved a good mystery."

A weight tugged on her heart. Papa had fanned the flames of her inquisitive mind, giving her puzzles to solve and sending her on scavenger hunts. What would he say now about her writing as Lady M?

"Emersyn dear, it's time to go on an adventure."

As the evening progressed, they continued to sip their cozy drinks and chat as if time had never passed. Kelly talked about her balance between writer and mom, and Emersyn discussed her new job at Maplewood Prep.

"I have something I want to tell you." They both blurted out the words at the same time.

Kelly giggled. "You go first."

Emersyn stared down at her stocking feet. She needed to confide in someone.

"What is it Em? Is everything okay?"

She lifted her chin, pulse skipping. "I met someone."

"You did?" Kelly grinned like a schoolgirl. "Tell me everything."

"His name's Reid. We met at a coffee shop."

"Reid. That's a great name for a leading man. What does he do?"

"He's a software designer. He designed an app, and it goes live in the fall."

"What kind of app?"

Emersyn explained what Reid told her about his online estate sale business and his ideas about connecting buyers with sellers. "I could tell he loves what he does. He had the same look you get when you talk about your characters."

"I do love my characters." Kelly's expression turned wistful. "You said you met Reid at a coffee shop, but how did you two get into a conversation?"

"There weren't any tables open, so he asked if he could share mine."

"Your booth?"

Emersyn laughed. "Yeah. My unofficial private booth." Heat wrapped around her as she relayed their initial meeting and how Reid returned later in the evening to help her with her website.

"It's funny, I run from technology, but I was drawn to him." Her voice wobbled. "While he worked on my website, his fingers danced across the keys like an artist sketching an intricate landscape. But he wasn't all algorithms and procedures. He was engaging and … a little shy. After he finished with the website we talked about books and the places we traveled."

"He sounds very nice." Kelly waggled her brows. "And maybe a little handsome?"

Prickly heat danced across her cheekbones.

"Oh, I see." Kelly flashed her a knowing look. "He's leading-man handsome."

She nodded, heart pounding. "Tall, with dark, wavy hair and gray-blue eyes."

"Great description." Kelly arched a brow. "But I sense there's something else. What *aren't* you saying?"

"I didn't give him my real name."

"Ah, so there it is. What pseudonym did you give him? A good pen name can make or break a story."

"Renée Landon. I'll be using Miss Landon at school. They were fine with it after I explained my desire for privacy."

"I love it. Now we really are sisters."

Despite Kelly's excitement, dread curled in her belly. "What am I going to do?"

"What do you mean?"

"After I ended it with Guy, I made a promise to myself to be more cautious."

"I remember Guy. The politician. Right?"

"Yes. Guy Arnold Atwater, the third. I thought he was a knight in shining armor. Turns out he was a devil in disguise."

"I'm not sure I'd trust a guy named Guy." Kelly snickered. "Who names their son Guy? I mean it's not very thought out."

"I think it was his grandfather's name or something. It doesn't matter. That relationship was a disaster. I was blinded by his charisma and those haunting brown eyes."

"He sounds like the perfect man. I've been duped by one of those before."

"Oh?"

Kelly waved her off. "It's a long story. What happened to Guy? One minute you were together and the next ..."

"I caught him on a call pretending to be my assistant to garner tickets for a private dinner at the governor's mansion." She leaned back and blew out an exasperated breath. "I don't even have an assistant."

"That's terrible."

"If he'd asked me, I would have checked into the event. Instead, he pretended the governor personally asked him to attend and I was his plus one."

"What did you do?"

"I know the governor's daughter. I told her what happened, and she passed it on to her daddy." She folded her arms with a shrug. "I went to the event sans Guy and made sure I got my photo taken with the governor for their social media post."

Kelly's lips tipped at one corner. "Aww. Poor, Guy."

Emersyn snorted at her play on words. "Now you see why I've vowed to keep my identity a secret. What if all Reid cares about is money? Or worse. What if he's just a software designer who doesn't want to be thrown into the chaos that comes with the Zucker last name?"

"What does his family do?"

She shrugged. "I didn't ask."

"I think you should find out. What if his family has ties to criminals? Like the Russian mafia?"

"That's a stretch. Even for *your* imagination." She picked up her mug and took a sip of her tea. "Have you ever met anyone in the Russian mafia?"

Kelly waved her off. "No. Of course not. I'm just saying, sometimes people aren't who they seem to be."

"I'm not who I said I was."

"Yes, you are. You told him you're a teacher. Right?"

"Yes." She set her mug back on the tray.

"And you're going by Renée Landon at school?"

"Yeah.

"Then it's not a lie."

She hesitated. "But how am I going to tell him who I really am?"

"Get to know him a little better, then break it to him. Maybe you could do the reverse Cinderella." Kelly's face brightened. "Rescue him from his laptop, slap a tuxedo on him, and fly him to Paris."

Emersyn groaned. "That could end in disaster. 'I'm here to sweep you away. Did I mention I'm a Zucker?'"

"What *did* you tell him about your family?"

"I told him the basics. I was raised by my great-grandparents, and now you and James are my closest family."

"If he's a computer guy, maybe he's already run you through some facial recognition software."

"He doesn't have my picture." A grin towed at her lips. "I think only *your* friend circle is that weird."

"You mean Henry?"

At the mention of Kelly's brother-in-law, they both folded over with laughter.

Henry Allen Taylor, James's younger brother, could hack into His Majesty's computer blindfolded.

Kelly settled back in her seat, stretched her legs in front of her, and wiggled her toes. "Henry means well."

"I'm beginning to think Henry works for MI6 or something."

"Nothing as glamorous as that."

"Right. The man can track down anyone." Emersyn smoothed out a wrinkle in her blanket. "Give him a laptop and he's lethal."

Kelly picked up her mug and took a slow drink. "Henry's boring. He works in IT."

"Sure, he does."

"Speaking of Henry, want me to have him look up Reid?"

"No."

"Why not?"

"I want to find out about Reid on my own."

Kelly tapped her fingernails on her mug. "But, what if he—"

"No. Listen, I just want to meet him again." Her heart deflated. What if he wasn't interested? "I want to get to know him face to face, not from a printed report Henry draws up."

"I might have better peace of mind if *I* knew." Kelly said.

"I'll be fine. I'm being so cautious he doesn't even have my name or number."

Kelly laughed. "Good point."

"If I do see him again, I'll just blurt out my name. Quick and easy. Isn't honesty the best policy?"

"Yes. It is." Kelly set her mug down and yawned. "I think I'll call it a night. I didn't sleep much on the plane."

How could she call it a night after sipping on coffee? "What did you want to tell me?"

"Let's talk about it later. I'm here for girl time." Kelly pulled off her blanket and stood. "When I get up, we'll discuss what you should wear to your next coffee date."

"Sounds good."

She waited for Kelly to exit the room before she went to the foyer, dug through her messenger bag, and pulled out Reid's business card and her phone. What did she have to lose?

She checked the time. It was past midnight. Probably too late to text someone she barely knew.

Shifting from one foot to the other she considered what she should say. A casual hello or an outright invite to meet up again?

She slid Reid's card into her back pocket and climbed the stairs to her room. She'd text him tomorrow morning. Maybe she'd start with something casual like thanking him again for his help on her website.

What happened after that would be up to Reid.

6

As the plane taxied into the Oklahoma City airport, Lucas switched his phone off airplane mode. He hoped the uneventful Monday morning flight would be a precursor to the week. Quick and easy.

His screen blinked to life with a trickle of texts. Two from Dad's assistant, one from the insurance adjuster agreeing to meet him before lunch, and a text from an unknown number.

As he scanned the last message his pulse quickened.

> Sent in my website for my final grade.
> Thank you again. BTW, this is Renée.

Punching out a response, he stayed rooted to his seat.

I'm glad. Do you want to meet for coffee?

That sounded a little eager. He deleted the text, then typed out another answer.

Good to hear.

He scrapped his words again. This wasn't working.

The person to his right nudged him. "There's a gap. You getting out?"

"Yeah. Sorry." Lucas slid his phone into his pocket as he stood and eased into the aisle. After grabbing his bag from the overhead bin, he joined the line leaving the plane. *How should I respond?*

When he cleared the jetway, he ducked into an alcove and pulled out his phone. Staring at Renée's words, he tried to decipher her mood. Did she want to start up a conversation? Why else would she reach out?

A buzz alerted him to a call. Sighing, he answered it. "Yeah, Dad. I just landed. What's up?"

Dad ran through a handful of last-minute instructions about meeting with the insurance adjuster. "Check your email. I have a lead on a possible new client. It's a large ranch, in a little town east of the city."

"I'll check my email when I get to the warehouse."

After he ended the call, he reopened the text from Renée. Would she want to see him again?

> Glad the website is working.

> Did your family get in from the UK?

Lucas pushed send and stared at his screen for what seemed like an eternity.

Nothing.

He raked a hand through his hair. She'll text back. Won't she?

Slipping his phone into his carry-on, he headed for the rentals. He'd been to the Oklahoma City warehouse three times. One to shadow his dad during an acquisition, and two quick visits for private showings. Each time he'd been more interested in catching a ballgame down in Bricktown than watching his dad at work.

After picking out the rental, he added the warehouse address to the GPS, then pulled out of the parking lot. As he drove through the steady traffic, he went through his mental checklist with Dad's additional tasks.

His phone buzzed, breaking his concentration. Lucas resisted the urge to check the text while he meandered through the streets downtown. According to the map, the warehouse was nestled between a retro bakery and an abandoned auto complex.

Finally, after finding the right street, he pulled into one of the parking spaces and fished his phone out of his bag. It was another text from Renée.

Yes!

He chuckled at the happy face emoji, followed by the plane and heart emoji.

Kelly flew in a few days early. James and Noah arrive at the end of the week. What are you up to this week?

Lucas stepped out of the rental and scanned the area. Sounds of construction floated through the air, coming from the building across the street. Pivoting to his left, he took a picture of a tall office building, then pushed send.

I'm out of town for work. Any guesses where?

A moment passed before she sent her response.

Dallas?

He smiled. She was close.

Go a little north.

A video blinked on his screen of a cowboy on a horse singing *Oklahoma!*

A chuckle rose in his throat. He sent a return text explaining about the impromptu trip his dad had sent him on, then his fingers froze. Take a leap. All she can say is no.

Would you like to grab a coffee when I get back?

57

The thrum of his heart rushed to his ears as he pushed send. Please say yes.

After a second, her answer filled the screen.

I would love to.

Her words were followed by a coffee mug emoji and a laptop emoji.

Releasing his breath, Lucas leaned against the car and sighed. "She said yes."

He told her to have a great time with her family then ended the conversation with a quick tip on how to add some elements to spice up her website. She assured him she wouldn't lay a finger on her website unless he was close by to fix her mistakes.

Warmth spread through his chest. He couldn't wait for that cup of coffee.

With renewed energy, Lucas unlocked the warehouse door and entered the code to disarm the alarm. Inside the warehouse, rows of shelving lined with books and knick-knacks stretched along one side of the building. On the opposite side, there were bulky pieces of furniture and architectural pieces from abandoned local buildings. At first glance, nothing looked as if it had been disturbed.

Lucas strode to the office and flipped on the lights. After dumping his luggage onto a table in the corner, he pulled out his laptop and set it on the desk. With a few hours to spare before he could check into his hotel, he decided to get comfortable.

Settling into the desk chair, he tapped on his keyboard and brought up the inventory report for the warehouse. He groaned. It was over one hundred pages long. It would take more than a hasty perusal to know if anything had been taken during the fire when their security had lapsed.

Clicking off the list, he opened the security camera's video file from the night of the fire. Several lightning strikes streaked across the background. Three seconds in, a shadow emerged from behind a dumpster in the alleyway. Lucas paused the video and zoomed in. Odd. The person was tall, dressed in black, and wore a mask covering everything but his eyes.

He stopped the video and opened the email with the police report. Scanning past the legalese, he zeroed in on the last couple of lines.

"A chair and an outdoor camp stove were found behind the dumpster. Most likely a drifter started the fire."

He returned to the paused video. Why would a drifter wear a face mask? In May?

He pushed play and continued to analyze the feed. The person threw what looked like a pan into the dumpster. Several seconds rolled over, then sparks leaped out of the metal doors and brushed against the outside wall.

Another bolt of lightning lit up the video as the streetlights blinked, then went dark. After several minutes, flashing lights filled the bottom half of the screen. Before the emergency vehicles crossed in front of the camera, the feed went dark.

Lucas sat back and released a long breath. It seemed all cut and dry but a clawing in his gut told him something was off. Why was the guy wearing a mask?

A firm knock at the door yanked him from his thoughts. After a quick check of the security camera showed a man with a briefcase, Lucas left the office and headed to the front.

When he opened the door, a lanky, gray-haired man stood in the doorway, holding out his hand. "I'm Tony Shelton, the insurance adjuster."

"Lucas Bennett." He shook Tony's hand, then motioned for him to follow him inside.

Tony pointed toward the exit door at the back of the warehouse. "Why don't we head out back and take a look around."

"Sounds good."

When they stepped into the alley, Tony examined the burn marks on the building, then walked over to the dumpster. "According to the report, the dumpster caught fire, we can assume from a passerby or someone sleeping out here." He motioned to a charred old cart turned upside down behind the dumpster.

Lucas pointed to the damaged outside wall. "The fire reached the wall but is contained there. There's no damage inside the warehouse."

"We had some crazy storms that night. Lots of wind." Tony joined him by the wall and ran his hand over the soot-painted brick. "By the time the emergency vehicles showed up the rain was coming down hard, which probably helped contain the fire. Three tornadoes were reported east of the city."

"Is that normal?"

Tony's mouth quirked into a grin. "The storms? Yep. In May, the weather can go from sunny skies to Dorothy's front yard in a matter of minutes."

Lucas shuddered. He'd seen bad weather in Virginia, mostly remnants of hurricanes, but they usually had days to prepare.

Tony motioned toward the door and glanced up at the camera. "I see in the report you lost security footage for about two hours that night."

"I've gone over the video. A person disappears behind the dumpster, then there's a spark, followed by the fire. After the emergency lights enter the video, it looks like the street loses electricity."

Tony shoved his notebook back in his briefcase. "The electric company had numerous reports of power outages downtown. Do you have a backup generator for your building?"

"We do. It clicked on, but it looked like it took another few hours for the cameras to come online." Lucas rubbed a hand across his chin. "One thing seems out of place to me."

"What's that?"

"The guy was dressed all in black, or dark colors, and his face was covered in what looked like a balaclava." He looked up at the blue sky, then back at Tony. "Why would someone cover their face like that in spring weather? It wasn't exactly cold that night."

"It's hard to tell." Tony shrugged. "Maybe he saw the storm coming and tried to stay dry."

Lucas's thoughts drifted back to the note his father showed him before they left.

I'll get my cut.

No one would be able to get their cut if the place burned down.

Tony pulled a manilla envelope out of his briefcase. "Look this over, and after you finish your inventory, contact me."

Lucas accepted the envelope, opened the back door, and walked Tony to the front. "I'll have the report to you by the end of the week."

"I'll keep an eye out for it." Tony shook his hand once more then headed for his truck.

Lucas's phone buzzed as he shut the door. He drew in a quick breath before he fished it out of his pocket and threw it on speaker. "Yeah, Dad. What's up?"

"Did you meet with the insurance adjuster?"

"He just left. Looks like it's going to be an easy claim. I'll make sure I have somebody started on the repairs before I leave."

"What about any missing items?"

He gave the warehouse a cursory glance. "Nothing looks out of place. I'll do a line-by-line and get back to you. Did you find anything missing in Denver?"

"Not yet. It looks like the fire was an accident."

Lucas gripped the phone. Two accidental fires?

"I reached out to Genevieve." Dad's tone turned resolute. "She's looking forward to meeting with you after you get back. Make sure you prepare. I want you to bring your A-game to the Renaldi family."

You mean bring my A-game to impress Genevieve. Before answering, Lucas schooled his emotions. "Remember, I'm leaving the country in a few weeks. I won't have time to finalize the Renaldi acquisition."

"I remembered. That's why I made the appointment for the day after you got back."

"Why can't you meet with her? When *you* get back."

"Letitia and I are heading to Albuquerque. Remember? To check on the other warehouse." Annoyance coated Dad's tone. "We're making it a mini vacation. It's gorgeous in New Mexico this time of year."

Lucas's jaw set.

"Meet with Genevieve. If she's open to it, go back to Renaldi's and look at the product. I've got three assistants at your disposal at the office. They're ready to give you estimates and write up a proposal. You're the boss. You don't have to be bogged down with the details."

He walked back to the office to start in on the inventory. Is this what it meant to be entwined with the business? Having his father call the shots of every aspect of his life? He needed to maintain a boundary.

"I have plans on Monday when I get back."

They weren't finalized, but Dad didn't need to know that. If all went well, he'd be in Newport News having coffee with a bright-eyed woman who made his heart beat faster every time he thought of her.

"Then change them. Genevieve made plans to be at her father's estate on Monday. Meet her in the morning then offer to take her out to dinner. Do whatever it takes to secure the acquisition."

Lucas slumped into the desk chair. Maybe he could meet Renée before he met Genevive. The Renaldi estate wasn't far from Newport News. How hard would it be to squeeze in a coffee? He stifled a groan. He didn't want to eke out time with Renée. He wanted their next meeting to be relaxed and not on the clock.

"Let me know ASAP if there's anything in the inventory that doesn't look right."

Dad's request yanked him out of his thoughts. "I will."

He finished the call, set down his phone, and tapped his fingers on the desk. Were the mishaps in Denver and Albuquerque connected to the one in Oklahoma City?

He printed the inventory from his laptop. His father would approve of doing it the old-fashioned way. Walking to the front of the store, he began in section A and started checking off items.

One Louis VI chair. One 18th-century French armoire with gold inlay. Two Waterford candlesticks. One marble-topped chess table, which included a full set of marble chess pieces.

Halfway through the section, his stomach rumbled. He checked his watch. Somehow it was already one in the afternoon. The idea of a couple of ounces of red meat and a plate full of hearty sides made his mouth water. Glancing back over the list, he finished walking through section A.

As he put the last check on the list, his stomach roared again. "Time to go."

But before he could turn away, a circle in the dust on one of the shelves caught his attention. His gaze traveled over the section as he counted the items present. He checked his list. Eleven items on the shelf. Eleven items on the list. Was there something missing?

He studied the dust ring again. It was behind a vase worth over two thousand dollars. If someone had taken something, then why'd they leave that?

He lifted the vase. Underneath was a small circle outlined in a layer of dust. He placed the vase in the open ring. The circumference of the dust ring was twice as big. From a glance, the other items weren't the right size either. Something hadn't been moved, it had been taken.

After he replaced the vase in its original spot, he glanced around the warehouse. How many more discrepancies would he find?

Shaking his head, Lucas pulled out his phone and snapped a photo of the dust ring. How do you file a claim for something there wasn't a record of?

He slid his phone into his pocket and made a notation on the inventory. As he did, his thoughts wandered to the drifter camped out by the warehouse. Something about him was off.

Stalking back to the office, he grabbed his keys. Without proof of lost inventory, his gut feeling led to a dead end. *What am I missing?*

For now, the gnawing at his gut told him to find a barbecue joint, then he'd scour the warehouse for any other missing items.

He armed the alarm, pushed through the front door, and walked out into the warm sunlight. If Buster Cavanaugh was in on this, he probably wanted to rattle him. But if Professor Carlson somehow had a hand in the fire ... Carlson wouldn't dare go after *Bennetts*. Would he?

Lucas unlocked the rental, jerked open the door, and slid into the driver's seat. When he pushed the start button, the two-seater's engine rumbled to life as more questions roared through his brain. Maybe he'd have more answers once he finished combing through the inventory.

One thing was for sure, he'd get to the bottom of this. Whoever was messing with *Bennetts* had poked the wrong hornet's nest.

7

Emersyn joined Kelly and James in the living room after reading three superhero bedtime stories to Noah.

Sinking into the club chair across from Kelly, she released a contented sigh. Since James and Noah's arrival, the weekend had been a flurry of laughter and activity following her graduation.

It warmed her heart to have family meals around the large table again and a row of shoes by the door. Living in a house full of rooms and no one to occupy them, her days had become entirely too lonely.

Kelly glanced up from her laptop. "Did he go to sleep for you?"

"He did."

"How many books did you need to read?" James walked in from the kitchen carrying a mug of tea.

"Three." She could've skipped the third one because Noah had drifted off to sleep, but it was about a man in blue tights—research.

A flutter floated in her belly as thoughts of Reid did pirouettes in her brain. What was he doing right now? Saving the world from computer viruses with a simple click of his mouse? Her cheeks heated. She needed to stop daydreaming about Mr. Americano.

"Only three?" James set his mug down on a coaster, then sat next to Kelly. "You got out early. The little guy's beat from traveling."

"Or maybe it's from the hike we went on today." Kelly closed her laptop and slipped it into the satchel at her feet. "His legs were working overtime to keep up with his daddy."

"Until I turned into the kid hauler for the last bit." James winced as he rubbed his neck and shoulder.

Kelly patted his arm. "You do your job as kid hauler quite well, Mr. Taylor."

"Thanks, luv." He gave Kelly a knowing look, lifted his brow, then reached for his tea.

Kelly cleared her throat and looked away.

"You two look like you're sending each other secret spy signals or something." Emersyn glanced from Kelly to James, then back to Kelly. "What's going on?"

"Nothing." James shifted in his seat and sipped his drink.

"It's not nothing. We have …" Kelly shot James a worried look, then looked back at her. "We have something we need to tell you."

"What's wrong?" Emersyn's guts twisted. "Is there something going on? With you guys? Or with Henry?"

She'd overheard James on the phone with Henry after lunch. From what she'd gleaned, the hushed conversation sounded tense.

James replaced his tea on the coaster and waved a dismissive hand in the air. "Henry's fine. Ordered and tidy as usual."

"Then why do you both look as if someone drank spoiled milk?"

Kelly reached inside her laptop bag and pulled out an envelope. "There's something Abram wished for me to discuss with you."

"What?" Hair lifted on the back of Emersyn's neck as she

took the envelope. She trusted Kelly, but it had been years since her papa's death. Why wait to give her this letter now?

"Read the letter first."

She ran her fingers across the salutation written in Abram's hand.

> To Emersyn
> With love, your Papa

Tears gathered in her lashes as a picture of Abram's kind, wrinkled face slid across her mind. The hole in her heart from missing him had yet to close.

She tugged at the wax stamp, and the circle with the raised letter Z separated from the flap. Heart pounding, she withdrew the contents of the envelope and read his words.

> *Dearest Emersyn,*
>
> *I hope this letter finds you well today. You are the shining star of my life, and I'm blessed for the time I had with you.*
>
> *There are so many things I wish to tell you, but I know you have questions about your mother.*
>
> *Your mother was a beautiful soul, and she left your life too soon. She chose your name, and I believe it suits you. Emersyn means brave.*
>
> *Before you arrived, she shared with me a bit of her history. I've given a journal to Kelly Landon, the author I worked with, detailing your mother and father's story. I hope it comforts you in your times of loneliness.*

Emersyn glanced up at Kelly and James. Their expressions remained taut. She returned her attention to the missive and continued to read.

> *Your mother was adopted and never knew her birth mother. I've asked Kelly to research her family lineage and share with you all*

that she's found. Family is important, and so is our history. Maybe unearthing more of your background will help you to understand your calling. Who knows, maybe you'll be able to reunite with someone on your mother's side one day.

Emersyn sat back and took a breath. She'd kept a picture of her mother by her bedside. She was beautiful, with an angelic face and sparkling eyes that danced with hope and a hint of mischief. With no explanation, her mom's heart gave out several days after giving birth. The doctors said it was an unexplainable condition. An anomaly. Whatever the reason for God taking her mother home, it didn't erase the void that tugged at her soul from never having known her.

A tear trickled down Emersyn's cheek. As she swiped at it with the back of her hand, she brought her attention back to her papa's words.

On to the main matter of this letter.
As a young man, I was part of an underground society whose main purpose was to track down missing religious heirlooms.

Emersyn froze. What? Blinking past the moisture in her eyes, she continued to read.

For security purposes, I will not list the name of the group. Kelly can give you that information.

She jerked her chin up. "Papa was part of a secret society?"
Kelly nodded. "Many years ago."
Emersyn continued reading.

This group has survived for ages, and the mantle is passed on through family connections. With great consideration, I'm passing the mantle to you.

She lowered the letter into her lap as she worked to tame the wild horses galloping through her veins.

"Abram asked me to give you this letter after you turned twenty-one—and at my discretion." Kelly's expression softened. "I wanted to wait until you finished school and had decided on a career path."

Emersyn lowered her gaze back to the letter and studied the last few lines.

> *You have a choice to make. To join the society, or to leave that connection in the past.*
>
> *Should you decide to join the society, you'll commit to preserving the guidelines and integrity of the group.*
>
> *Don't make this decision without considering the cost. However, if you choose to step away, you do so for life.*

Her pulse thundered in her ears as she lifted her gaze. "What is this society? What do they do? Is it illegal?"

"No, nothing illegal." Kelly's expression turned animated. "They're a clandestine group, known as H & G, made up of a diverse group of members from around the world. The society has been around for centuries, and those connected to H & G use their time and talents to track down missing religious heirlooms."

Emersyn's throat dried. She'd just graduated college. Joining an underground society had not been on her to-do list this summer. "How long do I have to decide?"

"There's no expiration." James leaned forward and rested his elbows on his knees. "But if you turn your back on H & G, there won't be a second invite."

Missing family heirlooms. Secret legacies. Clandestine societies. These were the things of fiction, not real life.

"I don't understand." She waved the letter in the air. "How does this all work?"

James sat back and tugged at his collar. "I know you have a

lot of questions. We were thinking perhaps you could come back with us this summer and go over all the details."

"Are you both involved?"

They nodded.

"Both of our fathers worked for H & G." James took Kelly's hand. "Kelly's father died before he could tell her about the society, but an event in our past caused our paths to cross and opened the door for us to work together on a mission."

She folded the letter and placed it back in the envelope. "How does that work?"

James's brow quirked. "What?"

"If you'd never told me, how would I have known about H & G?" She flicked her gaze toward Kelly. "Had you considered not telling me?"

"Yes."

Kelly's answer stunned her. "Why?"

"Abram stepped away, and I don't know why. It may have been to raise you. It may have been another reason. He gave me the option to tell you about H & G or keep it a secret." Kelly's expression fell. "I don't know why he gave me that responsibility, but I wrestled over the decision for years."

She turned Kelly's words over in her mind. Maybe it would've been easier if she'd never known. *But what if this is my calling?*

"What does it entail? Joining H & G."

"Consider the groups prepared to rally in a disaster. Like the Red Cross." James spoke up. "Those volunteers go about their daily lives, but when disaster strikes, they're called up to lend a hand. Missions come in, and based on members' location and availability, they're assigned the mission."

Kelly flashed her an encouraging smile. "In the meantime, you hone your skills."

"My skills? What skills?"

"According to Abram, you can solve a puzzle with your eyes closed." James's lips curved into a grin. "You're a black belt. You can read music. Kelly's informed me you've taken over the Lady M column." He shot her a bemused look. "Posing as Lady M will give you some on-the-job training."

Emersyn considered James's words. Could basic, everyday skills be used for something as important as tracking down religious heirlooms?

"What about Henry? Is he a part of this?"

James nodded.

"There's something else." Concern infused Kelly's tone. "I found out some information about your mother's adoption. She had a brother. Two brothers. They were twins and were born many years after her adoption. I suspect to a different father. One is no longer living, and one—"

"The other one is in jail." As James finished Kelly's sentence, his expression darkened. "The bloke's a menace."

"What? In jail? Why?"

Kelly frowned. "He was involved in the black-market trade of stolen antiques."

"Who is he? What's his name? Does he know about me?" A shudder racked her spine. *I have an uncle.* "Did my papa know about him?"

"His name is Declan." Kelly's voice lowered. "Declan McNeary."

James stood and stalked over to the mantle. "There's a reason why we're telling you about him now." A weighty silence lingered before James spun to face them. "He's getting out on parole."

"He's getting out of prison?" A boulder landed in Emersyn's gut and settled.

"Em, the bloke's not a nice guy. He's trouble." James walked back and claimed the chair next to her. "Henry's been keeping tabs on him for years. Declan claims he's turned over a new leaf and is getting out because of good behavior." A spark of fury ignited in his eyes. "I don't buy it. Not one bit. The guy's a master manipulator."

A prickle danced across her scalp like a brush of a hundred tiny fingers. She had family. Alive. But he was a criminal.

"Em, listen." Kelly's tone remained calm. "Your uncle doesn't know anything about you."

"How can you be sure?"

"I can't." Kelly hesitated. "But it took me a while to connect the dots, so unless he had a reason to go looking, I don't see Declan unearthing this mystery. He'd never even think to look."

With one letter, her life had gone from mundane to something ripped right out of a mystery novel. She folded the envelope and placed it in her pocket. "This is a lot to take in."

"I know it is. But remember, you're not going through this alone." Kelly glanced at James, then back at her. "We're here, just tell us what you need."

"We may not be blood, but we are your family." James gave her shoulder a gentle squeeze.

"Right now, I think I'm going to turn in early." She rose from her seat, stomach knotted. "Let's revisit this tomorrow after I've had some time to untangle my thoughts."

As she turned toward the door, moisture gathered in her eyes. *I have an uncle, but he's a convict.* The family she'd dreamt of having had morphed into a nightmare.

What about Papa's connection to H & G? Trudging to the stairway at the back of the kitchen, she paused and glanced out a window, staring into the ebony sky. *Is this my calling, God? Should I join H & G?*

If she said no, life would carry on as if nothing happened. But if she said yes …

She rubbed her temples. Lady M for the *Yorktown Courant.* Miss Renée Landon at school. Now what? Treasure hunter over summer break?

Releasing a sigh, she turned and trekked up the stairs. At least one thing in her life wasn't complicated. Reid.

He was all zeros and ones. Ordered. Sequenced. Dependable.

And when he got back from his business trip, they had a coffee date.

A shiver tickled her neck as she stepped onto the landing, and Reid's handsome face flashed in her mind. Maybe she should put the idea of romance on the back burner. It would be tricky keeping all these secrets from him.

A smile tugged at her lips. She'd cross that bridge when she came to it. Spending time with Americano, two sugars, might be just the distraction she needed right now.

8

E mersyn slowed her car to a roll and pulled into a parking spot across the street from *Fraiser's Deerhound Pub*. For a Monday evening, the place was packed.

Using the Lady M column as an excuse, she'd sequestered herself in her SUV that afternoon with a honey latte and drove around aimlessly. She needed time to think. To breathe.

She turned off the car and released a long breath. After a weekend of revealing family secrets, her nerves were frayed. "God, help me. What am I supposed to do about H & G? About my uncle?"

She shifted in her seat and studied the people going in and out of the pub. Maybe solving this mystery would take her mind off the one that had become her life. Digging through her messenger bag in the passenger seat, she withdrew the file she made about the restaurant and scanned her notes.

A letter to Lady M had reported the theft of a century-old deerhound statue. A gift to the original owner.

Emersyn picked up her phone and perused the blog post about the theft on the local Scottish association website, taking in the details. Her gaze shifted to the pub's dark-stained antique door. She'd eaten at the restaurant a few times and recalled the statue sitting outside the entry. It had to have weighed a few hundred pounds. This was no snatch-and-grab—this was premeditated.

Drumming her fingers on the wheel, she returned her thoughts to what James said about the skills she might bring to the table with H & G. Did she have any special talents? She doubted tapping out a tune on the ivories would solve any mysteries. Or, what about her black belt training? That might help her defend herself and stay fit, but how would it track down a family heirloom?

"Am I really considering this?"

She pulled her bouncy curls into a ponytail, then tugged on the frayed ball cap she always wore hiking. She'd think about H & G later. Tonight, her goal was to speak with the pub's owner and get his firsthand take on the missing deerhound.

As she reached for the door handle, a blacked-out limo pulled up close and pinned her in.

Feeling like the paparazzi, she watched for the limo's passengers to appear. Were they an older couple celebrating an anniversary? Or was it a bunch of teens on a group date?

When a sharply dressed couple stepped out of the double doors of the swanky steakhouse next to the pub, her heart sank. It can't be.

Hand trembling, she lifted her phone and took a snapshot of the pair. Don't let it be him. Please don't let it be him. She held her breath as she zoomed in on the photo. He wasn't wearing his glasses, but it was Reid.

Emersyn tugged her ball cap down and sunk back into her seat. Wasn't he supposed to be out of town? He'd rescheduled their coffee date but hadn't specified why.

She watched the couple as they drew closer. Reid was dressed to kill in a tailored charcoal-gray suit while the woman, who walked with her arm draped in the crook of his, wore a glitzy, ebony knee-length cocktail dress.

Emersyn's stomach twisted as the driver opened the limo door. Posture rigid, Reid released the woman's arm and waited for her to step into the vehicle. When he glanced up, heat blanketed Emersyn's skin. He couldn't see through the tint. Could he?

After a moment, he ducked into the limo, and she released her breath. She'd never considered he might be in a relationship. Why would she? He didn't wear a ring or mentioned he had a girlfriend. *Hadn't he invited me for coffee?*

She stared at the photo on her phone. Was meeting her for coffee just a friendly gesture? Maybe he only wanted to meet to make sure her website was still running smoothly. What about the spark? The magic?

Reid had been adamant about being a down-to-earth guy. Had that been a mask as well? Did a down-to-earth guy wear designer suits and use a chauffeur for dinner?

As the driver slid into the limo, an electrical pulse surged through her veins. "Sorry, Fraiser, the deerhound story will have to wait."

As the limo drove away, she started her car and pulled out behind them. "What am I doing?"

A quick look at her side mirror, and Emersyn brought her gaze back to the windshield. "You're honing your detective skills. Just like Kelly and James suggested."

The limousine meandered through several side streets, and she continued to follow, giving at least two car lengths between them.

Flipping on her turn signal, she veered onto the main highway and turned up the radio. As the pulsing notes of a saxophone floated around her, she pressed the gas pedal and ignored the warnings tumbling through her brain.

The limo made its way through Yorktown and over the toll bridge leading into Gloucester Point.

She glanced out her window as the terrain changed from a cityscape to neighborhoods with sprawling, manicured lawns and shady trees.

The limo banked right and turned onto a highway edged with affluent homes and gated driveways.

As the limousine slowed, it turned at a sign that read, *Renaldi Equestrian Center*. Continuing past the entrance, she drove a few more feet, turned off onto the gravel shoulder, and put her SUV in park. She used her phone's camera to follow the limousine as it pulled in front of a sprawling black and white colonial.

The driver opened the door, and Reid and the woman stepped out. The woman slipped her hand into the crook of Reid's arm before they both walked up the short flight of stairs to the front door.

The woman walked inside, and only after a moment's hesitation, Reid followed.

Tears stung Emersyn's eyes.

Turning over her phone, she scrolled through her texts and stopped on the last one from Reid.

> My business was extended. I'll call you
> soon to reschedule our coffee date.

As she deleted his text, heat blazed through her veins. There wouldn't be another coffee date. Ever.

Glancing back at the stately home's ebony door, a single tear trickled down her cheek. At least she didn't need to worry about keeping secrets about H & G from him. Or sharing her real name.

She turned her SUV away from the shoulder and retraced the highway back to the toll bridge.

It was better this way. She'd spend the summer with Kelly and James in London and learn what she could about H & G. Then when she returned, she'd focus on her first year of teaching and what to do about her prodigal uncle. Papa's letter had turned her life upside down. She didn't need Mr. Americano and his secrets to complicate things.

9

Lucas stepped out of the shower and wrapped a towel around his waist. It was the first week of June, but instead of feeling excited about his upcoming annual guys' trip, he wanted to skip it altogether.

He trudged to his room, sank onto his bed, and swiped his phone off the bedside table. After his fourth desperate text, Renée still hadn't responded.

A weight pressed against his chest. He'd done his research, and according to an online men's magazine, four texts to someone with no response was one too many. He needed to take the hint. Renée had been grateful for his help with her website, but she was way out of his league.

He glanced at the time. His flight to Tokyo left in less than twelve hours. If he had any hope of getting a wink of sleep before his driver showed up, he'd need to dump all thoughts of Renée out of his mind. Not only for tonight—but for good.

With a huff, he raked his fingers through his wet hair. A few trickles of water dripped down his back, making him shiver.

Finding his soul mate in a coffee shop. What a joke. Like Dad said, that only happens in movies.

He stood and trekked back to the bathroom. After rounding up his travel-sized soap and shampoo, Lucas chucked them into his toiletry bag on the counter. *But what about when my fingers brushed against hers? Didn't she feel it too? The jolt?*

"Don't be an idiot." He shook his head and beads of water flung off the tips of his hair dotting the mirror. His heart might have been palpitating like a man rounding the bases the day they'd met, but hers was not.

Yanking a pair of sweats off the hook by the door, he quickly replaced the damp towel with his pants. As he raked a comb through his hair, his phone buzzed. "Maybe it's her."

Dropping the comb, he ambled back into the room and checked the number. Not Renée. He put the call on speaker and flopped onto his mattress.

"Hey, Skip. What's up?"

Skip Greenwood, part of his foursome group of friends heading to Tokyo, heaved a sigh. "I've got some bad news."

"What happened?"

"It's my dad." Skip's voice hitched. "He had a heart attack."

"Oh, no. I'm sorry. What's your plan? Are you heading out to Sacramento to see him?"

"Yeah. I'm making reservations as we speak."

"I understand. Family first." A knife twisted in Lucas's gut. Was that really how he felt? Then why act like a punk when Dad asked him to meet with Genevieve?

"My sister is there now but can only stay for a week," Skip said. "I'm mobile, so I can stay for as long as it takes for Dad to get back on his feet."

"The perks of our job."

"True." A beat of silence hung in the air. "I have a favor to ask."

"Anything."

"I wouldn't be so quick to agree until you hear what I'm asking."

"Okay. What are you asking? You're already leaving me to babysit Todd and Grady on this trip."

Skip's laughter soared across the line. "They shouldn't get into too much trouble. I heard Grady's decided to settle down."

"I'll believe it when I get the wedding invite. Out with it. What's the favor?"

"I'm not sure how long I'll be gone. Dad's doctor thinks recovery may take a few months." Skip blew out his breath. "I just signed a hefty contract with a private school in Newport News to set up their IT for the new school year." Skip explained his position and how the job fell into his lap. "Most of the job is remote, but I agreed to host an in-person training for the teachers at the end of July. I don't want to rush Dad's recovery, so—"

"Did you say a private school? In Newport News?"

"Yeah. Why?"

"What's the name of the school?"

"Maplewood Preparatory Academy."

"I'll do it."

"Really?"

"Yep." Would this be considered stalking? Lucas brushed off the thought. "Need a house sitter while you're gone?"

"Sure. I could use someone to check in on the place every so often. You know the codes to get in and the guest room is ready for you."

"I also know all the food delivery places within a ten-mile radius of your condo." His pulse ratcheted up a notch. And the best coffee spot in Newport News. "When I get back in town, I'll head over to your place and check in."

"You sound … excited. What's going on?" Skip drew out his words. "Wait. Is this about the girl you met at that coffee shop?"

"Yeah, but …"

Skip snorted. "Here I thought Grady would be the first of us to tie the knot."

"Don't rent the tux yet. She's been ignoring my texts for weeks."

"What? What did you do?"

"I'm not sure." Heat crept up Lucas's neck and folded over

his ears. Out of the four of them, he was the least apt in the ways of women. "Got any advice for me?"

"Grand gesture."

"What do you mean?"

"Reservations. Somewhere no one can get in on a whim. Use all the ammo you got in that Bennett arsenal of yours."

"What about showing up to her school to teach the IT class?"

"She's a teacher?" Skip choked on a laugh. "At Maplewood?"

"Yeah. It's her first year."

"She's not texting you back, and you're going to just walk in and say hi?"

Lucas's stomach flipped over. This was a bad idea.

Skip let out a low whistle. "That's epic."

"You think?"

"Well, it's gutsy. You'll have to let me know how it goes."

"I will." Lucas ended the call and climbed into bed.

Maybe God had opened a door for him to see Renée again. Or maybe he'd just planned the worst move ever.

10

The late July sun warmed her skin as Emersyn stepped out of her car and walked across Maplewood Prep's parking lot. After spending the summer with Kelly and James in London, she'd come back to Virginia burdened with more questions than answers. Was teaching her calling? Or working with H & G? What about Declan?

As she pushed through the double doors leading to the library, skittish butterflies danced in her middle. She wanted to honor her papa's legacy, but she also wanted to make her own imprint on the world. Was it possible to do both?

She found a seat at the front of the room. Today, she'd focus on teaching.

"Did you get your room set up?" Penny Banks, the drama teacher and her classroom neighbor, slid into the chair next to Emersyn and opened her laptop.

"Mostly. My first-year jitters are still at full throttle."

"Don't worry too much about being perfect the first year." Penny pulled up her home screen, then pivoted to face her. "The kids want to know you care. Once you form a relationship with your students and their parents, everything else will fall into place."

Emersyn fished out her laptop from her bag and placed it

on the table as more teachers filtered into the room. Penny's reassuring words sent a ripple of warmth through her. This was her calling. She could feel it. She'd dreamt of teaching since she was little, and now, in a couple of weeks, she'd have her first classroom full of students. *Please, God, help me be a good teacher.*

Their assistant principal, Kari Woods, walked to the front of the room and turned on the interactive whiteboard. "How's everyone's first day back?"

Murmurs of excitement skipped around the room.

As Kari repositioned the height of a metal podium, she added, "Wait until the students show up. Then things will really get busy." She glanced at the back of the room and motioned for someone at the door to join them. "Come in, Mr. Greenwood. We're about ready to start."

All heads turned as a man walked through the door carrying a leather satchel and looking lost.

Emersyn's heart crawled into her throat and settled. What's *he* doing here? And why had Kari call him Mr. Greenwood?

Reid strode to the front of the room. When he reached Kari, he stuck out his hand and flashed a winning smile. "Good morning. My name's Reid. I'm standing in for Skip today."

For a second, Kari looked confused, then she glanced over her notes on the podium. "That's right, Mr. Greenwood emailed me a few weeks ago. I'm sorry about the mix-up. How's his father doing?"

Reid laid his messenger bag on a table and pulled out his laptop. "Better. Skip will be back in town by the end of August." Without looking up, he unfurled a cord and plugged his laptop into the interactive whiteboard. "Skip set up everything for your school remotely, so I don't foresee any problems while he's gone."

"Perfect." Kari checked her watch. "We'll start in about five minutes."

Reid placed his laptop on the podium and opened the cover.

After a few seconds, his home screen, a picture of a baseball diamond, appeared on the whiteboard.

"He's charming. And tall." Penny nudged her. "He's got that wholesome, geek thing going on."

Emersyn pulled her eyes away from Reid and glanced at Penny. "What? Who?"

"The IT guy. Up front. He's adorable." Penny waggled her brows, eyes sparkling. "I'm pretty sure my website will need *a lot* of help this week."

Emersyn's cheeks prickled as she turned back to face the front. Reid conversed with Kari while he pointed at something on his laptop. She loved the way the crease on his brow came together when he concentrated. *Stop. Remember the limo?* She blinked, trying to focus.

Kari looked out over the crowd of teachers. "It looks like we're ready to begin." She flipped on the microphone and waved a hand toward Reid. "This is Reid. He'll be leading you through the steps to connect with the school's server. We want to make sure everyone's emails are working as well as your website and message boards.

"After Reid's done with his presentation, feel free to ask any questions." Kari glanced at Reid. "You'll also be in the rest of the week for a few hours a day. Is that correct?"

"Yes." He pushed his glasses onto the bridge of his nose. "I'll be available all week."

Emersyn looked down at her screen, mouth pinched. This can't be happening.

"He'll be here all week." Penny squealed under her breath. "I wonder if he's single."

Emersyn's attention shot back to Reid. *Yeah, I wonder.* When his gaze met hers, warmth pooled in her belly. After a smoldering few seconds, he glanced away.

"What was that?" Penny purred in her ear while she fanned herself with her hand. "He looked at you like he knew you. Or wanted to get to know you."

"We're in the front row." Her hand shook as she pulled a pen and notebook out of her bag. "He happened to look at our table."

Penny stared back at Reid. "And I thought training was going to be boring."

Emersyn's stomach dipped. She'd give anything to have boring in her life right now. Maybe she could skip training and have Penny give her the synopsis.

Kari rattled off a pep talk about the theme for the new year, then she turned to Reid. "They're all yours."

Reid nodded. "I'll do a few hours of training, then break for lunch."

"Sounds good. Let me know if you need anything." Kari gave a cursory wave to the room, then rushed out the door.

"Let's have everyone bring up their websites." Reid typed in a few keys before the school website appeared on the whiteboard. "I need to make sure every teacher is connected with the school software."

Penny shot her hand up like an enthusiastic first grader. "I'm having a few issues with the buttons on my website. Would you be able to help me after class?"

"Sure." Reid tugged on his collar as his gaze slid from Penny to Emersyn.

Emersyn jerked her chin down and stared at her keyboard. After lunch, she'd sit in the back with the PE teachers.

"Let's go over a few things first." Reid's deep voice circled the library, tickling her ears. "In a new tab, type in the school web address and bring up the home screen. We'll discuss how you enter your students' names into the portal."

The sound of clicking keyboards trickled across the room. Emersyn brought the home screen up on her laptop and stole a look at Reid as he moved his mouse around the whiteboard to navigate the screen.

When he looked up, she inhaled a quick breath.

He flashed her a tender smile, then went on to explain to the group how the student portal worked and how parents could pay for lunches on the meal tab.

After his presentation, Reid checked his watch. "According to the schedule, we have about an hour for you to input your students' names, then we'll break for lunch." He looked up and glanced around the room. "Throughout the week, I'll look at your websites to make sure they're all working properly. Please come see me if you have any questions."

Penny's eyes brightened as Reid approached their table and took the seat across from her. She pushed her hand toward him. "Hi, Reid. I'm Penny."

Reid shook her hand, then took a swipe at the ebony curl that had fallen across his forehead. "Nice to meet you, Penny."

Feigning interest in the school website on her screen, Emersyn watched Reid from beneath her lashes. Penny was a handful, but he took her flirting in stride.

When she first met Penny during her student teaching, they'd bonded over a closet full of old stage equipment in the basement of the school. A brilliant playwright, with a doctorate in performing arts, Penny's main goal in life was to acquire her *M.R.S* degree before she turned thirty.

Emersyn bit back a smile. With his stable career and superhero good looks, Reid gleamed like a solitaire diamond in a velvet box.

"I can't seem to get my messaging button to work." Penny turned her laptop to face Reid. "Can you help? Or do you need to spend some time on it after hours?"

Reid scrolled through the pages. "This isn't too bad. I've seen worse."

The urge to kick his shin under the table jolted through her.

Reid continued to tap on the keys while Penny rattled on about how it took her forever to find a good headshot for her bio page.

"I wanted to find one that made me look dramatic, but not over the top. Or old. I mean, I'm not even thirty."

His lips tugged at one corner while he remained focused on Penny's screen.

This was torture. She should pack up her laptop and leave. Her website was fine—thanks to him—and she wasn't going to ask him any questions. About anything. Ever.

As if reading her mind, Penny laid a hand on her arm. "What about you? Did you get headshots taken or did you use the standard faculty photo?"

"I … uh …" Heat grew across the back of her neck like a forest fire.

"Your pic looks amazing." Penny scooted closer and pointed at the picture on her screen. "What do you think Reid? It's not even fair that she has all those natural waves in her hair."

Like a moth to a flame, Emersyn searched for his reaction.

Reid glanced up, color staining his cheekbones. "Her picture's great."

Pulse igniting, Emersyn's gaze fell back to her screen. Had someone turned off the air conditioner?

Reid cleared his throat as he rotated Penny's laptop to face her. "You're all set. You needed a few adjustments."

Penny typed on the keys and scrolled through her pages. "It works."

"Do you want me to take a look at *your* website?" Reid pivoted and shot her a teasing look. "Or do you have another IT guy on retainer?"

"I … no … my website's fine."

"Do you have a business card, Reid?" Penny held out her hand, palm up. "In case I have any problems after school hours?"

"I'm standing in for Skip this week. He's the one you'll contact if you have any issues."

Penny pouted. "Okay. Hopefully, Skip's as helpful as you."

"Skip's great." Reid's face flashed with amusement before he stood and walked to the podium. "How's the student portal working for everyone? It's easy, right?"

Mumbles of agreement traveled around the library.

"Let's break for lunch, and when we return, we'll go over how to put grades into the student portal."

Penny clicked her laptop closed and sighed. "I'm going to head to my condo over lunch. I'm babysitting my brother's puppy this week, so I need to take him for a quick walk." She swept a hand over her laptop. "Can you push some buttons or something, so my website's broken by the time I get back?"

Emersyn laughed. "Leave it out with the puppy tonight."

"Good idea." Penny swiped her laptop up along with her purse. "I'll see you after lunch."

As Penny walked away, a message box appeared on Emersyn's screen. The sender's name was RC. She glanced around the library. She'd not met all the teachers yet, so she wasn't sure whose initials were RC.

She opened the message.

I'm sorry.

Her chin jerked up, and Reid's mournful stare shot an electrical pulse through her. *RC. Reid Clark.*

She typed out a reply.

For what?

A return message came through.

I'm not sure.

Her fingers hovered over the keys as an image of Reid stepping into a limousine with another woman flew into her mind. Maybe she should ask him about the woman instead of filling in the blanks herself.

Another message appeared on her screen.

Would you like to join me for lunch?

Her pulse sped up. Seeing him again had wrecked her resolve. Maybe he'd been on a blind date. He didn't even look like he was having fun. What if the roles were reversed? Wouldn't she have wanted to explain her side instead of having him jump to conclusions?

An additional notification from RC blinked in the message box.

> I hear it's chicken sandwich day in the cafeteria.

She risked another look at him. Penny was right, he *was* charming.

Reid kept his gaze zeroed in on his laptop while he worried his bottom lip between his teeth. Against her better judgment, she'd thought about him all summer. Maybe God had opened this door so she could get some answers.

She typed out her response.

> I have a better idea. How do you feel about Thai food?

When she looked up, his expression brightened. Another message appeared on her screen.

> I'll meet you in the parking lot in five.

Reid closed his laptop and slipped it into his bag. Walking past her table, he shot her a wink and strode out the door.

Feeling like a teenager who'd been asked out by the star quarterback, she waited five minutes, which felt like a lifetime, before she packed up her things and scurried out of the library.

Lucas's heart thundered in his ears. The risk had paid off. At least she'd given him another chance. Arms folded, he leaned against his car and waited.

After a few minutes, Renée pushed through the double doors and scanned the parking lot.

He waved and the smile she gave him made him feel like he'd won the World Series. *Don't mess this up.*

She wove through a row of cars, stopped at a black SUV and dropped off her laptop. When she approached his car, his pulse sharpened its rhythm.

"Hi."

"Hi." She repeated.

He wanted to run his fingers through her soft curls and pull her close, but instead, he dropped his hands and tugged on his shirt cuffs.

"There's a Thai place two blocks over." She motioned across the parking lot. "It's not too hot today. Do you want to walk?"

"Sure." Unable to fight the longing to be close to her, he reached for her hand.

She didn't pull back. Instead, she intertwined her fingers with his.

"How's your summer been?" His heart bounced in his chest as they walked through the parking lot hand in hand.

"Busy. Yours?"

He gave her fingers a light squeeze. "The same."

When they arrived at the restaurant, he released her hand and opened the door for her. As he followed her to a table by the window, questions swirled in his brain, crowding his thoughts. Why did she stop answering his texts? Should he ask?

Lucas pulled out a chair and waited for her to sit before grabbing the seat across from her.

After the server took their drink orders, Renée folded her arms and shot him a questioning look. "How did you know?"

"How did I know what?"

"What school I was at?"

He averted his eyes and pretended to scan the menu. "That was easy. Your website. I just wasn't sure what to do with that information." When he lifted his gaze, the surprise in her expression made him smile.

The server dropped off their drinks and jotted down their

lunch orders. When she walked away, Renée continued to eye him like a trained interrogator.

"First of all, I'm not a stalker." He grinned, then took a long drink of his soda.

"Isn't that what all stalkers say?"

"Do they? Maybe I should lead with something else."

"Maybe you should." Her expression softened.

He chuckled, enjoying her playful mood. "My buddy, Skip, is contracted to work with Maplewood Private Schools. He had an emergency and needed me to step in for him. Your website mentioned you worked for Maplewood. I prayed you'd give me five minutes to ask if you'd reconsider our coffee date."

"Really?" Her cheeks turned bubblegum pink.

"Really."

A second of silence loomed between them.

"I'm not good at this ... telling someone how I feel. I wanted to see you again. I didn't want to cancel our coffee date." His voice hitched, and he cleared his throat. "My dad, who's agreed I should take over the family business sooner rather than later, filled up my calendar when I returned from my business trip in Oklahoma City."

"What's the family business?"

"Estate and antique sales." He leaned back in his seat and huffed out a sigh. "The day after I got back from Oklahoma, I had a meeting with one of my father's clients. He wanted me to wine and dine her so we could acquire her estate. I didn't want to fit our coffee date in between a business meeting. I wanted time to spend with you and—"

"I'm sorry I went dark." Her eyes glistened, and she looked away.

Lucas reached across the table and took one of her hands in his. "If I've done something to upset you, I wish you'd tell me."

She turned back to face him, expression solemn. "No. You didn't do anything. I had something come up with my family, and I ... I needed some time to think things over."

"Is everything okay with your family?"

Her lips turned up into a soft smile. "Yes. They're good."

Releasing her hand, he took another drink of his soda. "Kelly and James, right? They live in London?"

"Yeah. Kelly's an author, and James teaches physical education at a primary school. I know I've told you Kelly and James aren't really my relatives, but they both knew my papa. Kelly treats me like a younger sister, and James, well, he acts like an older brother."

He tried to conjure up an image of James, and concern circled in his belly. How intimidating could a British PE teacher be?

"Did something happen during their visit?"

"Nothing big. Just some family drama." She fiddled with her napkin. "I have some life path decisions to make. My great-grandfather raised me, and he left some stuff behind for me to sort through."

Lucas thought about his own family and the struggles between him and his father. Keeping *Legacy* a secret felt criminal. Not to mention the tension with his stepbrother. "I can understand. My family's pulling me in one direction, and I'm trying to go another."

"Exactly." Her expression sobered. "One minute you think you have your life mapped out, and the next—"

"*Bam.*" He balled his fist and slammed it into his palm. "Something comes out of left field."

"Yep. A takedown."

Lucas laughed as his heart lightened. He could handle family drama. At least he hadn't done anything to make her stop answering his texts.

The server brought their dishes and placed them on the table. After refilling their drinks and asking them if they needed anything else, she walked away.

"I'm glad you agreed to go to lunch with me today." He stuck his fork into his noodles and took a bite. The aromatic spices tantalized his tongue, making his stomach rumble.

"I am too." She tipped her chin down and looked at him through lowered lashes. "I thought about sabotaging my website."

"Why?"

"This summer, I went back to London with Kelly and James and had a lot of time to think. I realized I should've taken you up on that coffee date even after you rescheduled."

Warmth rushed through him. She'd been thinking about him all summer. "Well, I have a confession too."

"Uh-oh. What?" She took a sip of her soup, then dabbed her mouth with her napkin.

"I considered inserting a bug into your website, so you'd need to call me."

"How do you know I would've called you?"

"I'm your IT guy."

She laughed and the happy sound floated across his ears like a cool breeze.

"What else have you been up to this summer?" They both asked the question in unison.

Lucas set his fork down. "You first. I want to hear about London."

"London was great. Kelly and I did a lot of shopping and sightseeing. I have a whole new wardrobe for the winter." Her expression brightened. "We all took a train to Germany and spent a week looking up my papa's family history."

"Unearthing family history is fun."

"Sometimes." She shifted in her seat. "I also participated in a martial arts competition over the summer. I even brought home a few medals."

"I'm impressed. You're a black belt. Right?"

"Yeah." She held up her hands and wiggled her fingers. "These are deadly weapons, so don't try anything, Mr. IT."

He held his hands up in surrender. "Don't worry. I won't."

"School starts next week. I'm excited and nervous." She took a bite of her mango rice, then relaxed back in her seat.

"You'll do great. Did you get your curriculum loaded onto your website?"

"I did."

"Remember, if you need help, I'll be here all week."

"Penny's looking forward to it." She shot him a playful look. "She asked me to cripple her website during lunch. She's got plans to ask you a few more questions."

He scrubbed a hand across his jaw. "Penny's scary."

"Not scary. Enthusiastic. She's a trained opera singer. Are you sure you don't want her number?"

"No. Thank you." He leaned in and whispered. "I've already got one girl's number. If she would only text me back."

She snickered then sipped on another spoonful of her soup. "What have *you* been up to this summer?"

"I went on two business trips. One to Oklahoma, that you knew about, and one to Seoul."

"Wow. That's exciting. Which place did you prefer?"

"If you're looking for good barbecue, I suggest Oklahoma. If you're looking for an exciting nightlife, head to Seoul." He rested his elbows on the table and steepled his fingers. "I prefer barbecue."

"I'd love to go to Seoul to watch a martial arts competition."

"You wouldn't participate?"

Her eyes widened. "No way. That's where it all began. After one round, I wouldn't be able to get off the mat."

"Takedown?"

"Definitely." She placed her spoon on the table. "You mentioned your dad sent you on an errand to OKC. Why were you in Seoul?"

"I went with a couple of friends. They're in tech as well. We go on an annual trip for fun and to network. Remember the app I told you about?"

She nodded.

"It goes online in the fall. I met with a few last-minute investors while I was there."

"How did that go?"

"I hit a few snags. The competition's fierce, but let's just say I took out the competition." He held up his hands and waggled his fingers. "These hands are weapons too. At least with a keyboard and a couple of layers of code."

She bit back a laugh. "Tell me more about your app."

"It will be a worldwide shopping portal for estate items like antiques and other heirlooms."

"It sounds like your family's business, but on a wider scale."

"You could say that." His neck muscles tensed. "My father doesn't approve of my path for the business."

"Yikes. That's not good."

"Yeah. He doesn't even know about the app going online. I need to be honest with him, but every time I bring up the subject, he explains his disapproval of my *hobby*."

"What are you going to do?"

"For now, I'm going to wait. I'll juggle my role as an app developer and continue to learn the family business."

"Won't that be tricky?"

"Only time will tell." He checked his watch and sighed. "I guess we should get back." Standing, he said, "Thanks for suggesting this place. The food was great."

"I'm glad you liked it." She rose and dug in her purse for her wallet.

"Let me get lunch." He laid several bills on the table. "*I* asked *you* out. Remember?"

"True. But you suggested we eat a chicken sandwich."

"I haven't had a school sandwich in years. It sounded tasty."

"No. Just no." She shook her head as they walked out of the restaurant.

Lucas laughed as he reached for her hand again, and they strolled back to the school. Her palm was warm, and her fingers curled around his as if they'd been carved out of the same mold. He could walk for miles like this.

When they reached her SUV, he spun her around, so she faced him. "I want to see you again."

"You will. In about ten minutes."

"True." He glanced over her head at the line of trees flanking the parking lot. "This week's going to be difficult."

"Why?"

When he looked back at her, he tugged her closer. "Because I need to focus on teaching this class and not on you."

"Do you want me to sit in the back? With the PE teachers?"

"No. You need to sit near Penny and rein her in."

Her eyes sparkled. "I'll be sure and tell Penny how much you love musicals."

"Don't you dare." Pulse thumping, Lucas resisted the urge to wrap his arms around her and press his lips against hers. "Would you consider going out to dinner with me tonight?"

She brought a finger up to her chin and flashed him a coy smile. "Maybe. I need to check your socials and make sure you're not a stalker."

"Go ahead. I've got nothing to hide." His heart sputtered. *Except my real identity.* "What about you? Do *you* have any aliases *I* should know about Miss Renée Landon?"

She held his stare for a second then pivoted out of his arms and opened the back of her SUV. "None you should know about." After she grabbed her messenger bag, she closed the hatch and turned back to face him. "I can do a late dinner tonight. Will that work?"

"Works. Would you prefer me to pick you up, or would you like to meet me?"

"I'll meet you."

"Fair enough. I could be a stalker."

Her expression turned serious. "Or worse."

"What could be worse than a stalker?"

"A politician." She slung her bag over her shoulder. "I'm going to stop by my classroom and freshen up before training starts."

Folding his arms, Lucas relaxed against the side of her SUV. "I'll see you in the library. Up front."

"I'll try not to distract you." Batting her eyelashes, she turned and sashayed toward the school.

"Too late." As Lucas watched her retreat, he smiled. Finally. A date with Renée.

He'd made the right choice, coming here today, unannounced.

Now, if he could figure out the right time to tell her he was a Bennett.

11

S weat seeped out of Emersyn's sparring helmet and slid down her temple. The heat coursing through her body had nothing to do with the unusually warm September weather. Or her thoughts about Reid. Today, perspiration dappled her skin because of the quick responses of her sparring partner.

She rolled her shoulders and returned to her ready stance. Today's workout had one purpose—to clear her head.

Bouncing on the balls of her feet, she concentrated on the quick, limber movements of her martial arts instructor, Jaeden Park.

He drove a strike to her jaw, then followed with a kick to her midsection.

She grunted and hopped back.

Towering several inches above her and weighing nearly forty pounds more, it wasn't his size that made him a formidable opponent, it was his speed. Even in his sixties, Jaeden moved like a jaguar on the prowl. Steady and light on his feet.

Lunging forward, her glove sailed through the air and struck Jaeden's temple. She drew back, swung again.

He slid, raised his left glove to block another hit, then landed a blow to her middle with his right.

She huffed. Charging forward, she aimed a kick at his left side.

He deflected, swatting her foot away.

She recovered quickly, bringing herself back to the balls of her feet.

"Good idea. You need to move faster." Jaeden stayed in motion as he handed out his instructions. "Keep your eyes on mine. You looked down and gave yourself away."

She ground her teeth against her mouthguard. Sparring didn't come naturally to her. She preferred the lithe, poetic movements of the ancient, choreographed forms.

Sparring had too many variables. Too many outcomes.

Her left glove sliced through the air rocketing toward his jaw.

He ducked, then clipped a strike to her gut.

Groaning, she sidestepped. If they were keeping score, she would've bowed out five minutes ago.

"You announced your strike." His brow scrunched. "Again."

Emersyn pressed her eyes shut. *I need to focus.* Blinking away her frustration, she shook out her arms and returned to a ready stance.

Jaeden shot her a concerned look. "Do you need a break?"

"No, sir. Just some water." Her gaze flew to the clock on the wall. Her lesson had only started, but her heart pounded like she'd run a marathon.

Jaeden bowed, and she returned the motion.

Stepping away from the ring, Emersyn yanked off one glove and stowed it under her arm. After pulling out her mouthguard, she picked up her water bottle and let the icy liquid trickle past her lips. It soothed her parched throat but did little to quell the anxious thoughts circling through her brain. *Reid. H & G. Teaching. My wayward uncle. Repeat.*

Ever since she'd returned from London, she'd gone in circles about joining H & G and tracking down her uncle. Then, with Reid reappearing last month, harnessing her thoughts had been a struggle.

100

She swiped the back of her hand across her lips, erasing the remnants of perspiration and water, then took another swig of her drink. *I can't wait to see Reid again.*

After their first dinner date, Reid had divided his time between house-sitting for his friend Skip and driving back to Richmond to work with his dad. No matter how hectic their schedules were, they'd spent every weekend they could acting like tourists around Hampton Roads. Spending time with Reid made everything mundane feel new again.

Jaeden cleared his throat.

A surge of heat raced through her as she pushed away the image of her handsome tech guy.

After quickly tucking her water bottle back in her bag, she replaced her mouthguard, then shoved her hand back into her glove.

"Time to focus, Sparrowhawk." Jaeden grinned as they faced each other on the mat and bowed.

She nodded. The name he'd given her after her first year as his student yanked a memory to the forefront of her mind.

"Look at me, Papa." She demonstrated her first-year forms with *agility and grace.*

Abram smiled at her from his seat in the waiting area. "Like a melody, sweet girl. You move like a melody."

She readied her stance and held her gloved hands level with her face. A melody. A rhythmic order of movement. A sparrowhawk moved with the same grace. Gliding toward its prey with unwavering speed and focus.

Leaning forward slightly, she bobbed back and forth, laser-focused on the liquid onyx pooling in Jaeden's eyes. He'd taught her for years how to clear her mind when she stepped into the ring. Today, she needed to execute.

The corner of Jaeden's upper lip twitched. He lunged and threw a punch.

She twisted out of his reach, then hcisted her leg to sweep a kick to his temple.

He bounced back, regrouped, and took another shot. This one made contact.

Emersyn shook it off, rolled her shoulders. Thighs burning, she returned to her stance and refocused. *One, two, three, four. One, two, three, four.* The song of their sparring circled through her brain as they continued to strike, kick, slide, and retreat.

Jaeden took a step back and lowered his hands. "Very good."

"Thank you, sir." Panting, she stuck her gloved hands out and bumped them with his.

After a few more rounds, she stepped out of the ring, stripped off her gloves and headgear, and took out her mouthguard.

Today's session was meant to silence the chatter in her brain, but instead, the exercise brought to the surface her need to make order out of the chaos in her life. *God, what am I going to do?*

As she slipped off her uniform jacket, cool air feathered over her sweat-soaked T-shirt, sending a chill across her skin.

Slumping into a folding chair, she pulled off her padded foot covers and shin guards. If Papa had stepped away from H & G to raise her, maybe he'd only given her the choice to join out of obligation.

While she sipped on her water bottle, Jaeden sat beside her and removed his gear.

"That's my first medal." He pointed to one of the photo frames on the wall.

A young boy in a martial arts uniform had a gold medal around his neck, his expression beaming.

"What did you get the medal for?"

"Sparring."

She chuckled as she twisted in her seat to face him. "You started young."

"So did you." He shot her a bemused look. "I still remember when Abram brought you in for your first class."

"I do too."

Her heart squeezed. It had been the day before Mother's Day.

A holiday she tried to ignore. Blinking away the sting in her eyes, she sighed. Why did everything pull at the wound of losing her mother?

"Do you remember what you said to me when we met?" Jaeden glanced back at the wall of pictures.

She tugged at the memory, unable to free that cord. "I don't."

"I asked you if you were ready to try something new. Something that, if you put in the time and commitment, would make you strong and brave." Once more, he shifted to face her. "You looked at me, with the fire of battle in your eye, and said, Mr. Park, I'm already brave. I've had to learn to live without my mother."

A lump expanded in her throat.

"Do you know what?" Jaeden patted her knee. "You were right. You *are* brave. Heart tears *can* make us strong and brave, but only if we allow God to work with them."

Moisture filled her eyes, and she turned her gaze back to the row of photos on the wall.

Within the first year of their meeting, Jaeden had grown from an imposing martial arts instructor to a mentor. Heart tears were his way of explaining events that rip pieces from the heart and leave people feeling broken. Not having any memories of Mom had torn a wound in her heart that had yet to heal. Maybe it never would.

"You seem burdened today, Sparrowhawk."

She worried the inside of her cheek, afraid to speak.

"Do you want to talk about it?"

"I'm having trouble quieting my mind. It's been ... well, it's been an interesting summer."

"You just finished your first month of teaching. Right? How's that going?"

She rolled her shoulders, trying to break up the tension in her neck. "Teaching's been great."

She paused, needing to share more but hesitant.

"I've recently found out something about my family. Something I need to sort through."

"Nothing bad, I hope."

She fiddled with the drawstring at her waist. "No. Just confusing."

After a moment, Jaeden rose and walked over to a cluster of black-and-white photos bordering his office door. "These photos tell of my family's lineage. A story not without its fair share of heart tears."

She joined him, examining the pictures. She didn't recognize the faces, but each photo reflected a snapshot of Jaeden's DNA.

"My family's legacy is steeped in history from Korea to Europe, then finally to America. It's a mixture of faith, sacrifice, and peril. Sometimes it can be confusing to understand where God is working in your life. What His purpose is."

He gestured to a picture of two men, one in a military uniform and one in a suit. "That's my great-uncle." He pointed to the man in the uniform. "He fought in wars he wanted no part in and risked his life for what seemed like a lost cause."

Emersyn leaned in and studied the photo. The two men smiled as if they held the key to the same secret.

"The man beside him was his best friend. He was a missionary in Korea at the time of the great revival. Two very different paths, but two very important callings."

A solemn quiet pressed in around them as he continued to stare at the photo. "I never met either of them, but my family continues to share stories about their lives and their legacies. They had a few brushes with death and a few victories, but they both lived out their calling in their own way."

Jaeden pivoted to face her. "Your story, my story, like my uncle and his best friend—they're all unique."

Emersyn blinked back the sting in her eyes.

"God has an incredible story for you, Sparrowhawk. He does for all of us. But I wonder, whose story are you living right now?"

She jerked her chin up. "What do you mean?"

"You live in the shadow of Abram Zucker, but you teach as Renée Landon." His expression remained stoic. "Here, you're Sparrowhawk. And to your friends? Who are you to them?"

Feeling caught, she looked away. How could he understand what she was going through?

"I've been there. Standing in the shadow of my family, trying to find my way." He laid a hand on her shoulder. "Don't be afraid to step into your calling. Whatever that is, God will give you the strength and wisdom to move forward."

She inhaled a deep breath, then released it.

Jaeden withdrew his hand and turned back to the photo of the two men. "Ask yourself this question. If today, at this moment, you lived without fear, what would you do? What would you say yes to?"

She swallowed hard. She wasn't sure that was a question she was ready to answer.

12

Lucas pulled onto the half-mile drive leading to his family home in the sprawling green acres west of Richmond. September drew to a close, and *Legacy* was going online in one week. Dad still didn't know. Or approve.

His stomach twisted as he drove closer to the house. *Can I balance being a Bennett and still make Legacy a success?* And keep it a secret? He turned up the radio to drown out his concerns.

When he reached the house, he threw his two-seater into park and tapped out the final chorus of *Livin' on a Prayer* on his steering wheel. The song always reminded him of his childhood. When his parents were in love and his dad still smiled.

With this song playing in the background, his dad would grab whatever he could find to use as a microphone. Mom would shake her head and roll her eyes, but she'd always draw him in for a long kiss after he finished singing the chorus.

Mom had been gone for ten years, but the hole in his heart still burned with the pain of her absence. *Will I ever be able to let the pain go?*

When she'd died, his dad changed. Everything in their home changed. Heartbroken and wading in his own grief, Sinclair had met Letitia. She wasn't the stepmother dark fairytales are made of, but Letitia wasn't loving either.

As the song faded to local commercials, Lucas forced away the memories and turned off the engine. Why did his life feel so off-kilter? He twisted his neck from left to right, hoping to break up the tension gripping his shoulders. *Because I'm lying to Dad.*

Guilt gnawed at Lucas as he stepped out of the car and took the steps two at a time to the front door. Walking into the house, silence greeted him.

"Dad?"

Maybe he'd need to come back. He'd received a call from an estate manager of an orchard outside of Lynchburg. The owner had passed away, and the family was ready to part with his possessions. It would be a perfect acquisition for *Bennetts.* He'd love it for *Legacy,* but he wanted to give his dad the first option. Besides, if all worked out as planned, *Legacy* and *Bennetts* would be one in the same very soon.

He closed the front door, and the soft thud of his steps echoed around him as he walked down the dimly lit hallway to his father's office.

A light shone from under the office door, and he picked up his pace. Good, he'd catch Dad before his afternoon tee time.

"I don't see it anywhere." Preston's voice jarred him to a stop.

Lucas listened, waiting for his father's response.

Instead, he heard Preston again. "I'm not sure where to look next."

The muscles in Lucas's neck wrenched as he pushed through the office door. "Is there something you're looking for?"

Preston turned from the row of filing cabinets. "Lucas. I didn't know you were stopping by today." He tore the phone from his ear, ended the call without notice, then slipped the phone into his pocket.

"I don't need an appointment to talk to my father." His gaze traveled around the room, then landed back on Preston. "What are you doing in here?"

"Sinclair asked me to pick up a file." Preston yanked open one of the drawers.

"And take it to the golf course?"

"No. He asked me to take it to the downtown office."

"Was that Dad on the phone?"

Preston swiveled and shot him a daggered glare.

"Is there something going on here?" Lucas stepped farther into the room. "Dad doesn't usually like *anyone* poking through his office."

"Are you accusing me of something?"

"We've lived together long enough for me to know when you're trying to hide something." He folded his arms, bracing for battle. "What's going on?"

"Nothing." Preston shoved the cabinet closed. "I told you. I'm looking for a file."

"Look, when we were little, I'd cover for you when you acted out, but if you're in here snooping for no reason, you've crossed a line."

Preston pulled out his phone and slammed it on the desk. After he punched in a number he pushed the speaker button.

Dad answered. "What is it? I'm in the middle of something."

Preston kept his gaze level with his. "Sir, I haven't been able to find that file."

Dad grumbled. "I left it on the table by the door."

"Got it." After he ended the call, Preston picked up his phone and slipped it back into his pocket. "Satisfied?"

Lucas bristled. "Sorry."

"Sure, you are."

Lucas slid into the leather wingback flanking his father's desk and crossed an ankle over his knee. "Listen, Press, you have a reputation. You had a betting racket going on in the dorms."

"You knew about that?"

"Of course, I knew. You and that low-life Ronald Hutchins you hang out with. I did my best to keep it from getting back to Dad."

Preston stiffened. "Did you turn Ron in?"

"It was either him or you. I decided Dad didn't need to deal with it."

"You decided?" Preston stomped to the table by the door and picked up the file. "That was years ago. I was a freshman in college, and Ron's my friend." His stepbrother drilled him with a hardened stare. "And it's not illegal to bet on sports."

"It's only legal to bet if you're over twenty-one." Lucas gestured around the room. "We have a reputation to uphold. Dad spent years securing his legacy. Why did you do it? Why would you risk making him look bad? I know you don't need the money."

"I was bored." Preston folded his arms and let the file dangle in his hand. "I get it. Mr. Righteous, firstborn golden child, has never done anything wrong. You've never kept a secret from Daddy. Have you?"

Heat seared Lucas's chest as he held Preston's gaze.

"We're different. We don't share an ounce of blood." Unfolding his arms, Preston slouched into the chair facing him. "Let me ask you a question. Is there a place for me at *Bennetts*?"

"Do you want there to be?"

"Don't answer me with a question. What's Sinclair got up his sleeve?"

Lucas dropped his foot to the floor and straightened his posture. "He doesn't have anything up his sleeve."

"Really? From what I can see, you've taken on more responsibility. Making more decisions and leading more meetings. Sinclair hasn't asked me to do anything." Preston waved the file in the air. "Except be his errand boy."

"You're still in college."

"I graduate in May. You'd think if he wanted me to learn the business, he'd bring me in more often."

"Do you *want* to work for my father?"

Preston smirked. "I wouldn't be working for Sinclair. I'd be working for *you*."

His gut clenched. Did he trust Preston enough to hire him?

"Will I end up as your errand boy too? Or do you have another menial job planned for me?"

"Here's the deal. If you came to work for me, one mess up, that's all it would take, and you'd be gone."

Preston's smirk faded. "I can see you've already made your mind up about me."

"Like with any new hire, you'd have a six-month probation."

"New hire? What about the family clause? Oh, I forgot, we aren't actually family. Are we?"

"Don't start down that road, Preston. It's above you."

Preston released a low chuckle. "But is it above Sinclair?"

"What are you talking about?" Lucas forced his shoulders to relax. He hated battling with his stepbrother.

"All the world's been laid out for you. You have nothing to worry about. You can make mistakes, and you'd still have something to fall back on. You're Sinclair's *real* son."

Preston might not take the lead at *Bennetts*, but his father wouldn't push him out completely. Would he?

"I need to get this over to the office." Preston rose and shot him a scathing look. "I wouldn't want Sinclair to think I'm a screwup."

As Preston stomped down the hall, Lucas struggled to untangle their conversation.

In middle school, when Preston moved in, he'd played the part of his brother's keeper. And now? Instead of covering for Preston, he outright accused him of doing something nefarious in his father's office.

Lucas huffed out a groan. With the recent problems at the warehouses, he was jumpy. At a time when his father was handing over the ship, chaos swirled at the helm.

His father trusted him to treat *Bennetts* as his own, but with his deception about *Legacy*, was he doing what was best for *Bennetts*? Or what was best for himself?

Maybe instead of pointing out the speck in his brother's eye, he should take the plank out of his own.

13

Emersyn warmed her fingers around a stoneware mug while she stared out the coffee shop window and waited in her booth for Reid. It was her favorite time of year. October. With grey skies and cooler temperatures, the crisp air beckoned her each morning to go for a hike through the fall colors.

As she took a long drink of her pumpkin pie latte, she thought about her last trek with Reid. It had been a sunrise hike with a picnic breakfast at the end of the trail.

Setting her cup down, she sighed. That day, over a Thermos of hot chocolate and a paper sack of homemade granola bars, they'd laughed about her fear of spiders and his aversion to paintball while they shared glimpses of their dreams for the future. *Am I falling in love with him?*

Reid walked through the door and flashed her a dimpled grin.

Her heart flipped, dipped, twirled, then took a bow. *Yep. I'm falling. Hard.*

He approached, bringing with him the heady scents of his rustic cologne and the fall breeze. "Do you mind if I share a bit of your booth?"

"How do you feel about an Americano, two sugars?" She pointed to the mug across from her.

"Did you steal my drink again?"

Did you steal my heart? She cleared her throat. "Technically, I didn't steal it, just mistook it for mine."

"Ah, that's right." Reid placed a quick kiss on her temple before sliding into the seat across from her. "What did you tell me that day? You liked cinnamon. And spice?"

Heat radiated through her. Something like that.

After flashing her a captivating smile, he took a sip of his coffee, then set his cup down. "Did you see the 'for sale' sign in the window?"

"It's been there for months. I hope whoever buys it keeps it a coffee shop." She feathered a hand over the soft fabric covering the vintage bench seat. "I'd miss this place."

"I would too." He reached across the table and took her other hand. "This is *our* place."

Our place. She loved the sound of that.

"How's school going this week?"

"Great. We're scheduled for a field trip to the zoo."

"I remember those days. I'd run around with my friends, make silly faces at the gorillas, then scarf down a sack lunch at the picnic area." He released her hand and relaxed back into his seat. "We should go on a zoo date sometime. I hear the behind-the-scenes tours are amazing."

"That would be great." She took a sip of her latte. "So … tell me the news. I'm dying to know."

"News? About what?"

"*Legacy* went online last week." She set her mug down and pinned him with a stare. "How's it going? Did you get any customers? Tell me everything."

"Well …" He looked away. "It's going okay."

"Just okay?" Her body deflated.

When he glanced back, a surge of excitement sparked in his eyes. "I'm kidding. I put the first week's numbers together last night." He pulled his phone out of his pocket, punched a few commands onto his screen, and a row of colorful charts appeared. *"Legacy's* doing great. Sales are up twenty-five percent more than projected. I've got purchases going out worldwide, and I just put a bid on another acquisition."

She wasn't sure what the charts were telling her, but the enthusiasm in his voice made her skin tingle. When was the last time she'd shared a win with someone who made her heart sing?

"That's amazing. I'm so happy for you." She withdrew a wrapped box from her messenger bag and slid it across the table. "I got you something. To celebrate."

"What's this?"

"Open it."

He ripped at the paper like a kid at Christmas and opened the box. Pulling out a coffee mug, he read the painted words aloud. "I got these biceps coding." Reid glanced up and shot her a teasing look. "Are you checking out my biceps, Renée?"

Heat rushed over her cheeks, and she looked away. "No. I mean ... well ..."

When she turned back, she swept a glance at the navy-blue sweater hugging his well-defined arms before looking back at his face.

His brows shot up. "I saw that."

"Stop it." She slapped him playfully on the forearm, praying her makeup disguised her flaming face.

Reid's dimpled grin widened. "I love the mug. Thank you."

She took a quick drink, still feeling the heat on her face. "I thought it would remind you of me while you're working."

"Not sure I need the reminder. You're *all* I think about lately." The cobalt flecks in his eyes turned electric. "But I do love the mug."

Her pulse skyrocketed. *I need to start drinking decaf.*

"Speaking of work." Reid cleared his throat. "I'm stepping into a larger role at Dad's office while running *Legacy.*"

"He still doesn't know about the app?"

"No."

"When are you going to tell him?"

He frowned. "It's complicated."

"Family can be."

She thought about the family secrets *she* was keeping. When would be the right time to tell him about those?

"I have something I want to ask you."

His words broke through her thoughts as he pulled a postcard out of his back pocket and slid it across the table.

"Would you go with me to the Howl-oween Masquerade Ball on October thirty-first? It's a charity event for the Richmond Animal Shelter. Have you heard of it?"

"I have." She'd attended the event years ago with Sam. "And I'd love to go. But I do have one stipulation."

"What's that?"

She pulled a flyer out of her bag and handed it to him. "How do you feel about kids?"

"Is this another boyfriend test?"

She shook her head, laughter tugging at her ribs. "No."

"Too bad. I'm great with kids."

"A lot of kids?"

"How many kids are we talking?" He studied the flyer and read the announcement aloud. "You're invited to the Maplewood Fall Fling." After he finished reading the details, he glanced at her. "Are you inviting me to the school fall festival, Miss Renée?"

She nodded. "I'm signed up for trunk-or-treat, and I'd love to have help handing out candy."

"Do we need to dress up?"

"Yes, but—"

"I'm in."

"You haven't heard my plan for my trunk theme."

"What is it?"

She held her hand up. "Here me out. He's a superhero. He's got great hair and a girlfriend who's a journalist."

Reid leaned back and folded his arms. "I've heard this story before."

She stole another look at his biceps. He'd have no problem pulling off the costume. "You can dress like a journalist unless you want to wear—"

"No, way." He shook his head, a chuckle rumbling in his throat. "I draw the line at blue tights."

Too bad. "Okay you could wear a suit, glasses, and ..." She stopped herself. *And that adorable curl that always falls across your forehead.*

"And?"

"And you could bring a couple of bags of your favorite candy."

"I can do that."

"I thought we could dress the trunk up like a newspaper building. My friend Sam works in the theatre. I'll see what I can borrow from her."

He rapped his fingers on the table while he threw out ideas. "Newspapers. How about some fake skyscrapers?"

"I've got plenty of newspapers." She pointed to his phone. "I know technology is taking over the world, but there's something about the feel of a regular newspaper in your hands. The smell. The ink."

"I have to agree with you."

"Really?"

He nodded. "I get everything online, but after a while, it's nice to take a break from screens and flip through something tangible. I prefer paperbacks instead of those downloadable books."

"You're kidding? I envisioned your house to be sort of sterile. Like a smart house. Where everything's connected to one of those wired assistants whose voice sounds like a robotic kindergarten teacher."

Reid pursed his lips together.

"Wait. Your house *is* like that. Isn't it? Everything's connected to voice command?"

He held his palms up. "You got me. If I could connect it, I did. You'd be amazed at how tech can streamline your household."

"What if somebody hacks your system?"

"The chances of somebody hacking into my system are like one in a million."

"How did you get that statistic? I heard that one in three Americans gets hacked. Doesn't that bother you?"

He shrugged. "Most people don't have the proper controls. They use the same passwords or out-of-date software. Or the breach is for financial reasons." He folded his hands and laid them on the table. "My finances are locked up tight. Preventing my lights from coming on or blocking my refrigerator from ordering groceries isn't a big motivation for hackers." A twinkle danced in his eye. "Trust me, I know some of them."

"Wait. Did you say your refrigerator orders your groceries?"

"Yep."

"That's too much."

"Let me guess, you go to the store with a list and a pencil, marking off your items as you go."

"I use a pen to mark it off, but the list is in pencil." She leaned back and folded her arms. "You should try it sometime. Lists are very therapeutic."

His laughter circled them. "Maybe I will."

"I'll hold you to it." She uncurled her arms and pulled out a notebook and a pencil from her bag. "Let's finalize our plans for the trunk-or-treat and the masquerade."

He plucked the pencil out of her grip. "How about I make a note on my phone?"

"You do that, but I'll make a list in my notebook." She snatched back her pencil and started to scribble. Candy. Newspapers. Building cut-outs. Blue tights.

He picked up his phone and, with a voice command, he

ordered it to pull up a notetaking app. "I'll make my own list in case yours gets lost or smudged with coffee."

She bit back a giggle. Her lists always had coffee rings on them. "I'm going shopping next week. Do you want to join me?"

"Sure." He waggled his phone. "I'll bring my list."

"You do that." She thumped her pencil on the table. "What's the dress code for the masquerade?"

He flipped over the postcard and pointed to the description. "Woodland creatures. Looks like an enchanted forest theme."

"I love that. What should we dress as?"

He returned his phone to his pocket. "Let's surprise each other."

"That sounds fun."

A masquerade where she had to search out her woodland prince. Her heart did a little jig.

He gestured to the door. "There's a new antique shop down the street. Do you want to go check it out?"

"You must be reading my mind."

They scooted out of the booth and discarded their cups in the dish rack before exiting.

Reid gripped his gift box in one hand and reached for her hand with the other. "You know, if you want me to wear the blue tights …"

Laughter rose in her throat like a spring morning. Fresh. Alive. Hopeful. *Thank you, God, for putting someone in my life to make me laugh.*

She looked up at him and a dark wave of hair fell across his forehead.

Was it possible that she'd found her happily ever after?

Or was falling for Reid her kryptonite?

14

Emersyn's pulse jumped as her driver, Thomas, pulled up to the circle drive of the hotel ballroom. She'd spent days working on her costume, employing Sam and the rest of her theatre friends to help her pull off the perfect look—a glamorous sparrowhawk.

She tied on a gilded filagree mask and slipped her phone into the pocket of her dress as Thomas circled the blacked-out sedan to open her door.

Like he'd done since she was little, he slipped a small, gold-wrapped butterscotch into her palm as he helped her out of the car. "You look very fetching tonight, Miss Zucker."

"Thank you, Thomas." The front of her cinnamon-colored skirt brushed against her knees, while the back of her dress cascaded to the floor with layers of tulle and glittery copper feathers. "You don't think it's too much?"

He flashed her a tender smile. "Not at all."

"I'll call when I'm ready to be picked up." She slipped the candy into her pocket and prayed the current in her belly would cease.

"I'll be waiting." Thomas's gaze focused behind her, and the edge of his mouth ticked up. "It looks like another bird of prey has stepped out of the shadows."

As she turned, the waves in her middle cascaded over a cliff.

"Have a good evening, Miss Zucker."

Thomas's words floated away in the breeze as a man wearing a satiny brown tuxedo approached her.

"Good evening, Renée." Reid glanced at her dress, then lifted his gaze. The gilded Venetian hawk mask he wore tantalized the gold flecks in his eyes. "You look stunning."

"Thank you."

She studied the sharp contours of his jawline, taking note of the weeks' worth of stubble. The wild look complemented the metallic accents in his mask. A combination of luxury and enchanted forest.

Reid's lips tugged at one corner as he held out his arm to her. "Shall we go in?"

She nodded, skin tingling. After she slipped her hand into the crook of his arm, Reid led her into the hotel.

"Wow, this looks amazing." Emersyn's breath caught as they stepped into the opulent ballroom and fell into a fantasy.

Above them, several wooden trellises dangled from the ceiling, covered in loose greenery and vines of twinkling lights.

She pointed to the rustic lanterns hanging from the chandeliers. "Those are beautiful. The lights look like real flames."

"They do." Reid redirected his gaze to an alcove with a circle of whimsical mushroom couches and a backdrop of thatched-roof cottages. "Ever wanted to lounge on a fungus?"

She laughed as they continued their perusal of the ballroom, where bird song mixed with the soft melody of a live string quartet.

"Would you like to dance?" Reid nodded toward the dance floor.

"I'd love to."

After several turns around the floor, they walked to a pub table where they took two sodas from a server dressed like a woodland fairy.

As they stood talking and sipping their drinks, a tall figure wearing an obsidian wolf mask approached her. "Could I interest you in a dance with a wolf?"

"I thought wolves hunted in packs." She looked past the brooding pup. "It looks like you're lost."

The wolf's smooth, tan features molded with his gilded mask. "I'm more of a lone wolf."

"You decided to attend." Reid shot her an apologetic look. "This is Preston. My brother."

She studied the wolf, trying to decipher the resemblance, but came up short.

"Preston, this is—"

"Renée." Preston shot out his hand. "My brother talks about you incessantly."

She cut a glance at Reid.

He flashed her a smile, then looked at Preston. "Where's your plus one?"

Preston shrugged. "She's around. I wanted to meet your beautiful date."

After a few minutes of small talk, a lanky man with a fox mask stepped out of the shadows and gripped Reid's shoulder. "If it isn't the young entrepreneur."

Reid's lips pressed into a hard line. "Professor. Can I help you with something?"

The man leaned in and whispered something to Reid.

He jumped to his feet. "Renée, I'll be right back." He pointed a finger at Preston. "Be good."

Preston saluted, then relaxed his elbows on the table. "That fox is a menace."

"Who is he?"

"My brother's old professor."

She hoped Preston would expound on his answer, but instead, he shifted the conversation to her.

"I heard you're a teacher."

She nodded as she took a sip of her drink. "I teach art appreciation. To high schoolers."

"Art appreciation. Our family dabbles in a bit of that as well."

Reid returned to the table, jaw set. "I'm sorry about that."

"Is everything okay?" She reached for his hand. It was trembling.

"Yes. Just a misunderstanding between old friends."

Preston snorted a laugh. "Don't let Carlson get under your skin. He's more bark than bite." He straightened and shot her a cheeky grin. "It was nice meeting you. Let me know if you change your mind about that dance."

Reid gave him a shove on the shoulder. "Get out of here." After Preston melted into the crowd, Reid turned to face her. "I'm sorry. He can be such a child."

"I can handle him. I teach high schoolers. Remember?"

"That's about his maturity level."

The music faded to a track of an ancient grandfather clock broadcasting twelve deep gongs.

Reid tugged at her hand. "The best part of the evening, midnight in the enchanted forest."

They wove through the crowd until they reached the center of the room.

She scooted closer to Reid, her body feeding off the energy emanating from his anticipation. "This *is* the best part."

He glanced at her, surprise in his eyes. "Someone forgot to tell me they've attended this ball before."

"It was a few years ago."

"Should I be jealous?"

She shrugged. "I don't know. Should you?"

He leaned down and whispered. "You can keep your secrets, Renée. I can handle them."

Secrets. So many secrets. Could he handle them? "My date was my best friend. Sam decided we needed to dress like peacocks."

"I would love to have seen that."

"It was terrible. We couldn't sit down the whole night."

He laughed and glanced at her dress again. "Whoever designed *that* number deserves an award. You look amazing."

"Oddly enough, same best friend."

A man walked to the center of the ballroom, holding an unrolled scroll. "Here ye, hear ye. It's the stroke of midnight and the wee beasties have come out to play on Howl-oween night."

The emcee rattled off a few rules for engaging with the dogs and thanked the attendees for their support of the downtown animal shelter.

At his last word, the double doors opened at the front of the ballroom and a surge of dogs and puppies, dressed in costumes, flooded the floor.

Lucas followed Renée through the canine chaos, rubbing pups behind their ears, patting furry heads, and scratching fuzzy chins.

She stooped to cuddle a miniature schnauzer puppy with grey and white markings. "Look at this one. He's so fluffy and little."

"What's his name?"

She checked the tag dangling from the collar. "*Her* name is Daisy May."

"Daisy May suits her."

As Renée straightened, a bulky Siberian husky bumped into the back of her legs, making her wobble.

Lucas caught her elbow, keeping her upright. "Are you okay?"

"Yeah. Thanks. That dog's enormous." She pointed to her copper-colored heels. "And I'm not used to these."

"I can imagine. You're almost as tall as me in those."

Glancing behind her, he caught another group of oversized canines heading their way. "Time to move."

Whirling her around, he guided her to a secluded area behind a column, avoiding the stampede.

"Thanks. Again." Leaning against the column, she kicked off her heels and hooked the straps in the crook of her forefinger. When she looked up, the gold dust in her eyes sparkled, causing his blood to flame.

"Renée, have I … uh … umm …" Had he forgotten how to complete a sentence? His attention dropped to her lips. What would it be like to kiss her? For weeks he'd thought of nothing else. He coaxed his gaze back to her eyes. "Have I told you how beautiful you look this evening?"

Her lips parted with a hint of a smile. "You might have mentioned it."

"I'm going to tell you again. You're stunning." Warmth flooded his chest as he lazily brushed a thumb beneath the curve of her bottom lip. "Would it be okay if …"

She nodded, answering the question he couldn't complete.

Pulse racing, he rested one hand on the column, while he carved his other hand around the silky skin at the back of her neck. In a whisper-soft movement, his trembling lips pressed against hers.

Sighing, her lashes fell closed. She kissed him back, tender and responsive, their mouths moving like two instruments playing one song.

Lucas closed his eyes. Everything he'd longed for hung in the melody of this kiss. Love. Passion. Forever. He didn't want this song—their song—to end. Ever.

After several heartbeats, they parted. Eyes fluttered opened, gazes locked. The only sound between them was the mingling of their shuddering breaths.

"I wondered where you two ended up."

Preston's voice sliced through the moment.

Perfect timing. As always. Arms dropping to his side, Lucas

stepped back and twisted to face Preston. "Did you need something?"

"Yeah. A ride home." Preston peeled off his mask, giving it a twirl around his finger.

"What?" Lucas scanned the ballroom. The dogs were corralled, and only a small crowd of partygoers lingered in the room. He stole a glance at Renée's mouth, then his gaze lifted to meet hers. "I guess it's time to go."

She nodded, cheeks rosy. "I guess so."

"Am I calling a ride for all of us?" Preston tugged his phone out of his suit jacket.

"No. I'm good." Renée reached into the pocket of her dress and produced her phone. "My driver will be here in five."

"It's late." Lucas took off his mask. "I'd feel better if you rode with us."

She replaced her phone in her pocket and slipped on her heels. "Don't worry. I know the driver. Sam and I have been using Thomas for years."

He reached for her hand. "Okay, but I'll walk you out."

Fingers intertwined, the air remained charged between them while they exited the ballroom and stepped into the hall.

"Our ride will be here in ten." Preston followed behind like a stray puppy. "My date decided to leave with some of her friends."

When they reached the hotel portico, Renée took off her mask and pointed to a blacked-out sedan. "That's me."

Before the driver hopped out, Lucas opened the back passenger door. "Tonight was ... um, what I mean is ..." Stifling a nervous laugh, he gripped the back of his neck. "I had a great time tonight."

A dreamy look covered her expression. "Me too."

"When will I see you again?" He lowered his arm and reached for one of her hands. "Next weekend?"

"James and Kelly arrive in town next weekend. They're staying through Thanksgiving and Christmas."

His shoulders sagged. In two weeks, he'd head off to Vermont to visit family. The time apart, after that kiss, would be unbearable. "Let's plan to get together after Thanksgiving."

"I'll be counting down the days."

"Me too." He kissed her cheek before she slid into the back seat. "Call me when you get home."

"I will."

After he closed her door, Lucas stood on the curb until the car pulled away.

Preston ambled up next to him. "Do you like her?"

"Isn't it obvious?"

"You might want to warn her about Sinclair."

He jerked his head to look at Preston. "What do you mean?"

"Sinclair has his own plans for your future." Preston laid a hand on his shoulder. "I'm not sure marrying a teacher will fit into his agenda for the Bennett legacy."

"Dad doesn't have a say in who I marry."

"That's not what he thinks."

As Preston's ominous words rolled through his thoughts, their ride pulled up to the curb. Preston was right. Dad liked to meddle.

Now, not only did he need to stand up for *Legacy*, but he'd also need to hold the line when it came to Renée.

15

E mersyn clutched her phone, pacing in the entryway, and occasionally peeking out the window. Kelly and James would arrive any minute. They were staying for—how had James said it? A proper American Thanksgiving and leaving after they chimed in the new year.

With all her chairs filled around the dining table, Christmas would be magical this year. Maybe someday, she'd get to set an extra plate.

Her phone buzzed. She read the message from Reid as tingles traveled over her skin.

> Have a good time with your family. I
> miss you.

> I miss you too.

> Can't wait for our after-Thanksgiving date.

> Counting the days.

Warmth ribboned through her like melted chocolate as she traced a finger over her lips. After their masquerade kiss, her thoughts had been preoccupied with little else.

Enjoy your Aunt Rosemary's turkey.

He answered with a happy face and a turkey emoji.

Do you want me to bring you some back?
It's her famous recipe.

Pausing a beat, she sent a return text.

Have you ever cooked your own turkey?

No. Is this a boyfriend test?

Her toes curled in her ankle boots. A husband test.

Minus one point.

Three laughing emojis skipped across her screen.

You wound me. I'll have Aunt Rosemary
give me some pointers.

Her cheeks flamed. Imagining Reid with his cuffs rolled up, cooking a holiday meal, did crazy things to her middle. *I wonder if he can cook as well as he can kiss.*

Reid sent a picture of a chef's hat.

I can see a cooking date in our future.

Me too.

She let her finger hover over the picture of the kissing lips, then landed on the heart sticker and pushed send.

I'll see you soon.

Tires crunched over the gravel drive, pulling her thoughts away from Reid.

She slid her phone into her pocket, shrugged on her jacket, and threw open the door. When she reached the driveway, Kelly and James had stepped out of their rental.

"How was your flight?"

Kelly walked over and brought her in for a warm hug. "Long."

"I bet." She stepped out of Kelly's embrace and turned to James.

"Hey, Em. How have you been?" His melodic accent carried through the breeze as he gave her a quick hug.

"I've been good. I'm so glad you guys are here."

"Kelly's been talking about this for months." He walked to the back of the vehicle and opened the door. "I think she's packed for months as well."

"I heard that." Kelly ducked into the back seat and unbuckled Noah.

"Aunt Em!" Noah catapulted out of the car and ran into her arms. "It's almost Christmas."

"It is." Emersyn picked Noah up and gave him a squeeze. "How was your plane ride, little man?"

Noah slithered out of her grasp, landed on the ground, and folded his arms. His serious expression mirrored his father's. "Long."

She barely contained her snicker.

"There was a lot of water under us." He eyed his dad. "Daddy called it a pond, but I think it's too big for a pond."

She tousled Noah's hair. "It is a bit big for a pond."

James shook his head as he lifted out the final piece of luggage and set it on the gravel drive. Everyone grabbed the handle of a bag, including Noah, who clutched a kid-size bag covered in pictures of superheroes.

As they trudged to the house, she gestured to Noah's luggage. "You really like superheroes. Don't you, buddy?"

He nodded and pointed to the man in blue tights. "He's the best."

"Yes, he is." Emersyn winked at Kelly, then brought her gaze back to Noah. "Wait until you see the room you're staying in."

She'd bought a few special toys for Noah's extended stay and added superhero sheets to his bed.

"Can you show me now?" Noah bounced on his toes like a spring.

"Of course. Let's get these bags inside, and I'll take you to your room."

Noah sprang inside the door and after they all settled into their rooms, Kelly and James met her upstairs in the sitting room. A fire roared in the hearth, and they each claimed a seat facing the fireplace.

"I love a cozy fire surrounded by family." Kelly pulled a blanket off the side of the chair and tucked it around her lap.

Emersyn snuggled with her own blanket. "Me too."

Donna swept into the room with a tray of tea and hot chocolate and a plate of chocolate chip walnut cookies. "It's so good to have you guys back in town. Where's little Noah?"

"He's playing with his new toys." Kelly snatched a cookie off the plate and took a bite. "These are delicious. You make the best cookies in the whole world."

"Oh, stop." Donna waved her hand in the air. "You're being —how would you say it, James? Cheeky?"

James chuckled.

Kelly held a hand over her heart. "Me? Never."

"I'll take these to Noah, with a cup of milk." Donna piled two cookies on a small plate. "If that's okay?"

"Of course." Kelly poured herself a mug of hot chocolate. "Are you spending Thanksgiving with us this year?"

Donna's cheeks turned several shades of pink. "Yes."

Kelly looked from Donna to Emersyn then back at Donna. "Am I missing something?"

Emersyn grabbed her own mug and poured a spoonful of marshmallows into the cup before adding her hot chocolate. "Donna *and* Frank will be joining us this Thanksgiving."

"*Oh?*" Kelly's brows lifted.

"Frank Collins?" James poured tea into his mug and added a square of sugar. "I haven't seen him in a while."

"Donna bumped into him at the grocery store." Emersyn grinned. "He asked about you and Kelly."

"Frank mentioned not having anyone in town this Thanksgiving, so I ..." Donna blew out her breath. "I invited him."

Kelly looked at James. "Didn't his wife pass away a few years ago?"

"Yes." James took a sip of his tea then set it down on a coaster. "He has two older boys. They live in Maine with their wives and children."

"Well, from what I remember, he was quite handsome." Kelly dunked her cookie in her hot cocoa, then took a bite.

James's brows shot up. "Oh, really?"

"Is he?" Emersyn sat back in her seat. "Why don't you describe him for me, Donna?"

Donna waved them all off as if they were a bunch of naughty children. "You three, stop it. I didn't want him to spend Thanksgiving alone." She squared her shoulders. "And if you must know, he's quite handsome."

The three of them chuckled as Donna glided out of the room.

"I'll enjoy catching up with him." James's brow pinched together. "So, Em, Kell tells me you're seeing someone."

She eyed Kelly, then looked back at James. "I am."

"What's his name?"

She straightened, bracing herself for the interrogation. "Reid."

"Is it serious?" James dipped his chin. "If it is, I'd like to meet him."

Kelly laid a hand on his knee. "James, we've been in Virginia only a few hours. You have the next two months to act like an overbearing brother."

"I'd like for you to meet him, but ..." Emersyn picked up a cookie and took a bite.

"But what?" Leaning back, James folded his arms. "Is there something wrong with him?"

She swallowed her bite, then set the rest of her cookie down on a napkin. "No, Mr. Taylor. There's nothing wrong with him."

"I'll find out if there is."

"He's kidding." Kelly turned to James. "Aren't you?"

He shrugged.

"Kelly, you promised." Emersyn's cheeks heated.

Kelly took another drink of her cocoa before setting the mug on the coaster. "I did promise—we promised." She shot James a chiding look. "We trust your judgment, Em."

"I was thinking after Thanksgiving, the four of us could go out to dinner." Emersyn twirled the silver ring on her middle finger. Was she ready for Reid to meet her family?

"Good plan." James uncrossed his arms and snatched a cookie off the plate.

"There's one thing. He doesn't know I'm a Zucker."

A surprised look crept across Kelly's face. "I thought you were going to tell him after our visit."

"I'm not ready."

"You've been seeing each other for a while," Kelly said. "Don't you think you should tell him who you are?"

The room quieted. James finished off his cookie and gestured to Emersyn. "Let's hear her out. She might have a good reason for keeping secrets."

"Secrets are never a good idea." Kelly's brows crinkled. "Are you two getting serious?"

A shiver tickled her middle as the memory of their kiss flashed in her mind. She cleared her throat. "Reid and I see each other a few times a month. We text and talk on the phone, but it's not like we live in the same neighborhood."

"Texting?" James poured more tea into his mug. "That's considered dating?"

She shrugged. "Yeah."

"I must be getting old. That's a weird way to date."

"You're not old. Maybe old-fashioned, but not old." Kelly glanced at him with a dreamy look. "Which I don't mind at all."

"Honestly." Emersyn curled her legs up under the blanket. "I'm scared."

"Scared of what?" James swung his attention back to her.

"Once he knows," she gestured around the opulent room. "That this is where I live, this is who I am, I'm afraid things will change between us."

"I get it. But don't you want to know how he'll respond?" Kelly reached out and took James's hand. "We know from experience it's good to get everything out in the open before you try and have a relationship with someone."

"Kell's right," James said. "What if he's only interested in your money?"

Her guts twisted. Her secrets were piling up. Would Reid understand? Would he still want to be with her once she confessed?

"Is there something else?" Unease coated Kelly's question.

"What about H & G?"

"What do you mean?" James asked.

"Do I tell him about it?"

A sharp line formed on James's brow. "You don't need to mention the society. Some members don't even tell their spouses."

Kelly frowned. "That's not advisable either."

"I'm confused." Emersyn pulled the blanket snug, warding off a chill. "I thought I needed to be completely honest."

"This is different." James stood and walked over to the fireplace. Grabbing the iron poker, he stoked the glowing wood. "Have you decided you want to be involved with H & G?"

As the wood crackled and flamed, she worried her bottom lip between her teeth. Did she really want to commit to something she doubted she was qualified for? "I haven't decided yet."

James replaced the poker and turned to face her. "There's no expiration date. Kell and I would love for you to be a part of H &

G, but it's a big decision." His expression softened. "Until you decide, Reid doesn't need to know."

She swallowed back the lump forming in her throat. What would Abram have her do? What would Mom have wanted?

"There's something else we need to talk to you about." James's hands rested on his hips. "Declan's been released."

"My uncle? When?" Firey panic shot through her. "Do you know where he is?"

"He's been assigned to a reintegration house in Chesapeake." James's expression hardened. "They sped up the timetable of his release."

"I still don't think you have anything to worry about." Kelly looked from James to her. "I doubt he knows about your connection."

James gripped the back of his neck while he paced in front of the fireplace.

"James." Dread laced through Emersyn. "What aren't you telling me?"

"It's just …" He stopped and folded his arms. "We're working on something. A case with H & G. It picked up speed around the time Declan was released."

She looked from him to Kelly. "What does that mean?"

"I think it's a coincidence," Kelly said. "James disagrees, but I don't think Declan would risk going back to jail."

"A leopard doesn't change its spots." James returned to his seat and scrubbed his hand down his jaw. "Maybe Declan's slipped right back into the life he's comfortable with. Money is a strong persuader."

Emersyn shivered. Who was this uncle she'd never met? Would he ever find out they were related? If he did, what would he do?

"I want you to consider hiring security. At least until I know for sure Declan's not involved in this latest case." James's suggestion sliced through her thoughts. "When I see Frank over Thanksgiving, I'll speak with him about checking in on Declan."

She flung off her blanket, jumped to her feet, and plodded over to the large bay window. Grey clouds had rolled in, hiding the sun and mirroring her bleak mood. "Papa never wanted me to live in a bubble. I know I need to be cautious. I've always known that." After a beat, she turned to face Kelly and James. "Unless there's a direct threat, I'm not going to live hiding behind a wall."

Kelly stood and joined her, taking her hand. "Look, I understand where you're coming from. I've been there. Just be aware of the situation and remain vigilant. If something changes, we'll let you know."

She gave Kelly's hand a squeeze, then looked at James. "I'll keep my guard up, but for now, no security."

Noah pushed through the door with a cookie in one hand and an action figure in the other. "Dad, look at what I found in my room."

James gave her an understanding nod. He opened his arms to his son. "Let me see. Is that your favorite superhero?"

Noah giggled as he jumped into James's lap. "Yes. He's the best. He can fly, and he's super strong."

As she watched James and Kelly playing with Noah, a longing tugged in her heart. She wanted this. Family. Marriage. A bond so strong nothing could sever it. *Could I have that with Reid?*

Tears stung her eyes. She needed to be honest with him. About everything. He'd shared his family—and the secrets about *Legacy*. If he could open up to her, she needed to take a step of faith and trust him.

Then, if God allowed, maybe she'd finally find what she'd always wanted. A happily ever after and a family of her own to circle her table.

16

Lucas walked through his front door and dropped a stack of mail on the entry table. His Saturday morning flight from Vermont had been quick, but Thanksgiving had been the longest holiday of his life. He missed Renée. And burying his excitement about *Legacy* while his dad discussed his new role at *Bennetts* didn't help.

I'm a terrible son. His overnight bag slid from his shoulder and landed with a thud on the floor.

Shuffling into the living room, he shrugged out of his jacket and set his laptop bag down before slumping onto the couch. *Legacy* was doing well, and he wanted to share it with his dad. But he couldn't.

Raking his fingers through his hair, he huffed out a groan. Keeping *Legacy* a secret was a risk. A gamble that might get him booted out of *Bennetts* for good. Maybe even struck from the will.

His phone buzzed. Pushing away his scattered thoughts, he fished his phone out of his jeans and accepted the call.

"Preston. What's up?"

"Are you going into the office Monday?"

"I hadn't planned on it." Dad had suggested he take a few

days off. With the holiday sales ratcheting up, he'd use that time to work on *Legacy*.

"Maybe I could shadow you a day or two," Preston said. "While I'm on break from school."

Lucas pursed his lips together. For weeks, Preston had probed him about *Bennetts*. He'd started asking more questions and showing genuine interest in the history and the day-to-day activity of the family business, but he couldn't get this nagging feeling to fade—Preston wasn't right for *Bennetts*.

Was he prejudiced because Preston wasn't blood? He hoped not.

"Let's shelve that idea until after the first of the year. My schedule's sporadic right now."

Preston paused a beat. "Yeah. Okay."

After another minute of small talk, Preston ended the call.

Lucas tossed the phone on the couch. Preston was a conundrum. One minute he acted like a prodigal, the next a dutiful son.

Rising, he walked back over to the stack of mail. Most of it junk, but an unmarked envelope at the bottom of the pile caught his eye.

He ripped open the letter and scanned the note.

> *How does success feel?*
> *Remember, I'll get my cut one way or another.*

Heat raced through his veins. He thought after the chat at the masquerade ball, Carlson would've backed off. *Legacy* was his. End of story.

He shoved the letter back into the envelope. If he gathered his family's lawyers to silence Carlson, his dad would need to know about *Legacy*. But if he did nothing ...

He thought back to the fire outside the warehouse in Oklahoma City. After combing over the inventory, he'd discovered no discrepancies. However, shapes left in the dust, over twenty of them, where products should've been, still kept him up at night.

He sat on the couch and pulled his laptop from his bag. After a few clicks, he brought up the inventory lists from Oklahoma City and scanned the dates. The updates were all from this year.

"Maybe I need to look at last year's report."

He picked up his phone, ready to call Marc, the assistant dad had assigned to him, but a gnawing in his gut made him pause. *Can I trust Marc?*

Slamming his laptop shut, Lucas sighed. He doubted Carlson was stealing inventory. That would hurt *Bennetts*. Not *Legacy*.

"I'll get my cut one way or the other."

The words scribbled on the note surged through his thoughts. Stealing inventory and selling it for himself would allow Carlson to get his cut.

He set his laptop aside, picked up his phone, and sent Preston a text explaining plans had changed. They'd both be in the office on Monday.

If Preston wanted to prove his worth, he could help find the anomaly in the inventory. Then, maybe he'd consider giving him a position at *Bennetts*.

After a quick back and forth with Preston, Lucas checked his watch. He had several hours before he was supposed to meet Renée and her family for dinner. His pulse kicked up a notch. It's only dinner. Not an interrogation.

Rising, he stretched then brushed a hand down the stubble along his jawline. He needed to shave and decide which suit to wear. *Renée likes blue.* Decision made. With a bolt of energy, he leapt to his feet and made his way to the shower.

Tonight would be just what he needed. No drama, just dinner. For the next couple of hours, he could put his rift with Carlson in the rearview and focus on what really mattered to him—Renée.

17

Emersyn sipped her water as she glanced at the door of the restaurant. *Did I send Reid the right address? Yes. Of course I did. Relax.*

Setting her glass down, she made a mental note to stop staring at the door. Tonight was going to be perfect.

"He's late," James grumbled as he drummed his fingers on the table.

"He's not late." Kelly placed her hand over his, silencing the rhythmic thud. "We're early."

James slipped out of Kelly's grip and checked his watch. "You're right. He's got five minutes." He relaxed his posture and took a drink of his water. "Fill me in again, Em. You mentioned Reid's a software designer. Sounds like he'd get along with Henry."

"She told me he was leading-man handsome." Kelly's expression turned coy.

James's brow shot up. "Is that so?"

Emersyn forced a smile. Tonight was going to be ... interesting.

Before her mind could devise an escape plan, Reid stepped through the door.

"He's here." She waved him over. *Please, God, let this dinner go smoothly.*

James stood and stuck out his hand. "You must be Reid."

"Yes, sir." Reid shook James's hand, then stole a glance at her. "Hi."

Her insides squirmed. "Hi."

After James introduced Kelly to Reid, they both took their seats.

"You look amazing." Reid leaned close, bringing with him the fresh scents of a recent shower.

"Thank you. So do you."

Reid slipped his hand under the table and curled his fingers around hers. A zing bolted through her. However tonight unfolded, they'd walk through it together.

A sharply dressed waiter interrupted her thoughts when he approached the table with menus and took their drink orders.

"Renée told me all about the Howl-oween masquerade." Kelly sipped her water, then glanced at her menu. "That's such a great fundraiser."

Emersyn exhaled. At least Kelly had remembered to call her Renée. Maybe she and James had more experience in duplicity than they'd let on.

"Have you attended the ball?" Reid gave her hand a quick squeeze as he directed his question to Kelly.

"Yes. Years ago. I used to live in Virginia." Kelly looked up, eyes bright. "I could've taken home every puppy. They were all adorable. Do you have any pets, Reid?"

"I don't." He paused a beat. "Wait. Do horses count? I have a few horses, but they stay on my dad's property."

Emersyn's pulse slowed to a normal pace. At least tonight's interrogations centered around pets.

James leaned forward, steepling his fingers on the table. "Renée mentioned you're in IT."

"I am." Reid released her hand and relaxed back in his seat.

"A few months ago, I worked at Renée's school setting up the software for their grades and curriculum."

The server reappeared, carrying their drinks. After he took their dinner orders, he motioned toward a glass-enclosed patio aglow with twinkling lights. "We've opened our terrace this evening. It's heated and includes live piano music with one of our local musicians. There's a dance floor and lounge seating under the stars. I hope you enjoy your evening, and if there's anything you need don't hesitate to ask."

"Thank you." James waited for the waiter to leave before he rose and reached out his hand to Kelly. "Would you like to dance, luv?"

"Yes." As she rose, Kelly flashed Reid and her a smile. "What about you two? Want to join us?"

With an inviting look, Reid stood and offered his hand to her. "Dance with me?"

"I'd love to."

They followed Kelly and James out to the terrace where the gentle notes of the ivories mingled with the fairy lights and the starry sky, filling the glass-walled garden with an ethereal magic.

Still holding her hand, Reid twirled her toward him and slid his other hand around the small of her back. "This is one of my favorite things. Dancing with you."

She looked up at him, swaying in time to his lead. "What's your *most* favorite thing."

"That's easy." Leaning in, his breath feathered across her earlobe. "Kissing you."

She gazed around the room. Was there anywhere they could escape to share a few stolen kisses?

Reid's voice turned husky. "I already looked. Nothing."

She turned back to him, cheeks flaming.

"I've missed seeing you." He continued to move in rhythm with the music, practiced and languid. "This has been the longest November of my life."

"I've missed you too." She melted into him, wishing the song would never end. "Thank you for coming tonight to meet James and Kelly."

"They seem really great." He glanced at the Taylors, who swayed together in time with the music.

"They are. I don't know where I'd be without them."

Tenderness covered his expression. "I'm glad you had them to lean on when you lost your great-grandfather."

"Me too."

The airy notes of the ballad circled them, and Reid continued to lead them flawlessly in time to the music. "I hope I pass tonight."

"Pass?" She glanced up at him. "This isn't a test."

"It isn't?" His mouth tugged at one corner. "I wouldn't be surprised if James has already lifted my fingerprints off the water glass."

She tipped her head back and laughed as Reid twirled her in a circle, then brought her back snug against his chest.

"Trust me. Tonight's a test." His expression turned serious. "When you told me he was Kelly's bodyguard years ago, I almost canceled."

"Don't worry. James isn't here to interrogate you. Just to get to know you."

Reid pushed a curl away from her cheek, grinning. "Honestly, the interrogation doesn't bother me. After he runs my prints, they'll find I have nothing to hide."

As the final notes of the song filtered through the air, he released her and led her back to the table.

"This place is great." Kelly sank into her seat as James held it out for her.

"It is." Emersyn relaxed in her chair as James and Reid took their seats. "I can't believe I've never been here before."

A few moments later, the waiter approached with two other servers, and with a bit of fanfare, placed their plates and a loaf of warm crusty bread in front of them. Emersyn's mouth watered.

"Let's say grace." James took Kelly's hand.

They all bowed their heads as he said a short prayer thanking God for great food and friendships.

"Amen." They ended the prayer in unison.

As they ate, James regaled everyone with his thoughts on the latest historical docuseries about the Middle Ages. Kelly gushed about little Noah and his obsession with superheroes as well as his anticipation for Christmas Day.

Reid pitched in and talked about his antics with Preston.

"He tried to get me to break into the school computer and change his grade. In home living. He could never get a handle on cooking an egg over easy."

"Did you do it?" James wiped his mouth with his napkin. "Change the grade?"

"No. I paid someone to teach him how to cook an egg. Then I forced Preston to cook me breakfast for a week."

Everyone laughed and Emersyn's heart soared. The night progressed exactly as she'd hoped.

"You'd get along well with my brother Henry." James reached for a slice of bread and buttered it. "There isn't a computer he can't hack."

"I'm not into hacking. I prefer to build things with code rather than try to break them." Reid looked at her, then back at James and Kelly. "I don't know if Renée told you, but I started my own app."

"She mentioned it." James glanced at her as he took a bite of his bread, then laid what was left on his plate.

"My family acquires antiques for resell. We work mostly in the family estate business." Reid placed his fork beside his plate and eased back in his seat. "I designed an app to connect buyers and sellers worldwide to priceless antiques and unusual family heirlooms."

"Is your app active online?" James asked. "Maybe I've heard of it."

"It's called *Legacy*."

James coughed, then straightened his posture. "Did you say *Legacy*?"

"Yes, sir." Reid held James's gaze. "It went online at the beginning of October. The first week, we had over a million downloads."

"Is that so?" James's voice dipped into a growl. "Impressive."

Emersyn jerked her head to look at James.

James kept his eyes trained on Reid. "Are you the sole owner of the app?"

"I am. Owner and developer."

Kelly cleared her throat. "That's quite an accomplishment. Especially for someone so young."

For a moment, a tense silence ribboned around them.

Emersyn reached her hand under the table and curled her fingers around Reid's. Why had James's expression turned stormy when Reid told him about *Legacy*? She glanced at Kelly, imploring her with a look to explain.

"Tell us more about *Legacy*." Kelly dabbed her mouth with her napkin, then slid it back into her lap. "It's an online market for antiques. Correct?"

Reid turned his attention to Kelly. "Yes. I deal with large estates from all over. I've also started a database of interested buyers and their preferences. Part of my background includes verifying provenance for family heirlooms."

"Provenance brings in a better rate. Doesn't it, Reid?" James squared his shoulders. "Especially if the origin story is especially dark or steeped in intrigue."

"Well, I ..." Reid released her hand and gripped the cloth napkin in his lap. "I don't know if I've stumbled across anything like that. Usually, it's as simple as uncovering if a past president used a desk or a famous painter left behind an unregistered painting."

Their server returned with the check. "Is there anything else I can bring you?"

"No. Thank you." James pulled out his wallet and placed his

credit card in the leather bifold. The waiter picked up the payment and scampered away. "Reid, I do have one more question for you."

"What's that?"

"Does your *father* know about *Legacy*?"

Reid's face paled.

"I didn't think so." James shot up and pushed his chair in.

A tremor worked its way across the back of Emersyn's neck.

When the waiter returned with James's card and receipt, James scribbled his signature, then handed it back. "The service was top-notch. Thank you, again."

Reid cut a glance at her, confusion blanketing his expression.

She shrugged. She'd find out what James was up to, then call Reid later to explain.

"Thank you for meeting us for dinner." Kelly stood, and James helped her with her jacket. "We need to get back and make sure Noah's okay."

Reid rose and smoothed the imaginary creases in his sports coat. "Thank you for inviting me." He held out his hand to Emersyn and shot her a mournful look. "May I walk you out to your car?"

"Yes." Emersyn took his hand as she got to her feet.

"That won't be necessary." James blasted Reid with a hardened stare. "We left the SUV with the valet." Jerking a look at her, James said, "It's getting late."

Reid helped her with her jacket, then she picked up her clutch purse. Glancing at Kelly, she started to protest.

Kelly's face paled as she shook her head.

Turning her attention back to Reid, Emersyn tried to convey her apology with a look. "I'll call you tonight."

He cut a glance at James, then returned his attention to her. "Okay."

They left Reid standing by the table as they hurried to the valet exit. When they all climbed into the waiting SUV, James looked like he wanted to implode.

"What happened back there?" Heat bubbled in Emersyn's veins. "One minute you're treating Reid like he's your new pal, and the next you were acting like a complete—"

"I'm sorry, Em." James pulled the SUV out of the parking lot and onto the highway.

"We'll discuss it at home." Kelly turned in her seat and sent her a pleading look. "It's a little bit more complicated than we can explain in a car."

A text notification came in, and she pulled her phone out of her purse.

> What just happened?

Emersyn pinched her eyes shut, mortified at how dinner had ended. *What am I going to say?*

She opened her eyes and, with a trembling hand, punched out a reply.

> I'm not sure. I'll call you when I get home.

Staring out the window, she rehashed their conversation. James had been out of line, and nothing he could say would excuse his behavior. Nothing.

18

Emersyn stepped into the living room with Kelly and James ready for battle.

"What happened tonight?" She curled her hands into fists and rested them on her hips. "Why did you treat Reid like that?"

James scowled. "Why don't you take a seat?"

"But ... I ..."

"Please." He turned and gestured to the loveseat. "This is going to take some time."

Reluctantly, she sat down.

Kelly gave James a nod then left the room.

James cleared his throat. "Remember how I told you Kelly and I are working a case with H & G?"

"What does that have to do with how you treated Reid?"

"That's not an easy answer." Kelly returned with a laptop and took the seat next to her. "We've uncovered something we think you should know about."

Emersyn's insides boiled "I asked you not to check into Reid."

"We didn't." Concern painted Kelly's features. "But we've discovered something about him. Inadvertently."

"What do you mean?"

James walked over and handed her his phone. A picture of a weathered Bible filled the screen. "We're currently working to retrieve this Bible."

Emersyn studied the photo. The inscription on the front appeared to be written in Korean. A script she recognized from Jaeden's dojang.

"This Bible is over one hundred years old," James said. "It's recently been smuggled out of North Korea."

She whipped her chin up. "Out of North Korea? I thought people smuggled Bibles *into* that country."

"Typically, yes." He took the phone from her and flipped it to another photo. It was a screenshot of one of the inside pages. "The dialect is ancient. Nobody uses it anymore. When the underground church in North Korea finds one of these archaic heirlooms, they attempt to move it across the border." James took a seat across from them on the couch. "It's their silent way of letting the outside world know they're still there, but they need new Bibles with updated dialects."

"What does this have to do with Reid?"

"This Bible was passed to an H & G member at the Chinese-Korean border." James took the laptop from Kelly. "The H & G member had plans to transport the Bible out of China and take it to Seoul. After that, another member would hand carry it to London."

"What happened to the Bible? Did it make it to Seoul?"

"I'm not sure." After typing on a few keys, he set the laptop on the coffee table and turned it to face her. A photo filled the screen. "Before we lost track of the Bible, our contact sent us this list. It was written in the front of the Bible."

She reviewed the list of names. "I don't understand. The names are in English."

"This Bible belonged to a missionary living in Korea during the time of the Great Korean Revival. At one time, missionaries studied at a seminary in Pyongyang."

"Really?"

He nodded. "After the seminary shut down, the missionaries dispersed. Some returned to their homeland, while others stayed at the risk of their lives to continue to spread the gospel."

James relaxed back in his seat. "Kelly and I've been working through the names on the list. When the Bible made it to London, we wanted to pass it on to a living relative." He hesitated. "If we could find one."

"What did you find?"

"So far? A bunch of dead ends. Then, over the summer, we had an unfortunate incident." James turned the laptop to face him, tapped on a few keys, then spun the screen back to her. "Read this."

"Two missionaries, with ties to underground Bible smuggling, were found dead in a hotel room in Seoul." Acid crawled up her throat as she read through the rest of the article.

"One of those men was H & G. We believe both men were murdered."

She looked up. "What happened to the Bible?"

"We assumed it was confiscated." James glanced at Kelly then looked back at her. "Or stolen."

A shiver rolled over her spine. She knew working for H & G could be risky, but murder?

"As for why things took a turn at dinner tonight," James took the laptop, and when he swiveled it back, an email was open. "This is from H & G headquarters."

Emersyn read the missive aloud. "As we mourn the loss of one of our own, we've had another shocking discovery. Evidence points to a planned event. Lost item found at the Widow's House. High currency." She skimmed ahead, reading the remainder of the veiled message to herself.

Begin research on Legacy. Heirloom hidden beyond the veil.
Next step, retrieve that which is lost.

"H & G is investigating *Legacy*?" Her mouth dried. "What does all that mean? Beyond the veil? The Widow's House?"

"I've told you enough." James closed the laptop. "You need to know that *Legacy* is on my radar. I'd think twice about trusting your boyfriend. Better yet, stop seeing him."

Kelly sent James a narrowed look. "James."

"Kell, you know as well as anyone how these things work." He crossed his arms and shot both a scowl. "Em needs to pledge her loyalty to H & G before I can tell her anymore."

"In this case, you need to make an exception. She's involved."

James turned his attention back to her. "How close are you and Reid?"

If she were honest, she'd dreamt of Reid sweeping her off her feet and proposing.

"We're … well, I like him." *A lot.* She cleared her throat. "But that doesn't mean I can't look at this without bias."

James pursed his lips. "From my experience, you can't."

Kelly shot him another chastising look, then pried open the laptop. "James and I are going to tell you everything we know about *Legacy*. After that, you can decide about Reid."

"Can't I just tell you I think he's of a bad lot, and you delete his phone number?" James asked.

Emersyn fisted her hands. "No."

"I'll get some tea steeping for you." Kelly stood and patted James's shoulder. "It might be a long night."

As Kelly left the room, James uncrossed his arms and exhaled. "I don't think you're going to like what I have to say."

"What do you mean?"

"Reid's been lying to you."

He bent toward the laptop, typed for a moment, then turned the screen to face her. "Your boyfriend's name isn't Reid Clark. His real name is Lucas Bennett."

19

Emersyn stared at the photo on James's screen. "What's this?"

"That's the Bennett family." He pointed to the picture of a group of well-dressed people in front of a backdrop of a sprawling mansion. "That's Sinclair Bennett, his wife Letitia, Lucas, and his stepbrother Preston. The others are a set of grandparents, an uncle, and a few cousins and their spouses. He's not just a software engineer, Lucas is a very wealthy heir to a century-old family business."

Hot coals raked across her chest. He wasn't just a normal guy. He'd lied. Or had he only omitted the truth? *Like I did?*

"Tell me the whole story. About the H & G investigation. About the Bible. Everything." She couldn't believe Reid, or Lucas, or whoever he was, had anything to do with the missing Bible. Or the death of those two men.

James pulled the computer into his lap and nodded to the seat next to him on the couch. "Buckle up. This will be a lot to take in."

Heart hammering, she rose and took the seat next to him. *I can do this. I can be objective about Reid.*

James brought a photo of a man up on his screen. "This is Lee. He retrieved the Bible at the Chinese border."

She stared into the man's eyes. His expression was lively. Hopeful. Kind.

"Lee wanted to get the Bible out of China as soon as possible." James opened an email from Lee and explained the contents. "Lee worked in IT and had registered for a tech symposium in Seoul. This would give him a reason to travel. He'd made plans to meet another H & G contact in Seoul, so he could pass on the Bible."

"Was Lee ..." She hesitated, afraid to voice her question.

James nodded. "He was found with the other man. Killed before he made the transfer."

"Why would someone kill him over a Bible?"

"Henry suspects it has to do with the names on the list. If anyone related to that list is still living in North Korea, they could lose their life. Or worse, get sent to a labor camp." James hesitated. "Even children are sent to these camps, Em. And most don't make it out alive."

Her stomach twisted. "Did you know him? Lee?"

"I did. But Henry knew him better. They were both computer guys. Gatherers. Lee was used to research, not handling artifacts. He didn't know he was being followed or that he was in any danger."

Kelly brought in a tray with three mugs and set it on the table. "Here's your tea, James. I brought hot chocolate for us, Em."

Emersyn took a mug of hot cocoa from the tray, relishing the warmth of the stoneware in her hands. "Where's the Bible now?"

"Last month, it was listed on *Legacy*. Before I had a chance to make a bid, it was gone." He took a sip of his tea, then glanced at Kelly. "It's perfect, luv. Thank you."

"Of course." Kelly settled back into the loveseat. "How's the debrief going?"

"I'm going to show Em what Henry found on *Legacy's* website." James placed his mug on a coaster. After a few taps on his keyboard, *Legacy* appeared on the screen.

He hovered his mouse over the grandfather clock in the *Legacy* logo. Nothing happened. He double-clicked on the Roman numeral twelve, and the hands on the clock started turning together.

"Wait." Emersyn pointed at the clock. "What's happening?"

James's mouth twitched at one corner. "Watch."

Shifting her gaze back to the screen, she watched the clock hands rotate three times until both hands came to a stop at the Roman numeral twelve.

James pushed control, alt, the number one, then the number two. A mouse ran out of the center of the clock and scurried to the right corner of the screen.

"What's the mouse doing?"

"Taking us behind the veil." James hovered the cursor over the rodent and clicked. "In three, two, one ..." An array of falling stars filled the screen before it went black.

James started to count again. "One, two, three ... When he reached twelve, the website returned to the screen, this time its border was red instead of gold.

"What just happened?"

"Think of it like another level in a video game." James clicked on the icon of items for sale. "We call this the Widow's House. Or the dark web."

"What does this have to do with the missing Bible?"

"Last month, the Bible showed up here for sale. After three days, it was listed as no longer available."

"Reid, I mean, Lucas explained to me how he acquires products for *Legacy*. It seemed legit. Is it possible he acquired the Bible and didn't know what he had?"

"Let's take the Bible out of the equation. Why does he have a hidden page to sell some of his products?"

She bristled at his question. "Is everything on this page legal?"

"Henry's checking. So far, yes."

"Would it be illegal if Lucas had acquired the Bible?"

James released an exasperated breath. "Not technically. But the last person who had the Bible lost their life trying to get it to H & G."

She tugged on a strand of hair. "What am I supposed to do with this information?"

James shut the laptop. "Nothing. This isn't your assignment. You're not with H & G." He paused, then added, "I can't tell you to stop seeing him, but I will caution you to be careful. I don't know yet if Lucas had any interaction with Lee, but if he lied to you about his name …"

As his words trailed off, her blood chilled. Reid might be keeping secrets, but there was no way he was capable of murder.

20

The January wind whipped at her cheeks as Emersyn unlocked the *Yorktown Courant* building and walked to her office. James and Kelly had left early that morning for the airport, and unable to crawl back into her bed and get any sleep, she decided to get a head start on this month's Lady M column.

She turned on her light, pulled her laptop out of her bag and set it on the desk. Christmas and New Year's had flown by, but the lingering questions about what to do about her relationship with Reid—or Lucas—still plagued her.

After slumping into her chair, she released a sigh. Her heart ached. And despite what James had told her, she longed to see Reid again.

"His name is Lucas." She huffed and opened her laptop. "I still can't believe he's—"

"Knock, knock."

Emersyn jerked her chin up. Sam leaned on the door jamb, wearing a pointy party hat and waving a paper horn in the air.

"Happy New Year!" She blew into the horn, sending the gold and silver streamers flying. "You're here early."

"Happy New Year to you too." Emersyn relaxed back in her seat. "Kelly and James left early this morning."

Sam removed the party hat. "You look like you had a rough holiday."

"You have no idea."

"Want to talk about it?"

"Not really."

Sam flopped into the chair next to her desk. She was dressed like she stepped out of a Renaissance fair, with brown leggings, a flowing white tunic top, and two golden feathers hanging from ribbons in her hair.

"Did the fam meet the boyfriend?"

"Yep."

"And?"

She closed her eyes and exhaled. She wanted to tell Sam everything. But she couldn't. She'd need to figure this riddle out on her own. Emersyn forced her eyes to open and leaned forward, resting her elbows on the desk. "Let's just say it was … tense."

"Family can be a little tense sometimes."

"James practically interrogated Reid. He's convinced Reid's keeping something from me."

Sam's eyes widened. "You're kidding. Like an evil plan to take over the world?"

"Something like that."

"Are they just being overprotective?" Sam fiddled with the gold moon dangling on a chain around her neck. "They aren't blood relatives. Are they overstepping?"

"They aren't blood, but Papa asked them to step in when he passed. He trusted them, and I do too."

"Okay, so *is* Reid hiding something?"

"I don't think so." She nibbled on one of her fingernails, a habit she'd thought she'd abandoned as a kid. "What about me? How can I judge him when I haven't even told him my real name?"

"You'd think Mr. IT would have figured that out by now."

"He's too busy with his new app." And hiding that from his dad. And smuggling stolen heirlooms. She rested her cheeks in her hands. What a mess.

Sam shot out of her seat, and a whoosh of air followed her. "I have an idea." Floating out of the room, she returned a moment later with her laptop and reclaimed her seat. "Does Reid work from home? An office?"

"Both. And his name is Lucas."

Sam's brows lifted. "What?"

"Long story." Emersyn waved her hand in the air as if wielding a magic wand. "Let's forget I said that. *Poof.*"

"Your wand doesn't work on me. We'll come back to that later." Sam looked at her screen and pecked at the keyboard. "So, he's mobile and rents an office?"

"He rents an office space at some place called Telespace or Mobilespace. Something like that. How's that important?"

Sam muttered something incoherent. After a few moments, she glanced up. "*Mobile Solutions*? It's downtown Richmond. A five-story office space."

"That's it. He's got a two-room office. He went on about how it came with the free use of meeting rooms and geeked-out lounge space."

Sam placed the laptop on the desk and pointed to the website. "This is it. There's a gym on the first floor, a few trendy restaurants in the basement, a spa, a small convenience store, a drop-off daycare, and an event space on the top level."

Emersyn leaned closer. "Nice place. Rent's got to be crazy expensive. What's your grand idea?"

"Send Lady M to investigate your bcyfriend."

"What? No."

"Why not? Your crazy British uncle—"

"He's not my crazy British uncle." She pulled a mint out of the candy jar on her desk and plopped it into her mouth. "James is a good guy. He's just—"

"Overprotective?"

"Yes."

"Okay, so you're overprotective, quasi big brother, thinks Reid—Lucas—is hiding something. Besides his name." Sam pointed to the sleek building on the screen. "Go be the journalist and find out what."

"How?"

"Pretend someone wrote to Lady M about the *Legacy* app." Sam shrugged. "Act like your letter writer is concerned it's a front for the Russian mob or terrorist cell."

"I doubt anyone would write a 'Dear Lady M' letter to investigate espionage."

"What exactly is James accusing Lucas of?"

"Not espionage."

Stolen antiquities. Illegal sales. Murder. She bit down on her mint and crunched it.

"Do you like him?" Sam asked.

"What? Who? Reid? I mean Lucas." She finished off the mint. She needed to remember not to call him Lucas to his face. Another lie.

Before the holidays, she believed she'd fallen in love with him. She still couldn't stop thinking about holding his hand or that amazing kiss. Reflexively, she held her hands up to her cheeks. They were on fire.

"So, that's a yes." Sam sent her a knowing look. "Prove to Uncle James he's wrong about Lucas. Prove Lucas is just a hot, geeky software developer who picks up his grandmother's groceries and coaches Little League on the weekends."

Her shoulders slumped. Wouldn't that be nice? Sure, he might be rich, but he's got his own business and attends church on Sundays. Was it possible he wanted the same things she did? A simple life, a family, and maybe even a dog or two.

"What do I do when I get into his office? I'm not even sure what I'm looking for." That was partially true, She needed to find that Bible.

"Is he going out of town any time soon?"

"At the end of this month. He's going on a father-son ski trip to France."

"Whoa. He certainly goes on a lot of trips overseas."

She cringed. He did. Did that mean anything? He went to Seoul over the summer, and somebody ended up murdered.

Sam crossed her legs and smoothed her skirt out into a fan. "Do a sweep of his office. Does it appear to be a shell company? Is it a front for something illegal? Does he have pictures of himself shaking hands with menacing-looking men on yachts?"

"Your imagination is more outlandish than James's." She glanced at the building on the screen. How hard could it be to get into his office? She could rent a space herself or have lunch at one of the restaurants. *How can I get in there and not look suspicious?*

Emersyn pressed her lips together while she scanned the amenities. When she came to the end of the list, she smiled. "I think I know how to get in."

Sam leaned forward and rested her chin in her hands. "What's your plan Lady M?"

She pointed to the screen. "Overnight janitorial staff."

Sam squealed. "It's perfect. Are you going to apply for a job?"

"I have a better idea."

"What?"

"I'll use Lady M as a front. Not for espionage but just some basic, old-fashioned journalism."

Sam eased back in her seat and fingered one of the feathers in her hair. "I'm listening."

"I'll poke around and see if anyone on the janitorial service wants to do an interview. Maybe a human-interest piece on wages. Or find a college student trying to balance a full class load and hold down a job. There's got to be something."

"You should go undercover. I've got just the wig to cover that gorgeous hair of yours."

"You're not thinking about that *Dolly* wig I saw in your backseat, are you?"

Sam slipped into a southern drawl. "Girl, ain't nobody would mess with *Dolly* in a janitor's uniform. It would be perfect."

"Perfect if I want to end up as content on social media. No, thank you. I'm trying to keep a low profile, not break the internet."

"Okay, okay. We'll forget about *Dolly* and get you something plain-Jane."

Her phone rang and she held her finger up to Sam while she answered it.

"Hello … Reid."

"Hey, how are you? Did your family make it home okay?"

"They left this morning."

"Oh, good. I hope they have a safe trip." A moment of silence hung between them. "I, uh … I need to talk to you about something."

"What's up?"

"Not over the phone. In person." He cleared his throat. "Our last dinner was a little, well … rushed. I was wondering if you'd like to have dinner tomorrow night."

His shy tone made her heart do a little flip. "I'd love to."

"Great. There's a new place along the river I want to take you. Can I pick you up?"

She glanced at Sam and mouthed '*Help*.'

Sam pointed to herself and whispered, "My place."

Relief washed over her. Sam's condo would be a believable option for a teacher's salary. "You can pick me up. What time?"

"Really? Great." Excitement coated his words. "How does six-thirty sound?"

"That works." She rattled off Sam's address, and they said their goodbyes and ended the call. "I don't know if I can do this."

"Do what?" Sam closed her laptop and set it on the desk.

"Go out with Reid while I pretend I don't know his name is Lucas and plan to break into his office."

Sam sat back in her seat and shot her a sassy look. "It's called acting, baby. Acting."

Emersyn shook her head. She was sure this was one role she wasn't qualified to play.

21

Lucas stepped out of the limo and eyed the condo. Number 2024. Navy blue with white trim. It was the right one. Now he had to walk the fifteen or so steps and knock on the door.

Tonight, he'd tell her everything. *Please, God, help her understand.*

The driver opened his door, and Lucas gave him a slight nod. "I shouldn't be long."

He walked to the front door and the porch light flickered on. What if she refuses to speak to me after tonight? He shook off the thought like a catcher calls off a bad pitch. Push the doorbell.

Renée opened the door, and the scent of her floral perfume circled in the breeze. "Hi."

"Good evening." His gaze traveled over her silky emerald dress. "You, look stunning."

"Thank you." She waved him inside. "I heard it might rain tonight. Let me grab my coat and purse."

He stepped over the threshold and glanced around the tidy living space. It looked more spacious than he imagined, with an open concept living room that led to a kitchen and a dining room.

"I wasn't sure what to wear tonight." She glanced at his suit, then pulled an ebony swing coat off the hook by the door. "If I'm being perfectly honest, I tried on five dresses before deciding on this one."

Laughter tickled his throat as he took the coat from her and motioned for her to turn around. "I'm sure whatever dress you chose would've been perfect, but *green* is definitely your color." He slid the coat over her arms, then she twisted to face him.

"You're not wearing your glasses." Her eyes twinkled. "It's … different."

"I don't need them, but they help when I'm looking at screens all day." He wrapped his arms around her waist and drew her body against his. "Do you prefer the glasses?"

"I prefer you." She trailed a finger down his temple then across his jawline. "Glasses or no glasses."

His skin heated, her touch making him lightheaded. "I want to kiss you."

"Then why don't you?" She slipped her hands behind his neck and threaded her fingers.

He didn't need any more encouragement. As their lips met, the intoxicating mixture of strawberry and mint mingled with their kiss, making him groan.

She snuggled closer.

When they parted, his pulse soared. *No more stalling. You need to tell her.*

"We have, uh … dinner reservations." He tightened his hold, not wanting to let her go. "We should probably head out."

"We should." Her tone was flirty while she remained encased in his arms.

He leaned down and brushed his lips against hers once more. *Please, God, let her forgive me.*

When he released his hold on her, she gifted him with a lazy smile, then turned out of his arms and grabbed her clutch off the entry table.

"Do you like surprises?" He opened the door, and a whoosh of air circled between them cooling his skin.

"I do."

"Good. I've got a few planned for this evening." His stomach roiled when he took her hand and led her down the steps to the limo. *I hope one of those surprises doesn't ruin the evening.*

"This is a fun surprise." She pointed to their ride, then glanced up at him. "A stretch limo? What are we celebrating?"

"Us. The new year. New beginnings."

The driver opened their door, and Lucas waited for her to slide into the back seat before he joined her.

"Did you know we've been dating for almost six months?" He shifted on the bench seat to face her. "This might sound silly, but I grew up with a mom who loved any excuse to celebrate."

"That doesn't sound silly." She scooted closer to him and took his hand. "We never know what tomorrow brings. Right? It's good to celebrate the little things."

"I agree." He brought her hand up to his lips and placed a kiss against the inside of her wrist.

As the limo wove through the city streets and highways, they talked about the holidays and what they did with their families.

"Noah's obsessed with superheroes," she said. "He loved the hero-themed room I set up for him."

"I would have liked to meet him." He wasn't sure if he should bring up the night James quizzed him about *Legacy*. After that meeting, he realized his secrets were catching up to him.

"Noah would've loved to have met you too." A hopeful expression lit up her face. "They're coming back in the summer. Maybe you can meet him then."

A bitter taste landed on his tongue. He wondered if James would ever want to see him again. He couldn't help the lingering feeling that he'd made a bad impression. How had James known he'd kept *Legacy* a secret from his father? He shifted in his seat. *Should I ask her?*

No. Tonight wasn't the right time to inquire about her family. He needed to come clean about who he was, then he could worry about winning over James and Kelly.

Emersyn glanced out the window as the limo came to a stop in front of a circular courtyard.

"Have you tried *Monaghan's* yet?" Reid pointed to the white clapboard building tucked behind a large fountain. "They had their soft opening last month."

"I haven't." With school and James and Kelly's visit over the holidays, she'd not even heard about the restaurant. "What do they serve?"

"They're calling it Irish fusion. Think Irish Pub meets French cuisine."

Her stomach rumbled. "That sounds amazing."

When the driver opened their door, Reid stepped out of the limo and held his hand out to her. "I'm sorry it's so cold. It's only a short walk through the courtyard."

A frigid breeze whipped at the tendrils of her hair as she stepped out of the vehicle and slid her hand into his. "It's okay. You can't control the weather."

"You're right, but I *can* use the weather to my advantage." Releasing her fingers, he wrapped an arm around her shoulders and tugged her to his side.

"Are you sure you didn't plan this cold front?"

"Maybe I did."

They hurried across the frost-covered brick path to the restaurant. When they reached the door, Reid released his hold, making his body heat gallop away with the wind.

"You're going to love this place." He opened the door and waited for her to step across the threshold.

As they walked into the restaurant, the inviting glow of candlelight and calming aromas of rosemary and fresh bread enveloped her in a comforting embrace. She murmured a sigh. "It's so cozy."

"Good evening, Mr. Bennett." The man standing behind the

weathered podium looked up and stuck out his hand. "How's your father been?"

Emersyn gripped her clutch. *Mr. Bennett?* She glanced at Reid but he didn't flinch.

"Good evening, Finn." Reid shook the man's hand. "My father's well. He wanted me to pass on his regards and mentioned he'll be reaching out to you soon. We have a business dinner he'd like to have *Monaghan's* host."

"Wonderful."

Reid looked in her direction. "Finn, I'd like you to meet Renée."

"Good evening, Renée." Finn bowed his head. "It's nice to finally meet you."

"It's nice to meet you too."

Finn gestured to the man walking toward them, dressed in a crisp white button-down shirt. "This is Tyler. He'll take your coats, then show you to the private room upstairs." Finn flashed her a warm smile. "It's not supposed to rain until later this evening, so you'll both enjoy a lovely view of the river over dinner."

Tyler took their coats and hung them on hooks by the door, then turned and gestured to the stairway. "Follow me."

They followed him up a narrow set of wooden steps to an open room with a wall of windows facing the moonlit river.

"Your table, sir." Tyler motioned to a table set with a white linen cloth, a bouquet of lavender, and a lit hurricane lamp as the centerpiece. "I'll bring up some water and a board of our fresh Irish soda bread."

Reid thanked him as he held out her chair. "I've been wanting to bring you here since they opened. Finn's an old family friend and has dreamt of opening his own restaurant for years."

His words mingled with her racing thoughts. *He called Reid Mr. Bennett.* She pushed away her warring emotions and focused on her surroundings.

"I feel like I've taken a step back in time." Taking her seat, she gestured around the room. A Hoosier cabinet stood against one wall, while an ornate fireplace with a roaring fire anchored the other. In the corner by the window, a stack of steamer trunks and a spinning wheel sat as if they'd just been carted off a docked ship. "Look at all the antiques in here."

Tyler returned with two glasses of water and placed a wooden board with bread on the table. After a brief explanation about the evening's specials, he stepped away to give them time to read over the menu.

She glanced up after reading the options. "Everything sounds amazing. What are you going to try?"

"I'm going to order the steak." Reid closed his menu. "What looks good to you?"

"I'm torn between the Irish stew and the roasted chicken."

He motioned for Tyler to join them. "Finn's menu looks amazing. Can you bring us all four of the main dishes for us to sample and the steak special?"

"Of course." Tyler's eyes lit up. "Can I get you anything to drink besides water? Maybe some coffee?"

Reid turned his attention back to her. "I could go for something warm right now. What about you?"

A lingering chill traveled across her shoulders. "That would be great."

Tyler gave them a quick nod. "I'll put in your order and have those drinks brought up shortly."

After Tyler left the room, the soft whistling sounds of the wind and the crackling wood in the fireplace ribboned around them.

"A sampling of every main dish? That's a lot of food."

He pinned her with an impish grin. "I have an ulterior motive."

"*Oh?* What's that?"

"I love leftovers."

"You do?"

Leaning back, he took a drink of his water. "I might even share my leftovers and send some home with you."

"You might?"

"We'll see."

She stifled a laugh.

"What do you normally eat at home?" Placing her cloth napkin on her lap, she bit back the urge to probe him about being called Mr. Bennett. "Besides leftovers. Do you like to cook?"

"Sometimes." He picked up a slice of soda bread and slathered it with butter. "My mom taught me how to cook the basics. You know, scrambled eggs, or roasted chicken. I don't have a lot of time to cook, and it's hard to prepare something for one person. I have a chef come in once a month and fill my freezer."

"You're kidding?"

"I'm not. Is that terrible?"

"No." She toyed with a sprig of lavender while she imagined his freezer lined with labeled dishes. *I wonder what his favorites are.* "I think it's a great idea."

"What about you?" He took a bite of bread, then set it on the small plate next to his drink. "Do you like to cook?"

Sorrow clutched at her throat. Donna had taught her to cook some things, but she wished she'd grown up with a mom in the kitchen. "I've never really thought about it. Like you said, it's difficult to make a recipe for one person. I can throw together a salad or make a grilled cheese, but I don't spend much time cooking."

Tyler ambled in with two oversized mugs and a pitcher of cream and placed them on the table. "Finn's working on your meals. Is there anything else I can get for you?"

Reid glanced at her while he took a drink of his coffee. "Need anything?"

"I'm good."

When he turned his attention back to Tyler, he smiled. "I think we're good for now. Thank you."

Tyler nodded, then scurried from the room.

She picked up a slice of bread and tore off a piece. While she nibbled on the tangy soda bread, she worked through what to say. *Just ask him.* She placed the bread on the side plate and straightened her shoulders. "On the phone, you mentioned that you wanted to tell me something."

His expression fell.

She waited and fiddled with her napkin.

"I've been keeping something from you."

She bunched the napkin in a fist, praying her pulse would slow.

"My real name isn't Reid Clark. I use that moniker online to keep my business life separate from my family life."

She released the napkin and attempted to smooth out the creases on her lap.

"My full name is Lucas Reid Bennett. My dad is Sinclair Bennett, owner of *Bennetts Estates and Antiques*." He stared out the window toward the moonlit bridge stretched out across the river. "I've been struggling lately. Juggling my personal life and business. I'm not proud of the secrets I've kept from my family." When he turned back to face her, pain filled his expression. "And from you."

Her shoulders relaxed. He'd been honest with her, and she'd not even had to probe him about it.

Keeping his gaze on her, he continued. "The plan is for me to take over *Bennetts*. I've had my life mapped out for me since I was born, but I wanted to do something different. Something that could be my own. My legacy. So, I became someone else." His voice dripped with regret. "Can you ever forgive me? Can you forgive me for keeping up this charade for so long?"

Her chest ached as her own secrets threatened to spill out of her. How could she not forgive him? She was guilty of the same thing.

"I ... uh, I forgive you, Reid—I mean Lucas."

As she held his stare, she realized how much the name Lucas suited him. She'd already researched its meaning. It was a strong yet tender name, meaning *bringer of light*. The identity fit. The light he'd brought into her life made her feel loved and secure. Cherished.

"You do? You can forgive me?"

She nodded, afraid her voice would betray her if she spoke. She wanted to confess her own deception, but with H & G investigating *Legacy*, this wasn't the right time.

"I'm so sorry for the dishonesty." His eyes glistened as he reached across the table and took her hand. "It's not who I am. I never wanted to keep anything from you."

Eyes burning, she sniffled. *It's not who I am either.*

"As you already know, I've kept *Legacy* a secret from my family." He released her hand and huffed out a frustrated sigh. "I'm trying to prove *Legacy* is a success. Then maybe I can convince my father it would benefit *Bennetts*."

"Do you think that will work?"

"I don't know. I feel like I'm running in a hamster wheel, and I don't know how to get off." He scrubbed a hand down his cheek. "I've made some business decisions I'm not proud of, things I wish I could go back and do differently."

"Like what?"

"If *Bennetts* passes on an estate, then I pick it up for *Legacy*."

"How is that bad business? It's not like you're taking it from *Bennetts*."

"No, but ..." A sheepish look blanketed his face. "I'm a provenance researcher. And I'm good at it."

"What does that mean?"

"Dad taught me everything about the business, like how to offer estimates and keep track of inventory. He's great with numbers, but I love history and learning about the origin of family heirlooms. It's a passion for me. A calling." He motioned around the room. "I helped Finn find all of this. It's not some random backdrop to yesteryear, but these items also have a backstory. Real people touched these things and used them in their everyday lives. There's added worth in the present when you know the connection to the past. That's the value of provenance."

Her heart swelled. The enthusiasm he carried for the past reminded her of Papa. "It sounds like you have a gift. Your father can't fault you for that."

"True. But the battle to make *Legacy* succeed while playing the dutiful heir is wearing on me."

"How so?"

"Remember when I told you I went to Seoul last summer?"

She nodded as bile rose in her throat. He'd been there at the same time the H & G operative's body had been found.

"I was there for a technology conference, but also to make some connections for *Legacy*. I met a man who wanted to work solely with my dad." Lucas took a quick drink of his water. "This man had a couple of rare items he wanted to sell us. Family heirlooms. Lots of history. One of the items was a once-in-a-lifetime piece. Wars could be fought to keep this item out of the wrong hands."

Sweat dappled her palms. *Please, God, no.*

"Do you know what I did?"

His question jerked her back to the conversation. "What?"

"I hesitated."

"Hesitated?"

His expression turned doleful. "For a split second, I wanted to keep the product for myself. To list it on *Legacy*."

"Did you?" Her gut twisted into a pretzel. "Did you list it on *Legacy*?"

Tyler entered the room with a tray, followed by Finn. They carried a set of steaming plates and laid them on the sideboard as well as a stack of empty plates and bowls.

Finn walked over to their table and waved his hand in the direction of the impromptu buffet. "I envisioned you enjoying a family-style meal after Tyler mentioned you'd ordered each main course." His face beamed. "If I remember correctly, Mr. Bennett, your favorite dessert is anything chocolate."

Lucas's expression brightened. "That's correct."

"How do you feel about chocolate, Miss?" Finn shot her a coy look.

She forced a smile trying to recover from their interrupted conversation. "I love chocolate."

"Ah, perfect." Finn squeezed Lucas's shoulder. "I'll send up my wife's famous chocolate mousse at the end of your meal."

Lucas patted his abs. "After we sample all your dishes, you might want to package it to-go."

Finn winked at him. "I'll do that. And when you're ready, I'll bring up a few additional to-go containers."

Tyler topped off their waters and followed Finn out of the room.

"It smells delicious." Lucas glanced over at the sideboard. "Should we say grace?"

She nodded and placed her napkin on the table as their conversation turned over in her mind. *God, help me to discern what's going on here.*

Lucas reached across the table and took her hand in his. After he said a brief prayer, he stood and helped her with her chair. "Let's shelve the business talk. I've got a lot to work out with my dad, but I have a plan."

Her heart struggled as thoughts of what Lucas was doing in Seoul flooded her mind. She'd seen the remorse in his eyes when he revealed his name and explained his strained relationship with his dad. How could someone with such a tender heart hurt anyone? It didn't connect with his personality. Seoul's a big city. His being there had to be a coincidence.

They filled their plates, grabbed a bowl of stew, then returned to the table.

She took a bite of the stew and sighed. "This is the perfect meal for a cold night."

"I couldn't agree with you more."

While they ate, they talked more about his relationship with his mom and how she'd been the glue that kept him and his father on equal footing.

"Do you and your stepbrother get along?"

"We can. At times, he pushes my buttons, but I've learned not to get so riled up when he does."

When they'd finished their meal and Tyler had boxed up their leftovers, Lucas glanced at his watch. "It's almost time for us to go."

"Go where?"

"The next part of our date." His eyes twinkled like a thousand stars. "If you like history, you're going to love our next stop."

Her throat constricted. She loved history. Papa had given her that. But tonight, the only history she was interested in was Lucas Bennett's.

22

Emersyn cuddled with Lucas in the back of the limo. "Thank you for dinner. Finn's great, and his wife makes a delicious chocolate mousse."

They'd decided to share one serving of the mousse and save the other.

"I'm glad you enjoyed *Monaghan's*. When I saw the inside for the first time, I knew I wanted to share it with you." He nodded to the stack of foil containers on the seat beside them. "We scored a ton of leftovers."

"We? Have you decided to share?"

"Maybe." He placed an airy kiss on her temple. "Do you have any dinner plans tomorrow?"

"I don't. My Saturday's free."

"Good. Come over, and we can heat up some leftovers."

Laughter tickled her belly. Sharing leftovers with someone brought with it a comfortable intimacy. A calm. A sense of belonging. Like when you find a mate to a sock.

"Do you know what?" Lucas's whispered words feathered over her neck. "I've decided winter is my new favorite season."

"Why's that?"

"It gives me a reason to keep you close." He pulled her tighter to his side.

"I think I like winter too." She settled into the warmth of his chest, as cozy feelings stirred inside her. "Are you going to give me a hint as to where we're going?"

"Nope. You can try to guess though."

"Okay. Let's see. It's almost ten o'clock. A movie?"

"No. There's nothing good playing."

"True." She laid her hands on her stomach. "And it can't be anything with food. I've eaten enough for a week."

Twisting to look at her, he shot her a boyish grin. "Ah, but you promised me a date with leftovers." He leaned in and kissed the tip of her nose. "Even if you're not hungry, I'd still like you to come over. I'm heading out of town on Monday. Remember?"

How could she forget? That's when she'd planned to infiltrate his office. *Can I do that now? Can I go behind his back and investigate him like he's some kind of criminal?* "I did remember. Ski trip, right? With your dad and Preston."

He frowned. "Don't tell anyone, but I wish I could leave Preston behind."

"You're secret's safe with me." She reached for his hand and intertwined her fingers with his. "So … are we going dancing? If so, I might need to leave these behind." She raised her feet and clicked her heels.

"No, not dancing. Although, that's a good idea. Maybe next time." He turned her hand over and drew lazy circles with his forefinger in the middle of her palm. "I do love dancing with you."

Goosebumps traveled up her arm and she sighed. His touch was clouding her thought process.

After a few seconds of enjoying his touch, he pulled away and reached for a small gift bag beside the seat. "We're almost there, so I'll give you a hint."

"What's this?" Taking the bag from him, she peeked inside.

"It's a clue."

She pulled out a pair of gold socks. "This is the strangest gift I've ever received."

"Where we're going, you need to have cool socks." He tugged up the hem of his pants. His socks matched the pair she was holding.

"Now I'm intrigued."

"You can put them on when we get there." He glanced out the window. "Which should be in about ten seconds."

She turned in her seat to orient herself to where the limo had taken them. Up until this point, her only thought—cuddling with Lucas. "Where are we?"

They'd driven for over an hour and were now passing a row of warehouses in downtown Norfolk. After they turned a corner, several structures emerged dotting the landscape with their diverse architecture and colorful murals.

The limo pulled up to an art deco building with two bronze peacock lights on each side of the door. Above the entrance a gold and black geometric sign read *Roil with the Presses*.

"What is this place?"

"We're just outside of the arts district downtown. Several investors are trying to pull these dated buildings out of the grave and revamp them."

The driver opened their door, and she followed Lucas onto the curb.

"Years ago, this was a newspaper building." He took her hand, leading her up the walkway and through the door. "Now it's a by-reservation-only bowling lounge."

She glanced around the opulent room, her senses sparking to life. "This place is amazing."

Geometric gold chandeliers hung from the ceiling, while paintings of tall, linear buildings edged in gilded frames lined the walls. Behind a row of velvet circular settees, couples sat together at brass curved tables.

A stocky man with dark hair stepped out of the shadows and stuck out his hand toward Lucas. "Lucas Bennett. How have you been?"

"Good." Lucas turned to her. "Vincent, I'd like you to meet Renée."

Vincent's mouth pulled into a slow smile. "It's nice to meet you Renée. Lucas has talked a lot about you. I'm Vincent Santori, and this is my place." He turned back to face Lucas. "How was Finn's tonight?"

"Great. We tried the menu."

"I bet." Vincent's bushy brows lifted. "I could eat my weight in warm Irish soda bread." With a wave of his hand, he urged them to follow him. "I have the scarlet lounge ready for you. If you need anything off the menu let me know."

They walked into a room with two polished bowling lanes, a vintage printing press repurposed into a table with a glass top, and a sitting area with a blood-red tufted L-shaped couch.

"Do you have your socks?" Lucas reached beside the couch and picked up two pairs of bowling shoes.

After she set her clutch on the table, she pulled the socks out of her coat pocket. "Got them."

"Gold socks. Nice touch." Vincent took both their coats and hung them on the hooks by the door.

He pushed a button on the wall and a row of sculpted brass sconces blinked to life on each side of the wooden alley. "You have the lanes for as long as you like." He pointed to a row of switches framed in a filagree plate. "These control everything in the room. You can dim the lights, or make them brighter, call to order snacks, and there's a switch to turn on the music." He shot Lucas a furtive grin. "There are five preset stations, depending on the mood you're going for."

Lucas studied the switches then dimmed the lights and turned on the one labeled 'jazz'.

Vincent winked at her. "I like Lucas's style."

Her cheeks rushed with heat. So did she.

"We have the coffee bar open until 2 a.m., and they serve cold drinks as well." Vincent pivoted to face her. "Make sure you ask Lucas to give you a crash course in the history of this place. If it wasn't for *Bennetts* and Lucas's expertise in antiques, I wouldn't have found half of these furnishings."

After Vincent left, Lucas shed his suit coat and rolled up his cuffs. "What do you think?"

"This place is incredible." She gave the room another cursory glance, taking in all the baubles and décor. When her gaze landed on the printing press-turned-side table she smiled. "I'd love a table like that. The design is amazing."

"It's yours. I'll talk to Vincent." Lucas's lips quirked. "Although, it won't fit in the limo."

"You can't take Vincent's table."

He chuckled. "He owes me a favor. Or two. He wouldn't mind."

She waved him off. Was he serious? He'd reclaim the table for her. "If you ever come across another press let me know."

"Printing press. Got it. Now I have a mission." He sank into the couch and patted the space next to him. "Let's get our shoes on and see who's going home with that serving of chocolate mousse."

"We're playing for leftovers?" She sat down, kicked off her heels, and slipped on her socks and shoes.

"Good try." He tied his bowling shoes, then relaxed back against the cushions. "Just the mousse. Those leftovers are going home with me."

Flopping back against the cushions, she folded her arms and pushed her bottom lip out in a pout. "In this dress, I might not have much of a fighting chance."

"In that dress," He snuck a quick kiss, covering her pout. "I might let you win."

"The leftovers?"

He cupped her face with his hands and kissed her like he didn't have anywhere else to be.

Skin tingling, her arms fell limp as she melted into him. What was she trying to win again?

When Lucas released her, he blinked slowly. "You can have

the leftovers. I forfeit the bowling score as well. You win. Let's sit here listening to jazz and do *that* all night."

Heat prickled her cheeks. Kissing Lucas. First prize.

"On second thought, maybe that's not a good idea." He rolled his palms over his knees and released a nervous laugh. "I mean it's a good idea, but …" Rising, he reached his hand out to help her up. "How's your bowling game?"

She slipped her hand in his and got to her feet, knees wobbly. "I think I can hold my own."

Could she? Not if he kept distracting her with his lips.

Emersyn replaced her bowling ball on the shelf at the end of the lane then whirled around to face him. "I think we need a rematch."

After they'd finished two games, Lucas came out the winner.

"Deal." He wrapped his arms around her and brought her in for a quick kiss. "I don't want tonight to end, but I should get you home before the sun rises."

"That's only in a few hours." She yawned and rested her head on his shoulder as the soulful sounds of Ella Fitzgerald and Louis Armstrong singing *The Nearness of You* ribboned around them.

Lucas drew her closer, swaying to the melody. "This is a great song."

"It is." Closing her eyes, she joined the rhythm, moving her body in time with his.

He whispered the last stanza in her ear, then placed a gentle kiss on her neck. "Have I told you how much I love dancing with you?"

"You might have mentioned it." She tilted her chin up, smiling. "I'll head up to Richmond after I freshen up and take a nap."

"Deal." Resting his forehead against hers, he sighed. "Have I mentioned I don't want this night to end?"

"You have. A few times."

His lips found hers again. When he pulled back, desire kindled in his expression. "Let's get you home."

They both took a seat on the couch and removed their bowling shoes.

"I dread putting these back on." She picked up her heels and dangled them from her fingers.

"I bet." Lucas slipped his dress shoes on, then stood. "It's not a long walk to the curb, just leave your socks on."

She rose and wiggled her toes in the golden socks. "Works for me."

After they slipped on their coats, Lucas reached for her hand, and they walked to the front of the building.

"Did you two have a fun night?" Vincent met them at the door.

"The best bowling experience I've ever had." She squeezed Lucas's hand.

Vincent waggled his brows. "It must have been the jazz."

Pink flashed across Lucas's neck, and he nodded. "That was it."

While Vincent talked to Lucas about his idea to open the back courtyard for a wedding venue, she looked at her hands. She had her heels in one and held onto Lucas's with the other.

"Oh, hey, I left my clutch on the table. I'll be right back."

Lucas released her fingers. "I'll call the car around."

When she returned, Lucas and Vincent had their backs to her and were talking in hushed tones.

She padded closer. Her stocking feet made it easy for her to slip behind them unnoticed.

"I'm starting something new. VIP. Private showings with items not on sale to the public." Lucas slipped a card into Vincent's open palm. "This summer, while I was overseas, I acquired a few things you might be interested in."

Vincent shoved the card into his shirt pocket. "I'm in the market for some jewelry. Something upscale. It's a gift for someone."

Lucas nodded. "I'm heading to France next week. I'll see what I can pick up." When he noticed her, he turned and reached for her hand. "Are you ready?"

She nodded, afraid to speak.

They walked to the exit, and Lucas held the door for her. When they stepped outside, droplets of cold rain dotted the pavement.

He glanced at her stocking feet. "That's not going to work." With a swift motion, he scooped her into his arms and cradled her close to his steel chest.

The rain quickened, along with her pulse. She looked up at him, savoring the mingling scents of fresh rain and, well, him. "Thanks. You're my hero."

Lucas glanced down, his rain-soaked hair clinging to his brow, and flashed her a sexy grin. "Anytime, sweetheart."

After tonight, one thing was clear, he could sweep her off her feet any day of the week—rain or shine. But she needed to make sure he wasn't pulling the wool over her eyes as well.

23

Heart thumping, Emersyn parked her rental in the parking lot a block from *Mobile Solutions* and turned off the engine. Lucas had been gone for almost two weeks, and she'd finally found a way into the building. Legally.

Am I sure I want to do this? With shaky hands, she smoothed down the raven-colored wig she'd borrowed from Sam, then yanked a lightweight beanie cap over her head securing it in place. *I need to do this.*

Before she lost her resolve, she stepped out of the car and surveyed the quiet downtown street. The early morning sun cast an orange glow over the city, reminding her of a photograph. Emersyn pulled her jacket snug.

This would work out. It had to. And Lana Granger, a first-year college student who worked for *Midnight Maids*, had been an easy sell.

Not willing to go into debt for her education, Lana worked two jobs to make ends meet, often sacrificing sleep to do so. Over email, they shared a couple of stories about college life, and when Emersyn explained her desire to write her story, Lana agreed.

Emersyn walked down one block to the alley behind the

office building and knocked on the employee's entrance. Today's task was simple: dress up as a janitor and take notes about Lana's typical day. While she played the part of journalist, she'd pop into Lucas's office and snoop around.

A noise sounded from behind a dumpster making her jump. A cat peeked out, greeting her with a yowl.

"It's just a stray cat." She knocked on the door again. "Come on, Lana. Open the door."

After a few moments, the door cracked open, and Lana greeted her with a smile. "You made it."

"I did." Emersyn fought back a yawn. "It's early."

"You're telling me." Lana waved her in, then shut the door behind her. "I've been here since two in the morning."

"What time does your first class start?"

"Ten. I've got two today. After that, I head to the café for my evening shift."

While she followed Lana down a long corridor, Emersyn pulled a small notebook from her back pocket and made some notes. Even though she was here to investigate Lucas, she'd write this story. What Lana was doing, attempting to get her education without any debt, was gutsy.

Lana pushed open the door to the lady's bathroom and handed her a bubblegum pink uniform. "You're a little taller than me. Maybe keep your leggings on with the skirt."

"Good idea. Is the beanie a problem?" She pointed at her knit hat hoping she'd not have to part with it.

"No. I wear a ball cap sometimes. They aren't too picky about headgear. You know, personal rights and all." She gestured toward one of the empty lockers. "You can stow your coat and clothes in there."

"Got it." Emersyn entered a stall, did a quick change, then joined Lana in the hallway. "You got approval for me to be here?"

"Yeah. I said you're from my church and needed to shadow someone for a college project."

"Perfect. Where do we go first?" She had to play the part of investigator for at least a few minutes.

"I'll get your cart. We need to do the bathrooms on each floor, and it's window day."

"Why don't you show me the ropes on the first floor." Emersyn tapped on her cheek pretending to pull the idea out of thin air. "Then I can go up to the third floor and do that one on my own."

"Are you sure?"

"Yeah. I'm here to shadow you, but I'm also here to help. I want to immerse myself in your daily life. If I get you out of here a few minutes early, that works too."

Lana grinned. "That would be great. I have a test today."

"One more thing." Emersyn took a few more notes about the cleaning schedule. "After I'm done, where should I dump the uniform?"

"When you go back to the lady's bathroom, next to the showers you'll see a sign that says, 'Employees' Laundry.' That's where we throw our uniforms at the end of the week."

"Got it."

For the next hour, Emersyn followed Lana around the first floor and helped her clean. While they worked, she asked Lana about her dreams and aspirations and learned more than she ever wanted to about bleaching grout, loading soap dispensers, and scraping gunk off window ledges.

When they finished on the first floor, Lana turned and pulled a card key out of her pocket. "This is for the third floor. It'll get you into each office so you can wash the windows. There's a supply closet next to the stairway that has all your soap refills."

Emersyn shoved the card into her pocket. At least she wouldn't be breaking and entering. "What do I do with the key after I'm done?"

"The slots on the lockers are big enough to slip the key in. I'm locker four A."

"Okay. Thanks for all the info you've given me. It'll take a few weeks to run your story. I've decided to give it to the *Yorktown Courant*."

"That's great." Lana adjusted her ponytail. "Maybe it will shed more light on the everyday struggles of balancing college and work."

After a few more instructions, Emersyn grabbed her supply cart and jumped into the elevator for the third floor. While she sped through her cleaning list, her mind turned like cogs in a clock, ticking off thoughts with each minute that passed.

Finally, she pushed her cart into the room that held Lucas's offices. "Let's do this."

She tugged her beanie hat against her skull and surveyed the space. The front room had three desks, but only two of them looked used. She walked to a door in the back corner and swiped her card over the lock screen. A green light blinked. She turned the handle. Success.

When a creak reverberated from the hallway, she stopped. Emersyn stared at the closed door leading to the hall. Maybe someone had entered another office. Or maybe the heater kicked on.

Releasing her breath, she entered Lucas's office. After she washed the large window overlooking the street, she skirted around the desk and slipped into the leather chair.

"What am I doing? I can't invade his space like this." She jumped up and grabbed the duster off her cleaning cart.

Moving around the open space behind Lucas's desk, she dusted a row of pictures.

In one photo, Lucas stood in a group of three other men, leis around their necks and palm trees in the background. Behind that photo sat a diamond-shaped glass plaque. *STEM award.* That didn't surprise her.

Her gaze landed on another picture with Lucas on a yacht, his arm around his father's shoulders. Both wore serious expressions.

"There's your yacht photo, Sam."

Whispered voices floated in from the hallway. She spun around and eyed the door. After a few minutes, the sounds quieted, and she slipped back into the office chair.

Waving her pink duster around with one hand, she used her other to pull open the desk drawers. The top two held basic office supplies, while the bottom, larger one, was packed with a treasure trove of childhood collectibles.

Using the handle of the duster, she poked at the contents of the drawer. An old baseball mitt, a clear plastic container of yellowed baseball cards, and a stack of antique books—but no Bible—filled the space.

Emersyn closed the drawer with a huff. James was wrong. Nothing in Lucas's office screamed criminal. But maybe he'd planned it that way.

Dropping the duster on the desk, she twirled around in the chair chasing her thoughts. Slowing to a stop, she eyed the filing cabinets in the corner. Maybe the files would shed light on the antiques Lucas had acquired for *Legacy*.

She jumped out of the chair and walked over to the cabinets. As her fingers wrapped around the handle, her gut tightened. She couldn't do this. If Lucas ever found out she'd been here … A sour taste wiggled in her throat. *But if I walk away now …* She gave the handle a yank.

"I wouldn't do that if I were you."

Emersyn froze as a melodic accent crawled into her ears. Irish brogue if she guessed correctly.

A thousand scenarios raced through her mind and none of them had a pleasant outcome. She slid the cabinet drawer back into place. The click of the latch broke through the quiet. Great. Just great.

Forcing her lips into what she hoped was an innocent smile, she turned to face the intruder. "Do what? I'm cleaning the cabinets."

A pair of cat-like eyes threw her a chastising look. "Don't play coy with me, Miss Zucker."

She bit down on her bottom lip. Miss Zucker? Reflexively, her hand tugged her beanie over the ebony wig.

Snatching the duster off the desk, she brandished it like a sword. "I think you've got me mixed up with someone else."

"I don't think so."

She held the man's stare. "I think I may have lost an earring." Dropping to a crouch next to the desk chair, she planned her next move. "I didn't see it over by the filing cabinet. Maybe it's under here."

She stared through the gap under the desk. The man tapped his foot.

"Do you see an earring over there? By your feet?" If she could get him sidetracked, she might have a chance of escape.

He stopped tapping but didn't answer. He wasn't taking the bait.

"I found it." She took a quick breath, then stood, pretending to shove something into her pocket. "Do you work here?"

His mouth twitched. "Hardly."

She glanced at the door. It was shut. How had he snuck up on her and closed the door?

"Do *you* work here, Miss Zucker?"

Her guts twisted. There's no way he recognized her. She pointed to her uniform. "Actually, I do. And it's … Ellie."

He leaned over the desk and studied her name tag. "That says Lana."

"I mean Lana."

"You're not very good at this. Are you?"

"Cleaning?" Lifting her chin, she took a few swipes with her duster around the desk. "I can hold my own."

"What did you hope to find? A sticky note with a password? A chest of stolen treasure?"

She huffed. Maybe try the direct route. "Look, I'm a journalist. I'm following a hunch."

"Is that so? Who do you write for? Maybe I've heard of it." He walked around the desk and pointed to a baseball bat leaning in the corner. "Well now, there's your story. That's worth a fortune." Shaking his head, he made a tsk sound. "And Mr. Bennett has it just lying around. What a shame."

She followed his gaze. "It's just a baseball bat."

"It's not just any bat. It's signed by the Babe himself." He curled his gloved fingers around the bat, hefted it to his shoulder, and gave it a low swing. "This bat is worth a pretty penny. I can't believe it's not in a case."

Her gaze rested on his gloves. She gripped the duster. As a weapon, it would need to work. Choke him with feathers or whack him with the handle?

"I'm partial to Rounders." He laid the bat on his shoulder, as if waiting for a pitch.

"What?"

"Rounders. It's a game I played in Ireland. Years ago." He returned the bat to the corner and shoved his hands into his pockets.

She was right about the accent. She'd need to tell Sam it was the Irish, not the Russians she needed to worry about.

"Are you going to turn me in?"

A low chuckle escaped his lips. "I'm the last person to do that."

"Could you maybe go away? Forget about us meeting."

"Not in a million years." A glint of humor flashed in his bottle-green eyes.

"Why?"

"For one thing, you don't know what you're doing. For another," he held up his hands and waggled his smooth, leather-wrapped fingers. "You're touching everything."

She glanced down at her hands. "I have a duster. I can swipe away my prints."

He nodded to the filing cabinet. "Don't forget the handle."

Rolling her eyes, Emersyn walked around to the front of the desk. After stowing the duster in the cleaning cart, she opened the door. "Today was a wasted venture. I need to return my cart."

He wrapped his hand around her arm. It took a split second before her martial arts training kicked in. She turned, wrenched his arm, and pinned it behind his back. "Do not touch me, sir."

"You've got some fire in you. Reminds me of a best-selling author I once knew." A low hiss escaped through his lips. "Of course, that was after her bodyguard taught her how to defend herself."

Emersyn released her grip. "What? How do you know them?"

"I'm a friend of the family." Turning, he straightened his suit jacket.

"How close of a friend?"

"Close enough to know about H & G."

Fear trickled through her, followed by a surge of anger. "Are you one of them? Did James send you to watch over me?"

"No, I'm not one of them. Good thing too. They have too many rules." He motioned around the room. "What are you looking for? Maybe I can help."

"I don't need your help."

"Really? I just got out of prison. I took a ton of how-to classes while I was in there."

She stilled. "You're ..."

"Declan McNeary. Otherwise known as your Uncle Declan." He grinned like a Chesire cat. "That has a nice ring to it. Family means everything to me."

She shivered. Her uncle had found her. Maybe she *did* need a bodyguard.

"How did you find me?"

"Research. Lots of it. Kelly decided to not let me in on this little secret." Shoving his hands back into his pockets, Declan lifted his brow. "As far as finding you today, I followed you. I wanted to get an idea of your daily life. See what we might have in common. Bridge the gap so to speak." He paused, looking her over. "It seems we have a lot in common."

"What's that supposed to mean?"

"You're trespassing. Already headed for a life of crime."

She dug through her pocket and waved the key card in the air. "I have a key. Not trespassing."

"I thought that way, too, once." Declan sunk into the office chair and cracked his knuckles. "What do you need me to look for?"

"I told you—"

"Let's cut to the chase, I'm here to help." Holding a hand over his heart he added, "I promise."

Can I trust this guy? Can I afford not to? Her pulse raced as she cut through the static buzzing in her ears. "I need info on some inventory. I'm looking for … something. I'm trying to prove that … well, I need to prove that Lucas Bennett doesn't have what H & G thinks he has."

Declan held up a hand. "Wait. Are you in love with this guy?"

Her cheeks rushed with heat.

He shook his head. "Oh, no. That's not good."

"What? Why?"

He stood and walked over to the filing cabinet. "Did you say H & G is investigating him?"

"Yes. But …"

Pulling open the drawer she'd previously touched, he smoothed his gloved fingers over the handle. "H & G doesn't usually investigate anyone without cause." Taking his time, he flipped through the files reading off the notations on the tabs.

"I don't believe Lucas is involved in—"

A door opened out in the hall followed by a bustle of chatter.

Declan shut the drawer and turned to face her. "I didn't see anything about an inventory. My guess? Mr. Bennett keeps everything like that locked up on a laptop."

She pursed her lips together. He was right. This had been a pointless trip.

The voices in the hall multiplied.

"We need to leave." She reached for her cart. "What's your plan to get out of here?"

"My plan?" He shrugged. "This was your idea."

She glanced at his clothes. He looked like he'd walked out of a men's fashion magazine. "The lawyers work on the second floor. You could look lost and pretend to be new."

"I hate lawyers."

"You're hardly going to fit in with the janitorial staff."

He brushed his hands together as if wiping away dust. "That is a true statement."

Emersyn pushed her cart closer to the door leading out to the hallway. "This building houses tech guys, lawyers, a catering company, and a mid-level modeling agency." She threw him a smirk. "Headshots for commercials and romance book cover models. Cheesy stuff like that."

"You've done your research."

"I'm a journalist. It's what I do."

He shot her a skeptical look.

"Okay. A part-time journalist."

"I've spent some time in the gym, I'll say I'm a model."

Emersyn stifled a laugh. "A prison gym."

"Does it matter?"

She shook her head. "I'm going to push my cart out into the hallway. Once I get the group's attention, you can come out and escape down the back stairway."

"Sounds good to me." He motioned toward the hall. "Ladies first."

She secured her beanie and opened the door. The group loitering around the alcove turned and looked at her. Pasting on what she hoped was an angelic smile, she gave them a quick nod.

Lifting her clipboard off the side of the cart, Emersyn pretended to make some notes while she devised a plan. She needed to get to the elevator and get them all to look at her.

She pushed her cart past the group and sashayed to the metal doors. Don't blow this.

When the doors opened, she shrieked. Several of the young men in the group came running to her aid.

"Are you okay?" A man, about her age, with a face that screamed made-for-television, held the elevator door open.

She opened her eyes wide pretending to be scared. "I saw ... I saw something crawling in the elevator."

From behind the sea of well-dressed bodies, she watched as Declan stepped out of Lucas's office. Crisis averted.

She turned back to the man holding the door. "Do you see anything in there?"

The man shook his head. "I don't."

"Is everything okay?" Declan's words sliced through the hall.

She jerked a look over her shoulder and frowned. Crisis not averted.

Flipping back into character, she batted her lashes. "Yes. I'm so embarrassed. I thought I saw a large spider dart across the elevator floor."

Declan shot her a bemused look, then stepped into the elevator. When he turned to face her, he winked. "I believe your eight-legged nemesis is gone."

Holding back an eye roll, she forced a smile. "Thank you."

She joined him then swung her cart around.

"Mind if I squeeze in here?" The man who'd held the door for her threw her an award-winning smile. "I'm heading down to the lawyer's floor."

Her face heated. "Oh. Sure."

"I'd grab the next one." Declan shot the man a glare. "Her cart's taking up half the space."

The guy stepped back and sent her a mournful look.

Declan hit a button, and the doors closed. "I think he was sweet on you."

Emersyn groaned.

She didn't need another overseer in her life. Especially not one who'd just got out of prison.

24

Emersyn juggled a latte in one hand while she turned the key with the other to open the door to the *Yorktown Courant*. Keeping the lights off in front, she stepped into her office, set her drink down, and shut the door. She needed a new plan.

Yesterday's research trip had been a bust. Except now she'd met her ex-con uncle. Life was getting more interesting by the minute.

Her phone vibrated in her back pocket. When she pulled it out, she groaned. Wonderful. Big brother. She answered the call. "Hey, James."

"Morning, Em." A slight pause hung on the line. "How have you been?"

"Good." She flopped into her desk chair and took a sip of her latte. "Everything okay with Kelly and Noah?"

"They're good."

She set down her coffee and twisted the cup in a circle.

"What have you been up to?" James asked.

Breaking and entering. The normal stuff. *Oh, and I met Declan.* "Nothing too exciting. I'm at the *Courant's* office early today. I had an idea for a story."

"Is Lucas out of town?"

"Yeah." A pang struck her chest. If James knew she'd snooped around Lucas's office alone ... "He gets back sometime this weekend. Why?"

"Did he happen to tell you where he was going?"

"Skiing. In France. Why the interrogation?" She glanced at her watch. "It's not even eight in the morning."

"It's well past morning here."

"I guess you're right." She plucked a pencil out of the mason jar on her desk and started to doodle on a sticky notepad. "Why are you asking about Lucas?"

"I've tracked Lucas to a ski resort outside of Paris."

"You're tracking him on vacation?"

"I told you H & G's investigating him."

She waffled between wanting more info and not wanting James to know she was interested. "Did you find anything?"

"I did."

She waited.

"Did you decide? About H & G."

"Look, James—"

"Never mind. It doesn't matter. Kelly made me promise to tell you anything I find."

"Held your feet to the fire, huh?"

"Something like that."

"Okay, let's hear it. Did the Bible show up on *Legacy* again?"

"No, but there was a party not far from the chalet where Lucas was staying."

"And?" She gripped the pencil. Was Lucas seen with another woman?

"It was an upscale party. Black tie. Lots of important people." James paused. "A few pieces of jewelry were stolen." Another long pause. "One of the pieces we found for sale."

"Where? On *Legacy*?"

"No. Another site."

She bristled. "So why does this concern Lucas?"

"Lucas and Preston attended the party."

"That doesn't prove anything." She dropped the pencil back in the jar.

"No. It doesn't. I just wanted to pass it on to you."

Tension coiled in her gut.

"I want to give you a description of the jewelry, in case ..." James hesitated. "In case Lucas gives you any of the pieces."

"What?"

"As a gift."

She gripped the phone as James rattled off the descriptions.

"One of the pieces has a gold pendant in the shape of a jaguar. The jaguar has emerald eyes, diamond-studded stripes, and a pearl collar."

Sam pushed through her door wearing an eyepatch and a floppy pirate's hat. "Argh. Was your undercover mission successful, matey?"

Emersyn held her finger up to her lips suppressing a laugh. She pointed to her phone and mouthed 'James.'

"What undercover mission?" James's question jolted her.

Sam's eyes widened as she mouthed 'Sorry' and slipped into the chair next to her desk.

"Sam's got a pirate gig." Emersyn's shoulders tensed. "She's practicing her lines."

Silence floated through the phone.

"You should see her. She's got an eye patch on and a hat with big feathers. I know how much you like pirates." She cut off her ramble afraid James would see right through her façade.

"Em." James leveled his tone. "Promise me something."

"Sure. Anything."

"Be careful when it comes to Lucas."

Her heart crumpled. "I will."

After she ended the call, she released a long breath.

"Sorry about that." Sam grimaced. "I didn't realize you'd be on the phone with James."

"No problem. I'm sure he doesn't suspect a thing."

Sam leaned forward in her seat. "So ... tell me everything.

Did you get into Lucas's office? Did you find anything? Did anyone catch you?"

Emersyn held up a hand. "One question at a time." Then pointing to the hat, she said, "I can't take you seriously in that getup."

Sam laughed as she pulled off the hat and the patch. "Is that better?"

"Much."

"Okay. Spill."

Emersyn finished off the last bit of her latte before pouring out her story. "It was easy. Lana gave me a uniform and a key, so I walked right in."

"Is Lucas living a double life?"

A weight pressed against her chest. The only duplicity in their relationship was her own. "No. Nothing odd. Vacation photos with his family and friends. A picture of some T-ball kids and a signed baseball bat."

She recalled Declan's words. *That bat's worth a pretty penny.*

Kelly had told her about Declan's past with black-market antiques. Would he be an asset? Or a hindrance?

"So, nothing weird happened?" Sam asked.

"Huh?" Sam's question yanked her back to the conversation "No. Nothing weird."

Her phone buzzed with an incoming text.

Guess where I'm at?

Lucas sent a photo of a coffee cup on the table in their booth. Her heart soared.

When did you get back?

A few hours ago.

Give me twenty minutes.

She glanced at Sam. "I'm heading to the coffee shop. Do you want anything?"

Sam pointed at the cup on her desk. "Need another one? Or is there something hotter than a latte waiting for you?"

Her skin heated. "Lucas is waiting in our booth."

"Our booth?" Sam slapped the pirate hat back on her head. "Argh. The boyfriend's back and he's tempt'n ya with the liquid gold."

Emersyn giggled as she shot out of her seat and grabbed her purse.

Missing heirlooms. Stolen jewelry. Secret societies. Wayward uncles. Maybe she'd fallen into one of Kelly's suspense novels.

Now, if she could convince James that Lucas wasn't the villain.

25

Emersyn turned into the parking lot of the Newport News baseball complex as excitement bubbled inside of her. Spring had brought with it sunnier skies and a steady stream of baseball-themed dates with Lucas. They'd shared hot dogs and popcorn while picnicking at the local minor league games and even traveled with a couple of friends to take in a major league game in DC.

Like music or martial arts was to her, baseball was a part of Lucas, and today he invited her to meet his Little League team.

A pang of guilt poked at her. The missing Bible had yet to reappear, and despite James's concern, Lucas hadn't gifted her any stolen jewelry. *How could I have ever believed he was involved in anything criminal?*

As she edged farther into the complex, thoughts of H & G swirled in her mind. If investigating innocent people was included in their mission, she didn't want any part of it. *So, why haven't I told James?*

She chewed on the inside of her cheek as she pondered the question. Walking away from something connected to Papa wasn't going to be an easy decision.

While she followed a minivan with *Get 'em Tigers* scribbled in bright orange paint across the back window to an open row of parking, pockets of pint-sized baseball players poured out of cars and gathered along the grassy walkways. Laughter and shouts circled in the air.

She'd shelve her anxious thoughts and enjoy this moment. This moment with Lucas and his team.

Emersyn parked and turned off the car.

While she waited for a group of energetic kids to exit the car next to her, she reapplied her ruby-red gloss and checked her phone. She had ten minutes to wade through the throng of players, parents, and siblings to find Lucas.

When she made it to the front gates, her gaze narrowed on a man with Lucas's build. He wore mirrored sunglasses and a red ball cap and stood in a circle of animated children.

She approached the huddle. "Lucas?"

He turned and flashed her a boyish grin. "Hey. You found us." He gestured to the kids. "Renée, I'd like you to meet my little Hawks. Hawks, this is my friend Renée."

"Hey, we're not little." A kid with a smattering of freckles and eye black smeared on his cheeks folded his arms. "We're going into fifth grade."

Lucas crouched and playfully pushed the boy's hat down, so it covered his eyes. "This is Will. He's, my shortstop."

Will shoved his hat up and flashed her a toothy grin. "Best short stop in the city."

She stuck out her hand. "Nice to meet you, Will."

Will shook her hand, then refolded his arms.

Lucas stood and introduced each kid along with their field position. "We've got a great team this year. We might even make it to the big game."

The kids gave high-fives to each other as they whooped and hollered.

A little girl with long braids raised her hand. "Coach, is Renée your girlfriend?"

A swarm of giggles erupted from the group.

"Well, Nicole," Lucas addressed the little girl. "She's my friend, and she's a girl."

Nicole rolled her eyes. "That's not answering the question, Coach."

Emersyn laughed, enjoying the playground banter.

"To answer your question," Lucas bent and pulled a Hawks hat from the duffel lying on the ground next to his feet. "Renée's a new teammate."

"What position is she playing?" Nicole narrowed her eyes. "It can't be third base. I play third base."

He slipped the hat on Emersyn's head. "She's going to be my assistant."

"Assistant? Are you sure about that?" Emersyn pulled her hair through the hole in the back of the hat and straightened the cap on her head. "I don't know much about the rules of baseball."

"Don't worry. We'll teach you the ropes." He winked at her, then glanced back at the kids. "Won't we, Hawks?"

Will leaned toward Nicole. "She's totally his girlfriend."

Lucas laughed as he tilted his head and whispered in her ear. "You *are* totally my girlfriend." He turned back to the kids and clapped his hands together. "Okay. Move in."

The team took a few steps in, tightening their circle around her and Lucas.

"We're here to play nice, and we're here to have fun, but we're also here to learn how to play the greatest sport on earth."

The children jumped up and down with enthusiastic shrieks.

Lucas held up a hand and they quieted. "What's our number one rule?"

Their pitcher, a tall, blue-eyed boy Lucas had introduced as Matt, raised his hand while he spoke. "Watch out for your buddy."

"That's right, Matt." Lucas squatted, making himself eye level with the kids. "If your buddy's having a bad day, you look them in the eye and say, 'You're doing great and you're not alone'. Everyone matters on this field. Got it?"

"Yes, Coach." The kids answered in unison.

While Lucas continued his pep talk, Emersyn studied him. As the kids peppered him with questions, he answered each one with encouragement and kindness. They weren't just a team. They resembled a patchwork family.

They even dressed the same. Lucas's red and white pinstriped jersey and grey baseball pants matched the kids' uniforms, but instead of tall socks and cleats, he wore his pants to his ankles with black running shoes.

She liked this side of him. Lucas wearing a baseball uniform made her think of relaxed Sunday afternoons. Or of sunshine, fresh-cut grass, and a double-dip cone all wrapped together in one appealing package. Homerun.

After Lucas finished giving a few more last-minute directions about today's tournament, Will raised his hand.

"Yes, Will. What's up bud?"

"You forgot the quote, Coach."

"You're right." Lucas folded his arms. "Today's quote is from Yogi Berra. He was one of the greatest catchers in history."

The kids pressed in, zeroing in on their coach.

"Before I give you his quote, here's one of my own— remember, no matter how many curveballs life throws you, take a swing, and keep moving forward."

Matt smiled. "That's a good one, Coach. I got a mean curveball."

Will playfully punched Matt on the arm. "I like your slider better."

The rest of the team chuckled.

"Okay, here's Yogi's quote." Lucas dipped his voice into a gravelly, East Coast accent. "It ain't over 'til it's over."

A second passed before laughter erupted from the players.

"That's easy to remember," Will shouted over the hoopla.

"It is, and I expect you to quote it back to me next week."

Lucas picked up his gear bag and gestured toward the row of tables by the entrance. "Let's get these kids checked in and find out what field we're on."

The players followed them like a cluster of distracted bear cubs crossing a street. When Lucas finished at the sign-in table, they walked to a small patch of open grass by field three.

He turned and motioned for the kids to huddle up. "I want you all to head to the field and start warming up with your partner. Our game starts in thirty minutes." He handed his gear bag to Matt. "Will you get this to the dugout for me?"

The boy nodded. "Sure thing."

The team scurried across the gravel walkway to the field with a big number three strapped to the fence.

Lucas took her hand and twirled her to face him. "You look good in that hat."

"Thanks." Reflexively, she smoothed down the poof of curls she'd pulled through the back of the loop. "You don't look so bad yourself, Coach."

"I'm glad you think so, because I have a whole closet full of hats at home." He flipped his hat around, bill to the back, then leaned in and gave her a quick kiss. "You ready to assist today?"

She resisted going in for another kiss. With him, in that backward hat, she'd be tempted to linger. "Three strikes and you're out. Right?"

"Right. And make sure nobody swings a bat at anyone's head."

"Got it." She nodded to the Hawks on field three. "You're good with them. There's a lot of personalities to balance."

Lucas slipped his hand in hers and led her toward the field. "The kids are great. Did you know they're all in foster care?"

"They are?"

"Yeah. This tournament's designed to give the local foster kids a place to play with others who can relate to what they're going through."

"That's wonderful."

"There'll be a few foster families in attendance, but all the coaches are volunteers wanting to give back to the foster care community." As they approached the fence overlooking the field, he pointed at the other team warming up. "That team, the Blue Dogs, is coached and sponsored by one of the police departments."

She glanced over at the team clad in blue and black. Two men and two women hit ground balls to their team while the kids raced to catch them.

"I hope these kids, even if for one day, feel like someone took the time to focus on them. I want them to know they're worthy and have something to contribute to the game."

She looked up at him. "Thank you for sharing this today with me. And inviting me to meet the Hawks."

"I wouldn't want to be out here with anyone else."

Warmth traveled through her. *James is wrong about Lucas.*

"Let's go. I need to hit some grounders to my team." He tugged her toward the gate, and they walked into the home dugout. "And my assistant needs to get this dugout organized."

She laughed and looked around at the scattered bat bags and water bottles. "You got it, Coach."

He released her hand, grabbed his glove and bat out of his bag, and jogged onto the field.

As she hung bat bags on the fence and helmets on the wooden pegs, her heart soared like a fly ball.

Lucas had pulled back another layer of himself today. Hopefully, she could open her heart enough to do the same.

26

"Hawks, make sure all your trash gets thrown in the can, and don't forget your helmets." Emersyn stood, hands on her hips surveying the flurry of activity in the dugout.

After two wins, the Hawks had moved to the semi-finals, and the energy emanating from the team made it feel like they were heading to the World Series.

Lucas jogged into the dugout after a quick conversation with the other coaches. "Listen up, Hawks."

The kids stopped their packing and turned to face Lucas.

"We've got an hour and a half for lunch, bathroom breaks, and"—he pointed to Will, who was yawning—"a nap. The dugout looks clean, so grab your bags, and let's head over to the concessions."

Cheers erupted from the kids as they shoved the rest of their gear into their bags.

"Great job today." Lucas picked up his bag and slung it over his shoulder. "They never clean up this well for me."

"You've got to be firm, Coach." Leaning in, she whispered, "I may have bribed them with bubble gum."

His brows shot up. "Got any more?"

She dug into her pocket, pulled out a piece, and held it up. "Did you clean up your mess?"

He swiped the gum out of her hand and grazed her cheek with a kiss. "Always."

With a giggle, she withdrew a piece for herself and popped it into her mouth. "What happens after lunch?"

"There's a big-league game, then the final games of the tournament start at four."

"Sounds fun." She threw a water bottle into the recycling bin. "What's the big-league game?"

"You'll see." He gestured for the kids to follow him to a line at the concessions. "Let's go get some hot dogs."

More shrieks erupted.

After Lucas picked up the players' lunches, he pointed to a picnic area by the playground.

"Hawks, grab your lunch, then head over to the tables. After you clean up your mess, you can play. When you hear the announcement for the big-league game, get to the stands, and I'll have Renée do a head count."

"Yes, Coach." The Hawks answered in unison as they grabbed their food and their bags and took off for the row of picnic tables.

"Let's go get our lunch." Lucas pointed to the concession line with a few other options besides hot dogs.

Her stomach grumbled. "Sounds good."

They threw their gum into the trash and opted for two barbecue sandwiches, chips, and sodas. After they found a picnic table facing the playground, Lucas dropped his bag on the grass, then set down their meals, and handed her one of the drinks.

"How long have you been coaching?" She slipped onto the wooden seat across from him and took a long drink, enjoying the cool bubbles on her throat.

"A few years." He dipped his head for a second. When he glanced back up sadness covered his expression. "My mom was friends with Layla Canton." He nodded to the metal sign hanging above the playground. "Both her and my mom were involved in several charities across the state."

She read the plaque aloud. "In memory of Layla Canton, for her love and dedication to children." When she turned back to Lucas, she asked, "What happened to Layla?"

"Layla was killed in a car accident about a year before Mom got sick."

While Emersyn waited for Lucas to continue, she took a bite of her sandwich.

"After Mom died, Mr. Canton and my dad organized this tournament in their honor."

"That's sweet. What a great legacy to leave for both ladies."

"I know it sounds crazy, but somehow being here, coaching these kids, makes me feel like I'm honoring Mom as well."

She reached out a hand and placed it on his. "That's not crazy at all. I have things like that in my life to honor my Papa."

"Like what?"

"I ... well ..." She hesitated. Was it the right time to tell him about the *Yorktown Courant*? Not yet. "My family always donated to a Bible translation group. Papa had a passion for getting the Bible translated into as many languages as possible."

"I like that." Lucas took a bite of his sandwich, then munched on a few chips.

Ask him about the Bible. She pushed the thought aside. No, it's not the right time.

"We have another tradition our family's kept up for years in honor of my mom." Lucas finished off his chips, then chucked the empty bag into the trashcan.

"What's that?"

"Have you ever heard of Richmond's Garden Week?"

"I have. Upscale homes around the state open their gardens for public view." She'd heard of it, but Papa didn't think it was wise to have strangers traipsing through their private property. "It's for a good cause, right? Don't the proceeds go to community gardens?"

"That's it. It starts next Friday." His look turned sheepish. "My family goes all out. I was wondering if you'd like to tour our gardens next weekend and …" He paused. "… meet my family."

"I … uh …" Meet his family? Her stomach flipped over.

"We have five guest cottages on our property. You'd be welcome to stay in one of those. I'd stay at the main house with my dad and Letitia." An inviting smile tugged at his lips. "There are different events planned each night. We kick off Friday night with a formal dinner, then Saturday there are poetry readings, and—"

"I'd love to." *Maybe I'll search for clues about the Bible.* The fleeting thought floated into her mind, and she quickly shoved it away. *I'm not working for H & G. Am I?* Had she become some rogue treasure hunter without even realizing it?

"Great. I'll have one of the cottages reserved for you."

Lucas's words yanked her out of her thoughts. "Great. Sounds perfect."

"Big-league players, please report to the field in ten minutes." The announcer's words boomed across the entire complex.

"Duty calls." Lucas stuck the last piece of his sandwich in his mouth, then followed it up with a drink. After he threw away his trash, he unzipped his bag and pulled out a jersey.

"Are you playing today?"

"Yep." He removed his sunglasses and hat and set them on the table. With a quick tug, he drew his Hawks jersey over his head, leaving him standing there in a compression shirt that molded his abs like a second skin.

She looked away.

"I pitch for the Sluggers. We're a recreational league baseball team."

When she brought her gaze back to him, Lucas had slipped on a blue and red jersey and was buttoning it closed.

"Our team's made up of guys who played in college and a few who went to the minors." He rolled up his Hawks jersey and shoved it and his Hawks hat into his bag. "We play in fundraisers and summer travel leagues. We try to use our mid-level baseball skills for good."

"That's awesome. You're like baseball superheroes."

He chuckled as he flopped onto the bench next to her and yanked off his running shoes. "I love playing baseball, but I knew it wasn't going to be much more than a hobby for me."

"Why's that?"

"I'm good, but not *that* good." He unzipped a side compartment of his bag and pulled out a pair of cleats. "Besides, my passion is in tech. Baseball's just a side gig." After he tugged on the cleats and tied them, he grabbed another hat from his bag. This one was blue with a large *S* on the front.

She bit back a giggle. Maybe he'd throw on a cape. "A side gig that also allows you to make a difference in kids' lives."

"That's the best part." He stood and tucked his jersey into his waistband. "It's a legacy I hope I can leave for my kids to follow one day."

"That's a great goal." Emersyn jumped to her feet and wrapped her arms around his waist. "I'll be in the stands cheering you on, slugger."

He skimmed a knuckle down the curve of her cheek. "Try not to cheer too loud, I might get distracted and throw a wild pitch."

She lowered her voice to a whisper. "You won't even know I'm there."

"I'm kidding. You can cheer as loud as you want." His mouth quirked at one corner. "Once I'm in the zone, nothing distracts me."

"Nothing? That sounds like a challenge."

He tipped his head back and laughed. "Don't worry. I've been distracted by you all day."

She fluttered her lashes. "Time to focus. Slugger."

"I am focused. On you." He tickled her waist, and she giggled as she backed out of his grip.

"What time does the game start?"

"Two. On field one."

She straightened her ball cap. "I'll go check on the Hawks and get them to the stands."

"Good idea." He chucked his shoes into his bag and slipped on his sunglasses. "I need to go throw some practice pitches. Make sure you sit near the home team dugout." He grabbed his bag and flashed her a quick smile. "And remember, cheer as loud as you want."

"Don't worry. I will." She blew him a kiss as he strutted off.

After Emersyn got the Hawks situated and sitting with another team, she scooted onto the bench behind the home team's dugout.

Both teams, the Jays and the Sluggers, walked out to the baseline and lined up. She scanned the players until her gaze landed on Lucas. When he winked, her heart melted.

This is my new favorite sport.

"Welcome to the annual *Swing for the Fence* big-league game." The speakers above her crackled to life. "Please welcome the founders of this great tournament, Mr. Sinclair Bennett and Mr. Michael Canton."

The crowd erupted in applause as the two men walked to the pitcher's mound.

Sinclair took a moment to explain the heart and purpose of their charity. Then the crowd rose, hands over heart, as the National Anthem echoed around the field. After the song ended, Sinclair threw out the first pitch, and everyone cheered.

As the players walked back to their dugouts, Lucas ambled over to her and stretched a few fingers through the fence. "So, it's tradition."

"What's tradition?" She wrapped her fingers securely around his.

"A quote. Before the game." His lazy grin made her pulse zing. "Do you have a quote for me, Assistant Coach?"

"A quote? Let me think." *I found him whom my soul loves.* She smiled. She'd save that one for later. "I've got one. You're doing great, and you're not alone. Everyone matters on this field. Coach Lucas."

The sun glinted off his shades. "I wish I could kiss you right now."

"After the game, slugger."

"Bennett." An older man stepped out of the dugout and waved him over. "Stop mooning over your girl like a schoolboy. Time to warm up. These balls ain't gonna pitch themselves."

"I'll see you after the game." Lucas squeezed her fingers, then ran into the dugout.

When his hand slipped away, her palm tingled.

Rolling his shoulders, Lucas took the mound, pivoted, and let the ball sail out of his hand. Each pitch landed with a thwack against the catcher's glove.

She rubbed her hands together, the tingle evaporating. In a few weeks, she'd meet his family.

After that, she'd need to gather the courage to tell him about hers.

27

Emersyn set her overnight bag by the front door and checked her watch. One o'clock. If she wanted to miss Friday's rush hour traffic and get to the Bennetts' in time for dinner, she'd need to leave by three. Thankfully, the parent-teacher conference schedule today required her to work only until noon. Now she had plenty of time to prepare to meet Lucas's family.

She released a long breath. What if they didn't like her?

A knock at the door yanked her out of her thoughts. Peeking through the peephole, a ribbon of tension coiled around her neck. "What's *he* doing here?"

Emersyn took a moment to collect herself, then swung open the door. "Mr. McNeary. How did you find my house?"

He threw her a nonplussed look. "Really?"

"Yes. Really."

Declan tugged on his shirt cuffs as if bored by her inquiry. "Can I come in?"

"I guess. For a minute."

He scooted past her and stepped onto the checkered tiles.

"Mr. McNeary—"

"Why don't we drop the formalities?" He turned to face her,

grinning. "You can call me Uncle Declan. Or Uncle Dec, or some other endearing term."

She shut the door and folded her arms. "I hardly think I know you well enough to start with the *uncle* stuff."

A pained look flashed across his face before he waved a hand around the room. "I missed this place. Abram always had the best taste in décor."

"I believe my great-grandmother did most of the decorating."

"Ah, that's right. Rachel, was it?"

Emersyn rapped her fingers on her arms in tempo with her rising pulse. "What are you doing here, Declan?"

"Direct. I like it." Leaning against the stair railing, he slid his hands into his pockets. "Have you found what you needed? To clear Mr. Bennett's name."

"I … well …"

"Do you know what you're looking for?"

"I have an idea." She eyed him, trying to decipher his motives. "Why?"

"Because I want to help. You're family. And family means—"

"Everything to you. So, you've said."

"Despite what Kelly or James might have told you, I do have a heart." Declan arched a brow. "What *did* she tell you? Better yet, what did her bodyguard—I mean her husband—tell you about me?"

"How do you know they said anything?"

"Because you looked horrified, but not surprised, when I said I was your uncle."

"They told me some things, but I'm beginning to think they didn't tell me everything."

"Do they know I got out on good behavior? That's got to count for something. Right?"

Emersyn snorted. "Or the prison needed room and chose someone with less baggage than say a—"

"A murderer? Or a serial killer?" His baritone laughter

galloped around the entryway. "I never killed anyone. But James has."

She stilled. *He had?* "We're not here to talk about Kelly and James."

"You're right." Declan straightened, then walked over to the wall of paintings at the bottom of the stairs. Running a gloved hand along one of the gilded frames, he said, "I want to help you because I want to prove to everyone that I've turned over a new leaf. I want to rewrite my legacy, so to speak."

"Look, Mr. McNeary—Declan, I appreciate you coming here and offering me your services, whatever those services might be, but you're a criminal and—"

"*Ex*-criminal." He spun to face her.

"A recently released criminal." She uncurled her arms and took a step toward the door. "I have a busy afternoon planned, so I'm afraid you'll need to leave."

"What do you have on the docket today?" His gaze dropped to her bag. "More breaking and entering?"

"No. And I wasn't—Never mind."

"More investigating for H & G?" A sneer tugged at his lips. "Don't tell me you've decided to join their ranks. Those Brits can be a real pain when they—"

"No."

His brows shot up. "No?"

"I haven't decided to join H & G. Not yet."

"Interesting. What do Kelly and James think about your hesitation?"

"They support me in whatever decision I make."

"Of course they do. So, why are they going after your boyfriend?"

"They think he's connected to something they're searching for. I don't believe he's involved." She turned and reached for the doorknob. "I appreciate you stopping by. If I ever need a kidney or anything like that, I'll be sure to look you up."

"I'd be glad to hand over a kidney. If that's what you needed."

She dropped her hand and twisted to face him. Was this guy serious?

Declan's expression sobered. "Right now, you need help locating something, and I can help."

"How do I know I can trust you? I don't know anything about you. Except that James thinks you're a menace."

"He's right. I was. When I first went to prison, I was bitter and angry. I wanted revenge. But I had a change of heart. I decided that if I was ever free again, I wouldn't waste my second chance. Let me prove that to you."

She studied him for a second, then asked, "Why do you wear gloves?"

"I have an injury." He glanced at his hands. "I prefer to keep the scar concealed."

"What happened?"

"That's a story for another day."

"How can I trust your intentions if you won't share some of your life with me?"

"For one thing, I don't want to go back to prison. Everything I do to help will be above board. On the right side of the law this time." He straightened his mossy-green tie. "I'd consider it an honor if you'd let me help in your crusade to clear your boyfriend's name."

"Why were you in prison?"

"I'm sure Kelly filled you in on all the details."

"I want to hear *your* version."

"I was blinded by a decade's old vendetta to search for …" He waved a hand in the air. "That detail doesn't matter. At my lowest point, I took out any obstacles that got in my way and hurt many people in the process."

"What do you mean by 'took out'?"

"Remember, I never killed anyone. I extorted, twisted the

truth, bribed, and did some other things I'm not proud of, but I paid my debt, and I'm hoping you'll give me a chance to prove I'm on a different path now."

She shifted on her feet, considering his plea. *What do I have to lose?* Maybe everything.

"Okay. You can help."

"Really?" Surprise coated his voice.

"Yes. But if you go rogue or make any more disparaging comments about James or Kelly, we're done. Understand?"

"Can you leave the floor open for James? He annoys me."

"No."

"Fine. I'll keep my James comments to myself." Declan flashed her an impish grin. "Where shall we begin? What great secret does H & G think Lucas is hiding?"

She checked her watch. She could spare a few minutes before she needed to leave.

"I need to show you something." Emersyn gestured for him to follow her into the dining room. "Take a seat. I'll go get my laptop."

After she retrieved her laptop from the office down the hall, she joined Declan at the table.

"Lucas designed an app called *Legacy*." While she gave a quick backstory, she sat next to him and walked through the steps James had shown her to open the secret page on *Legacy*.

Declan pointed to the screen. "What just happened?"

"This is a hidden portal in *Legacy*." She opened the product pages and started to scroll. "H & G is looking for a one-hundred-year-old Bible. James found it for sale on this site."

"I see why Sir James is riled. This stuff is fascinating."

She nudged him. "Focus."

"Okay, okay. Tell me about this Bible."

She shared what she knew. "I'm not sure I should tell you this, but James thinks *you* might somehow be involved."

Declan chuckled. "Me? Why?"

"The time frame. Your release and when the Bible was listed for sale."

"What do *you* think?"

"I think if you have the Bible, why are you trying to help me clear Lucas's name? He'd make a good scapegoat for you."

"Good point. You can tell Mr. Taylor I'm not the villain. This time."

This time? Shifting in her seat, Emersyn studied him. *I hope this isn't a mistake.*

"What's your next step?" Declan's words severed her thoughts. "To exonerate your true love."

She shivered. *Is Lucas my true love? Or the villain?* "I'm staying at the Bennett estate this weekend. Lucas wants me to meet his family. I plan to see what I can uncover while I'm there."

"Meeting his family." Declan let out a low whistle. "That's a big step."

Her skin heated. It *was* a big step.

"What if you don't clear his name?" Declan asked. "What if you find the Bible? Or something else to incriminate him? How much do you know about Lucas Bennett? Or his family?"

Worrying her bottom lip between her teeth, Declan's questions tumbled through her mind.

"Can I give you some advice?" He didn't wait for her answer. "Be careful. You're playing a dangerous game between deception and love. You may end up on a path you never intended to take."

A band tightened around her chest. She was investigating a man she'd fallen in love with, going behind James's back, and working with a reformed villain. There's no doubt she'd already wandered down the wrong road. *I can't stop now. I need to exonerate Lucas.*

"I'll be careful."

As she finished relaying to Declan everything she knew about the Bible, doubt crept into her belly and settled.

What would happen if Lucas found out she was investigating him? Would he believe she was trying to clear his name? Or would he feel betrayed?

No matter what the outcome, she prayed this path wouldn't lead to a broken heart.

28

Emersyn drove up the winding drive to the Bennett estate, enjoying the stunning view.

The sprawling acres were in full bloom with petals of pink, ribbons of yellow, and buds of red and white bursting from the ground, blanketing the entire landscape in a rainbow of color.

While the Zucker mansion had its orchards, spherical hedges, and a rose garden clothed in an array of different hues, the panoramic view of Lucas's family home reminded her of a scene from an art book.

As Lucas pulled up in a golf cart, she put her car in park, turned off the engine, and stepped out to greet him.

He flashed her an inviting smile. "How was the drive?"

"Easy." She closed her door before waving a hand toward the gardens bordering the main house. "I feel like I've stepped into a *Monet*. Your family's home is beautiful."

"Thank you." He jumped out of the golf cart and joined her next to her car. "I can't believe I have you all to myself for a whole weekend." Circling his arms around her waist, Lucas drew her in for a slow, tender kiss.

When they parted, her lips tingled. "I want you to show me everything this weekend. All your childhood haunts."

"I plan to." Still holding her close, he feathered a finger across her jawline. "I want you to know everything about me and my family. Everything."

Everything? Her throat dried, and she swallowed.

"Your chariot awaits, my lady." He stepped back and motioned to the golf cart.

She tamped her racing thoughts and took her seat. After Lucas grabbed her luggage and dress bag from her trunk, he set her items on the back seat.

"We have about an hour until dinner. Let's get you to your cottage, and you can get settled in."

Lucas slid into the driver's seat and maneuvered the golf cart off the driveway and onto a paved walking path.

"This is how we'll get around for the next few days." He cruised down the pathway, turned at a copse of trees, then drove toward a large, manicured courtyard.

As he pointed out landmarks along the way, he gave her a brief rundown of how the weekend would unfold. "We'll have caterers each day and security. We open several acres for the public to walk through and serve light refreshments in the center courtyard."

Lucas veered left and turned down a path with a sign labeled COTTAGE LANE and pointed to the gates leading to a row of cottages. "These gates will be closed, and I'll give you the key code to get in." He drove past several cottages painted in various pastel colors before pulling in front of the sage green one.

"The cottages are full this weekend, but everyone staying is either a friend of the family or works for *Bennetts*. I put you in the last cottage, so you'll have the most privacy."

He put the cart in park, grabbed her luggage, and led her to the front door. After punching in the door code, he deposited her bags on the bench in the entryway. "I need to change for dinner, but I'll pick you up in about an hour."

"That should give me enough time to get ready."

Lucas leaned in and feathered a soft inviting kiss over her lips. "If you need anything, call me."

She nodded and, with one final look back, Lucas hopped onto the golf cart and sped away.

Butterflies hatched in Emersyn's stomach as Lucas, clad in an ebony tuxedo, walked her up the front steps of his family's home.

"Who all will be here this evening?"

"A couple of Dad's friends and a few people from *Bennetts*." He opened the front door and followed her in. "Dad and his wife, my brother, a couple of other relatives, and ..." he pointed to a woman walking toward them wearing a shimmering floor-length gown. "My grandmother. Gigi is the nicest lady you'll ever meet."

Gigi's expression brightened as she approached them. "Lucas. I'm so glad you're here." She reached for Emersyn's hands and drew her gaze over her royal blue cocktail dress. "You must be Renée. That dress does amazing things to your eyes, sweetheart."

"Thank you." Emersyn relaxed at the woman's gentle tone. Gigi was an ally.

"My grandson has done nothing but talk about your visit all week. I'm so glad to finally meet you."

Emersyn glanced at Lucas, then brought her gaze back to Gigi. "It's nice to meet you as well."

Gigi released her and gestured to a group chatting in the center of the room. "You'd better go meet the rest of them." She leaned in and whispered. "Don't let them frighten you away, dear. Their bark is worse than their bite, and besides,"—Gigi pointed to Lucas—"this boy will be the one holding all the cards one day, so it really doesn't matter what they think."

With a wink, she whirled around and glided over to a group of ladies about her age.

"I do like Gigi. She's quite a character."

A boyish grin tugged at Lucas's lips. "I'm Gigi's favorite."

She chuckled as he led her over to the rest of his family.

"I was afraid you'd be late for dinner." Sinclair Bennett gripped Lucas's shoulder, then dropped his hand and turned to her. "Good evening. You must be Lucas's plus-one we've heard so much about."

Lucas circled an arm around her waist, drawing her closer to his side. "Renée, this is my dad, Sinclair Bennett."

"I recognize you from the baseball tournament," Sinclair said. "*Swing for the Fence* is one of Lucas's favorite events. I look to him to take it over one day."

"It's a wonderful concept." She caught the look of joy on Lucas's face. "The kids had a great time."

"They always do." Sinclair's expression turned serious as he looked back at Lucas. "Have you seen Carolyn Bixby yet this evening?"

A muscle in Lucas's jaw jumped. "No, I haven't."

"Too bad. She was asking about you. We have some business to discuss with her and her father." Sinclair leaned toward her and whispered, "Carolyn is practically family. She'll be staying with us this weekend along with a few of her friends. I bet you two will get along famously."

Emersyn's insides somersaulted. Was Carolyn the wealthy heiress Sinclair had chosen for Lucas to marry?

"Lucas, there you are." A woman wrapped in a dazzling gold gown floated toward them, trailed by a cloud of expensive perfume.

"This is Letitia." Lucas's tone tightened. "My stepmother."

Emersyn pasted on a smile as she faced Letitia. "It's nice to meet you."

"The pleasure is all mine." Letitia held out her limp hand as if she expected Emersyn to kiss it.

Ignoring the gesture, Emersyn zeroed in on Letitia's neckline. Resting just above the collar of her dress was an ornate pendant in the shape of a jaguar. Her guts twisted. Was that the necklace James had described?

"Lucas." Sinclair motioned to a group standing next to a bay window. "Come with me to say hi to Carolyn and her father. He's our link to acquiring the Sterling estate."

"I'll be right back." Lucas released her as an apologetic expression flooded his face.

After he stepped away, Emersyn pointed to the pendant resting on Letitia's neck. "That's a beautiful necklace."

"Oh, this? It's just a little trinket." Letitia fingered the jaguar like it was a pet. "My son brought it back from his ski trip. We had it appraised, and it's worth more than that art hanging over the mantel."

Her son. Which one? Emersyn's gaze darted toward Lucas. He was deep in conversation with whom she assumed to be Carolyn and her father.

"What is it you do for a living Renée?"

She pulled her gaze away from Lucas and faced Letitia. "I'm a teacher."

"Oh, how sacrificial of you. There's not much money in teaching. The last I checked, teacher pay is near poverty level." Letitia fanned her face as if the idea of low pay made her faint. "Teaching is a noble profession, just not a job I'd want *my* children doing."

She heaved a sigh and wagged a hand in Lucas's direction. "It's bad enough that Lucas volunteers so many hours with those foster children. Does he really believe playing sports with those kids is going to make a difference in their lives?"

Heat crept over Emersyn's skin. "I think it will make a big difference in their lives. Anytime kindness is shown to someone, it makes an impact."

Maybe she should inform Miss High-and-Mighty Letitia that as a Zucker, she didn't need to teach, but it was the calling she believed God had placed in her heart. She breathed in, then exhaled slowly. Calm down. This isn't the place. Or the time.

Letitia huffed and pulled her lips into a sneer. "Maybe so, but he has other things he should be focusing on. Like running *Bennetts*."

Emersyn's gaze dropped back to the pendant. *Remember why you're here.* "Lucas has a great eye for the unusual. Where did he get the necklace?"

"Here, Mother. A glass of champagne as you requested." Preston appeared at their side with two glasses and handed one to Letitia.

He turned and flashed Emersyn a roguish grin. "Renée. How are you this evening? Isn't it nice that none of us are wearing masks tonight?"

We're all wearing masks, wolf. "I'm well." She glanced back at Letitia. "Letitia was just telling me about her stunning necklace."

"Was she?" Preston's gaze flew to Letitia's neckline. "I told her it was too gaudy, but she insisted on wearing it tonight."

Letitia shot a glare at Preston. "Why do you have to be such a pain?"

"Pain is my middle name. Is it not?"

"No, it's Antonio." With an exaggerated sigh, Letitia pivoted on her heels and stomped away.

Preston's grin widened. "She gets flustered when I joke with her."

"Then why do you do it?'

He shrugged. "I overheard her talking about teacher salaries. I thought I'd save you from her badgering."

"I didn't need saving." Emersyn gestured around the room, upset at missing her opportunity to interrogate Letitia. "Are you a lone wolf tonight? Or do you have a plus one?"

"I brought a date." Preston took a long drink of his champagne. "But I think she's more interested in Lucas. The heir."

Emersyn glanced back at Lucas. A woman with jet-black hair had joined Carolyn and her father, her attention fixated on Lucas.

"Two women to resist. Maybe it's Lucas who needs saving." Preston leaned closer and the smell of champagne mingled with his cologne. "Carolyn's territorial. I'd keep a tight rein on my brother if I were you."

"Anything one needs to keep a leash on isn't very loyal."

Preston chuckled. "I like you, Renée. I think you and I are going to be great friends."

Lucas turned from the ladies and made his way over to her and Preston.

Before he could get to them, Preston lifted his glass in a mock toast. "I'll see you around, Renée." As he glided over to his date, he nodded at Lucas as he passed, then turned and threw her a wink.

She shook her head. What a flirt.

"Sorry about stepping away." With a light touch to her elbow, Lucas steered her to a quiet area near the fireplace. "Thankfully, you look unscathed. What do you think of my family?"

She spun to face him. "Let's see, your father mentioned Carolyn Bixby was practically family, Preston's date prefers your company to his, and Letitia's necklace is worth more than the art hanging over the fireplace."

His lips pressed into a thin line. "Wonderful."

"Tell me about Letitia's necklace. It's quite a unique piece."

"It's a ridiculous piece. My father made some connections in France on our last trip. I think that might have been a part of the haul. I'm not sure, though. It hasn't been added to the inventory." Lucas scowled. "Letitia's a narcissist who thinks flaunting my father's money makes her better than everyone else. I don't like her or trust her."

"She made sure I understood the scale of teacher pay."

"I'm sorry. Please don't judge me by them." He glanced over at his father, who'd joined Letitia at the punch table. "Dad never used to be this way. Not when Mom was alive." After a moment, his gaze swept back to her. "When Mom died, Dad outlined a script for my future: take over the family business, marry a wealthy heiress, and have a couple of kids to carry on the Bennett name."

"And now you're turning the script? By dating a teacher?" The words flew off her lips, and she wished she could take them back.

"No. It's not like that. I don't care about my father's plan. I want to make my own way. Make my own decisions for my life."

"And launching *Legacy* was part of that?"

Lucas folded his arms and leaned against the grand fireplace. Clad in a tux, and wearing a brooding scowl, he looked as if he'd stepped out of an Austen novel. "If I can prove *Legacy* is a success, Dad will finally take me seriously."

She considered his words. It was admirable that he didn't want to live hanging on the coattails of his family's wealth.

But how far would he go to make *Legacy* a success?

29

After changing out of her dress, Emersyn opted for a pair of nice jeans and a cozy, light sweater. Lucas had promised her a moonlit walk in the gardens, and she'd hoped for some uninterrupted time to find out more about his family. And the necklace.

As she ambled through the large hallway connecting the great room to the dining room, looking for Lucas, she scanned her surroundings. Everything looked neat and orderly, but criminals didn't flaunt their crimes. Did they?

"Reneé, dear. There you are."

She turned to see GiGi approaching.

"Lucas mentioned he took you back to your cottage after dinner. Is everything okay? I hope we didn't overwhelm you."

"Oh, yes. I'm fine." Emersyn gestured to her jeans and flats. "Lucas suggested a walk this evening. I wanted to change. Do you know where I might find him?"

Gigi's brow creased. "He didn't drive you up from the cottage?"

"I told him I'd walk back after I changed. The weather was perfect and I—"

"You needed some time to recover from us."

"No, really. I just ..."

A coy smile tugged at Gigi's lips. "I think my darling grandson is in Sinclair's office." The older woman's expression slackened. "My son can't go one day without talking business."

"Maybe I should wait for Lucas in the great room."

"No, no." Gigi waved her hand to the hallway. "Take this hall to the end, turn the corner, and Sinclair's office is on the right."

"Well, I …"

Gigi reached out and patted her arm. "You go rescue my poor grandson. He'd much rather be taking a moonlit stroll with his beautiful girlfriend than talking numbers with his dad."

"Are you sure I won't intrude?"

"What if you do?" With a flick of her hand, Gigi pivoted on her heels and left her standing alone in the hall.

Emersyn smiled. She wasn't sure if Mr. Bennett approved of her, and she had no doubt Letitia didn't, but what Gigi had said about Lucas was true. He needed rescuing. Even if it was from his own family.

She followed Gigi's instructions to Sinclair's office. As she approached the half-open door, Lucas spoke.

"You need to rein in your wife."

"Excuse me." Sinclair's annoyed tone floated into the hall.

"Letitia decided to give her opinion on Renée's profession."

Sinclair snorted. "You know Letitia. She's harmless."

"Really? Mom would've never treated a guest like that."

"Don't bring Mom into this."

"What about that necklace?"

Emersyn stilled, waiting for Sinclair's reply.

"What about it?"

"From a quick glance, it's worth thousands. Where did you get it?"

She held her breath.

"Does it matter?" Sinclair's tone hardened. "We had security at the dinner."

"It's not a good look. For *Bennetts*. Letitia flaunting your money like she's the Queen of England. Like you've always told me, we're a wholesome, family business." Lucas paused. "Aren't you worried about *Bennetts* reputation anymore? The future of *Bennetts* depends on our brand. At least, according to you."

"It's not her necklace. I already have a buyer. In fact, Letitia knows the buyer and helped me set up the private sale. She wanted to try it on for the night. You know her penchant for the dramatic." Sinclair huffed a curse. "Before you question my personal life, maybe you should examine your own."

"What's that supposed to mean?"

"It's time you get serious about settling down with someone who will complement you. Complement this family. You need to stop playing the field."

"Come on. Not this again." Frustration clung to Lucas's words.

"I spoke to Miss Renaldi." Sinclair's voice remained steady. "She mentioned you were seeing someone."

Emersyn's heart twirled. While she suspected him of dating someone else, Lucas had been thinking about her.

"I prefer to keep my private life private."

"And yet you brought Renée here this weekend."

A second of silence passed.

"What about Carolyn?" Sinclair's question oozed irritation.

"What about her?"

"You knew her family was going to be here this weekend to talk business."

"Just stop."

"I thought you liked Carolyn."

"I *tolerate* Carolyn. We're childhood friends."

"Old friends is a great place to start."

"Dad, I'm not having this conversation with you. I've already made it clear. My personal life is off limits."

Sinclair murmured something under his breath.

Heart pounding, Emersyn twisted and pressed her back against the wall. She needed an escape before Lucas stormed around the corner and caught her eavesdropping.

She glanced at the hallway. If she went back the way she came, she might encounter Gigi and face a line of questioning. If she went straight, she'd need to walk past Sinclair's office door. *What do I do?*

To her left was an alcove with a set of French doors. Wherever those doors led would be better than being caught standing out here in the hall.

When she pushed open the doors, she stepped out onto a well-lit deck overlooking a koi pond and a lush row of tall hedges. To her right, steps led down to a lower stone patio which housed a fire pit, an elaborate outdoor kitchen, and a circle of amber glowing torches.

She leaned against the wood railing and stared out over the moonlit landscape, thinking about the necklace. How had Sinclair acquired it?

As she wrestled with her thoughts, she walked down the deck steps and slipped into one of the Adirondack chairs that circled the fire pit. Leaning back, she stared into the starlit sky. "I shouldn't be here."

"But having you here has made this weekend much more enjoyable."

She jerked her head up as Preston emerged like a phantom from the shadows of the hedges.

"They can be a little overwhelming in there. Once they start talking business, I need to find my escape."

"Are your dad and Lucas—"

"Always butting heads? No, not really." Preston walked over to a pile of wood and gathered a few logs in his arms. While he wasn't as tall as Lucas, she noticed his black T-shirt hugged well-defined muscles along his back and shoulders. "It's my job to be the black sheep of the family. Not Lucas. He's the golden boy."

He laid the wood in a crisscross pattern in the fire pit, then walked over to the outdoor kitchen and pulled a lighter from one of the drawers.

"Sinclair's upset because Lucas brought you this week."

Preston shoved the lighter into his back pocket and opened a cabinet under the sink. He pulled out a blanket and brought it over to her. "Gigi makes sure this area is stocked with clean blankets and firewood every spring." His lips curved into a half grin. "It's her way of promoting a cozy, family environment for everyone who stays with us during our Garden Weekend."

She took the blanket and unfolded it across her lap.

"Did you know Lucas and I were both Wilderness Scouts?" He returned to the firepit and pulled out a handful of dry flint pieces from the wood pile and tossed them into the pit. "I remember one time, we went on a weeklong camping trip with our scout leader." He retrieved the lighter from his pocket and flicked it on and off. The white-orange flame blinked like a lightning bug. Flicking it on steady, Preston stared at the flame as he continued his story. "Lucas was always the rule follower, but that week ..." He paused and waved the flame over the kindling. "That week, he decided to break the rules."

"What did he do?"

Preston set the lighter next to the fire pit and blew on the kindling. The flames flickered and danced to life.

"Lucas went hiking in the middle of the night. Alone." Preston lifted his gaze and shot her a piercing look. "Lucas has an independent streak, but sometimes it gets him into trouble."

The French doors opened, spilling more light from the hallway onto the back deck. Lucas, now dressed in a grey university hoodie and jeans, descended the steps to the lower deck.

"Sorry I took so long." He sank into the chair next to her and reached for her hand. "I got held up."

Emersyn schooled her thoughts about the overheard conversation. "Oh? By what?"

"Dad and I were having a bit of a disagreement."

Preston snorted. "Is that what you call it? More like Sinclair's mad because the golden boy isn't obeying his orders."

Lucas tightened his grip on her fingers. "Stay out of it, Preston."

Preston kept silent as he placed another log on the fire.

"Preston told me a story about a scout who got lost in the woods." She hoped bringing up a childhood story might lighten the mood.

"Did he mention he nearly burned a couple of acres of private property attempting to find me?"

Preston shrugged. "No harm done. Just cleared a little brush." He grabbed the metal poker leaning next to the fire pit and nudged a glowing log. "I was a kid. How was I supposed to know fire had its own agenda?"

Lucas's expression softened as he turned to face her. "Preston thought I needed a rescue, but I was doing just fine out in the woods all by myself."

"A coyote might have eaten you if I hadn't come looking for you."

Lucas chuckled. "There were no coyotes in those woods. A couple of raccoons, but no coyotes."

"All this wilderness talk makes me want a s'more." Preston patted his stomach. "I'll go get the supplies. I'm sure Gigi's got the marshmallows ready to go."

After Preston sauntered back into the house, Lucas released a long breath. "Brothers. What does God say? They're made for adversity."

Emersyn bit back a laugh. "He's not so bad. A little cocky maybe."

"A little. The boy thinks nothing can touch him. I feel like I've spent most of my life running around putting out fires he starts. Literally and figuratively."

"What did he mean by him being the black sheep of the family?"

"He said that?" Releasing her hand, he stood and walked over to the wood stack. After finding the log he wanted, he placed it on the fire where the hungry flames licked at the edges.

"He's always had a chip on his shoulder. It's been tough for him. And Dad doesn't help. Dad's made it clear that I'm taking over the family business. Preston will have a job if he wants it, but he won't have any ownership in *Bennetts*."

"Does Preston even want a part of the business?"

"I'm not sure *I* do."

"Why not?"

"It's a long story."

Before she could press him for more, the French doors opened, and Preston stepped onto the back porch with Carolyn and a raven-haired beauty trailing after him.

"There you are, Lucas." Carolyn's nasal voice pitched higher. "Preston didn't mention you were out here with anyone."

Emersyn tugged at the blanket around her legs. If Carolyn thought she intimidated her, she obviously never attended an all-girls private school.

Lucas shot Preston a glare before grabbing another piece of wood and placing it onto the fire.

"I brought snacks." Preston laid a tray of marshmallows, graham crackers, and chocolate squares on the side table next to the fire pit.

Carolyn sashayed over to Emersyn and stuck out her hand. "I'm Carolyn Bixby. You may have heard of my father's company, Bixby Pharmaceuticals."

Emersyn shook Carolyn's hand. *Yeah, well, I'm Emersyn Zucker. I'm sure you've heard of my family.* "I'm Renée. The name Bixby sounds familiar, but I'm not quite placing it."

Carolyn's lips bent into an unattractive frown. "It doesn't matter. The Bennetts and Bixbys go way back." She swept her gaze over to Lucas. "We had play dates together right here in this very house. Lucas's mom, God rest her soul, was friends with my mom, so we were always together. Weren't we, Lucas?"

"I only remember you pouting because I wouldn't haul your dolls around in my remote-controlled Jeep." Lucas plucked a chocolate off the tray and popped it into his mouth.

Carolyn rolled her eyes, then motioned toward the other woman standing beside her. "This is Zara Tipton. She owns a boutique downtown. High-end stuff. Nothing off the rack."

Zara faked a smile. "Nice to meet you."

Carolyn pulled Zara over to the bench seat on the other side of the fire. "Lucas, would you grab us a blanket? If I remember right, Gigi keeps them in that little cabinet by the sink."

Obviously annoyed, Lucas lumbered to the kitchen area and pulled out a blanket. Turning, he hurled it at Carolyn. "Check it for spiders. They like to hide in the cabinets."

Both ladies screamed and threw off the blanket.

Preston chuckled as he slid into the chair Lucas had vacated. Leaning close to her, he whispered, "Carolyn's a brat. She thinks her new last name should be Bennett."

Emersyn turned to face Preston, matching his muffled voice. "She'd probably prefer to hyphenate Bixby-Bennett."

"True." Preston sighed. "My opinion? I don't think she has a chance since you showed up."

Emersyn let her attention trace to Carolyn. When their gazes met, Carolyn shot her a glare as she shook the blanket and laid it over her and Zara's lap.

She suppressed a giggle. It looked like Miss Carolyn Bixby had swallowed a bitter pill. Maybe she should ask her daddy about what remedy he'd recommended to cure jealousy.

Lucas leaned back against the metal cabinet and folded his arms, observing the scene around the fire pit. Too bad there wasn't a whole family of spiders hiding in that blanket, then maybe Carolyn and Zara would've jumped in their sports cars and gone home.

This weekend hadn't started out like he hoped. He wanted to show Renée everything he loved about his childhood home and for her to meet his family. Instead, Dad was trying to push him toward Carolyn, and Letitia was showing Renée the shallow side of her personality. He rubbed a hand over his jaw. This weekend was hurtling toward disaster.

Renée flashed him a tender smile, and his heart tumbled over. How was it that through everything she'd experienced with his family, she still looked at him like she wanted to be with him? *God, please don't let my family drive her away.*

He shoved himself off the cabinet and walked over to her. "I promised you a moonlit walk."

"You did." She glanced at Carolyn, then looked back at him. "What's your escape plan?"

"I'm not sure." He pulled her to her feet and wrapped his arms around her.

"Lucas, are you going to make s'mores with us?" Carolyn's sing-song voice broke through the quiet.

He bit back a groan as Renée turned into his chest, smothering a laugh.

Preston stood, putting a wall between them and Carolyn. "Want me to run interference while you two disappear?"

"Yes." They whispered their answer in unison.

"What do you want me to do? Take them out to the woods and lose them?"

Lucas grinned. That sounded perfect, but ... "No. Just show them how to burn a marshmallow."

"Fire. My specialty."

He slugged Preston's shoulder. "Thanks."

"What are brothers for?" Preston's lips pulled into a sly smile as he turned toward Zara and Carolyn. "What do you say we get this fire going?"

Carolyn squealed. "Show us what you got, Preston."

Lucas tugged Renée's hand and pulled her into the shadows. "Come on, let's go before anyone notices we're gone."

"You mean before Carolyn notices *you're* gone."

He chuckled as he led her down a path until they entered the hedgerow maze, and the darkness enveloped them like a thick fog.

Renée hesitated. "Won't we get lost in the dark?"

"I could walk this maze blindfolded." Turning to face her, Lucas drew her close, his lips hovering only a breath from hers. "I won't let you get lost. Ever. Do you trust me?"

"I … do."

Her breathy answer sent a shiver over his skin.

Did she trust him? For months he'd felt she was holding something back from him. A part of herself he longed to connect with. He hoped bringing her here, to his childhood home, and meeting his family would show her how much he wished to be a part of her life. But was it enough?

"Renée, I …" His breath hitched. *I love you.*

Afraid to utter the words his heart had declared, Lucas leaned forward and pressed his lips tenderly against hers. Pleasure and joy burst in his soul like an array of fireworks.

He loved her.

And no matter what life—his dad, Carlson, or *Legacy*—threw at him, he wanted Renée by his side. Forever.

He just prayed that after this weekend with his family, she'd feel the same way.

30

As Emersyn waited for Lucas in front of the martial arts center, his question from last weekend traced through her mind. *Do you trust me?*

Those words had pricked her heart, and she realized she'd not trusted him with anything. While she'd kept the walls she'd erected around her life secure and impenetrable, Lucas had done the opposite. He'd brought her into his business, his home, and his heart.

But what about the necklace? While she still wondered how the jaguar pendant had ended up around Letitia's neck, she also believed Lucas had nothing to do with it. *Maybe H & G needs to be looking into Sinclair.*

A wave of guilt surged through her as the memory of her eavesdropping at Sinclair's door filled her thoughts. Did Sinclair know the necklace was stolen property? Or had he acquired it through what he thought was legal means?

Questions swirled in her mind as she watched several students, a few she recognized and several she didn't, push through the double doors of the dojang.

From the outside, they were an unlikely crew, but Master Jaeden Park and her classmates had become like a second family to her. A family who'd given her a place to belong when she'd felt so alone.

Would Lucas understand what it meant to bring him here today? His openness had penetrated her walls, but sharing a part of her heart wasn't easy for her. *God, if Lucas is who You've chosen for me, help me trust him.*

As Lucas's sports car turned into the parking lot, she straightened her uniform. It was time for her to push aside her apprehensions and take a chance on love.

Lucas exited his car wearing gym shorts and a black T-shirt. He grabbed a duffle bag from the trunk and joined her by the door.

"Hi." His gaze traced her uniform. "You look adorable."

She lifted her hands and wiggled her fingers. "Cute, but deadly. Remember?"

His lips parted into a playful grin. "I remember."

Emersyn grabbed his hand, pushed through the door, and led him through a maze of people to the row of chairs along the back wall. "You can leave your duffle there." She pointed at an open space on the floor as she kicked off her sandals. "And take off your shoes."

"I feel like a kid on the first day of Tee Ball." Lucas dropped his bag and removed his shoes. "I have no idea what I'm doing."

"Don't worry. This Saturday is our open house. We have a lot of first-timers."

Kids shuffled around the room, while parents and siblings filled the seats along the wall.

Master Park bowed at the edge of the mat and walked to the front of the room.

"Good morning." His commanding voice called everyone's attention. "Thank you for joining us today for our open house. My name is Master Jaeden Park. Please take a moment to sign in. We'll start in three minutes."

Lucas leaned toward her. "He looks intimidating."

"He does. But he's a great guy. I'm not sure where I'd be without his leadership and direction."

Understanding filled his expression. "I've had coaches like that."

"During my loneliest days, missing my parents, this place became my sanctuary. A refuge where I could learn and grow and thrive." She nodded to the group wearing uniforms standing near Master Park. "We all start at the same level. No matter what your age, we begin together."

Once Master Park had given everyone a chance to register, he resumed his place at the front of the room. "If you're here for the first time, I'd like you to line up at the front on the blue line."

She gave Lucas a nudge. "That's you."

He blew out his breath. "Wish me luck. See you after class."

Chuckling, she watched him walk to the blue line and take his place among the kids.

After class, they grabbed lunch and spent the rest of the day perusing antique shops and acting like tourists. By the time they'd finished strolling through a local war museum, it was almost dinner time.

"I'm getting hungry again. What about you?" Lucas walked her back to the car and opened her door.

She nodded. "All that walking has made me hungry too."

"I've got the perfect place for us to try."

He drove her to a crab shack near the river. They wore bibs, cracked crab shells, and talked about martial arts and baseball. When they finally left the restaurant, the sky glowed with a warm, golden hue.

"Do you know what this time of day is called?" He reached for her hand and led her across the parking lot.

"What?"

"It's called the magic hour. It's the last hour before sunset and the best time to take photos." He guided her down a path to the rocky beach. When they reached the edge of the water, Lucas grabbed his phone, wrapped his arm around her, and took a picture.

She giggled, cuddling closer. "Send me that one."

"I will."

With his arm still around her, he spun them so their backs were facing the painted sky. He took a few more photos. Some of them smiling, some of them acting silly, and several of them kissing.

He slipped his phone into his pocket and reached for her hand, leading her down the craggy beach to a secluded alcove. "I think this is one of the best days of my life."

Renée looked up at him. "Really?"

He nodded. "I enjoyed getting to know another part of you. Your martial arts family is great." Lucas twirled her around to face the blazing sky. "Look at those colors."

"It's as if God painted it just for us."

"I like that idea." As they both faced the setting sun, he wrapped his arms around her middle and pulled her snug against his chest. "Which do you prefer? Sunsets or sunrises?"

"Definitely sunsets." She intertwined her fingers with his as their arms rested against her belly. "I'm not a morning person."

"I'll remember that." He nuzzled into her neck and placed a kiss below her earlobe. "Hot fudge sundaes or milkshakes?"

"That's a hard one."

"Why?"

"If I'm driving, milkshakes, but if I'm at home …"

"We'll say yes to both." He pointed to a seagull swooping in front of them. It dipped and dove toward the water. "Cabin in the woods or cottage on the beach?"

"Cabin in the woods."

He placed a kiss on her collarbone, imagining a future where they cuddled all day in a cabin next to a blazing fire. "I could go either way on that one."

"I have a question for you." She slid her fingers free and feathered them over his forearm, making him shudder. "What's your favorite season?"

"Spring. Easy question."

She craned her neck to look at him. "Why spring?"

"Spring training of course. What about you?"

"Fall." She looked back at the water. "I love hiking when the trees are changing color."

"I like those hikes too."

The bottom of the sun kissed the horizon, making the orange melt into the water.

Lucas released a contented sigh. "Bed and breakfast or swanky hotel?"

"Bed and breakfast. Any time someone makes me breakfast. I'm in."

"I'll take swanky hotel any day of the week."

She looked back at him. "Somehow I can picture you ordering room service in an oversized robe while you read the morning paper."

"Can you?"

Her cheeks pinked as she slapped his arm, then turned away. "You know what I mean."

"I do like room service." He placed a kiss on her temple. "Football or baseball?"

She twisted in his arms, so she was facing him. "Is this a trick question?"

"Maybe."

"Football."

"Football? Wrong answer." He tickled her ribs until she pushed away laughing.

"Okay, okay." She held up her hands. "I like them both."

He opened his arms, and she shimmied back into them. "I do have one more question."

"What's that?"

With the crook of a finger, he tilted her chin up and placed a row of kisses from her earlobe to her collarbone. "Do you prefer kisses here?" He moved from her neck to her lips. "Or here?"

When they parted, she asked, "Do I have to choose only one?"

"No." Pressing his lips against hers again, his pulse soared through his veins like a fastball.

They shared several languid kisses while the sun dipped slowly into the water. Finally, the sky darkened to a deep purple.

Lucas glanced around at the nearly empty beach. "We should probably head back to the car."

"Probably."

"Would you like to go to church with me tomorrow?" He reached for her hand and steered her back to the trail leading to the parking lot. "I realize it's a bit of a drive up to Richmond, but—"

"I'd love to."

"Really? Great. I hate going alone." He paused and turned to face her. "After service, would you like to see the *Legacy* warehouse?"

Her brows lifted. "I'd love to see *Legacy*."

The enthusiasm in her tone lightened his step as they continued up the trail. He hoped bringing her into every part of his life, even the secret ones he'd kept from his family, would prove even more how much he cared for her.

As they stepped onto the pavement of the nearly empty parking lot, a shadow darted behind his car.

"What was that?" Her voice quaked as she gripped his hand tighter.

He pulled her toward a truck parked under a streetlamp, tucked her behind him, and released her hand. Taking a step forward, Lucas peered around the back of the tailgate. The form hovered by the passenger's side of his car, then walked slowly around to the trunk. "Someone's walking around my car."

"What are they doing?"

"I don't know."

After a few minutes, the figure jogged through the shadows, jumped into a car, and sped off.

"They're gone." He turned to face her, his heart pounding.

"Did you get a good look at the vehicle?"

"No. It's too dark."

She pulled out her phone. "Do you want me to call the police?"

"No." He stepped out from behind the truck and surveyed the parking lot. "Maybe it was someone coming up from the beach." He reached for her hand again. "Let's get out of here. I'm sure it was nothing." *Please, God, let it be nothing.*

As they approached the car, he pulled out his phone and flipped on the flashlight. He drew the light over both sides of the car and the tires. Everything looked untouched.

"Do you think they were tagging your car? Like for surveillance?"

He scrolled through his phone and checked for any unwanted devices. "I don't see anything unusual on my phone."

Lucas walked her over to the passenger side and opened her door.

When she slipped into the seat, she pointed to the windshield. "They left a note."

He ripped the note from the windshield and stared at the words.

Does she know what you're hiding?

Closing her door, he balled the note into his fist and scanned the parking lot. Had Carlson been watching them?

This has got to stop. He sent a quick text to one of the private investigators on *Bennetts* payroll. Someone he trusted with his life.

I need your help.

Keep it discreet.

> Sinclair doesn't need to be
> bothered with this.

He typed a few more details, then walked around the car and got into the driver's seat.

"Who left the note?" Renée's question dripped with concern.

"I'm not certain, but I have an idea who it might be." He started the engine, then reached across the center console and took her hand. "Don't worry. I'm going to have someone look into it. It's just somebody trying to get under my skin."

Trembling, she squeezed his hand, and the compression shot to his heart.

If this was Carlson, he was going to pay.

31

Emersyn followed Lucas's sports car into a parking lot and turned off her vehicle. They'd spent the morning worshiping together, and now she was going to visit *Legacy*.

The understated row of single-story brick buildings was not what she expected for *Legacy's* headquarters. Somehow, she'd envisioned a downtown showroom with large windows displaying antiques. She glanced down the street. Almost all the warehouses looked the same, with tall security fencing and only a few windows.

They both stepped out of their cars at the same time, and she gestured to the grey building. "So, this is *Legacy*."

"For now. It's a rental." He reached for her hand and led her to the door. "Someday, I'll own my own warehouse and the land it sits on." He opened the door and waited for her to step inside. "Are you ready for the grand tour?"

"I can't wait."

While Lucas walked her through the building packed with antiques, he told her stories about each piece. In her mind's eye, she pictured the furniture, paintings, and baubles in the homes they'd come from and the families who'd made memories with them.

He directed her to a long hallway, where the walls were lined with framed paintings and antique photographs. Pausing, he pointed to a painting of a Parisian landscape.

"Imagine you're staying in an apartment in Paris and this painting greets you every morning. The memories you make in Paris will somehow translate to this image." He turned to face her, his expression animated. "It's like a song, smell, or taste. Memories have a way of attaching themselves to things so we can hold onto them longer."

Her thoughts traveled back to the jazz song they'd danced to at the bowling alley. She'd come to think of it as their song, and whenever she brought it up on her playlist, her heart would return to that moment.

"I grew up with antiques and art surrounding me." Lucas's statement pulled her back to the present. "Their history runs in my blood. It's not about the physical item, it's about the feeling you get when you know the origin. Provenance gives the present an anchor to the past."

"It's true. There's a comfort in it. Especially after you lose someone." She thought about her own home. She still sat in the same wingback chair Papa sat in to read his newspaper and used the tea set her great-grandmother had brought with her from Germany. These items were like warm hugs from the past, and the memories they evoked filled her home with love and joy.

A chime rang through the warehouse and Lucas's eyes lit up. "Wait here."

Before she had a chance to reply, he took off through the maze of old books and Edwardian chairs until he vanished around the corner.

She turned and studied the painting once more. With its vibrant colors, the picture pulled her in like a long-lost friend. She'd gone to Paris as a girl, but she longed to walk the *Champs-Élysées* again as an adult.

What would it be like to peruse the *Louvre* with Lucas? He had an artistic side that reminded her of Papa. *I miss you, Papa.*

Her chest burned as she glanced at the rows of antiques. Papa would've loved to have heard Lucas's stories of provenance.

Emersyn blinked back the moisture gathering in her eyes. *Why God? Why does the man I'm falling in love with have this suspicion hanging over him?*

Lucas's presence touched her before his hand brushed against her arm. "Is everything okay? You seem a little lost in your thoughts."

"I was just thinking about Paris." She leaned into him, and he wrapped his arms secure around her middle. "I'm trying to organize a fundraiser for a senior trip next year to Paris. I want my students to experience art in a city that's famous for some of the greatest creatives in history."

"Ambitious, but wonderful." He brushed a kiss against her neck. "Have you ever been? To Paris?"

"Years ago. When I was a girl." She rotated to face him. "I have wonderful memories of fluffy dogs in the park and yummy pastries. Papa bought me a sketch book while we were there, and I drew stick drawings of the Eiffel Tower."

"Those are wonderful memories." He tugged her closer and placed a gentle kiss on her forehead. "I wish I could have met your papa."

Her eyes misted. "Papa would've liked you."

"Maybe it's time you went back and made some new memories in Paris. Memories of kisses in the rain while the Eiffel Tower sparkles against the backdrop of a moonlit sky."

Her heart melted at his words. "Do you have those memories?" She hoped he didn't.

"No." He brushed a knuckle across her cheek. "No kisses in Paris. Not yet."

"Then you have quite the romantic imagination, Mr. Bennett."

"Only when you're around." He slid his fingers behind her neck and lowered his mouth to hers. Tentative at first, then with an ardor that promised those kisses in Paris would someday come true, he continued to caress his lips with hers.

When he pulled away, Lucas swept a thumb across her trembling bottom lip. "I have a surprise for you."

He took her hand and maneuvered her through the maze of furniture to a room in the back. Inside, an oak farm table was set with two place settings.

"How does lunch sound?" As he lifted the lid on a silver serving dish, the rustic aroma of French onion soup and crusty bread wafted through the air. "It's not Paris, but this is a century's old French farm table I picked up a few weeks ago."

She ran her hand over the distressed wood. "It's beautiful."

Lucas pulled out a chair and motioned for her to sit.

"What made you think of a French theme for our warehouse picnic?" Emersyn slid into the ornate chair, still sturdy after years of use.

"I noticed several Eiffel Tower stickers on the back of your laptop." His expression turned shy as he took the seat to her right at the head of the table.

"You definitely have an eye for details." She let her gaze wander over the decorative place settings. "Is this a snippet of the experience you hope to give your customers?"

"It's an idea I had. Having themed dinners for customers to relax and enjoy the product." He ladled soup into her bowl, then filled his own. "Is the experience working?"

"Maybe. Were you hoping I'd make a bid on this farmhouse table?"

He tipped his head back and laughed. "If you want the table, it's yours."

She blinked. "What?"

"I mean … I guess that would be a weird token of love, wouldn't it? A table." A flash of red covered his neck, then slowly faded as he picked up his spoon and tasted his soup.

Love? What was he saying? Warmth covered her skin as if someone had pointed a sunlamp at her.

She ran her hand over the tabletop again. It was beautiful. Well loved, well worn. She'd neglected sitting around her own table at home during most meals. It didn't feel right, sitting alone at a table for eight.

A flash of Thanksgiving dinner jumped into her thoughts. Her table was full, with James, Kelly, Noah, Donna, and Frank, but more than that, it was full of laughter and joy.

"Lucas."

When he looked up, he lowered his spoon to the side plate and picked up his napkin.

"A table is a symbol of family and togetherness. It's a perfect symbol of love."

His brows lifted. "It is?"

She motioned to the grey-blue provincial chairs situated around the table. "Can you imagine the stories shared around this table? The meals. The history. The relationships."

He followed her gaze, then looked back at her. "Like right now, the two of us sharing a meal in a warehouse full of castaway furniture." He ran his fingers along the knotty wood. "Our lunch today will be one of those stories."

"It's a wonderful story." She picked up her spoon and brought a serving of broth to her lips. The hearty liquid was aromatic and soothing. "And this soup is delicious."

"I'm glad you like it."

She lifted her gaze and caught him looking at her.

"What do you think of the warehouse?"

"I love it. There's so much to explore." Tearing off a piece of bread, she dipped it in her bowl and took a bite. The tangy taste danced on her tongue. "I think this kind of shopping experience is a wonderful idea. A meal like this could really work."

"Thanks. I appreciate you letting me bounce ideas off you."

"Any time."

After they finished their lunch, he gathered the soup bowls on a tray. "I have one more surprise for you today."

"You do?"

He stood and held out his hand. "Come with me."

"Is this another part of the shopping experience?" She rose, slipping her hand into his.

"Oh, no. What I'm going to show you my buyers will never see."

"Okay, I'm intrigued."

He gave her hand a squeeze as he escorted her to the back of the warehouse. "Are you afraid of the dark?"

A shiver walked across her spine. "Not usually."

"What about basements?"

"Basements?"

"Come on. You're going to love this part of *Legacy*." He tugged her hand, and she moved in step with him.

They took a sharp right and turned down a narrow corridor that was only illuminated by an exit sign. They passed the exit door and continued to another at the end of the passageway.

Lucas pushed on the metal handle, and a whoosh of cool air rushed over them. With a flick of a switch, soft amber lights lit up a cement stairwell.

Her pulse galloped through her veins. "Where does this lead?"

"You'll see." The metal door clicked behind them. "The stairs are narrow. Watch your step."

She kept a firm grasp on his hand as they descended the dimly lit stairs.

"This is an extra storage area. It's climate-controlled, so I keep it cooler down here." When they reached the bottom of the stairway, he let go of her hand and flipped on another light.

The illumination revealed a basement lined with furniture and shelves full of knick-knacks and books.

Lucas made a sweeping motion around the room. "This is where I keep my favorites."

She tamped her desire to run ahead and start searching for the Bible. "It's like a wine cellar for antiques."

"Something like that. Feel free to look around."

Her gaze scanned the space and landed on a shelf lined with books. She walked over and examined the spines. "My papa loved old books. I have a library full of his collections."

Lucas came up behind her and trailed his fingers over some of the titles. "If you see anything you like, let me know."

She didn't see what she was looking for, so she continued to move around the room and check out the antiques. In the back corner was another door. If it led to another room of hidden treasures, she didn't want to leave without checking them out.

"Where does that door lead?"

Lucas jerked a thumb over his shoulder. "Do you remember the row of warehouses in the parking lot?"

She nodded.

"Through this door is a long breezeway connecting all the warehouses on this street." He opened the door and pointed to the dark hallway. "It's a bit creepy and not very well lit, but it also serves as a fire escape, so you don't have to run back upstairs if the building's in flames."

She shuddered at the thought of running through spiderwebs to get to safety, but if that was the only option, it would be better than going up in smoke.

"Speaking of creepy." His eyes lit up as he motioned her to another corner of the room. "This is the freight elevator." He pushed a button, and a metal gate opened. After stepping inside, he motioned for her to join him.

"Is it safe?"

"It's original equipment but still works."

She hesitated, then stepped into the elevator.

"It's kind of a unique heirloom piece in its own right." Lucas pushed another button, and the gate closed. "I don't think I'd take any of my clients for a ride though. They might not come back."

The elevator's motor hummed as it started its ascent. Before reaching the main level, the light flickered and the elevator went dark.

Shooting her hand out, Emersyn grasped Lucas's arm. "I feel like I'm in a scene from a horror movie."

The lights blinked back on, and he chuckled. "At least the lights came back on this time."

Her heart sputtered. This time?

When they reached the main level, the motor stopped with a clunk. Lucas pushed the button, and the gate opened with a slow, shrill creak.

"I think I'll skip that part of the tour next time." She released her grip on his arm and stepped out onto the first floor.

With a boyish gleam in his eye, he shrugged. "If you insist." He waved a hand toward a closed door. "Our last stop on the tour. My office."

After he unlocked the door, she followed him into the sparse space where a large mahogany desk sat in the center of the room. There were no pictures on the wall, and a bulky black safe anchored one of the corners.

She nodded to the fake plant sitting on the floor. "I love what you've done with the place."

Leaning his hip against the desk, Lucas folded his arms. "I need a place to park my laptop." He pointed a finger at the coffee pot by the door. "And a subpar coffee maker."

She followed his gaze to the dilapidated single-shot coffee maker. "That's seen better days. I'm glad you didn't offer me any coffee today."

"Don't worry, I'm well aware of your coffee standards."

Her cheeks warmed as she stole a look at the freestanding safe. "What's in there?"

"State secrets. Objects too pricey for me to leave out in the open. A few rare books. Some legal paperwork. Jewels. Stuff like that."

"Sounds very clandestine, Mr. Bennett."

His grin widened, showing off his dimple. "You know us software guys, we've got our secrets, and we know how to hide them."

His phone buzzed, and he pulled it out of his pocket to check the screen. "I need to take this." Lucas pushed himself off the desk and walked out of the office.

Emersyn eyed the safe. Could she get him to open it?

"I told you to stop calling me." Lucas's heated words trickled into the room cutting off her thoughts.

She shuffled near the door and pretended to flip through a flea market magazine lying next to the coffee pot.

"Are you blackmailing me?" Lucas lowered his voice. "Because I've only begun to dig up dirt on you."

Ice trailed through her veins at the temperature of his tone. Scared. Angry. Threatening.

Who's he talking to? And did it have anything to do with *Legacy*?

Lucas ended the call and strode back into the office. "Sorry about that. One of my clients … well, he's got an issue I'm trying to resolve."

He's lying. She closed the magazine. "One of those 'the customer is always right' moments?"

"Something like that." He avoided her gaze and checked his watch. "I hate to end our tour, but I have a client meeting I need to prep for."

"I understand." She shot another quick look at the safe. If she wanted to look inside, she'd need to come back another time.

He walked her through the warehouse, then followed her to her car.

She had so many questions. Would he be willing to answer any of them?

"Let's talk this evening." He gave her a quick kiss and waited for her to get into her car.

"I'll be waiting for your call."

As she drove out of the parking lot, she thought about the warehouse tour. Lucas had held nothing back, but that phone call had rattled him. And what about the safe? Was the Bible in there?

She needed help. And so did Lucas. Hesitating only a moment, she dialed Declan.

He picked up after two rings.

"Hey, it's me, Emersyn."

"Hello Emersyn. What are you up to today?"

"Do you have any experience breaking into safes?"

His laughter bounced across the line. "I do but remember what I told you."

"What?"

"I'm not going back to prison. Not even for you."

She nibbled on her bottom lip. "Okay, so it was a bad idea."

"What happened?"

As she continued onto the interstate, she told Declan about the tour of *Legacy's* warehouse and the phone call she'd listened in on.

"What's your gut tell you?"

Declan's question jarred her.

Lucas had taken her into his confidence. Shown her *Legacy*. Now someone was threatening him. "My gut's saying Lucas isn't the villain in this story."

Declan snorted. "Sounds like something Kelly would say."

"Where do I go from here?"

After a few seconds, he replied. "I think you know."

They exchanged a quick goodbye and disconnected the call.

She did know. She'd need to uncover the real reason the Bible had been for sale on *Legacy*. After that, she'd convince James— no, H & G—to stop investigating Lucas and find the real villain of this story.

32

Emersyn opened the mini fridge in her classroom and pulled out her lunch. It had been over a week since she toured *Legacy's* warehouse, and she still couldn't push aside the phone call she'd overheard between Lucas and an unknown caller.

Are you blackmailing me?

She waffled between telling James about the phone call and asking Declan to reconsider committing a crime. Neither seemed like a good option.

Popping the lid off her salad, she sighed. Lucas was innocent. Why couldn't James see that?

As she drizzled creamy Italian over the mixed greens, her thoughts bounced back to the school board meeting she attended last night. With a plan in hand, she'd proposed a senior trip to Paris next year and how she'd raise the funds to get there. Everyone was on board and gave her the green light to plan her art fundraiser when the upcoming school year started.

Emersyn pulled up her notes on her laptop as she ate her salad. The concept was simple—have the art students donate original pieces and invite the public to purchase them at an auction. She'd also planned on asking local artists to donate to the cause or maybe garner a couple of gift certificates from the city theater to auction off.

A crackle buzzed on the announcement speaker. "Miss Landon?"

"Hey, Amber. What can I do for you?" Hopefully, they didn't need an extra body in the lunchroom.

"There's a delivery for you in the office. I thought you'd want to come get it on your lunch hour."

"Thank you. I'll be right down."

She finished her salad, then packed up her dishes and stuck them back into her lunch bag. Maybe the charcoal pencils she ordered last weekend had arrived.

After she locked up her room, she made her way down the hall to the office.

Amber pointed to a large box in the corner. "It's not heavy."

Emersyn picked up the box, confused. It was too big to be her pencils.

As she walked back to her room, Penny met her in the hall. "Did you already finish your lunch? I wanted to see if you wanted to brainstorm ideas for your fundraiser."

"I'm done with my salad, but I'd love to brainstorm."

Penny glanced at the box. "What's that?"

"I'm not sure." Emersyn punched the code on her door and pushed it open. "It has a P.O. Box for the return address and no name."

Penny followed her into the room and waited while she got a pair of scissors and sliced through the nylon strap.

After she pulled back the cardboard and a thin layer of foam, she gasped. It was the Paris landscape painting from Lucas's warehouse.

Rounding the desk, Penny peeked into the box. "Wow. That's gorgeous. Who's it from?"

"Lucas."

"Mr. IT?"

She nodded as she pulled out a small notecard and read it

aloud. "I wanted to be the first to donate to your fundraiser. I've included the appraisal for the painting and the provenance. Let me know what else I can do to help."

"That's one romantic gesture." Penny slipped into one of the students' chairs. "You only got the approval last night."

"I called him after the board meeting to let him know how it went."

"How serious are you and Mr. IT?"

"I don't know." She sighed as she slid into her desk chair, and a tingle spread from her neck to her cheeks. "He's so kind and thoughtful."

"And gorgeous."

Emersyn laughed. "Yes, there's that. But ..."

"But what? He overnighted you a painting."

"I'm just hesitant."

Penny waved a hand toward the box. "That gesture speaks volumes. He's obviously supportive of your career and your ideas."

Her chest squeezed. If only the H & G investigation wasn't looming over them.

She glanced at the painting, then looked back at Penny. "Rain check on the brainstorming. I want to call Lucas."

Penny got to her feet. "Of course." Before she scurried out of the room, she glanced over her shoulder. "I expect all the details about Mr. IT during our brainstorming meeting."

Emersyn laughed and picked up her phone. She had another thirty minutes before her next class. Maybe it was time for her own grand gesture? Or at least a bit of honesty.

After three rings, Lucas's deep voice carried over the line. "Renée. Hi."

"I just got the painting. I don't even know what to say, it's ... I mean, you sent it overnight. That's really thoughtful."

There was a second of silence.

"Lucas?"

"Yes, I'm here. I'm sorry, I … I was hoping you wouldn't think it was too over the top."

"No. It's perfect." *Just like you.*

"I'm glad the school gave you the green light to go forward."

"Me too." She studied the painting. "You've donated the first piece to auction off. The kids are going to be ecstatic."

"It's a great piece. It should bring in a good amount."

Emersyn fiddled with a pencil on her desk. "Are you at the warehouse today?"

"Yeah. I have a few client meetings this afternoon."

"Do you have dinner plans? There's something I want to discuss with you."

"Are you asking me out on a date?"

"I am."

"I'm all yours."

Her skin heated. "Perfect."

"I have a client coming in after five, but I should be done by seven. Where do you want to meet?"

"School's out at three. Since it's Friday, it won't take me long to get out of here." Emersyn picked up the pencil and doodled hearts on a sticky notepad. "I'll drive up your way around six. Meet me at the pizza place near your warehouse. I hear they have great Alfredo. I might even let you have my leftovers."

"I'll be there."

Her heartbeat slowed as they ended the call. Tonight was the night. She'd open the door to her world and let Lucas in.

She just hoped he'd still want to share leftovers after hearing her confession.

33

Lucas's heartbeat skipped faster as he finished packing a set of bone china dinnerware in a wooden crate for storage. Since he'd hung up the phone with Renée at lunch, he'd counted the hours until their dinner date. Why was time moving so slow?

Grinning like an idiot, he closed the lid on the crate, secured the corners, and walked back to his office. *Maybe I should tell her tonight?* He inhaled a quick breath. No. Stick with the plan.

Slipping into his desk chair, he scanned the document he'd left up on the screen. *Legacy's* proposal. He didn't want to wait another year to come clean to his dad about *Legacy*. His father would have to accept what he was doing, or ... Shoving away the thought, his mind skipped to another proposal. Was it too soon?

He opened the middle desk drawer and ran his hand along the back of the frame until he found the latch unlocking a secret compartment. Reaching in, Lucas pulled out the ring box. A zing of electricity shot through him. How would she react?

He flipped open the box and studied the platinum emerald-cut diamond engagement ring he'd acquired in Europe. The minute he'd laid eyes on the piece, he knew exactly who the next owner would be.

Replacing the ring box in the hidden compartment, he secured the latch holding it into place. Next month, he'd give his father the report on *Legacy* and state his case. With *Legacy* out in the open, Carlson and his threats wouldn't have a leg to stand on. Then he could move on with his plan. His plan to start a future with Renée.

Lucas closed his laptop, stood, and turned off the office lights. Renée had mentioned she wanted to discuss something with him tonight. Warmth spread through his body. Whatever it was, he couldn't wait to see her.

He checked doors and shut off lights. Before he reached the front door, the doorbell broke through the quiet. He froze. He wasn't expecting a delivery. Or another client. *Should I check the cameras?*

He shrugged off the thought. He had a dinner to get to.

When he opened the door, his blood iced. "Carlson."

"I'm here to chat."

"There's nothing we need to talk about."

"I think there is." Carlson slid his hand halfway out of his suit jacket, revealing a gun. "The Bennetts owe me money."

"The Bennetts don't owe you anything. Your issue's with me." Lucas glanced up. The security camera dangled from the door jamb like an eyeball hanging out of its socket.

Carlson snickered. "Looks like you need better security."

God, what do I do?

Carlson gave him a shove. "Step back inside, Mr. Bennett."

He held his stance, gaze flickering to the parking lot. His car was only a few feet away. Carlson wouldn't shoot him in the back. Would he?

Carlson shoved him harder this time, making him lose his balance. Before he could steady himself, Carlson crossed the threshold and slammed the door.

Lucas straightened. "You're going to pay for this."

"Not before you do."

Lucas was late. Emersyn flipped over her phone and stared at the screen. He's only ten minutes late. Don't panic. He's fine.

"Hey, Renée."

She jerked her head up. Preston stood near her table with two other guys.

"Hey, Preston."

"What are you doing here?" He scanned the room. "Are you meeting Lucas?"

"He was supposed to meet me here ten minutes ago."

Preston frowned. "That's not like him."

"No, it isn't." She glanced at her phone again. "Have you seen him today?"

"No." He motioned to the guys next to him. "Why don't you grab a table? I'll be over in a minute."

They nodded and walked away.

Preston slipped into the booth with her. "We're here to watch some sports and lament our dateless Friday night."

She forced a smile. "Maybe Lucas got caught in traffic."

"Maybe." Preston pulled out his phone, pushed a number in, and held it up to his ear. "Have you seen Lucas today?"

Her stomach knotted while she listened to the one-sided conversation.

He ended the call and shoved the phone back into his pocket. "Sinclair said he stopped by the office mid-afternoon but hasn't seen or talked with him since."

She fiddled with her purse strap. That was hours ago.

"When was the last time you heard from him?"

"Around noon."

"I'd give him another thirty minutes. If you don't hear from him, we can send out the hounds."

Her shoulders slacked. "Okay."

"I'm sure he's fine." Preston shot her a sympathetic look, then slid out of the booth and joined his friends.

Something's wrong. I know it.

She called Lucas's number one more time. Nothing.

When Preston went to the counter to order, she slinked out of the booth and sprinted to the parking lot.

34

Emersyn pulled up to the warehouse and surveyed the parking area. Lucas's car sat in the front spot. Why wasn't he answering her calls? She dialed his number one more time, but after three rings, it went to voicemail.

Tension coiled around her as she pocketed her phone and keys and stepped out of the car, an eerie quiet greeting her.

Emersyn quickened her pace to the warehouse.

When she reached the door, her attention flew to the broken security camera dangling over the door jamb. *Maybe I should call the police.*

Keeping Lucas's secret about *Legacy* was the only thing prodding her to turn the knob and walk over the threshold before making the call.

"Lucas?"

She scanned the dimly lit warehouse until her gaze landed on a sliver of light coming from the office. Please let him be okay.

Pulse-pounding, she tiptoed through the maze of antiques until she reached the office door. She turned the knob, peeked inside.

The safe was open, and a stack of old books littered the ground. She rushed to the safe, scanning the contents. Files, jewelry boxes, and more books lined the shelves, but no Bible.

Withdrawing her phone, she decided to call for help. Before she pressed nine, a distant clanking sound stopped her.

Emersyn dialed Lucas's number again. This time a quiet buzz drew her from the office to a row of bookcases. Using her phone's flashlight to scan the floor, she followed the noise to Lucas's phone. The screen had a jagged crack across the front.

"Lucas?" She whispered his name, getting no reply.

The clanking started again. Her gaze shifted to the door leading to the basement. Biting on her lower lip she weighed her options. Should she risk going into the basement herself or call for help and risk exposing *Legacy?*

She slipped Lucas's phone into her back pocket, crept toward the basement door, and pushed it open. A whoosh of cool air rushed around her, sprouting gooseflesh over her entire body.

Stepping into the stairwell, a creak from the front of the warehouse made her pause. Emersyn reeled around, heart pounding.

Shadows dripped down the walls like *Rorschach* ink blots. She waited, straining to listen for any movement from the front door. Nothing.

Another clang sounded from the basement, and her pulse skittered like a feral cat.

Turning back to the stairwell, she called out, "Lucas?"

As she stepped forward, a hand wrapped around her arm, yanking her back.

Emersyn screamed. Whirling around, she pulled out of the stranger's grasp and took a swing at the shadowy form.

"Whoa, Renée." The figure ducked, stepped backward, and held up his hands in surrender. "It's me, Preston."

"Preston? What are you doing here?"

"Following you. But not down *that* stairway." He pointed over her shoulder to the dark passageway. "Whose warehouse is this? It's not one of *Bennetts.*"

Her throat dried. "It's …"

The clanking started again.

Preston cocked his head to one side. "Did you hear that?"

Without answering him, she flipped on the light to the basement and took off down the stairs.

"Renée. Wait. Where are you going?" Preston caught up at the bottom of the staircase and grabbed her elbow.

"I think Lucas is down here." She tugged out of his grip. "He might be hurt."

"Wait. What?"

The clanging grew louder, and she zig-zagged through the room toward the service elevator, Preston on her heels. The iron gate was closed, but the elevator hung suspended about seven feet above the basement level.

"Lucas! Are you in there?" She yelled saying a prayer he'd answer.

The clanking stopped. "Renée? Is that you?"

"It's me."

"What's going on?" Preston cut in. "Whose building is this?"

A knot curled in her gut. She'd led Preston right to *Legacy*.

"Preston?" Lucas's voice hitched. "What are you doing here?"

Preston shot her a narrowed look. "I ran into Renée at the pizza place. She said you weren't answering your phone, so when she tore out of the restaurant, I followed."

Emersyn shifted her gaze away from Preston. There were too many questions in his eyes. None of them she wanted to answer. "Are you okay, Lucas?"

"I'm fine." Frustration clung to his words. "There's a control box to your right. See if there's a way to get this elevator moving again."

Preston hurried to a metal box secured to the wall. "It looks like the shut-off lever fell halfway."

He gripped the lever on the side of the box and cranked it up. There was a loud clunk, then the motor hummed to life, and the elevator made its descent. When it stopped, Preston pushed back the iron gate.

Lucas stumbled out and cupped her face in his hands. "Renée, I'm so glad you're okay. You are okay. Right?"

"What do you mean? I'm fine. You're the one stuck in an elevator." She lifted her hand and ran her finger across his bleeding and swollen lip. "What happened? Who did this to you?"

He stole a look at Preston. "Nobody. It's nothing."

"Nothing? Somebody locked you in an elevator." Preston gestured around them. "And whose warehouse is this?" His gaze jerked back to Lucas. "And why do you look like you were on the wrong side of a fight?"

"It's a long story." Lucas curled a trembling hand around hers. "One I don't want to tell. At least not right now."

She studied his battered face and neck. "We need to call the police and file a report."

Lucas's gaze fixed on hers. "We're not calling the cops. I'll take care of it." Releasing her hand, he staggered up the stairs.

Preston turned to face her. "Do you know what's going on?"

Ignoring his question, she waved a hand toward Lucas. "Do something. We need to call for help."

"If my brother doesn't want to call the cops, I'm not going to force him."

"He's not thinking clearly. He might have a concussion."

"Are you two coming?" Lucas turned halfway up the steps.

Preston swept an arm toward the stairwell. "Ladies first."

Emersyn shot Preston a scowl, then caught up to Lucas. When they reached his office, Lucas stepped over the mess and slumped into his desk chair.

"Are you going to fill me in? Or do I have to guess?" Preston folded his arms, swiveling a look between her and Lucas.

"It's nothing." Lucas pinched his eyes shut. "It was just a misunderstanding."

"A misunderstanding?" Unfurling his arms, Preston walked over to the safe and peered inside. "Are you doing something illegal?"

Lucas's eyes shot open. He winced. "No. But do me a favor, don't say anything to Dad about this. At least not until I tie up a few loose ends."

A second passed before a wry smile tugged at Preston's lips. "Keeping a secret from Sinclair. Oh, how the golden boy has fallen."

Lucas glared at him. "Leave. And keep your mouth shut."

"Okay, okay. I won't say anything." With a low chuckle, Preston glided out of the room and slammed the door.

Rounding the desk, she reached out and lightly touched Lucas's battered temple. "What happened? Who did this to you?"

"I don't want to talk about it. Not right now." He shot her a mournful look. "Give me a few days to figure this out."

Her throat thickened. She didn't want to give him a few days. She wanted them to figure this out now. Together.

Taking his phone out of her pocket, she laid it on the desk and turned to leave.

"Renée."

She glanced over her shoulder.

"I'm sorry. For all of this."

Why is he apologizing?

"Give me some time. I promise I'll figure this out."

She nodded, eyes stinging, then walked out of the office and through the dark warehouse to her car.

Whatever had happened tonight, one thing was for sure, Lucas was in way over his head.

35

Emersyn pulled into the parking lot of the nature park, hoping today's hike with Lucas would be the balm their souls needed.

She stepped out of her car, scanned the parking area, then checked her watch while her mind chased its tail. After a week, he'd not talked about what happened at the warehouse. She still wasn't convinced he was the bad guy.

But what part is he playing? She frowned. *Maybe I should ask myself the same question.*

Lucas pulled into the spot beside her, and after he locked up, he joined her, casting her a repentant look. "I'm sorry, I'm running a little late."

"It's okay. Traffic can be unpredictable."

He nodded, then reached for her hand as they walked in silence to one of the wooden piers. Finding a secluded spot, Lucas unwound his fingers from hers and rested his forearms on the weathered railing. "It's nice out here today. Peaceful."

She sidled next to him and let her gaze linger on the lake. Unlike her scattered thoughts, the water hovered like glass, reflecting the sky and a border of green, leafy trees.

After a moment, Lucas pointed out a family of turtles

relaxing on a log while a couple of Mallards sliced through the water and raced toward the muddy banks of the shoreline.

She envied them. Relaxed and unburdened. Swimming through life without a care in the world.

Her last day of the school year was yesterday, but instead of enjoying a lazy Saturday morning, her nerves were wound tighter than a bowstring. She had so many questions. Questions only Lucas could answer. *Do I really want him to?*

Impatience sprouted inside her. "What happened at the warehouse?"

"I don't even know where to start." He kept his gaze fixed on the water. "My life feels like a train wreck. I'm not even sure how it got to this point."

"Why don't you start from the beginning?"

He turned to face her, eyes weary. "Let's walk."

Lucas reclaimed her hand, and as they strolled toward the trail, the shrills and caws of the birds dimmed the sounds of the roadway. She breathed deeply, relishing the fresh air.

"It's all about *Legacy*. What happened at the warehouse. The note at the beach." Lucas's tone hardened. "A couple of months before *Legacy* went online, my old professor, Dan Carlson, reached out to me."

"What did he want?"

"He claimed he had rights to *Legacy*."

"Does he?"

"No." Lucas rubbed a hand across his days-old stubble. "During my senior year, I developed an app for one of my classes. It wasn't *Legacy*, but it was similar. Carlson gave me some pointers, and I ignored them."

He continued to relay more information about his conflict with Carlson as they stepped across a wooden bridge. Dragonflies dotted the rails and stared up at them with their beady, alien eyes.

"I wanted the program to be solely my own. Carlson acted

like a real jerk about it. Told me I was naïve, and if I ventured out on my own, the app would fail."

"What happened after you graduated?"

"He must have heard I'd developed *Legacy* because about six months before it went online, he started badgering me. Calling. Sending emails."

"Why didn't you go to the authorities?"

"I didn't want to involve Dad. He's made it clear how he feels about my 'hobby.' He still doesn't know *Legacy* is online, let alone that I've been doing business right alongside him."

She winced. Lucas was playing both sides of the fence. They both were.

He led her over to a fallen log just off the path, released her hand, and sat down. "There's something else."

"What?" She took a seat next to him, concern snaking through her.

"Carlson's been following me—following us." Lucas released an exasperated breath. "He mentioned you at the warehouse."

"Me? Why?"

"He threatened to tell you I've stolen *Legacy* from him. He says he's got proof."

How could Carlson have proof? What was Lucas holding back? She reached out a hand and rested it on his arm. "I wouldn't have believed him."

"Carlson's dangerous Renée. I don't want him anywhere near you." He turned to face her, eyes darkening. "I'll do whatever it takes to keep Carlson away from you. And *Legacy* out of his hands."

Lucas's resolute tone shot a chill down her spine. Whatever it takes? Did that include selling stolen goods? Or something worse? She shoved away the uneasy questions.

"Didn't you hire a private investigator? Can't he prove Carlson's threatening you?"

"The PI didn't uncover much." Lucas picked off a broken

piece of bark and flung it into the trees. "Carlson's done well at covering his tracks."

She eyed his bruised cheek. "What about the attack?"

"There's no security footage. It's my word against his."

"There's got to be something you can do."

He shrugged. "Carlson has gambling debts. He needs money. I offered to write him in as a consignor on a high-dollar item I'm about to list and give him half of the proceeds."

Her ears perked. "High-dollar item? What is it?"

"It's a piece I acquired last summer. I did some research. The history of the item is bound to bring buyers out of the woodwork." Lucas got to his feet and scanned the trail. "I'm supposed to meet with Dad in a few weeks. I just need to hold Carlson off for that long. Once I tell Dad about *Legacy* and Carlson, I'll have all of *Bennetts* arsenal at my disposal."

"Why can't you tell him now?"

"Dad's on a cruise with Letitia." He twisted to face her, his expression bleak. "Betrayal isn't something I want to confess over the phone."

She winced. What about her own betrayal? She pushed herself to her feet and brushed the dirt off her shorts. "What if your dad doesn't respond … positively?"

"Dad might disown me, but he won't let me take on Carlson by myself."

For the next hour, they continued hiking, while Lucas explained his theories about the warehouse fires, the missing products, and the threatening notes.

When they circled back to the parking lot, he walked her to her car and wrapped her in a warm hug.

"Thanks for meeting me this morning and letting me talk this out." After he placed a wispy kiss on her forehead, a smile towed at his lips. "With all this going on, I've realized how much having you in my life has changed things for me—for the better."

She held his gaze, her heart melting from the warmth she saw kindling there.

"I don't know what I'd do without you, Renée." He brushed a knuckle down her cheek, his tone turning husky. "Knowing I can trust you with this means the world to me."

Trust. The word carved a valley through her soul. She needed to tell him everything. She swallowed past the lump in her throat. Maybe not the part about investigating him.

He leaned in, his lips caressing hers like an artist's brush gliding over a canvas.

When they parted, a kaleidoscope of color burst in her soul, sending tingles over her skin. She loved him. And she needed to tell him who she was before their hearts intertwined any more.

"Lucas ... I ..." She inhaled and exhaled, attempting to settle her fear. "Are you heading back to Richmond now? Or do you have a few minutes?"

He glanced at his watch, then returned his tender gaze to her. "I need to head back. I have a meeting with a client for *Bennetts*. With Dad out of town, I'm in the lead." He bent his head, so their foreheads touched. "Come up tomorrow. We'll go to church, then we can spend the rest of the day together."

"Okay." Hot coals raked across her chest. She'd tuck her confession away for another day.

Lucas stepped back, his expression turning sheepish. "Would you like to look at a few condos with me next week? In Newport News?"

"You're looking at condos? Here?"

"This drive's becoming unbearable. I want to be here. With you." He gripped the back of his neck and flashed her a boyish grin. "Are you okay with that? Me moving closer?"

"Yeah. I'd like that." A flutter erupted in her belly. With him moving closer, there'd be no more secrets.

Relief washed over his face. "Okay. Good. You can help me scope out the best neighborhoods." He opened her door and waited for her to slip into the driver's seat. "I'll see you tomorrow."

After he got into his car, he waved, then drove away.

Emersyn sighed. Before she came clean with Lucas, she'd need to make a phone call.

She dialed. After three rings, James picked up. "Hey, Em."

"James, I … I need to tell you something." She quickly caught James up on everything that had transpired between her and Lucas. "I'm sorry." Her voice caught. "I'm sorry I didn't tell you sooner about Letitia's necklace or about snooping in Lucas's office. I thought maybe—"

"You thought you could clear Lucas's name. On your own." His voice dripped with frustration. "Do you know how much danger you've put yourself in? Not to mention how much you might have hindered our progress to track down the Bible. If the names in the Bible fall into the wrong hands, people will lose their lives."

"I know. I'm sorry."

James huffed out a breath. "In a region desperately trying to thwart the plans of God, one lost link in the chain can cause a ripple effect." After a heartbeat, he added, "This is why H & G exists, to help stop that from happening. You're not working for H & G, unless your involvement means you've made your decision."

A chord yanked on her heart. Why was she hesitating? Wasn't she already playing the part? She shook off the thought. There were so many parts she was playing with Lucas, James, and herself, balancing them was becoming a chore.

"I need more time to think about H & G. I know I shouldn't have been keeping information from you, I just don't believe Lucas is involved with the missing Bible." Her heart sprang into overdrive. *Because I love him.* Clearing her throat, she tamped down the thought. "What about Dan Carlson? Lucas's old professor. Do you know anything about him?"

"I'm already looking into him. There's not much there."

"What? How?"

"Private investigators talk," James said. "Word got around. Frank Collins heard Lucas hired someone."

"But Carlson's stalking Lucas."

"What do you mean?" James's tone turned steely. "Did something happen?"

"Carlson followed us one night and left a note on the car." She told him what she knew about Carlson threatening Lucas over *Legacy*.

"Em." James paused. "Have you considered Lucas has created this mess he's in? How much do you really know about him? Or his family? His stepmother wore stolen property that you claim Sinclair Bennett acquired."

"Alleged stolen property. I never got a photo. Maybe it only resembled the one you described." She paused, collecting her thoughts. "Have you seen the Bible back for sale on Legacy?"

"No."

"What about the stolen necklace?"

"No, but—"

"James, Lucas isn't the bad guy. Please, just check again on Carlson."

"I will. But Em, I want you to consider hiring security. What if Carlson contacts you?"

Her stomach turned. James wouldn't be just suggesting security if he knew Carlson had brought her name up in the scuffle with Lucas.

"I'll consider it."

After James rattled off a few more warnings, they ended the call.

As she contemplated all that James had said, she watched a bird do lazy swoops around the treetops. That's what her life felt like, a continual loop of secrets and what-ifs.

James and H & G believed Lucas was involved in the dark side of *Legacy*, but her heart told her he wasn't.

Choosing which one to listen to would be the hard part.

36

E mersyn pulled into a parking spot near the coffee shop and turned off her car. Today was the day. *My real name is Emersyn Zucker, and I know about the hidden rooms on Legacy.* Her heart hammered against her ribcage. He'd forgive her. Wouldn't he?

Flipping down the visor, she examined her reflection. Makeup flawless. Sundress. A healthy dose of courage. Maybe this would be a celebration. *Or maybe I'll leave in tears.* She picked up her purse and stepped out of her SUV.

Last night on the phone, Lucas's voice sounded cheery. Relaxed. A change from their conversation during their hike. He'd mentioned he had something important to share with her. She had something important to share too.

As she walked up to the door her mind wandered. Had he decided on an apartment? They looked at a handful. All of them nice. Or had Carlson given up his claim to *Legacy?* Whatever his news, she'd explain her story first.

Emersyn reached for the door handle and halted. The blinds were drawn, and the closed sign dangled in the window. She checked her phone. *Am I late?*

She brought up Lucas's number but before she could press

send, the lock clicked, and the door swung open. Lucas stood in the doorway dressed in a navy-blue suit that did crazy things to his eyes.

"Hi." She glanced at the closed sign, then brought her attention back to him. "Did they close early?"

A lazy grin tugged at his lips as he motioned for her to come in. "You're right on time."

The alluring draw of jazz and candlelight greeted her when she stepped over the threshold. Heart tripping, she spun to face him. "What's all this?"

"A coffeehouse picnic." Lucas took her hand and led her to their booth. After she sat down, he shot her a wink. "I'll be right back."

As he walked behind the counter, a text jumped onto her phone screen.

The Bible is back on Legacy.

She swallowed hard and read the next incoming text.

I believe Lucas is working with Carlson.

Her gaze flew to Lucas. He'd set a chilled bottle of French Lemonade on the counter along with two glasses. *Please, God. This can't be happening.*

When her phone pinged again, she glanced at the screen. Staring back at her was a picture of Lucas shaking hands with Carlson in front of *Legacy's* warehouse.

This was taken three days ago.

"Can I have this dance?"

She snapped her head up.

Lucas stood next to their booth, hand outstretched, while Elle Fitzgerald and Louis Armstrong belted out the notes to *The Nearness of You.* Their song.

"I … uh, sure." She slid her phone into her purse before

scooting out of the booth and taking his hand. *What am I going to do?*

Lucas guided her to the center of the coffee shop and wrapped his arms snugly around her. "Have I ever told you how much I love dancing with you?" Swaying, he coaxed her to move with him in time with the song's tempo.

"Yes … you have." As she leaned her head on his shoulder, the picture James sent flashed across her mind. *I can't believe it. I won't believe it. Lucas isn't—*

"I wanted to tell you, it's over."

She jerked her chin up to look at him. "What?"

"Carlson's backed off."

"He has? What happened?"

"It's nothing you need to worry about. I've taken care of everything." His expression turned serious. "When Dad returns from his cruise, I'll explain about *Legacy*, and the chaos in my life will finally be over."

Chill bumps floated over her skin. *But what about the Bible?*

"Now, for the reason I brought you here." Lucas leaned in, his breath brushing against her ear. "I have something I want to give to you."

"What?"

He released his hold on her and stepped back. "I bought our coffee shop. For you. If you want it."

"You bought me a coffee shop?"

Nodding, his lips bowed into a shy smile. "I replay the day we met over and over. For me …" His breath hitched. "For me, it was love at first sight. A divine appointment. A day that's forever changed my life."

Her stomach twirled and dipped like a ballerina. *But why is the Bible back on Legacy? Why were you shaking hands with Carlson?*

"Renée, I love you. I want to sit around that old French farm table and make more memories with you. I want to kiss you in Paris and support your dreams."

Withdrawing a ring from his pocket, Lucas dropped to one knee and held it toward her. "I want to build a legacy with you. *Our* legacy. And I want to share my leftovers with you every day of my life."

Her eyes misted. She wanted all that too. But how had he acquired the Bible?

"Renée Landon, would you do me the honor of becoming my wife?"

Renée? Landon? Lucas was offering her everything she'd ever dreamed of, but he didn't even know her. The *real* her.

"I …" Acid coated her throat. "I can't."

"What? Why? I thought that we …" He rose and shoved the ring back into his pocket. "Talk to me, sweetheart. Did I do something wrong?"

The hurt in his eyes ripped her soul in two. "No … it's just … Lucas, I can't."

She pulled her hand from his grip, grabbed her purse, and bolted out the door. How could she explain? There were too many secrets between them.

Retrieving her phone from her purse, she considered calling James. She shook off the thought. He already believed Lucas was guilty. What would he say about the proposal? Or that for a moment she'd considered saying yes?

Her eyes burned as she continued across the parking lot. Her secrets had finally caught up with her, and now her heart lay bleeding out in the coffee shop.

Stomach in knots, Emersyn dialed the one person she thought might understand the mess she was in.

After two rings it connected.

"Declan, I need your help." She sniffled as she climbed into her SUV.

"Is everything okay? You sound upset."

"I'm … fine." With the back of her hand, she wiped her eyes, then started the ignition. "Can you meet me at my place?"

"I'll be right over."

She needed to find out the truth. The truth about Lucas's connection to the Bible and Carlson.

After that, she'd put any thoughts of joining H & G and finding true love out of her mind. Forever.

37

ow could I have read the situation so wrong? Lucas reached into the shower, waved his hand in front of the digital panel, and started the water.

Tomorrow was Monday. After sulking in his condo for a week, working on *Legacy*, and praying Renée would call, he needed to regroup and prepare for his meeting with Dad.

Was buying the coffee shop too over the top? *Did I rush the proposal?*

Jets blasted from the shower stall ceiling and walls, filling the enclosed space with steam. When the green light appeared on the panel, the water had reached its perfect temperature.

Lucas shucked his robe and stepped into the shower. Standing under the rainfall, he prayed the streams of water would wash away his melancholy thoughts. Does she even miss me?

He moved the temperature three degrees higher and finished washing. The heat pelting his skin mirrored the fiery ache searing his heart.

"Why, God? Why did You let me fall in love with her?"

As he rinsed the last of the soap out of his hair, Lucas scrubbed a hand across the days-old scruff dotting his cheeks.

Did I miss something? Something that would've stopped me from losing my heart?

Despite the steam circling him, he shivered. Sleep had evaded him for days, and fatigue plagued his muscles as if he'd just played a doubleheader. How did anyone recover from a broken heart?

He pushed the red button on the panel and reached for his towel. He'd shave later. Maybe. Maybe he'd let the beard grow in. It could be a new look. A look that when he glanced in the mirror wouldn't remind him of before. Before, when he thought Renée loved him.

After he dried off, Lucas shuffled to his room and threw on a pair of lounge pants and an old baseball T-shirt. Swiping his phone off the dresser, he checked for any new messages, then scrolled through the photos of him and Renée at the beach. His eyes burned. Should he delete them? Or keep them as a reminder of when his heart didn't feel as hollow as a piece of driftwood.

With an aggravated sigh, he chucked the phone onto the bed and grabbed his laptop. *How can I delete them? They're all I have left.*

He descended the stairs like a man on death row. When he got to the dining room, he slumped into a chair and raked his hands through his damp hair. "I need to get out of this funk before I meet with Dad."

Firing up his laptop, Lucas punched a few keys and brought up the report on *Legacy*. The numbers looked good, and after a recent acquisition, he'd be even more in the black.

"What's the point?" He slammed the lid shut. "Dad's going to reject the idea anyway. He already has." Curling his hands into fists, the ache in his chest grew. *Just like Renée rejected me.*

A hard knock on his front door interrupted his lament.

It better not be Preston. I cannot deal with his drama right now. He rose and stomped to the door.

The knocking continued.

"I'm coming. Just a minute." When he opened the door, his heart jammed in his throat. "What are you—"

"Where's Emersyn?" James Taylor pushed past him and marched over the threshold, scanning the condo like he'd lost something. When he turned to face Lucas, he scowled. "Well? Where is she?"

"Emersyn? Who's Emersyn?" Lucas shut the door, pulse racing. "Mr. Taylor—James. What are you doing here?"

"I'm asking the questions here. When was the last time you spoke with her?" James yanked off his sunglasses and slid them into the V of his button-down shirt.

"Who?"

"Emersyn. Renée."

Lucas's guts roiled. Had she told James about his tanked proposal? Could this week get any worse?

"I haven't seen Renée in over a week. Why are you calling her Emersyn?"

James paced in front of the sofa. "Her housekeeper said she went camping with a girlfriend, but her mobile's been off for days."

"Like I said, she's not contacted me for a week."

James halted and pinned him with a hard stare. "Why? Did you do something to upset her?"

"What? No. I mean …" He rubbed a hand across the stubble blanketing his jawline. "We had a misunderstanding."

"What kind of misunderstanding?"

Lucas straightened when the man got in his face. He was a bit taller than James, but James Taylor looked like he wanted to throw a punch.

"Look, you probably already know this, but I asked her to marry me and—"

"You did what?"

"Don't worry. She said no. It was a disaster. I haven't talked to her since."

James stepped back. "She can't marry you, mate. She knows everything."

"Know's what?"

"Oh, come on. The hidden virtual rooms. I bet your father's so proud." James got back in his face. Lucas stepped back. "Are you going to deny you're selling stolen goods on *Legacy*?"

"What are you talking about?"

James pulled his phone from his pocket and showed him a picture of a tattered Bible. "This Bible was stolen. The man who had it last is dead. Now, it's listed on your app."

Cold sweat beaded on Lucas's brow as he studied the photo. The item number didn't match anything he recognized. His inventory numbers were twelve digits long, this one was six. "That's not *Legacy*."

James flipped through a few screens then showed him the home page. "Looks like your app to me, mate."

Lucas stilled. It was *Legacy's* homepage, but it wasn't *his Legacy*. "How did you get to the Bible?"

"Where's your laptop?"

He showed James to the dining room where he parked himself in front of the laptop. Lucas sat beside him, slid the laptop over, opened the lid and logged in, then slid it back.

After James clicked on a few keys, *Legacy's* homepage appeared on the screen. "This is *Legacy*. Right?"

He nodded.

James touched the top of the grandfather clock, and a mouse ran across the screen. After a few more clicks, another homepage popped up.

Bile coated Lucas's throat. "Someone's hacked *Legacy*." He twisted the laptop to face him.

"Tell me about Carlson."

"What?" Lucas jerked his chin up. "How do you know about him?" He turned his attention back to his laptop. "Never mind. It doesn't matter. Carlson's a jerk and most likely behind this." He skimmed through his files trying to find an anomaly.

"I'm giving you a chance to tell me what's going on with you and Carlson, or I'll figure it out myself. Either way, I'm staying in town until I talk to Emersyn, in person, and I find that Bible."

He looked back at James. "Are you going to tell me why you keep calling Renée, Emersyn?"

James drilled him with a hardened stare. "Are you going to tell me about Carlson?"

Lucas huffed out a breath. "Carlson's convinced he's part owner of *Legacy*."

"Go on."

"He's not." He turned back to the screen and tapped on the keys. "It's *my* design."

"You expect me to believe Carlson's working independently?"

"*Bennetts* has had two warehouse fires and one break-in since I developed *Legacy*." Lucas glanced up. "I can't prove it, but I think Carlson's connected."

"Why would he go after your dad's warehouses?"

"I don't know. To get my attention?" Lucas rubbed his temples trying to sort through the tangles in his mind. "He's been reaching out, and I've ignored him."

"Your theory is Carlson's hacked *Legacy* and selling black market goods behind your back?" James sat back and folded his arms. "You expect me to believe you don't know what's going on with your own app?"

"I can't force you to believe anything." He turned his attention back to the laptop and continued to scroll through *Legacy's* code. "Found it."

Lucas turned the screen to face James. "Here's how he did it." With a few clicks on the keyboard, he explained how Carlson had made a mirror of *Legacy*, then added functions to open the pages. "According to this, it's only been online sporadically. He must still be working out the bugs."

James waved him off. "My brother's the techy. None of that

makes sense to me. But why would Carlson use your site and not start his own?"

"Two reasons. One, to get to me. He took my idea and manipulated it. What better way to get back at me? And two, look who this incriminates. Me."

James scowled. "Did Carlson ever make a threat toward Emersyn?"

"Carlson threatened to tell *Renée* I stole *Legacy*." Heat seared his chest like a firebrand. "I don't think ... I can't imagine Carlson would go after her."

"How well do you know Carlson? Is he violent?"

Flashes from the attack in the warehouse sparked in his mind. "He's ... well, he's got a temper. But it was always directed at me."

James's jaw hardened like granite. "Does Carlson know about your botched proposal?"

"I don't know. It's not like I rented a billboard. My brother doesn't even know she rejected me."

James got to his feet and strode to the front door. "I'm going to pay Carlson a visit. I'll get him to talk, and if he's done anything to Emersyn—"

"Do you think he has her?" Lucas jumped out of his seat, following James. "I'm going with you. It's my fault if he does."

"No need to play the hero, mate." James gave him a once-over. "You look like you haven't slept in days. When was the last time you left the house?"

Glancing down, Lucas frowned. "I'll go change. You can't show up at Carlson's place and ... well, do whatever you're planning to make him talk."

"Do I look like I'd hurt anyone?" James slipped on his shades.

"Actually, yes—*mate*. And maybe even enjoy it."

James snorted. "Go put on some pants."

Lucas turned to go upstairs, then stopped. "Why do you keep calling Renée, Emersyn?"

"Get dressed and meet me out front in five minutes." James reached for the door handle. "I'll explain on the way."

38

Four minutes later, Lucas slid into the passenger seat of James's rental. "What's our plan?"

"*Our* plan?" James punched Carlson's home address into the GPS then backed out of the driveway. "Don't interfere, or I'll leave you on the side of the highway."

Lucas swallowed. *Is this man sane?*

Once they were on the interstate, James accelerated past the limit. "Tell me again about the last time you saw Emersyn. Was she distracted? Distraught?"

"First, I want to know why you keep calling her Emersyn."

James jerked a look his way. "That's her name."

"She told me her name was Renée. Renée Landon."

James stared out the windshield, thumping his fingers on the steering wheel. "Renée's her middle name."

Lucas waited.

"Her full name is Emersyn Renée Zucker. As in the Zucker Family Foundation of the Arts."

"What?" His neck turned clammy. "Why did she tell me her name was Renée?" All this time, he'd been trying to impress her. Had the great-granddaughter of one of the richest men on the East Coast been laughing at him?

"Look, this is Em's story to tell, not mine. She has this shield …" James cleared his throat. "She's built a wall around her. To keep the piranhas from trying to get close to her because of her money."

"Is she even a teacher?"

"Yes. She loves teaching. Wouldn't trade it for all the money in the world." James switched lanes and pushed the pedal down. "Em and you have a lot in common."

"How so? She lied to me. I was nothing but honest with her. About everything. My family, my dreams, and … *Legacy*." His gut clenched, He'd fallen in love with an illusion.

"As I recall, when we first met, *your* name was Reid."

Lucas gritted his teeth.

"That's not any different, mate." James slowed for the exit. "You're both trying to make your own stamp on this world, and your last names don't define you."

A war raged inside him. He understood Renée's, or Emersyn's, decision to be cautious, but to keep that deception around him for a whole year—*I can't believe I asked her to marry me.*

They wove through the upscale neighborhood and parked two houses down from Carlson's.

Lucas surveyed the street, then turned back to James. "What are you going to do? To Carlson?"

"It's simple. I'm going to ask him if he's seen Emersyn. His answer will determine my next move."

"You're going to waltz up to the door and accuse him of kidnapping? That will go over well."

James frowned. "Do you have a better idea?"

"I'll ask him about *Legacy*. It won't surprise him that I've uncovered the anomaly." Lucas scratched at the back of his neck. "I can't believe I didn't see it sooner. I guess I've been a little distracted."

"Okay, *Romeo*. We'll try it your way first."

When they made it to Carlson's door, Lucas gestured behind him. "Hang out a few steps back and let me do the talking."

"How are you going to explain my presence?"

"I'll say you're my bodyguard."

James shrugged. "That works. If Carlson gets out of line, I'll step in, and we'll do it *my* way."

With his pulse pounding in his ears, Lucas blew out his breath, lifted the circular door knocker, and let it fall.

Emersyn checked her watch as she loaded her bags into the back of her SUV. After a weekend glamping with Sam, she still didn't feel any better about how things had ended with Lucas. *Did I make a mistake?*

"You seem distracted today." Sam bounded down the stairs of the cabin, a bag in one hand and a mini-cooler in the other.

"Do I?"

"Yeah. A snake slithered by your tire, and you didn't flinch."

"A snake?" She side-stepped, then peeked around her car. "How big?"

"It was little and green. Harmless." After Sam threw her stuff into the back seat of her car, she clicked the door closed and turned to face her. "Are you going to tell me what's going on? We just spent a weekend getting massages and communing with nature, and you don't look refreshed. What really happened with you and Lucas?"

Emersyn closed the back of her SUV and considered how she should answer. "I told you—Lucas and I had a falling out."

"Have you talked to him about it?"

"No."

"Can you work it out? Or is it a deal breaker?"

Her shoulders slumped. Until she figured out how *Legacy* played a part in the missing Bible and told Lucas who she was, their whole relationship was a deal breaker.

Sam folded her arms and leaned against her car. "Do you like him?"

"Yes. Of course, I do."

"Does he like you?"

A picture of him on his knee holding up a ring flashed across her mind. Tears stung her eyes. "He … he told me he loved me."

Sam's brows shot up. "Isn't that a good thing?"

Shaking her head, Emersyn took a swipe at a rogue tear. "He's in love with Renée Landon. Not *me*. Not the real me."

"Oh, Em. Love doesn't care about names." Sam wrapped an arm around her shoulder. "Do you love him?"

She sniffled. "Yes."

"Then you need to tell him. Everything."

"I just … I just made such a mess of things. I snooped around his office and—"

"And you told me you didn't find anything." Sam released her grip and placed her hands on her hips. "Does James still think Lucas is part of some nefarious plot to take over the world?"

"No. Not really." Her heart shrank. Now she was lying to Sam too.

"Talk to Lucas. Explain who you are. Let him decide how he wants to take the news." Sam wrapped her in a hug. "Lucas is a good guy. He'll understand why you were so guarded."

Was he a good guy? Would he also understand me investigating him?

Sam stepped back. "It's almost dinner time. Let's go find a greasy burger, and we can hash out how to reveal your secrets to Mr. Americano."

Emersyn checked her watch. "I've got some business in Richmond tonight. Let's chat tomorrow at the office."

"You're going to Richmond?" Sam waggled her brows. "My pep talk worked."

She forced a smile as they said their goodbyes, but as she slipped into her vehicle, a pit opened in her stomach. She'd made plans to go to Richmond, but not for the reasons Sam suggested. *God, please guide my steps tonight. And heal my heart.*

Emersyn started up her car and headed toward Richmond.

After tonight, there wouldn't be any more secrets left between her and Lucas.

Or a relationship to repair.

39

Lucas banged the knocker again, then checked over his shoulder. This day hadn't progressed as planned. His plans for today were simple, prepare his presentation to sell the idea of *Legacy* to his dad, sulk on the couch, eat some caramel popcorn, then catch up on a few cop shows before he crawled back into bed.

James shifted behind him. "Maybe he's not home."

"He's home." As soon as Lucas said the words, the door swung open.

"What do you want?" Carlson glanced past him to James. "Who's your sidekick?"

"He's my bodyguard. I thought after our visit at the warehouse, I'd better hire security."

James stepped up next to him, tugging at his shirt cuffs. "What happened at the warehouse?"

"Nothing." Lucas shot James a look. The man needed a warning label. He turned back to Carlson. "Let's go inside. I'd hate to have this conversation where your neighbors can watch."

Carlson glanced at the street, then back at him. "Say what you need to say, Bennett."

Grinding his molars, Lucas withdrew his phone from his

pocket, and ran through the steps to the hidden virtual room on his *Legacy* app. "Do you want to explain this?"

Carlson's brows rose. "I've never seen it. Pretty impressive what you did there."

"Don't play dumb with me. I didn't add this to the app, and you're the only one who's seen part of my original design."

"What are you saying?"

"You're manipulating *Legacy*. Admit it."

Carlson smirked. "Per our agreement, I'll expect my first payment in two weeks."

"I'm not giving you a dime."

"How's your girlfriend doing? The teacher from Newport News?"

A blaze sparked inside Lucas. "If you've done anything to her …" He launched himself at Carlson and pushed him inside the house.

James rushed behind them, shoved Lucas out of the way, and pinned Carlson against the wall. "I suggest you leave the teacher alone, mate."

"Call off your watchdog, Bennett." Carlson struggled under James's grip.

"Or what? You'll call the cops?" Lucas slammed the door shut. "Where's Renée?"

"Who?" Carlson tried to push out of James's grip.

James slid his hand up and curled his fingers around Carlson's throat. "The teacher, mate. When was the last time you saw her?"

"A week ago. Maybe two. I … I didn't go near her. I swear." Carlson panted under James's hold. "I only … manipulated *Legacy*."

James loosened his grip. "Go on."

Carlson rubbed his throat as he explained how he mirrored the webpage to sell products and skim the funds. "There's a bug, though. The page crashes—a lot."

Lucas snorted. "That's because you're a subpar developer."

"Tell me about the products. The ancient Korean Bible, specifically." James continued to pin Carlson against the wall. "How did you obtain it?"

"I didn't." Carlson's gaze darted from James back to him. "I'm not the one acquiring merchandise."

Lucas got in Carlson's face. "Then who is?"

"Your stepbrother."

"Preston?" He took a step back as a weight fell in his gut and settled. "You're working with my brother?"

James released his hold and jabbed a finger at Carlson's chest. "Don't leave town, mate." He pulled out his phone and pushed in a few numbers. "Frank. Lucas Bennett is innocent. Dan Carlson's been manipulating *Legacy*. I'll send you his address."

Carlson shot James a glare.

James ended the call, then yanked open the door and motioned for Lucas to follow. "We need to find Preston."

In a daze, Lucas trailed after James to the SUV. *Preston's working with Carlson. How had I not seen that?*

"Where would Preston be on a Sunday night?" James unlocked the vehicle, and they slid into their seats.

"I'm ... I'm not sure." Lucas clicked his seatbelt into place. "Let's head to his apartment. Downtown." He typed the address into the GPS, then shifted to face James. "Can you fill me in on the Bible you're looking for? How did Preston obtain it? And how much is it worth?"

"You're not going to like what I have to say." As James drove out of Carlson's neighborhood, he shot him a glance. "If Preston acquired the Bible, he murdered someone to obtain it."

The sun's orange rays dipped below the horizon as Emersyn pulled her SUV into the empty parking lot in front of *Legacy's* warehouse.

She turned off the engine and studied the message from the website. The directions were clear. Meet at the warehouse, be ready to transfer the payment, and pick up the product. She checked her watch. This was the place and time. Why was nobody here?

Exiting her car, she pocketed her keys and phone. When she reached the door, her attention landed on the blinking green light from the new camera hovering above the doorjamb. She swallowed hard. Was Lucas surprised to see her?

With shaky hands, she punched in the code she received in the message from the seller and walked inside.

"Hello."

Silence answered her.

Heart pounding, she shut the door. "Is anyone here?"

Lights blinked on in the back of the warehouse, and she froze. Get the Bible and get out.

Emersyn picked up her pace, walking past a weathered carousel horse, a stack of porcelain dolls, and a shelf of wooden marionettes whose mouths hung open like cavernous black holes.

She shivered. Who would want to buy those?

As she turned the corner, a form stepped out of the shadows and blocked her path.

Heart charging, Emersyn shrieked. "Preston?"

"Renée?" Preston frowned. "What are you doing here?"

"I … uh, I'm here to … purchase something." Her gaze darted behind him as another man stepped out from the shadows. She recognized him as one of Preston's friends from the pizza shop.

"You're the buyer?" Preston folded his arms. "How does a teacher have that kind of money?"

Ignoring his question, she pointed to a leather-covered parcel sitting on a table to his left. "Is that it? Is that the Bible?"

"You didn't answer my question." Preston uncurled his arms

and shoved his hands into his pockets. "How do *you* intend to pay?"

"I have inheritance money."

"You expect me to believe a schoolteacher is willing to spend her inheritance on a century-old Bible? That you can't even read?"

The other man took a step toward her and cast her a hateful look. "She's wasting our time."

Emersyn shifted on her feet and looked back at Preston. "How do you know I can't read it?"

"Now you want me to believe you can speak a dialect that's been practically wiped off the face of the earth." Preston's tone dripped with sarcasm. "Come on, Miss Landon, you can do better than that."

She stared into Preston's obsidian eyes and took a step back. *Which exit can I reach first? And which one involves less spiders?*

Faking a smile, she reflexively felt for her phone in her back pocket. "You know you're right. Why do I want to spend all that money on an outdated relic?" She lunged to the right and sprinted toward the exit by the office.

With the speed of a falcon, Preston's sidekick swooped next to her, grabbed her wrist, and spun her around. "You're not going anywhere, honey."

She lunged forward, striking his nose with her palm.

He yelped a curse but didn't loosen his grip.

Rotating her hand, she curled her fingers around his wrist, strengthening her hold. With a jerk, she pulled him close and landed a knee to his middle.

The man released her, falling to his knees with a groan.

She spun and sprinted for the exit.

Pounding footsteps closed in on her. As she reached out to push on the metal handle, Preston's strong arms wrapped her in a bear hug and yanked her back.

With a guttural cry, she stomped her heel onto his boot. "Let. Me. Go."

"I asked you a question, Miss Landon." Preston tightened his grip as his warm breath glided over her neck. "How do *you* have that kind of money?"

Unwilling to accept defeat, Emersyn struggled in his arms like an ensnared rabbit.

"You're feisty. I'll give you that." Preston slid a hand up to her neck, clamped down, and cut off her air. "I'd stop fighting if I were you."

Sparks flashed in her eyes. Don't black out.

As he pulled her across the floor, she fought to draw air into her lungs.

"I can't let you leave. Not now." He stopped, loosening his grip. "How would Lucas feel if he found out I was the one who betrayed him?"

"Lucas is ..." She labored to suck in a long breath as her pulse soared through her veins. "He's going to find out ... eventually."

"What are we going to do with her?" Nose bloody, the other man limped up to Preston and shot her a glare.

"She's a handful, but I'll take care of her." Preston readjusted his grip. "Go make contact with the other buyer and set up a meeting. I want this Bible gone. It's been nothing but trouble since I acquired it."

"Will do." The man threw her another heated look, then stomped through the door leading to the basement.

Panting, Emersyn fought to gather more air in her lungs. That's why there were no cars in the parking lot. They'd come in through the basement.

When she heard the door close, she gathered her energy and flung her head back into Preston's nose.

He snarled a curse.

Emersyn lunged forward hoping to capitalize on his pain and break free.

"Wrong move, princess." Preston pulled her tight against his chest. "That hurt."

"Good."

A low chuckle escaped his lips. "If I had known we were grappling, I would've brought a mat." He spit on the *cement* floor, spraying spittle and blood on her pant leg.

"I don't need a mat." She dug her nails into his arms, breaking the skin.

Winded, he pulled her a few more feet back, then he twirled her out of his arms like some twisted dance move and flung her into a chair.

Her head hit metal. She winced. Get up. Run. With the fight still left in her, she attempted to stand, but stars danced in her eyes.

"We need to have a little talk, Miss Landon." Preston pushed her back. Holding her hand against the wooden armrest, he wrapped a leather strap around her wrist. With a yank, he tightened the hold. Moving to her other hand, he repeated the process.

What kind of chair was this? Her gaze went to the metal apparatus hanging over her head. An electric chair? Sweat sprouted on her forehead. Is there a market for vintage electric chairs?

Preston squatted in front of her and drew a pair of straps tight around her ankles. "That should hold you."

Her heart raced as if a current had already been forced through her veins. *God, please get me out of this.*

"Don't worry, there's no power." Preston winked at her as he stood. "But that would've been entertaining."

"What's your plan? Leave me tied up in the warehouse? Eventually, someone *will* come looking for me."

He yanked at his tie and glided it out of his collar. "I've got something more exciting in mind for us."

"What … what did you have in mind?"

With slow deliberate movements, he slid off his jacket, unbuttoned his cuffs, and rolled up his sleeves. "You'll see, sweetie." Leaning in, he wrapped the tie around her mouth and secured it.

The silky fabric soaked up her saliva, gagging her. She fought to protest, but the tie muffled her moans.

"Don't go anywhere. I'll be right back." With a low chuckle, he pivoted and walked away.

Fear cascaded over her as she jerked her head to the right, then the left, and finally she rested her gaze on the Bible.

If these names fall into the wrong hands, people will lose their lives. A part of the chain will break.

Tears filled her eyes as James's words seared her heart.

Is this my calling? To fight for believers I've never even met?

Peace spread over her like spring rain. Whatever Preston had in store for her, she couldn't let him leave with that Bible.

40

S he'd only been alone a few minutes before Preston reappeared.

"I've made a decision." He picked up a silver bowl off one of the shelves and set it on the sewing table to her right. "It's inconvenient, but you can't live."

Shaking her head, Emersyn whimpered in protest, but the gag hampered the sound.

"I know, I know." Preston grabbed an old book off one of the shelves and yanked out a few of the pages. Crumbling them, he tucked them into the bowl. "Lucas will be devastated."

Her eyes misted. *God. Please.*

As he pulled a box of matches from his shirt pocket, he started to hum. With a flick of his wrist, Preston struck the match against the side of the box. The orange-white flame flickered and danced.

"Did you know more people die from smoke inhalation than from the actual fire?" He placed the match in the bowl, and the flames licked at the paper. "It's a shame. The fire's the real masterpiece."

As if entranced, her gaze rested on the flames. *I'm going to die.*

Preston grabbed another bowl and added more pages from a book. "It's working out perfectly. Your face will be the last one

Lucas sees on the camera feed. There will be no need to speculate whose body's in the rubble."

He set the matchbox down, picked up the bundle and unwrapped the heavy oilcloth, exposing the tattered Bible. "I don't understand why this book is so important. I threw it up on the site on a whim." He glanced up, his expression darkening. "Mother acquired it for me. She doesn't mind getting her hands dirty."

Letitia? I need to tell Lucas. She squirmed in her seat, twisting her wrists and trying to break free.

"Not long after you offered, I got a counteroffer. Triple the price. Someone must really want this, Bible." He feathered a hand over the worn cover before replacing the cloth. "If I had more time, I'd hold out for more."

He set the Bible down, flicked another match, and set it in the second bowl. "I'd planned to leave a small token behind, but this …" He waved a hand around the warehouse. "This will be much better. Sending Lucas's dream up in flames as well as his true love. Poetic." He ripped a few more pages from a book before reading the spine. "Mary Alcott's, *Little Women*. I've never read it. Let's burn the whole book."

She moaned. For a moment she forgot she was about to die and wanted to avenge the books.

Preston glided over to another row of books and pulled one away from the group. "*Pride and Prejudice*. Rich boy falls in love with a nobody." He clucked his tongue, shaking his head. "Sinclair would've never let that happen. You and Lucas were doomed from the start."

Her stomach rocked like a ship in a storm. Maybe if he knew who she was, he'd hold her for ransom instead of torching her body. She tried to talk, but nothing got passed the fabric but a murmured growl.

"I'd save your oxygen. You're going to need it." He picked up a brass fruit bowl and proceeded to start another fire. "Did you know I shut off the sprinkler system this morning? It's about to get real hot in here."

God, please don't let Preston leave with that Bible. She pinched her eyes shut, and when she opened them, a dark form passed behind Preston.

Writhing against her restraints, she strained to see beyond the shadows. *Am I hallucinating?*

The form moved again. This time it drifted behind the bookshelf.

Preston pointed at another row of books. "What do you say? A children's book this time? Or maybe something romantic?" He walked in front of her and yanked down her gag. "You choose."

"Please, please just let me go." Hot tears saturated her cheeks.

"Wrong answer." Eyes narrowing, he shook his head like she was a naughty child. "Since you can't choose ..." He pulled a small flask from his pocket and unscrewed the lid. "I'll burn them all." After he sprinkled the contents over the entire shelf of books, he twisted to face her. "What a waste. The drink, not the books."

"You're sick." She tugged once more at her restraints. They didn't budge.

Preston chucked the empty flask at her feet, then lit another match. When he tossed it onto the bookcase, flames danced across the shelf. "You have to admit, that's beautiful."

Emersyn's throat burned as the air grew thick around them. "Are you going to be able to live with yourself knowing you murdered an innocent person?"

When he spun to face her, the flames reflected in his eyes. "I'm not taking your life, sweetie. The fire is."

As they took the exit downtown, Lucas checked his phone. Preston hadn't texted back. Where are you, brother?

He scrolled through Preston's social media, trying to get an idea of where he might be. Nothing.

Scanning his notifications, his pulse skipped. One had come in a few minutes ago from his security feed. He clicked on it, expecting it to be a delivery. When Emersyn stared back at him, he froze.

"Emersyn's at my warehouse." He held his phone up to James, showing him the camera feed.

"What? What is she doing there?"

"I'm not sure." He reversed the security video a few seconds and watched it again. "The time stamp says she walked in about the time we left Carlson's."

"How far away are we from your warehouse?"

"Not far." He pointed a thumb over his shoulder. "We'll need to turn around and backtrack."

James did a U-turn at the next intersection. "Put the address into the GPS, then call 911. Tell them there's been a break-in at the warehouse."

"What? I don't want Emersyn to—"

"She'll be fine. We'll explain later." James pushed on the pedal and sped through a yellow light. "If she's in trouble, we need to get someone out there."

Lucas punched in the address, then dialed the police. As he relayed the information to the dispatcher, James peeled around a corner and raced toward the direction of the warehouse.

When he jerked the car right, he pointed at the sky. "Is that smoke?"

Acid coated Lucas's throat. He told the dispatcher about the smoke, then disconnected the call.

"Go that way." Gesturing to a side street, white hot panic seized him. "Hurry."

41

Eyes burning, Emersyn stopped fighting her restraints. Her fate was sealed.

"It's been fun, dear." Preston coughed, then dipped his head in a quick bow. "But it's time for me to exit."

Something scraped against the floor.

Whirling around, Preston turned toward the sound.

"Emersyn, you haven't returned my calls." Declan stepped out of the shadows into the light of the fires, holding what looked like a long, flat wooden spoon.

"Who are—"

Before Preston finished his question, Declan sprang forward and wacked Preston's shoulder with the stick.

Preston grabbed his arm and yowled out a curse.

"I'm her uncle, you idiot." Declan charged again and landed another blow.

Stumbling back, Preston brought his arms up and hopped into a boxer's stance.

"Aye, a fighter." Declan shot her a wink as he spun and landed a strike against Preston's hip. "But not a very good one."

Preston folded, then staggered back into his stance.

"I haven't handled a hurling stick in years." Declan twirled the wooden stick in his palm. "Reminds me of my childhood."

Preston rushed at Declan, fist sailing through the air.

Declan ducked, then swung the stick and leveled a hit across Preston's cheek.

Preston growled another curse as he swiped blood from his face. "You're going to pay for that."

Turning toward the fiery bookcase, he gave it a shove. It toppled, landing on a stack of wicker chairs. The flames bounced from the bookcase to the chairs, and the heat in the room intensified.

Like an angry bull, Declan attacked again, this time driving the hurling stick across Preston's back.

Preston groaned, falling to his knees.

Declan wasted no time and brought another hit across Preston's shoulders. The hurling stick splintered.

Preston crashed to the floor.

"Declan." Emersyn pulled at her bindings as the flames danced like a wall around them. "Untie me. Hurry."

Declan dropped the busted stick and ran to her. "Keeping tabs on you has become a full-time job." With nimble fingers, he unstrapped the leather around her wrists and ankles. "Can I give you some advice? Don't do something this dangerous alone, ever again."

"I won't." She bolted from the chair and rubbed her wrists.

Preston groaned. As he pushed himself to his hands and knees, he let go a string of curses.

"We need to go." Declan grabbed her elbow and directed her toward the back exit.

"I'm not leaving without that Bible." She yanked her arm out of his grip as a rush of flames jumped to a stack of paintings.

"I'll get it." Declan pushed her aside, stepped around Preston and snatched the Bible off the table.

With a wail, Preston lunged forward and wrapped his arms around one of Declan's legs.

A scream tore from Emersyn's lungs.

Declan crashed to the floor, the Bible dropping from his hands.

"Declan! Get up!" She scanned the area, looking for anything to use against Preston.

"Take the Bible. Go." Declan shoved the Bible, and it slid across the floor. "Get out of here. I'll take care of him."

He kicked, and Preston lost his grip on his leg. Declan jumped to his feet.

Emersyn grabbed the Bible. Cradling it to her chest, she looked for an escape.

"That way." Declan gave her a shove and pointed to the side door. "Go."

She took off in a sprint, but before she reached the door, she looked back. Preston was on his feet and had his arms wrapped around Declan, wrestling him back to the ground.

"Uncle Declan!"

Declan's piercing gaze locked onto hers. "Emersyn! Go! Get to safety." His shouts carried over the ruckus before another bookshelf fell with a bang.

Her eyes misted. "But—

"Get. Out. Now."

42

Lucas gripped the dash as James accelerated through a red light, then barreled into the warehouse parking lot. Smoke billowed from the roof and the front door.

As James turned off the ignition, Lucas unhooked his seatbelt and scrambled out of the vehicle. "Come on. There's a side door."

"Be careful, mate." James sprinted after him as sirens wailed in the distance. "You don't know what you're walking into."

When they reached the door, it swung open. Emersyn darted out, clutching a book to her chest.

"Lucas? James?" Tears streamed down her face as she pointed toward the door. "Declan ... he's ... in there. He tried ... he saved me."

"Did you say Declan?" James pulled her away from the building and Lucas followed.

"Yes. He tried to ... help me." She coughed, then sucked in a quick breath. "Preston was—"

"Wait." Lucas reached for her arm, and she turned. "Preston's in there?"

"He had this." She held out the Bible. "I posed as a buyer. I didn't know it was Preston until I got here. I thought ... I thought it was ..."

321

She didn't have to finish her statement for him to know what she was going to say. *She thought the seller was me.*

He turned toward the door as black smoke spilled out around the edges. "Preston."

James grabbed his shirt sleeve, yanking him back. "You can't rush into a burning building, mate."

"He's my brother." He yanked free of James's grip. "I can't just let him die."

Sirens wailed louder as fire trucks, followed by two police cars screeched to a stop beside the building.

"Let the professionals do their job." James nodded toward the warehouse. "If you go in there, you won't make it out."

At the same time James finished his protest, a window next to the door shattered. Flames shot out and licked the side of the building.

"Let's go." James urged them toward the parking lot, past the emergency vehicles, and to an open space near the road.

Emersyn handed the Bible to James. "It's safe now. The chain won't be broken."

"You should've never gone after it yourself. You could've been …" James's voice hitched as he glanced at the warehouse, then turned his attention back to Emersyn. "You could've been killed, Em."

"I know. I'm sorry." She turned away from James to face him.

As he held her gaze a battle raged inside of him. Part of him wanted to gather her in his arms, the other part wondered if he was staring into the face of a stranger. *She lied to me. About everything.*

She laid a hand on his arm, eyes wide and face stained with tears and dirt. "Lucas, I'm so sorry about all of this."

"I need to let them know there are people in there." Eyes stinging, he broke free from her grip and took off for the emergency vehicles.

While *Legacy* burned, his heart split, and the thought of what he once had with her went up in smoke.

43

L ucas sank onto his couch and flipped his phone over in his hand. It had been three days since the fire, and Emersyn was already on a plane to London. She hadn't even called to say goodbye.

He tossed the phone onto the cushion beside him and groaned. Her statement to the authorities had been simple—she was lured to the warehouse under pretense to meet him, Preston had started the blaze, and tried to kill her in the process. She'd mentioned nothing about the Bible. Or her connection to Declan.

Lucas pinched the bridge of his nose. "What a mess."

When his phone buzzed, he reached for it and scanned the text.

Jacey Jones, a friend from college and local news anchor, had sent him a few last-minute instructions for their interview. He had ten minutes until he went on the air. Ten minutes until his plan unfolded.

Lucas slid his phone into his pocket and walked to the dining room, where his laptop was open on the table. After he punched in a few keys, the server linked him to the chat with Jacey.

"Here goes nothing." He tugged his headphones out of his pocket and slipped them into his ears.

"Good afternoon, Lucas." Jacey flashed him a made-for-TV

smile. "Thank you for agreeing to speak with me today. I wanted to check our connection before we go live. Can you hear me, okay?"

"Yes."

"Good. We'll go live in three minutes."

"Remember Jacey, no questions about *Legacy*."

"Of course. Just like we agreed."

Her tone warned him he'd need to keep his guard up.

"The desk will switch to us in less than a minute." Jacey sent him a reassuring look. "Follow my lead."

Within seconds, Jacey's expression turned serious. "I have with me this afternoon Mr. Lucas Bennett. Mr. Bennett, can you tell us what happened at the warehouse downtown?"

His palms turned clammy. "At this point, all I know for sure is that there was a fire."

"According to the police report, there was a body found. A man identified to be Mr. Declan McNeary. Did you know Mr. McNeary?"

"No. I didn't."

"Mr. McNeary was released from prison recently. He served time for the illegal sale of stolen antiquities. Do you believe he was there to steal anything?"

"I don't know why Mr. McNeary was at the warehouse." He swallowed past the half-truth. James had explained who Declan was, but not what he was doing there. Had Declan been there to help Emersyn or Preston?

"Mr. Bennett, I'd like to ask a few questions about your stepbrother, Preston Bennett."

His stomach knotted. "Due to the ongoing investigation, I can't answer any questions about Preston."

Jacey didn't blink. "According to the authorities, Preston is wanted for arson in the destruction of your property and possibly attempted murder." Her brows drew together. "Do you have any idea where he may be hiding?"

"Like I said, no comment."

She hesitated only a second before continuing. "Is it true, Mr. Bennett, that the warehouse was not one of Sinclair Bennett's warehouses? Instead, it's connected to a business run solely by you."

His jaw hardened.

"Is it also true that the warehouse held thousands of dollars of antiques?"

"I can't speak to that right now." *This is my chance.* "What I can speak to is the fact that a high-profile item from the warehouse has been recovered, unharmed."

"What did you recover?"

"A one-hundred-year-old Bible. It's a rare family heirloom."

"That's intriguing." Her brows shot up. "How did you acquire this Bible?"

"I didn't. I mean, I didn't know I'd acquired it. Sometimes when you purchase estate packages, there are ... surprises." He cleared his throat. "I plan to study the Bible's provenance and return it to a living relative."

"Wouldn't it be better in a museum?"

"Have you ever lost something precious, Jacey? Your grandmother's recipe box. Or letters from the past."

"Sure. I think we all have."

"This is a family Bible. One that's been lost, but now is found, and I intend to return it to someone who will cherish it."

Jacey asked a few more questions about the Bible then attempted to probe into Preston's actions leading up to the fire. Unsuccessful in her inquiry, she thanked him for his time and reminded the viewers to call if they had any information leading to the arrest of Preston Antonio Bennett.

After the live feed ended, Lucas pulled out his headphones and laid them on the table. Had Preston taken the bait? *What do I do if he did?*

Closing his laptop with one hand, he kneaded the kinks in his neck with the other. *At least I've taken the interest off Emersyn.* Now he needed to wait.

His phone buzzed, and he stilled. "That was quick."

As he withdrew his phone from his pocket, Lucas slumped into a chair and stared at the caller's name. It wasn't Preston. It was ten times worse.

"Hey, Dad."

"I want you in my office. Now."

The call disconnected and Lucas exhaled a lungful of air.

Before he worried about how he'd deal with Preston, he'd need to fight another battle—Dad.

44

As Emersyn and James's plane taxied to the gate at London's Heathrow International Airport, she switched her phone off airplane mode and brought up Lucas's number. *I should've called him.*

She shook off the thought. No. It's better this way. With Preston still on the loose, James's sole purpose was to get her and the Bible out of the country and keep them safe.

She swiped away Lucas's contact info, flipped to the local Virginia news app, and scanned the headlines.

PRESTON BENNETT WANTED FOR ARSON

MANHUNT UNDERWAY FOR STEPSON OF MILLIONAIRE SINCLAIR BENNETT

PRESTON BENNETT WANTED FOR THE MURDER OF ILLEGAL ANTIQUITIES DEALER, DECLAN MCNEARY

Sadness crashed over her like a rogue wave. Declan wanted to prove he'd changed, and all the press could display was his past sins.

While the plane rolled up to the gate, another headline caught her attention.

EXCLUSIVE INTERVIEW WITH LUCAS BENNETT

She brought up the video and pushed play. A picture of Preston flew up on the screen as the journalist discussed the manhunt. Staring into Preston's haunted eyes, Emersyn wondered how she'd never noticed his dark side.

After a minute, the news anchor announced the interview with Lucas, and the screen split between him and Jacey Jones.

Emersyn studied Lucas's reactions as Jacey drilled him about Preston. He appeared composed, but the taut line of his jaw proved he was anything but comfortable with her questions.

Lucas mentioned the Bible, and she stilled. "I plan to study the Bible's provenance and return it to a relative."

"Lucas, what have you done?"

James jerked his head to look at her. "What happened?"

She ran the video back a few seconds then turned the screen toward James and pushed play.

James shook his head. "Dumb move, Mr. Bennett."

"What's he doing?"

"He's baiting Preston."

Her mouth dried. "What? Why?"

"To draw the attention off you."

After the plane connected to the gate, everyone stood and pulled their bags from the overhead bins.

"The bloke's in way over his head." James shot to his feet and grabbed his backpack and her overnight bag. When he handed it to her, he scowled. "Your boyfriend should've stuck with IT. He's got no business wading into these waters."

"He's not my boyfriend. Not anymore." She rose, slipped her phone into her pocket, and flung her bag over her shoulder. She'd lied about her name, her family, and pushed Preston to almost burn down Lucas's warehouse. She doubted Lucas would ever speak to her again.

They followed the line of people out of the plane and through the tunnel. When they emptied into the airport, she fell in step beside James.

"Do you know who the second buyer is? Will they go after Lucas?"

James gestured to an empty alcove with a window open to

the tarmac. He pulled out his phone and thumbed through a few screens. "I'm going back."

"Going back where?"

"To the States." He glanced up, eyes darkening. "Lucas thinks he's drawing out Preston, but he's baiting someone even more sinister."

Nausea slinked around her middle. "Like who?"

"Not here." James sent a text, then gestured toward the escalator. "We need to go."

After gathering their luggage, they wove through the crowd until they reached the doors leading to a row of taxis. James darted for a black cab and opened the door. After he rattled off Henry's address, they settled into the back seat.

She turned to James. "Who's the buyer?"

He flicked a look at the driver and shook his head.

Emersyn pursed her lips together while a battle raged inside of her. James would need to answer her questions. Eventually.

After the cab delivered them to Henry's townhome, James punched in the code to his brother's door and waited for her to walk inside.

"Who wants the Bible?" She hung her bag on a hook in the entry way then whirled to face James. "Are they dangerous?"

"It's nothing you need to concern yourself with. It's an H & G problem." James shut the door behind them and called for Henry.

The soulful sounds of Ben E King's *Stand by Me* circled down the hall as Henry ambled around the corner.

"Welcome home, brother." Henry shot her a concerned look. "I heard *you* had a busy week."

Emersyn frowned. "I guess you could say that."

"I've got the Bible." James pulled his backpack off his shoulder. "But there's been a development."

"Since you left Virginia?" Henry's brows creased as he gestured for them to follow him into the dining room.

James laid his backpack on the table and pulled out the oilskin-wrapped book. "We need to get this into the vault."

Henry unfolded the oilskin and ran his fingers over the front of the cover. When he glanced up, pain etched across his face. "Lee lost his life trying to keep this book safe."

"We're going to do everything we can to keep the names in that Bible secure. We won't let Lee's death be in vain." James slid into a chair and pulled out his phone. "For now, we'll keep the Bible here while I head back to the States."

"Why are you going back?" Henry placed the Bible on the table and took a seat.

"Because Lucas Bennett is going to get himself killed." James glanced at her. "Show him the video."

Emersyn pulled out her phone and took the chair next to Henry.

After she showed him Lucas's interview, Henry frowned. "The bloke's made a mess of everything."

"He did." James looked at her, then back at Henry. "We had everything buttoned up. I hadn't expected the fire, but I was hoping to use it to our advantage. I even put word out the Bible had been destroyed."

Henry sat back in his seat and smoothed his hands down his sweater. "What's next?"

"I'm going to go back and shadow Lucas." James kneaded the back of his neck. "After that, I'm not sure."

Heat curled through Emersyn's veins. "I'm going back with you."

"No. You're not." James shook his head. "You've done enough, Em."

"But, I …"

Henry laid a hand on her arm. "I think what James means is—"

"Emersyn you're staying here. Where you'll be safe." James cut Henry off. "The North Korean government is looking for that Bible."

"North Korean government?" Her voice cracked. "Why?"

"One of those names is connected to a border guard in North Korea. He's a descendant of one of the missionaries, and he's been helping people during their escape." James sat back in his chair and scrubbed a hand down his face. "We offered to help him leave, but he refused. He wants to stay where God can use him."

"Now they think Lucas has the Bible." She jumped to her feet and paced to the window. "It's my fault he's in the middle of this."

Henry stood and joined her. "No, it's not. It's Preston's."

Emersyn's vision blurred. Henry didn't understand. Neither did James. She turned away from the window and wrapped her arms around her middle. "Lucas is a good guy. He doesn't deserve any of this. I need to go back and make things right. For Lucas. For Declan. For Mr. Lee and the border guard. Please ... help me do that."

After a moment, Henry walked back over to the table and picked up the Bible.

"It's our duty to make sure no one else gets hurt because of this Bible."

James nodded. "What's your plan?"

"I'll find out who's tracking the Bible and spread the word that Lucas is lying to catch Preston. I'll mockup a few photos showing the Bible burned and unreadable and throw them out in our chatrooms." Henry set the Bible down and secured the tattered oilcloth around it. "Call Frank, tell him what's going on, and have him keep an eye on Lucas." Henry swept a gaze her way. "Take Em back to the States. Let her save her prince."

Scowling, James sprang up and snatched his bag off the table. "I don't like it. Both Em and Lucas could end up in the crosshairs."

Henry's expression dimmed. "I'm afraid they already are."

The room quieted for a moment before James spoke up.

"Em, grab your bag. I need to go fill Kelly in on what happened before we head back to the airport."

Emersyn gave Henry a quick hug. "Thank you for understanding."

He kissed the top of her head, then gave both shoulders a squeeze. "Stay close to James. His main concern is keeping you safe." Henry nodded toward his brother, who'd already walked to the entryway. "James understands, too, but he'd never forgive himself if something happened to you."

Tears stung her eyes. "I know."

She followed James to the front door and retrieved her bag.

Let her save her prince.

As they left the townhome, Henry's words lingered in her mind.

Hopefully, her going back would fix this and not make things worse.

45

Lucas's stride slowed as he approached Dad's office. *God, give me the right words today. I know I've made a mess of things.* He breathed in, then exhaled. After one knock, he entered.

Dad sat in his desk chair facing the window, his fingers tapping the armrest.

"I'm sorry." Lucas blew out a long breath. "Have you heard of an app called *Legacy*?"

As he quickly explained how he'd developed *Legacy* and how Carlson had been blackmailing him, he prayed Dad would forgive him.

Dad's fingers stilled. "How long has this been going on?"

"Almost a year." Lucas swallowed past the gravel in his throat. "I was going to tell you this week. I hoped to prove *Legacy's* success and that you'd want me to bring it under the banner of *Bennetts* when I stepped into the lead role."

Dad rotated in his chair and shot him a daggered look. "Instead, I had to find out on the news that a Bennett warehouse nearly burned to the ground." His glare sharpened. "Funny thing though, I didn't recognize the address."

Lucas pressed his lips together. What could he say to make things right?

"The cops gave me the third degree about Preston." Dad's tone hardened. "Do you know where he is?"

"No, but we need to talk about Letitia."

"Don't." Dad held up a hand. "We're not discussing her."

"Dad, listen to me." Lucas slipped into the chair facing the desk. "Preston was working with Carlson to destroy *Legacy*, but I think Letitia's the mastermind."

"Letitia left me a few days ago."

"Left? We need to call the police. No, the FBI. This is way bigger than—"

"Stop." Dad slammed his fist on the table. "They already know."

Lucas's shoulders pinched.

"I suspected someone was skimming money from the business. When I hired a private investigator, she pointed to someone with access to my computers at home. That left you, Preston, or Letitia."

Lucas curled his fingers around the armrests and squeezed.

"I never suspected you, and I didn't want to believe it was Letitia. Why steal when she had everything of mine already?"

"Did she? Have everything. Or did you have a prenup?"

"We had a prenup." Dad's countenance fell. "But she could've asked me for anything."

"Even *Bennetts*?"

"No. Not *Bennetts*. That's *your* legacy to claim." Dad twisted his chair and stared out the window. "I'm sorry, son. For everything. I should've listened to your ideas."

Lucas wasn't sure how to respond, so he waited.

Dad swiveled his chair back toward the desk. "I've had a lot of time to reflect on things. I should've never let my marriage to Letitia interfere with my relationship with you." He opened the top drawer and pulled out a file. "I made a decision." He slid the folder across the desk. "I'm retiring, and *Bennetts* is yours. If you want it. You can make any changes you see fit with my blessing."

Lucas's pulse jumped as he leaned forward and scanned the documents in the file. He didn't deserve this. "I don't know what to say. Are you sure?"

"I'm sure." Dad's voice softened. "It was always intended for you."

Bennetts was his. Along with *Legacy*. He shot Dad a grin. "Do I need a lawyer to look over this?"

Dad laughed, and it was the happiest sound he'd heard in days. "You've got ten on retainer. Let them have a look at it."

Lucas closed the file. "I'd still like to work with you for the next year. You know, guppie in with the sharks and all that."

Dad's eyes brightened. "I think I can do that."

"Good." He picked up the file and stood. "I need to tie up a few loose ends with *Legacy*, but I'll see you in the office Monday. I have some ideas I want to run by you for the holiday season."

"Always thinking ahead." Dad smiled. "I'll see you Monday. First thing."

A weight lifted from Lucas's shoulders as he stepped out into the hallway. Preston and Letitia tried to destroy his family, but God had used this disaster to restore.

If only he could figure out how to repair what he had with Miss Zucker.

46

Lucas glanced around his rented office in downtown Richmond. After tonight, he'd no longer need the space. Monday morning, *Legacy* would rise out of the ashes and become a part of *Bennetts*, and he'd finally take his position with the family business.

Now, he needed to track down Preston. Until Preston and Letitia were in custody, a dark cloud loomed over him and his family. And Emersyn.

Slipping into the desk chair, he laid down his phone and fired up his laptop. His attempt to lure Preston out with the Bible hadn't worked. He checked his email and social media. Nothing. *Where are you, Preston?*

As if responding to his question, Preston barreled into his office with a man Lucas didn't recognize. "Where's the Bible?"

"Good evening to you, too, Preston." Lucas's shoulders tensed as his gaze fell on the irritated man standing directly behind Preston. "Who's your friend?"

"His name's Kai." Preston's voice quavered. "He's a buyer with very deep pockets."

Kai shoved Preston closer to the desk. "I have come for the Bible."

The man's harsh tone made Lucas bristle. Was this one of Letitia's henchmen?

"The Bible is no longer for sale."

"Just give him the Bible, Lucas." Preston's eyes sparked with fear. "He's paying double what your girlfriend offered."

Heat rushed to his brain. Even now, Preston's only concern was money. "You don't need the money, Preston. Why are you doing this?"

"Maybe *you* don't need the money, but Mother told me about Sinclair's plans to block me out of the business."

"Is this why you betrayed me?" Lucas stood to meet Preston face to face. "Did Letitia put you up to this?"

"Carlson made me an offer I couldn't pass up, and Mother gave me the means to make it happen."

Bile coated his throat. He'd taken Preston in as his brother and Letitia as a proxy for his beloved mom. Instead of loving him back, they'd betrayed him.

"I need that Bible, Lucas. After we turn it over, we can put all of this behind us."

"Behind us?" Grabbing a fistful of Preston's collar, Lucas yanked him halfway over the desk. "Have you forgotten you assaulted my girlfriend? You torched my warehouse and killed a man. We aren't in high school anymore. I'm not covering for you. You committed a crime, and you're going to pay for it." He pushed Preston back, causing him to stumble into Kai.

Kai shoved Preston aside, exposing the firearm he'd been holding against Preston's back. "I am here for the Bible. I do not care what you do with him." He wagged the gun toward Preston. "If he were my brother, I would throw him off a cliff. He is a disgrace to your family."

Lucas stared at the gun, pulse hammering. *God, please get me out of this.*

"Just hand over the Bible." Preston tugged at his rumpled collar. "What's the big deal? It means nothing to you."

It meant something to Emersyn. "Like I said during the

interview," Lucas whipped his gaze back to Kai. "It's a family Bible. I'm going to return it to the family."

Kai circled the desk and pressed the gun into his chest. "I am done asking nicely."

"Lucas, he's not playing." Preston's voice hitched. "He … he killed Carlson."

Carlson's dead?

"He is only stepbrother. Right?" Kai's lips tugged into a grin as he stepped back and aimed the gun at Preston.

"Yes. But …" Lucas bolted around the desk, and placing himself between Kai and Preston, he held up his hands. "Hold on. Let's discuss this."

"Just give him the Bible." Preston hissed in his ear. "Then this will all be over."

"I don't have it." He glanced back at Preston, then faced Kai's heated stare. "I mean, I don't have it … here."

"You imbecile," Kai growled as he glared at Preston. "You said he had it."

"Where is it?" Preston's voice dipped lower. "Your condo? Dad's—"

"No." Lucas rounded to face Preston. "Dad has nothing to do with this."

"My patience is growing thin with both of you." Kai waved the weapon between him and Preston. "The Bible. Now."

"His girlfriend has it." Preston squared his shoulders. "She was in the warehouse with me."

"She doesn't have it. I told you—"

"Her name is Renée. She posed as a buyer and—"

"Leave her out of this." Lucas spun and drove a punch across Preston's cheek. Opening his fist, he shook out his fingers. "This is between you and me."

"Wow. You still got that right hook." Preston rubbed his jaw. "By the way, Renée's a spitfire. She fought like a rabid cat."

Lucas's fingers curled back into a fist. Is this how Cain felt about Able? *God, forgive me.*

"Enough." Kai's voice boomed as he pointed the firearm at Preston's chest. "You are a liar and a disgrace to your family."

Preston blinked, voice trembling. "I can get you—"

"Too late." Kai pulled the trigger, and Preston's body dropped in a heap.

"No!" Ears ringing, Lucas fell to his knees and checked Preston's pulse. "You … you killed him."

"Tell me where you are hiding the Bible." Kai waved the gun at him, motioning for him to get to his feet. "You are the more honorable brother. I will let you live."

Legs shaky, Lucas stood and leveled a stare at Kai. If he was going to die tonight, he needed to keep Kai's focus on him and off Emersyn. "I told you, I don't have it here."

"That is unfortunate." In one swift motion, Kai holstered his gun, then slammed a fist into Lucas's jaw.

The room tipped, and he stumbled backward.

"I will ask again. Where is your girlfriend?"

"She … she doesn't have the Bible." He massaged his aching jaw, then drew back a hand covered in blood.

"Take a seat." Kai pointed to the desk chair. "We will find her together."

"I told you—"

"Enough." Kai assailed him with another punch.

The impact sent a tremor through Lucas's skull, and his vision blurred to black.

Wrapping a meaty hand around his arm, Kai jerked him around the desk and shoved him into the chair.

"We are going to play a little game."

"God, please help me."

"God?" In a cat-like motion, Kai produced a knife from his belt. "Where is your god? I've never seen him."

Lucas's stomach roiled.

"You see this?" Kai twisted the steel blade in front of his face, and it reflected the glow of the lights. "This is my god. It is with me wherever I go."

It is the Lord who goes before you. He will be with you; he will not leave you or forsake you. Lucas repeated the verse as his cheek swelled and a mixture of sweat and blood dripped from the corner of his mouth.

Kai held the blade to his neck. "The Bible, Mr. Bennett."

"I don't know …" He sucked in a quick breath. "I don't know where the Bible is."

"Where is your girlfriend?"

"She's not my girlfriend. Not anymore."

Kai pointed the knife at Preston's lifeless body. "According to your brother, she is."

"Stepbrother. And he didn't know me." Hot coals raked across his chest. Preston had betrayed him, and Emersyn had rejected him. Now he might die defending them both.

Kai shrugged. "Maybe he did. Maybe he didn't. He brought shame to your family. You should be thanking me." Kai pressed the tip of the blade into the tender skin below his jawbone. "I am growing bored, Mr. Bennett. Tell me where your girlfriend took the Bible."

"She left …" Lucas pressed back into the seat. "We haven't spoken in—"

A vibration on the desk cut him off.

His gaze darted to his phone. Emersyn's picture lit up the screen.

"Looks like your girlfriend is ready to talk." Kai nodded to the phone. "Answer it."

47

Lucas straightened as sweat dripped from his forehead. *I'd rather die.*

"Answer the phone, Mr. Bennett. And put it on speaker."

The phone continued to ring.

"Answer it." Kai waved the blade in front of his face. "Or I will make this *very* painful."

Extending a shaky finger, he answered the call.

"Lucas." Emersyn's worried tone permeated the air. "You shouldn't have done the interview."

"You're right." He shot a look at Kai. "That was a dumb move."

"Where are you? I think you might be in danger."

"I'm at my office. In Richmond."

Kai flicked the blade at his neck, slicing his skin.

Lucas gnashed his teeth.

"We're heading your way." Emersyn's voice shook. "Whatever you do, don't meet with Preston, or anyone who's looking for the—"

"What do you mean you're heading my way?" His gaze fell to wear Preston lay in a pool of blood. If Kai could shoot Preston, what would he do to Emersyn? *I need to keep her away.*

"I don't want you to come back. Do you hear me? You lied to me about everything. Don't come—"

Kai shoved him back in the seat. "Enough."

"That was a bad idea, mate." James's anger carved through the room. "She's worried about you, and you respond with an accusation?"

Kai stilled. His expression morphed from rage to surprise.

Does he know James?

"I'm heading back to Virginia. I suggest you watch your back until I get there." James ended the call.

Lucas blew out his breath. Maybe James would get on that plane alone.

"Looks like we are done here." A glint of amusement filtered across Kai's dark expression as he pocketed Lucas's phone, then slid the knife back into the sheath. "And it looks like I am heading to the airport."

No! I can't let him get to Emersyn. Head spinning, Lucas shot to his feet and barreled into Kai.

Kai swayed, but like a skilled warrior, he shrugged him off, pivoted, and landed another blow across Lucas's jaw.

"I told you, I do not want to kill you." Kai twisted him around and put him in a chokehold. "Last chance, Mr. Bennett."

Pinpricks danced across his vision as the suffocating darkness threatened to overtake him. "She ... doesn't ... have ... the Bible."

"You are correct." Kai cackled. "The man who is with her does. I will use her as leverage." Releasing his hold, Kai shoved him away. "Stay out of this. This does not concern you."

Stumbling, Lucas shot out a hand to grasp the corner of the desk. "I can't let you hurt her. I won't—"

Kai spun like a dancer, hurling a kick to his middle.

Lucas crashed to the floor. Curling onto his side, searing pain ripped through every muscle in his body.

"For a software designer, you are incredibly stupid." Kai

crouched next to him and patted his shoulder. "But I respect that you tried."

He rose, and turning to leave, Kai pulled out his phone and dialed. He greeted whoever was on the other end of the line in his native tongue, then, with a menacing laugh, he added in English, "I know who has the Bible."

I need to stop him. Lucas glanced around, looking for anything to use as a weapon. A trash can. A laptop charging cord. An old duffle bag. His gaze narrowed on the prize between the desk and the wall. *The Babe.*

With trembling hands, he reached for the bat and tugged it toward him. As he staggered to his feet, Lucas pulled the bat back and took aim.

"Swing for the fence." A crack reverberated through the room.

Kai fell to his knees, losing his grip on the phone.

The room tilted, and Lucas drew the bat back and prepared to take another swing. "Aim for the one in the middle."

Kai released a string of profanities while a wail of sirens echoed from the street below.

Lucas looked toward the window, then back at Kai. Please let those sirens be coming here.

"You are a dead man, Mr. Bennett." Tottering to his feet, Kai took a stuttered step toward him.

The sirens screamed louder.

With one eye swelling shut, and double vision in the other, Lucas dropped the bat and rushed at Kai. They fell, bodies entangled, with a hard thud to the ground.

Kai shoved Lucas off him, spun to his side, and jerked his weapon out of its holster.

"God, I need you." As Lucas prayed, the thunder of boots flooded the office.

"Drop your weapon!"

His head lolled toward the heated voice, trying to make sense of the mirage of SWAT team members with their guns trained on Kai.

"Drop your weapon!" The guy at the front of the battle-ready group yelled the command again.

Lucas's gaze fell back to Kai.

Kai's mouth twitched.

Lucas closed his eyes.

A shot rang out. And everything went black.

48

Emersyn nibbled on a fingernail as James pulled the rental into the hospital parking lot. "Are you sure Lucas is okay?"

Her imagination had circled through a terrifying loop of what-ifs ever since they landed at Norfolk.

James turned off the car, then shifted to face her. "Frank gave me the update when we landed. Lucas is banged up, but he'll survive."

"Do you think he'll want to see me?"

"It doesn't matter what he wants. *You* want to see him." James released a lungful of air. "Look, the bloke's been through a lot. From what Frank said, he put up a good fight to protect you."

"Protect me? What do you mean?"

"Just go talk to him."

She wrapped her fingers around the door handle and paused. "What am I supposed to tell him?"

"You can't tell him anything about H & G unless you two decide to—Never mind."

"You don't think he'll ask questions?"

"Not tonight."

Her eyes stung. How hurt was he?

"I'm going to call Kell." James retrieved his phone from the center console. "I'll meet you in the lounge."

She opened the door and stepped onto the pavement. *God, please let Lucas forgive me.*

"Em."

"Yeah." She ducked her head to look at James.

"Take your time. We're not in a hurry."

She nodded, then shut the door.

Taking a deep breath, Emersyn walked to the front entrance and found the elevator. When she got to the fourth floor, she approached the nurses' station.

"I'm here to see …" An ache tickled her throat. "I'm here to see Lucas Bennett."

The nurse frowned. "Are you family?"

"No. I … uh …"

"Emersyn."

She turned as Frank approached her. "Frank, hey. Is Lucas, okay?"

"He's doing better." Frank flashed a smile at the nurse. "She's with me." He guided her down the hall and gave her a quick update on Lucas. "He's the last door on the left."

As they approached the door, two guards eyed her with suspicion.

"She's authorized." Frank waved a hand toward her. "This is Miss Emersyn Zucker."

The burly men nodded as if their chiseled chins were connected to a conjoined string.

"Frank."

Frank pivoted to face her.

"Does Lucas know I'm here?"

"I told him you were on your way."

"Does he want to …" Her cheeks flamed. "Does he *want* to see me?"

"He added you to the visitor list. That's a good sign. Right?"

"Maybe." Or maybe he wanted a chance to tell her what a jerk she'd been. "Should you go in first? To make sure."

"He's awake. He's had coffee. Probably more than he should've. Lucas knew what he was doing when he added you to the list." Frank smiled. "He considered listing James as a threat."

Emersyn smothered a laugh. "I guess I'll go in." Gathering her courage, she eased open the door and slipped into the room.

Lucas looked up from the book he was reading, expression weary, face battered and bandaged.

"I, uh ..." She stood rooted to the floor. "I wasn't sure if you'd want to see me."

Lucas laid his book on the side table. "I wasn't sure what I wanted."

A heaviness filled the space between them. Part of her wanted to rush to him, the other part of her wanted to run.

"I'm sorry. About everything." As she studied him, her chest ached. Bluish-purple bruises covered his neck and spilled out from around the bandage on his cheek. The side of his face and the corner of his mouth were red and swollen. "You look ..." She inhaled a shuddering breath. "Lucas, you look—"

"Like I lost a fight with an assassin?"

"From what I hear, he didn't win."

"If the cavalry hadn't shown up, I would've ended up in a body bag."

Had he come that close to losing his life? She inched toward the bed. "Do you want to tell me what happened?" Her gaze flicked to the bandage on his neck. "If not ... well, I wanted to come back and make sure you were—"

"Renée, I mean, Emersyn, I want to tell you everything." He gestured to a spot beside him on the bed. "But I have a few questions first."

She sat down, relishing how comfortable it felt to be close to him again.

"Frank's already told me you can't tell me everything, but—"

"I'll tell you what I can."

"That works." His features relaxed. "Let's start from the beginning. What's your *real* name?"

She smiled and stuck out her hand. "Emersyn Renée Zucker. Abram Zucker was my great-grandfather."

He shook her hand, holding it a moment before releasing her. "The Zucker Foundation of the Arts. Right? But why use Landon?"

"I like to stay under the radar. College was a learning curve for me. Some people treated me differently as Emersyn Zucker, and I wanted people to get to know me for me. Does that make sense?"

"Makes perfect sense. What about your teaching job?"

"I've dreamt of teaching since I was a little girl. Well, that and being a journalist." She shifted on the bed. "I'm also part owner of the *Yorktown Courant*."

"Really?"

She nodded, shoulders relaxing. "It was a dying newspaper from another era. Papa would've loved it. After he passed, I was looking for something I could pour my time into. Grief makes you do crazy things." She shrugged. "I tried to resurrect an outdated periodical." Pausing a beat, she wondered if she should disclose that she was writing as Lady M. *I'll save that for another day.*

"It fits you. You have this old-school feel about you." He reached out and trailed a finger down her arm. The tenderness of his touch wrapped a warm hug around her heart. "What can you tell me about the Bible? What's so important about it? And why did someone try to kill me to track it down?"

Her stomach muscles twisted. There were certain doors she couldn't open for him.

"The Bible's a stolen heirloom. James wanted to recover it and return it to its rightful owners. In his research, he came across the Bible on your app."

"Is that why James was so hostile at dinner over the holidays?"

She nodded. "After James found out you owned *Legacy*, he warned me to stay away from you." Smiling, she added, "He plays the part of a big brother rather well."

Lucas snorted. "He does."

"I didn't want to believe you were the villain. My heart was telling me one thing, and James was telling me another." She fiddled with a loose string on her jeans. "But some things weren't adding up."

"Like what? I was transparent with you. I told you about *Legacy* and how I'd kept my business from my father. I took you to visit my family. I brought you into every facet of my life." He raked his fingers through his hair, mussing his waves. "But you ... well, you didn't tell me anything. You let me believe you were just a girl I met at a coffee shop."

Her throat thickened. "It was too soon for me when we first met. Then, after a while, I didn't know how to bring it up."

"The whole time we were together, James thought I was running a shady business."

"He had his doubts about you." She pushed off the bed, walked over to the window, and stared out at the parking lot. "And I wanted to prove James wrong, so I launched my own investigation."

"You were investigating me? Was it Frank? Did you hire him to spy on me?"

Emersyn twisted to face him. "No. Journalist, remember? I went to your office and snooped around."

"Did you find anything of interest?"

"No. And I'm glad I didn't." She wrung her hands together. "Declan, my uncle, offered to help me clear your name."

"You enlisted a crook to investigate me?" Lucas's face paled. "While I was falling in love with you, you were giving me a background check?"

"I wanted to prove you weren't connected to the stolen

351

Bible." She took a hesitant step toward the bed, heart pounding. "James sent me a picture of you with Carlson, then when you proposed, I didn't know what to do."

Pain filled his eyes, and he looked away. "Can we skip the botched proposal and jump to the part where you decided to meet with Preston?"

"Wait. Lucas." Reclaiming her spot on the bed, she reached for his hand. "Your proposal wasn't botched. It was … perfect."

He jerked his attention back to her.

"I didn't want to hurt you. It's just …" She swallowed past the burn in her throat. "I'd kept so much from you. I couldn't say yes. You didn't even know my real name."

"I understand." His shoulders slacked. "But it still doesn't erase—never mind, let's not rehash it."

A band tightened around her chest and compressed. How could she repair the pain she'd caused him?

"Are you staying in town?" His expression remained somber.

"No." She drew back her hand and stood. "Now that I know you're safe, and Kai's no longer a threat, I'm going back to London."

"For good? What about your students? I thought you loved teaching."

A shiver of hope danced through her veins. *Does he want me to stay?* "I'll only be gone for the summer. I need to decide … what I mean is …" She worked to steady her voice. "There are some decisions I need to make about my future and—"

"Emersyn." His voice turned husky as he waved her closer. "Come here, sweetheart."

She sat next to him, pulse sparking. Was there a chance he'd forgive her and give them a second chance?

"Take all the time you need." He lifted his hand and traced the contours of her jawline with his forefinger. "But please, if you have any more doubts about me, just ask."

"I'm so sorry for how I deceived you. I made …" Tears gathered in her lashes. "I made such a mess of things."

"Not a mess. If you hadn't met with Preston, I'd never have known he was manipulating *Legacy*. Or that Letitia was stealing from my dad." His lips tugged at one corner. "Next time you have questions, though, let's face them together. The thought of you being in danger ..." He sucked in a quick breath. "I can't go through that again. Ever."

She hung her head as tears cascaded over her cheeks. He was right. It was time to stop facing problems on her own.

"Promise me something." He lifted her chin, and with his thumb, he worked at wiping away her tears. "Promise you'll come back to me."

"I promise."

"Good. Because my heart wouldn't survive if you didn't." Leaning in, he carved his hand around the back of her neck and kissed her gently.

She relaxed under his touch, matching his tender offering with her own.

When he pulled away, his eyes filled with longing. "You'll be gone for the whole summer?"

Nodding, her cheeks warmed.

With an impish grin, he grabbed his phone off the side table and opened it to the calendar. "When does school start?

She pointed to the second Thursday in August.

Sliding his finger over one day to the Friday after, he typed 'coffee with Emersyn'. "It's a date."

"I'll be there."

He opened his arms, and she snuggled into them. This is where she belonged—in the arms of her love. But there was a summer between them.

A summer she'd take to decide if she also belonged with H & G.

49

Emersyn pushed through the doors of the coffee shop and breathed in the soothing scents of espresso and cinnamon. She'd waited months for this date. After a summer in London, it was good to be back home.

Home. The word brought a comfort she hadn't felt in years. She'd already made plans to invite Lucas over for dinner with Sam and her new boyfriend, Sir John. A knight she'd met at a Renaissance fair. She wanted to bring Lucas into every aspect of her life. Her work. Her home. And her heart.

As she stood in line, her palms itched to hold his hand again. To feel his embrace. To press her lips against his. Warmth dappled her cheeks. While she spent the summer learning about H & G, she'd also spent hours talking on the phone with Lucas, falling in love with him all over again.

She checked her watch. Couldn't time move quicker?

When she reached the counter, the barista threw her a wide smile. "What can I get for you today?"

Emersyn glanced at her usual booth. It was empty. Good. She'd grab it before Lucas got here.

Turning back to the barista, she returned her smile. "I'll try one of your English toffee lattes and a blueberry scone." The choice a nod to her H & G calling. A calling she'd embraced and was planning to share with Lucas today. *I hope he understands.*

"A name for the order?"

"Emersyn." Her thumb traced over the dime-sized pin in the shape of a shield attached to her messenger bag. No more hiding. No more secrets.

"Okay, Emersyn. We'll call you when it's ready."

She swiped her card to pay for her drink, then made a beeline for their booth.

Pulling her messenger bag strap over her head, she slid it onto the seat and scooted in next to it. *How should I begin?*

She was surprised James had given his approval to tell Lucas about her link to the society. After today, there'd be no more secrets. Except one. A smile towed at her lips. She secretly hoped he'd propose again someday, and this time she'd say yes.

"Emersyn."

The barista's voice sliced through her thoughts, and she walked to the front. On the counter sat a white porcelain mug with a frothy heart swirled in the center. A tingle walked across her skin. Was it a sign?

Before she picked up her mug, one of the baristas slid a small plate onto the counter with her scone. Her breath caught. Outlining the plate were the words 'Will you marry me, Emersyn?' written in caramel syrup.

She jerked her attention back to the barista, but she was gone. In her place, Lucas stood behind the counter, smiling.

Is this really happening? She looked back at the plate, then at him.

He walked around the counter and joined her. "I missed you."

"I missed you too."

The coffee shop quieted to a low hum. Emersyn glanced over her shoulder. Everyone in line and sitting at the tables looked their way as if frozen in time. A few ladies raised their phones, poised to take a photo.

Lucas cleared his throat.

When she turned back to him, he'd lowered to one knee and was holding out a ring.

"Emersyn Renée Zucker, I'm just a software developer, and" —he paused and looked around the room—"and a coffee shop owner. It doesn't matter who your family is, or who my family is, what matters is that I love you."

Her heart grew wings and flapped against her ribcage. Now there were no more secrets. Her dream had come true.

"I love how your eyes light up when there's a heart in your coffee, and I love how much you care about your students." He reached out and took her left hand. "I love how you have happy tears when you talk about your family, and I love how when you look at me, it feels like we've known each other for an eternity."

Her eyes misted.

"Will you start a new family legacy with me, Emersyn Zucker? Will you do me the honor of becoming my wife?"

A collective gasp enveloped the room.

"Yes, Lucas Reid Bennett." Happy tears trickled down her cheeks. "Yes. I will marry you."

He rose and slipped the ring on her finger. Then, drawing her close, he curved a hand behind her neck and kissed her like a man going off to war.

Applause erupted around them, and he drew back. "I forgot we had an audience."

Her skin tingled, wishing they didn't.

"I love you." He leaned in, and his whisper tickled her ear. "And I definitely love kissing you."

The milk steamer hissed to life and activity resumed behind the counter. Several people in line offered their congratulations and agreed to share photos of the engagement on the shop's media pages.

After the crowd returned to normal life, Lucas gestured to her coffee. "Your latte cooled. I'll make you another."

"You?"

"I got some training this summer." He threw her a sheepish look. "I figured if I'm the owner I better learn how this place runs."

"Latte artist and IT guy." She placed her hands on her hips and let her gaze linger over him. "You're just the guy I'm looking for, Lucas Bennett."

He tipped his head back and laughed. "That's good, because you just agreed to marry me." Scooting around the counter, he went to the sink to wash his hands. "I'll meet you at our booth."

Our booth. She slid into the seat and studied the ring on her left hand. *Am I dreaming?* Lifting her gaze, she watched Lucas behind the counter tamping down espresso and steaming milk.

He caught her looking and threw her a wink.

"Definitely dreaming". With a sigh, she settled back in her seat.

After a moment, Lucas carried her latte, an Americano, and two scones to the table. "I have something to show you."

"What?" She tasted her latte. It was perfect. Just like the man who made it.

He took his seat and pointed to a plaque above their booth.

She read it aloud. "This booth is reserved for teachers, hopeless romantics, starving artists, and daydreaming writers." Warmth circled her heart and squeezed. "It's perfect."

"There's one more thing." His expression turned shy. "James knew about the proposal. I called him a few weeks ago and asked for his blessing."

"You did?" No wonder James approved of her telling Lucas about H & G.

"I did." He took a sip of his coffee. "And Henry gave me a background check."

She giggled. "I'm sorry. Henry's like that with everyone."

"It's okay. Both of them made sure I knew what I was getting into."

"They did? Like what?"

"They told me you're headstrong and had a penchant for getting into trouble."

"Sounds like you might have your hands full, Mr. Bennett." She took another drink of her latte, relishing the nutty flavor.

He shot her a sexy smile. "After fighting an assassin, I think I can handle it."

She laughed. "That's true."

Her phone buzzed in her bag. She opened the flap and dug around in the bottom until she found it. When she read the text, her cheeks warmed.

Lucas touched her arm. "Is everything okay?"

"It's a text from James." She showed him the screen. "He says congratulations."

Lucas grinned. "He must have been sure of the outcome."

While returning her phone to her purse, another incoming text brought her attention back to the screen.

> I have your first assignment. Newport
> News. Bookstore.

Her heart jumped, and she looked at Lucas. "Lucas, there's something I need to tell you. About my family."

He laid his arms on the table and steepled his fingers. "Does this involve the Zucker family, your martial arts family, or your H & G family?"

"James told you?"

"He told me a little. He told me you were adamant about not having any secrets between us, and if I was going to marry you, I needed to know what I was signing up for." His mouth curved into a wry smile. "After that, Henry informed me he'd freeze all my assets if I broke your heart or betrayed H & G."

"He didn't. Did he?"

"He did." Lucas reached across the table, taking her hand. "What do you need to tell me?"

"I need to visit a bookstore tomorrow. Do you want to join me?"

"There's nowhere I'd rather be Em, than with you on a new adventure." He brushed a lazy circle in her palm with his thumb. "Now, let me ask you a question."

"What?"

"How do you feel about eloping?"

EPILOGUE

Newport News, Virginia
Two Months Later

Emersyn sat at her dining room table with James and Kelly, going through photographs. "These photos definitely tell a story."

James slid a black-and-white photo over to her. "This one's a picture of the seminary in Pyongyang. The families listed in the Bible were there when it started."

She looked at the photo, then turned her attention to the tattered Bible sitting in the center of the table. Over the past few months, it had been a source of intrigue and concern for all of them. Destroying it would make sense. But that would destroy a legacy. A hidden legacy. That's what James had called the revival that spread through Korea so many years ago. A legacy time had tried to snuff out.

She ran her hand over the Bible. The creases were worn, and traces of dirt and grime coated the pages. Buried for decades, unearthed, passed across dangerous borders, this Bible's story needed to be told.

The door to the dining room swung open, and Henry and Frank walked inside.

"The airport was crazy." Frank flopped into a chair at the other end of the table, facing James. "Next time, Henry can take a taxi."

Henry gave Frank's arm a good-natured shove. "Thanks, mate." Jabbing a thumb over his shoulder, he said, "Look who we found in the driveway. And he's got lunch."

Lucas walked in, holding a couple of pizza boxes and scanned the dining room. "I didn't realize *everyone* had flown in."

"I needed to see what all the hubbub was about in the States." Henry grinned as he rounded the table and took the seat next to Kelly. "So far, all I've seen is traffic."

"I know our visit was unexpected." Kelly glanced up from a photo. "We thought since it was almost Em's fall break, we'd surprise her."

Emersyn caught the stunned look on Lucas's face and mouthed 'I'm sorry.'

He laid the pizza boxes on the sideboard. "When Em mentioned she had company, I wasn't sure what to pick up, so I got several different toppings." After grabbing the seat next to her, Lucas kissed her cheek, then whispered, "This will be interesting."

Emersyn squirmed at his whispered words. Interesting was putting it mildly.

Donna stepped out of the kitchen carrying a tray with two pitchers. "Oh, good, lunch is here." As she set the tray on the sideboard, her gaze roamed to Frank. "I didn't know you were stopping by today. I hope you'll stay for lunch."

"I am now." Frank offered the seat next to him. "Join me?"

Her cheeks turned rosy as she settled into the seat and motioned to the counter. "There's lemonade and water, and there's soda in the fridge."

Noah burst through the door, wielding a coloring book and crayon with Daisy May nipping and barking at his heels. "Pizza. Yay."

Everyone laughed.

"Why don't we put Daisy May out back so she can run?" Kelly stood and scooped the wiggly Schnauzer into her arms. "Noah, go sit by your Uncle Henry."

"Yay! Uncle Henry." Noah jumped on the seat between Henry and Frank and settled onto his knees. "Uncle Henry, did you know superheroes eat pizza?"

"They do?" Henry scuffed his hair. "Does that make you a superhero?"

Giggling and nodding, he opened his coloring book.

When Kelly returned to her seat, James directed his attention to Emersyn. "Before we dive into lunch, I wanted to tell you why we showed up today unannounced."

Emersyn reached for Lucas's hand under the table.

"We found someone to give the Bible to." James's expression brightened. "And he lives here in Virginia."

Her pulse ticked up a notch. "Here? Who?"

James slipped a photo out from inside the Bible and set it in front of her.

"I've seen this picture before." She released Lucas's hand and picked up the photo. "At Master Park's dojang."

Lucas leaned in and surveyed the picture. "I remember seeing it there also."

"Jaeden told me stories about his family from Korea." Emersyn traced a finger over the two men in the photo. "The man in the military uniform is a relative of his."

James continued sifting through photos. "Yes, and the soldier was best friends with the man in the suit."

She nodded. "His friend was a missionary. In Korea. I don't recall him telling me his name."

James pointed to the man in the suit. "That's Edward Francis. He and his wife were the owners of the Bible. They were missionaries in Pyongyang before the seminary shut down." James opened the Bible and pointed to the list of names. Edward and his wife Young-Ja were listed first.

James read the inscription under the list of names. "Families knitted together by the legacy of spreading the gospel." He looked up, pain etched across his features. "We've only found one living relative of Edward Francis. The border guard."

Tears stung Emersyn's eyes. "Jaeden will be …" She sniffled. "He'll be so honored to receive the Bible and learn about the connection to his family."

James showed her a few more photos of the two men in front of the seminary. "When the connection led to Mr. Park, we agreed that he was the perfect choice to guard the Bible."

"So, this is what you do?" Lucas looked from Emersyn to James. "With H & G?"

James nodded. "It's the most satisfying calling in the world." His gaze traveled from Kelly to Noah. "That and being a husband and father." Turning his attention back to Lucas, he asked, "Are you sure you're prepared to join Emersyn in this life?"

"Yes, sir." Lucas looked at her, and the anticipation in his gaze shot a fire through her belly. "I can't wait to start a life with Em."

"Have you two decided on a date yet?" Henry asked.

"Well, we … uh …" A fire lit under her cheeks as she looked around the table, then cast her attention on Lucas.

Lucas cleared his throat, fighting a grin.

"Out with it." James folded his arms and shot them a probing look. "You both look like you're harboring more secrets than an Egyptian tomb."

"We're eloping." Lucas reached for her hand, his grin spreading. "Tomorrow."

"What?" James's brow quirked.

"Really?" Kelly's expression turned wistful.

Henry let out a low whistle. "Well, that was unexpected."

Emersyn glanced around the table, nerves tingling her belly. "Fall break starts tomorrow, and I have a whole week off. You all kind of surprised us by your last-minute arrival and—"

"You were going to run off and get married?" James frowned. "And not tell any of us?"

Henry snorted. "Sounds like somebody else I know."

James shot Henry a look.

"The ceremony is at the Shenandoah National Park." Lucas squeezed her hand. "Em's pastor is officiating."

"We wanted something small. Discreet." She glanced at Kelly. "You understand. Don't you? After what we just went through, we didn't want a big event."

"I understand." Kelly nodded, then eyed her husband. "Don't we, James?"

"Yeah. I get it. You two have been through a lot." James's expression softened. "Where are you going for your honeymoon?"

Lucas looked at her, and the whole world fell away. "I haven't told Em where we're going. It's a surprise."

"Aw, how sweet." Donna sighed. "Don't worry about us. Everything will be fine here. I'll take care of Daisy May and all your house guests."

Henry grinned like a Cheshire cat. "I bet I could figure out where they're going."

"Let them have their secrets." James shot Henry an amused look. "It's good to run away sometimes. To be spontaneous."

Henry scowled. "No, thank you. I prefer a plan."

Noah looked up from his coloring. "When are we going to eat?"

Everyone chuckled.

"I'll go get the plates." Emersyn shot to her feet.

"I'll help." Lucas jumped up and followed her into the kitchen.

When the door shut behind them, she spun to face him. "I think that went well."

"You think?" Lucas wrapped his arms around her, drawing her close. "It's not much of an elopement if everyone knows."

She buried her face in his chest, fighting off a string of giggles. "True."

"Oh, well. We tried."

Leaning back, she looked up at him. "I think we should invite all of them to the ceremony."

"I thought the same thing. Let's invite Dad too."

"Good idea."

"I can't believe they all showed up. Unannounced. Even Frank. It was like they knew something was going on."

She shrugged. "I didn't tell them."

"It doesn't matter. I can't wait for tomorrow." Lucas leaned in and teased her with a lingering, unhurried kiss. When they parted, his eyes sparkled. "Are you ready to become Mrs. Bennett?"

"I am." Emersyn batted her eyelashes. "Are you going to tell me where we're going for our honeymoon?"

"Hmm. Let me see ..." He curled a lock of her hair behind her ear. "Is your dress ready?"

She nodded. "Kelly mailed me hers as soon as we were engaged. It didn't take much altering. I hope that's okay?"

"I'd marry you if you wore a pink janitor's outfit."

Her brows shot up. "Who told you about that?"

"Sam."

"Traitor."

He chuckled. "You have something old." He rubbed his thumb over her engagement ring. "Circa 1920s."

"That works."

"What about something new?"

"I bought new shoes to match the dress." She kicked her foot, showing off her new hikers. "I bought new boots too. I've been breaking them in. Does that count?"

"Check. And check. And you have something borrowed."

She nodded. "Kelly's dress."

"What about something blue?'

"Let me think. I'm sure I have something."

"Will this work?" Lucas reached into his pocket and pulled out a sapphire tennis bracelet with an Eiffel Tower charm dangling from the clasp.

"Oh, Lucas, it's beautiful."

He undid the clasp, then secured it into place with a soft click. After he placed a tender kiss on the inside of her wrist he said, "Make sure you pack your passport."

"We're going to Paris?"

"*Oui.*" The smolder in his eyes turned her limbs to jelly. "And we'll share plenty of kisses in Paris for you to remember."

"That sounds perfect."

Lucas smiled as he opened the cabinet. "We better get out there, or they'll think we snuck out the back door."

"I'd be up for it."

Laughing, he grabbed a stack of plates. "With Henry and James both in town, we wouldn't make it two miles."

"True."

As she followed him into the dining room, Emersyn soaked in the scene around her.

Her family—her patchwork family—filled her table, along with her heart.

As she took her seat next to Lucas, Emersyn's gaze drifted to the Bible, and she thought about the border guard. His identity was safe. For now. And although miles separated them, the gospel connected them through eternity.

Warmth enveloped her. This was her heritage now. With Lucas. And with H & G.

Faith. Family. Love.

And all this came about because of one hidden legacy.

ACKNOWLEDGMENTS

First and foremost, I thank Jesus, the author and finisher of my faith, for the gift of imagination. Thank you to my husband, Steven. You rock at the kissing scenes, and I appreciate you sharing your ice cream with me while I stare at my laptop all hours of the day.

Thank you to my critique partner, Kristy Werner. Your endless hours of brainstorming and coffee dates help me get words on the page.

ABOUT THE AUTHOR

Christina Rost is an award-winning author, a mother to three amazing children, and is married to her high school sweetheart.

After spending twenty-four years as an Air Force wife, her husband retired, and she took this opportunity to pursue writing full time. While she currently lives in Oklahoma City, she's lived all over the US, a few years in the UK, and loves to travel.

An avid reader, she can still remember the first box set of sweet romance stories her mother bought her as a young teen— *The Canadian West Series* by Janette Oke. Reading about the rugged landscape of the west and handsome Canadian Mounties, Christina daydreamed about writing her own love stories.

Writing inspirational romance has always been Christina's

passion, and she loves to craft relatable characters with redemptive qualities that reflect the importance of her faith.

In 2021, her novel *Best Seller* took first place at WriterCon in Oklahoma City and in 2022, the same story was a finalist for the ACFW Genesis Contest. She's also won several awards in Flash Fiction and garnered a publishing contract by winning the GetPubbed contest for Scrivenings Press.

Her literary hero is Jane Austen, and, like Jane, she hopes her own contemporary romances can sweep her readers away for a swoon-worthy, enjoyable experience.

When she isn't spending time with her family or writing, you'll find Christina chatting with friends over creamy cups of seasonal coffee or perusing antique shops for tattered books and hidden treasures.

ALSO BY CHRISTINA ROST

Best Seller—H&G Mysteries Book One

When crime fiction novelist Kelly Landon agrees to write a memoir for an eccentric, elderly gentleman, her quiet life turns upside-down.

Unbeknownst to her, the memoir is peppered with clues leading to a rare collection of stolen jewels from World War II. After the memoir makes the best-seller list, Kelly finds herself in the crosshairs of a decades-old vendetta.

Now, instead of enjoying her rise to literary fame, she's thrust into the dangerous world of treasure hunting.

While Kelly struggles to win the game of cat-and-mouse, a secret family legacy is unearthed, forcing her to choose between trusting her charming literary agent or her vigilant bodyguard to keep her safe.

As the three of them become entangled in a web of deceit, it's a race to see who's the villain, who's the hero, and who holds all the pieces to solve the mystery of the best seller.

Get your copy here:

https://scrivenings.link/bestseller

The Decision

Running from her grief, interior designer Ava Stewart makes a hasty decision to join a missionary group heading to Uganda. She's in the country only a few days before tragedy strikes and a mistaken identity leaves her with an uncertain outcome.

Special Operator Blake Martin is assigned to a humanitarian mission when he's captured by a group of armed men. Wounded and miles away from his team, Blake's brought to Ava, and she's ordered to care for him.

Thrown together in chaos, with the threat of danger pressing in from all sides, Ava and Blake are forced to rely on each other—and God—to escape. An undeniable bond is formed during their flight to safety, but opening their hearts to love carries its own risk. A risk they aren't sure they're willing to take.

Now, miles apart and living separate lives, they need to decide if the connection they shared in the untamed, wilds of Uganda is strong enough to confront the future. A future where Ava's fragile heart and Blake's hazardous job collide, and only God knows the outcome.

Get your copy here:

https://scrivenings.link/thedecision

Get a **FREE** bonus epilogue, "From Africa, with Love" by clicking on this link: https://bookhip.com/SCQARPQ

YOU MAY ALSO LIKE ...

The Puzzle Within by Gina Holder

FBI agent Arizona Powers, recovering from a nervous breakdown, isn't ready to call it quits. Hoping to prove herself, she takes on a protection assignment for Bridgette Van Sloan, the spoiled teenage daughter of an ambassador.

Nick Trueheart, a former escape artist, joined DSS as a risk analyst after the tragic death of his wife. Consumed by his obsession to learn the identity of his wife's killer, Nick lacks the time and patience to handle the unstable field agent.

When Bridgette disappears from an escape room, Nick and Arizona become entangled in a dangerous game and a race against time. The risks are high as they confront their own failures and unravel secrets hidden within to save Bridgette—and themselves—from a sinister plot.

Get your copy here:

https://scrivenings.link/thepuzzlewithin

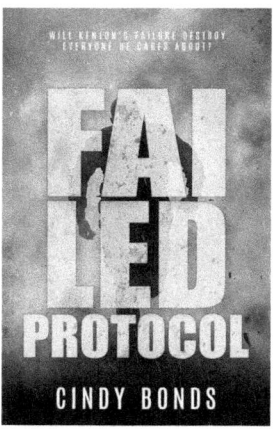

Failed Protocol by Cindy Bonds

Olivia Lloyd has left the U.K. to work in Texas as head of security for a tech firm. Her training in the British Army had given her a chance to get into the SAS—Special Air Service. But she washed out, with the help of her uncle and his contacts. Now, she was here at her uncle's request— miserable and lonely after running away from her last life-altering loss.

Kenton Matthews' Recon days are over as he now works as a detective in Dallas, offering assessments for security when high-value targets come to town. But a request from an old friend has his heart pounding, as the threat to the large tech firm holds more than just a breach of security.

Kenton is determined to battle the failed mission from long ago and will do everything he can to protect Olivia from facing the same torturous man her uncle did. But can Olivia trust the one man her uncle deems more than worthy?

Get your copy here:

https://scrivenings.link/failedprotocol

Frame of Reference by Amber Gabriel

One down, two to go.

The prima ballerina with the Grand Kyiv Ballet, Iryna is excited for her American tour—and the chance to reconnect with the brown-eyed American she hasn't seen since childhood. Her trip is just beginning when tragedy strikes, resulting in a close friend's mysterious death and a fear that she might be next.

Rick Carter wasn't looking to fall in love, but the moment he laid eyes on his sister's childhood friend all grown up, he fell hard. Their courtship, however, is haunted by unsettling threats and near-misses. Is someone hunting him and Iryna? And if so why?

As their newfound love deepens, so does the danger surrounding them. To survive they'll need all their wits but also their faith.

Get your copy here:

https://scrivenings.link/frameofreference

Stay up-to-date on your favorite books and authors with our free e-newsletters.

ScriveningsPress.com

www.ingramcontent.com/pod-product-compliance
Lightning Source LLC
Chambersburg PA
CBHW060616100726
47907CB00006B/1647